WEAPONS OF MASS DISTRACTION
LEXI GRAVES MYSTERIES

CAMILLA CHAFER

A

Audacious

ALSO BY CAMILLA CHAFER

The Stella Mayweather Series:

Illicit Magic
Unruly Magic
Devious Magic
Magic Rising
Arcane Magic

Lexi Graves Mysteries:

Armed & Fabulous
Who Glares Wins
Command Indecision
Shock and Awesome
Weapons of Mass Distraction

CHAPTER ONE

"I'm gonna die," I puffed as a bead of sweat slid down my forehead before plopping into my cleavage and joining a small puddle of water in my sports bra. To make matters worse, I voluntarily signed up for this spin class, and even suggested to my best friend, Lily, that we hit the gym during a rare moment of good intentions towards my body. Barely twenty minutes into it, my thighs were screaming and my lungs whimpered. "Yep, definitely going to die," I heaved as a faint wave of nausea hit me. Now, however, it was due to the up and down movement on the stationary bikes.

"Gears up!," yelled Anton, the hottest and meanest spin instructor in all of Montgomery, and, maybe, the world. "Up! Higher! You can do it! Think of those legs! Think of those buns! If you can't think of your own, look at the person in front of you. Their buns look better than yours! Do you want that? Nooooooo! You want hot buns! You need hot buns! And rise!"

Lily and I joined the rest of the class by pushing the gear up one notch, perching in our stirrups, and pedaling for all our fabulous legs were worth. I took a look around the twenty-strong class, stationed in three rows and facing a wall of mirrors that just misted ten minutes ago. Every single person was red-faced and drenched in sweat, their thighs straining as they hill-climbed their way to stronger lungs and tighter buns. To the front of me, an overweight white guy was bobbing in his saddle, with his huge butt in my face, and a lap pool of sweat surrounding his bike. Anton was wrong. I sure didn't want to look like that guy's butt, but kudos to him for trying to work his way towards a better one.

I looked from him to Lily, and her eyes dropped down as she stifled a giggle. I turned back to the butt, recoiling as the man swung his wet head, sending errant sweat droplets flying toward me.

"Do. Not. Sit. Down. Lexi. Graves!" screamed Anton. "Gears up! Uuuuuup!"

That's me. Lexi Graves. I'm not a gym bunny, not one bit, but I do have a rolling monthly membership to Fairmount Gym. Usually, I only attend the gym when Lily insists, a couple of times a week, or when I catch a less than flattering glance of myself in the mirror; but sometimes, I take an extra class when work is light. I'm a private investigator so that happens from time to time after I've closed a case and am waiting for a new one, like now. Since I just became a homeowner of the cutest buttercup yellow bungalow, a few days of downtime suits me fine, especially as I had a few boxes left to unpack. That task was finished last night, and I awoke with a newfound resolve to attend the gym. However, it was waning fast.

"I hate him," I whispered to Lily.

"Think of your jeans," Lily heaved. "Think of Solomon checking out your butt. Think of that dress you ate too much pizza to wear."

I thought of both, especially since I planned to wear "that dress" for Solomon, my boss slash boyfriend very soon. I didn't mean to multitask the main man in my life, but it turned out that way, and I was happy for it. He was a good boss and an excellent boyfriend. Once, he pretended to be my fake husband and was damn good at that too. "So now it's my fault you're a feeder?" I shot back.

"I don't think you reaching for the last two slices qualifies me as a feeder." Lily reached for her water bottle with a shaky hand and squirted liquid in her face. "Shoot. Missed." She tried again, this time firing the stream of water into her mouth.

"I... have... two... hands," I heaved. "One for each slice!"

"That's not an excuse and you know it."

"I rarely indulge. I should do more. I'm gonna die."

"You're gonna be skinny and gorgeous. You're gonna do this and you're gonna do it hard," Lily wheezed.

"That's right, everybody, listen to Miss Lily Shuler. She says 'You're gonna do this and you're gonna do it hard'," yelled Anton. "Are you with me? Are. You. With. Meeeeee? Aaaaand... back in your saddles!"

A chorus of yeses echoed around the steam-filled studio, along with a few whimpers that could have been affirmations. With twenty minutes left on the clock, there wasn't a whole lot of energy to go around, and most everyone looked like me, concentrating on getting through the next few minutes without wobbling off their stationary spin bikes, and collapsing onto the floor and crying. Not puking would be a bonus, although rumor had it Anton considered a vomiting episode as a personal best on a tough class.

I flipped the gears down two settings and continued to pump my thighs, hoping no one noticed.

"I saw that," hissed Lily. "Cheat."

"I need to walk the rest of the day, okay?" I hissed back. "And tomorrow too."

3

"You don't. You've been sitting on your butt, doing surveillance for two weeks."

That was true, and partly why I upped my gym hours because I really needed to compensate for all that sitting around. "I still need to hit the car brakes," I said, rising when Anton yelled again. "I need for my legs to work. Plus my surveillance job is done."

Lily stood a little taller in the stirrups and grinned. "I could drive for you. Let's be surveillance buddies."

"Yeah, that always works out so well," I replied. I was thinking about corpses, and suspected serial killers, along with the other things we discovered whenever she joined me on a stakeout. Not that she was a magnet for those sorts of things, but she didn't exactly deter them either. At least, I got paid for that kind of crap.

Lily was about to answer when one of the men in the front row wobbled off his bike and lurched forwards. The class would have inhaled a collective gasp, but no one had any breath to spare. All the same, several pairs of eyes followed the lurching body. If there was one thing Anton hated, it was a flake-out in his classes, and he had been known to ream people out. Anton was about to do his thing when the man took another wobbly step forward before sinking to his knees, both his arms limp at his sides. Blood seemed to drain from his face, giving his sweaty, red visage a ghostly pallor. He tipped his head upwards, his jaw dropping open and rasped out a breath.

Anton stepped towards him, reached one hand to his shoulder. "Are you...? Oh shit!" The man keeled forwards, his face hitting the studio floor with a dull thud. Instead of his eyes rolling back in a faint, they stared glassily ahead.

One by one, the class slowed down their bikes, gradually coming to a stop as the music thumped around us from the overhead speakers. They abruptly cut out as Anton pressed a button on his remote control.

We all leaned forwards on our handlebars as Anton reached for the man's wrist, his fingers checking for a pulse. After what felt like forever, with my heart thumping in my chest from exertion and waiting, Anton looked up and around. "He's dead," he said softly, almost inaudibly. Even without a word, his frightened eyes said it all. "He's dead."

"Oh my God, you killed him!" screamed a woman at the back. Our attention turned to her as she scrambled from her saddle and weaved through the bikes, her bag and towel bumping everyone in her path. "I am never spinning again!" she screamed, whirling around and banging out the double doors backwards.

"He's dead?" The big man in front of us turned to the man to his left, then to the woman at his right. "He's really dead? Oh my, I think I'm gonna…" And he did. He fainted. But as he fell, he leaned to his left and hit the handlebars of the next bike, toppling it before its rider could jump clear. That bike hit another, and that one hit another, as they all went down like dominoes. The last person had the good sense to jump off her bike when the others thumped to the floor, and dash towards the front of the room. She watched, with astonishment the crash of tangled limbs and bikes, their wheels still spinning.

"Let's always sit at the back," whispered Lily.

"He's dead," said Anton again, waving the remote. In the far left corner, someone began to cry. "I killed him! I killed a man!"

"Should we help?" asked Lily, sliding off her bike, addressing no one in particular.

"Can you get him off me?" squeaked the man under the big man who fainted. He was skinny and wore a sweatband around his head. "I can't breathe."

"I don't think so," said Lily, assessing the situation. "He's pretty big. Lexi, can we roll him together?"

"Yes, do that," said the man. "I can't feel my legs. Hurry, please."

"Just a moment," I said, holding a finger up to him, asking for patience. Grabbing my cell phone from the bike's tray, I hit "speed dial."

"Do you have to make a call right now?" wheezed the man. "Can't it wait until after…" He flapped a hand at the fainter. Behind Skinny Headband, several moans emerged from the other trapped spinners.

"If you can still talk, you're okay for another minute," I told him. Then the phone stopped ringing and my savior answered. "So, funny thing," I said. "I'm in my spin class, and a guy just died, and then this big guy knocked over all the bikes and now half the class is crushed. Can you send a couple of officers and maybe an ambulance?"

At the other end of the line, Maddox sighed. "How do these things always seem to happen to you?"

Adam Maddox was a detective with the Montgomery police department and knew better than to ask dumbass questions like that. I could have called a bazillion other police officers, but since I was related to a large portion of them, I thought calling my ex-boyfriend seemed like a better idea. He wouldn't bring this up at every family dinner forever after.

"I like to keep fit?" I replied, phrasing it like a question.

"Okay. How'd this guy die? Are you sure he's dead?"

"I'll double check, but I'm pretty sure. He's not moving and doesn't have a pulse."

"Good enough for me. He have a heart attack or something?"

"Maybe. It was a tough class."

"Remind me to never spin. Besides, overexertion through spinning isn't really a police thing. We like bullets, knives, heavy mallets. See any of those?"

I looked around, just in case. "Nope."

"I'll send a couple uniforms over. Need anything

else?"

"A hearse would be nice."

"Coming up. Stay put."

"It's okay," I told everyone, as I hung up the phone. I jumped over the first human domino, landing neatly a few feet from Anton. I should have been a ballerina. I felt really graceful doing that. "Help is on the way. Everyone needs to just stay calm."

"Easy for you to say," said Skinny Headband. "You're not under this guy and I think he just peed himself."

"It's probably just sweat," said Lily, taking Skinny's hand. He beamed up at her and I suspected maybe even fell in love a little. People seemed to do that with Lily, although, when I said people, I meant men. Until recently, that was great, but now she was all googly-eyed about my brother, which I found disgusting, but it was fine by me, especially since he finally reciprocated. They were even due to get married very soon after a whirlwind engagement that was a culmination of determination to get the guy on Lily's part, and giving in on Jord's.

Skinny's lip trembled. "I can feel it all over my legs."

"The good news is you can feel your legs," said Lily. She patted his hand reassuringly and wrinkled her nose. I glanced at the other spinners, noticing they too were rallying to help extricate the fallen from their stirrups and saddles.

I left them to their special moment, and crouched down next to Anton. "Hey," I said. "I think you can let go of his wrist now."

"Oh, right, yes. I need to call for help." Anton dropped the man's wrist and scooted backwards on his butt. "I can't believe this happened. I killed him. I shouldn't have pushed so hard. I should've…"

"No, you didn't kill him," I reassured him. "We all saw. You didn't lay a finger on him."

7

"I pushed you all too hard. I just wanted you all to have great asses. I shouldn't have gone so hard on everybody," Anton whispered, his voice thick with shock. He stared at the dead man, seemingly unable to look away.

"Our asses appreciate it," I told him as I picked up the dead man's wrist and felt for a pulse. Yeah, definitely dead. I reached for his other wrist. Yep, dead on both sides. Something about his hand caught my eye and I turned his palm over. I noticed a tiny smear of blood on his middle finger. With a shrug, I laid the hand down, and turned back to Anton. He had the walkie-talkie in his hand that all the instructors carried and was speaking into it in a panicked voice. Whatever he said must have been good because a few minutes later, white polo-shirted instructors swarmed the spin studio and started helping the people still lying on the floor and righting bikes.

As I sat with Anton, I watching the chaos, he staring at the body, only one thing occurred to me. I hoped this was the straightforward death he thought it was because otherwise, Maddox would be totally pissed that I allowed a crime scene to get trampled and compromised.

~

"Jeez, Lexi, how many people have been through here?" asked Maddox, surveying the chaos of the spin studio. I didn't expect him to turn up so I was pretty surprised when he sauntered through the double doors into the gym and purposefully entered the spin studio. Blooms of steam still coated the windows spanning the wall adjacent to the misted mirrors, and the bikes were in chaotic disarray, instead of the neat lines they were in at the start of the class. The floor… the floor was a mess of towels, sweat, shoe prints, and what smelled and looked suspiciously like pee. Poor Skinny did call it.

"What time frame are we talking?" I asked, even

though I knew what he meant. Yeah, I should have stopped people trampling all over, but really, what could I have done? People panicked and got stuck under bikes! And there was a corpse only a few yards from them and our instructor went into shock. Then, the gym staff added their footprints and the resulting mess was this. The room was now empty, but for the corpse, Maddox, and me as everyone else cleared out quickly. Lily reported that a few had grazed elbows and other scrapes, which were tended to by the EMTs in another studio.

Maddox raised his eyebrows and waved for a uniform to stand at the door, just to deter the curious from wandering over. "Let's say, since the class started."

"Okay, so, there was a full class of twenty, plus Anton, the instructor. That makes twenty-one."

"And after the guy died?"

"Six instructors and gym staff, their manager, four paramedics, and a whole bunch of nosy people. That makes…"

I started to count on my fingers, but Maddox was already there first with, "Thirty-two, plus."

"Thirty-one," I corrected. "One guy was dead, remember? I don't think he counts after his demise. Who was he anyway? I've seen him at the gym a few times."

Maddox checked his notepad. "Jim Schwarz, thirty-seven. Unmarried, no kids. Lives in Harbridge. Works as a lab tech." He looked up. "You've never spoken to him?"

"No." I tried to remember him. "I've seen him here with a woman a few times. She's a member too."

"You know her name?"

"No, but she was on the bike to the right of Jim. I saw them having a conversation before class started and she didn't look too happy. Anton might know who she is."

"I have their names. What does she look like?" Maddox asked.

"Around the same age as Jim, or a little younger. As tall as him too. Light brown hair. Oh, she was wearing a really cute, pink top. If you speak to her, can you ask where she got it?"

Maddox just shook his head as he snapped the notebook shut. "I'm just going to ask a couple questions for now, then I'm out of here."

"What? You're not going to interrogate anyone?"

"No reason too. From what I've heard, it looks like Jim just had a heart attack, but the ME will confirm. This isn't a murder, Lexi. Sorry. Don't look so disappointed. You did the right thing though in calling me."

That was disappointing, although in a way... not so much. I really didn't want to solve a murder at my own gym and since witnessing Jim Schwarz's death, I knew I would feel compelled to. This was where I sweated, relaxed, and checked myself out in the full-length mirrors. And not where I wanted to be on high alert for possible murderers. But on the other hand... "So what happens now?" I asked, seeking to learn how this would get wrapped up. The dead people I usually came across were murdered, so a natural death was new to me. I sincerely hoped, however, to encounter neither kind of death again.

"Jim's body will go to the ME and they'll want to do an autopsy since it is an unexplained death." I perked up. Unexplained! Called it! Maddox smiled, continuing, "Don't get your hopes up. He could have had a weak heart, or an aneurysm. These things happen, Lexi." He patted me on the shoulder in a friendly way, repeated the motion to the young uni posted on the door, and made for the exit. I followed him out, glad to escape the studio. I wondered if I would ever go in there again, and if this were a good excuse to make Lily choose some other kind of group exercise, something gentle, something non-life threatening like... yoga.

"I think I'm going to take up yoga."

Maddox paused and looked up from his notes. "Good to know. It's good for stress."

"How do you know?"

"Yoga club down at the station on Tuesday nights."

My mouth dropped open. "You guys do the downward dog en masse at the station?"

Maddox smirked and snapped the notepad shut. His blue eyes sparkled as he appraised me, eyebrows raised. "I'm imagining you doing the downward dog right now."

"Oh, please."

"Play hard to get, Lexi, don't plead," Maddox teased, laughing and I had to admit he looked as handsome as ever. It almost felt like old times, back when I first had a huge crush on him at my temp job, and way before I found out he was an undercover officer on the trail of missing millions. We closed the case together and I got the guy. Sometime later, when we worked separate cases, I lost him. It was sad, but it was life. "Hey, smile. It could be worse though I really don't know how. Now, can you point me towards the studio where the EMTs set up? I want to talk to this friend of Jim Schwarz's before I head back to the station. Figures she'll be in there, if anywhere."

While Maddox looked for the dead man's friend, I went in search of the manager, Michael Rivers. I found him by the coroner's van. It was parked in front of the gym, right where everyone could see it; and Michael looked like he was about to burst into tears. He was a bodybuilder, and around a foot wider than most normal folk. His dark skin looked like he buffed it, and his biceps appeared to have a bigger girth than my thighs. He was damned nice guy too with a sweet temperament and a sensitive disposition, that didn't sit quite right with his physique. He always took the time to say hi when I saw him. I suspected he once had a huge crush on Lily.

"You okay, Michael?" I asked, coming to a stop at his side. Behind me there was the sound of rattling castors and we turned to watch two attendants wheeling out a gurney, with a full body bag strapped on top.

"No, I can't believe this. No one ever died in my gym before," Michael said, reaching one meaty hand up to scratch his head.

"Bright side, you know how to deal with it now," I replied, trying to find a positive.

"I hope to never deal with it again. Detective Maddox said you called him?" Michael dragged his eyes away from the body bag to look down at me.

"It seemed like a good idea at the time," I said, feeling stupid now that Maddox emphasized just how natural this death looked, even if it was unexplained. We stopped talking for a moment and watched the morgue workers heft the gurney into the back of the van before banging the doors shut. It seemed a very final say on Jim Schwarz's life, and, I had to assume, not the way he planned on leaving the gym today. Or ever. "Did you know him?" I asked, nodding toward the van.

Michael shook his head. "Not really. Seen him around a few times. He came here a lot when he left his job, but he hasn't been here so much recently, so I assumed he was working again. Seemed pleasant. Always polite to my staff. Where's your friend, Lily? She back at the gym now?"

"Yeah. Making me suffer, too."

"Well, whatever she's making you do, it's working." Michael looked down and smiled. "You ever think about taking up weights?"

"Do bottles of wine count?"

"Sure, just don't drop 'em."

I feigned horror. "Never!"

"You could do some bikini athlete modeling; Lily, too, if you both worked at it, ate clean, lifted hard."

"Sounds awesome, but I'm all out of bikinis," I

replied, wondering what the hell a bikini athlete was.

The morgue van guy came over with a piece of paper for Michael to sign and I took the opportunity to snoop. It would have been ruder not to. "What happened?" I asked the attendant, hoping the all-encompassing question could glean some good answers. "Was it a natural death?"

"Maybe a heart attack," said the guy, squinting at me. "We won't know until we get to the morgue. Do I know you?"

"Nope," I said quickly, just in case he recognized me from any of my cases. I preferred to go incognito, which was tough, since at any given moment, someone could figure out I was a PI. It happened before and didn't always work in my favor. "What brought it on?"

"Couldn't tell you, sorry. Do you know the guy?"

"No, only in passing. Um, not that kind of passing. I didn't mean to pun," I added. "Just seen him around."

"Was he doing strenuous exercise when he collapsed?"

"Spinning. I told Detective Maddox already. He took statements."

"Thanks. I'll get in touch with him. Have a good day now."

"I'll try," I said as Michael harrumphed, clearly not having a good one.

We watched the van leave and Michael looked down at me as I looked up. "Another bright side, no more corpses at the gym," I said as we turned away from the van to head inside.

"I wish I could laugh. I gotta spin studio to clean, and serious PR to do. Don't want any members leaving. Also, Anton is a wreck. I'm gonna drive him home before he confesses to killing that poor guy and ends up with an angry family's law suit. He didn't kill him, by the way, and Jim Schwarz was a fit guy. Anton's just upset."

"I know that. I was there."

"If anyone asks, will you make sure to say the guy just keeled over and collapsed off his bike and was dead. Nothing to do with us. I hope the guy's family doesn't sue."

"Since that is exactly what happened, I will say just that."

"You're a good woman, Lexi Graves."

I bumped him with my shoulder. It was like bumping a wall. "Don't tell anyone."

Finally, a smile appeared on Michael's lips, but vanished just as fast. I patted his arm and resisted the urge to stroke the muscles that roped it. "Don't worry, okay? People die all the time. It's just unfortunate he died here. Everything will be back to normal tomorrow."

"Promise?"

"Hah. Um, no. Since I don't work here and am really just throwing out platitudes," I explained so another crappy day wouldn't fall back on me.

"At least, you're honest."

"If you keep saying nice things about me, I might start to think you like me."

"Nah. Now your friend, Lily…"

"I'll pretend not to be offended and Lily is engaged to my brother. But like I said, everything will be A-okay tomorrow." I gave him my brightest smile, and left to find Lily so we could spend the rest of our day somewhere with less corpses hanging about.

CHAPTER TWO

Everything was so not okay at the gym the following day.

After filing my report to Solomon on a simple surveillance job – successfully reuniting an old lady with her miniature Poodle after it was "appropriated" by a well meaning family on her street, which I completed a few days before – I hopped into my VW and drove to the gym. I parked within yards of where the morgue van was parked the day before.

"I can't believe you drive to the gym to use the treadmill," said Lily, as I took the machine next to her and settled my water bottle on the tray. The machines faced the windows and I could see my VW. I didn't take much notice, however since I could also see Lily's blue Mini parked in the corner of the lot. Taking a quick glance at the treadmill next to me, I saw a familiar-looking woman, my height and weight, at full pelt. She didn't look like she'd even broken a sweat, and I could hear the soft hum of music escaping her earphones. Without slowing her pace, she reached for her water bottle and took a gulp, depositing it in the console bottle holder when she was finished.

"If I ran here, I would have no energy to run *here*," I remarked, turning to Lily who was jogging without much conviction, her arms raised, while her legs pumped a gentle rhythm.

"This is true," Lily agreed. "And I like your outfit. Is it new?"

I checked out my running capris with black-and-pink piping and matching top. "Half price on sale," I told her. "Payday treat."

Lily hit a button and her treadmill slowed from a jog to walk, and I sped mine up to a fast walk. "We should go shopping."

"I wish. Right now, I have to save for new bathroom tile, a refrigerator that doesn't make a noise like a wasp nest, and curtains for every window that doesn't have them. That's all of them, in case you didn't notice."

"The pleasures of home ownership," sighed Lily. "Never-ending payments for stuff you never knew you needed."

"I'll drink to that." I took a swig from my water bottle. "How's the bar?"

"Awesome. I love running my own bar, but the paperwork! Sheesh! I thought getting the license was a tough call."

"At least it's making money."

"Barely, but breaking even is good enough."

I turned my head at hearing an odd noise next to me. The female runner was wobbling from side to side, her fingers clawing for the side bars and missing. She looked up at me with glazed eyes.

"Hey, are you...?" I started to say, slowing my power walk speed setting.

She gurgled something, and clutched her throat. Then she unexpectedly seemed to sink onto the treadmill, her legs giving way under her. Her face hit the

16

belt as it continued to rotate before spewing her several feet onto the gym floor. She lay motionless in a limp mess. For a moment, I simply kept pumping my thighs and continued my walk as Lily and I stared at her. She didn't get up.

"Oh my gosh," said Lily, slowing her machine. "Did she just faint? Ow, that had to hurt." She hopped off her machine as I stopped walking. I let it slide me off backwards until I could step off. We reached her at the same time as the gym floor monitor. Waiting silently as he crouched beside her, turning her onto her side into the recovery position, we ignored the sudden burst of chatter as people started to look. He checked her forehead with the back of his hand, then pried her eyelids open. When he checked her pulse, panic was visible on his face as he turned her onto her back.

"Call 911," he yelled, tipping her head backwards and commencing chest compressions. He paused intermittently to breathe into her mouth. There was no response. Her lips and face looked swollen and her skin was discolored. She didn't move at all when the instructor checked her eyes. He leaned over her, continuing to administer aid.

"I'm calling," said Lily, extricating her cell phone from the band wrapped around her upper arm. "What do I say? Hello. Hello? Yes, I'm at Fairmount Gym and a woman collapsed. We need an ambulance. No, right away. She's unconscious. Hold on. Lexi, is she unconscious? She looks unconscious."

"Looks that way to me," I said. "Tell them she's getting mouth-to-mouth."

"She's getting mouth-to-mouth and not in a sexy way," Lily told the operator. "And someone's doing chest compressions on her. Is she breathing? No, not you. Why would I ask you?" Lily rolled her eyes at me. "Lexi, is she breathing?"

"Is she breathing?" I asked, relaying the question to

the man resuscitating her.

He looked up from his chest compressions and shook his head before bending over her again, and breathing into her mouth. I shook my head at Lily, who shook her head at the phone. We waited. "Oh right," said Lily. "No, she's not breathing. Oh my gosh, she's not breathing! Is she…?"

"Yes," said the instructor, his tone dull, as if in shock. Around us, the whispering continued and I suddenly became aware of the pump of the air conditioning, the whirring motors of machines, and the soft thump of music trickling from the runner's headphones as they were disengaged from her ears. Above all that was my own racing heartbeat. "I think she had a heart attack. No pulse for a minute. Ask them what do I do?"

"They say to keep doing compressions," said Lily. "An ambulance is on its way."

The man nodded, leaning over to breathe into her mouth again, before restarting compressions. He continued without cessation until eventually, I walked around and tugged him away. It had been five minutes. Five minutes without her taking any breath. I knelt next to him and held his limp hand as we looked down at the woman on the gym floor. We stayed there, along with the small crowd that gathered before Michael ran in with the paramedics. The silence broke into commotion again as everyone waited for them to perform some kind of miracle. But moments after they ushered us out of the way, I heard someone declare her dead.

~

"Two apparently natural deaths in two days at your gym," said Solomon as he looked up from the menu. We were sitting in a Thai restaurant, which Solomon suggested we dine in downtown. The enticing smell of food wafted over us, making my stomach gurgle. It wasn't surprising since I skipped lunch. The shock of the poor runner dying in front of me managed to put me off.

"Do you want to join a new gym?"

"No, I want to know why two people died there in two days." I looked at the menu and the long list of unpronounceable names. Fortunately, I had my pointing finger and quite an appetite. "Are we doing entrees?"

"Yes. Want to share?"

"Silly question. Of course, I do. Solomon, what are the odds on two natural deaths occurring within a day of each other at the same gym?"

"I don't imagine anyone ever took the time to find out the probability on that, but I'm guessing low or…"

"Or?" I waited, ready.

"Or it's a really unlucky coincidence." The look on my boyfriend's face told me just how unlikely that was. However, as the owner of a private investigations agency, he rarely was convinced of the innocence of anything or anyone anymore.

"Neither of them looked unfit. Jim Schwarz, the guy from my spinning class, took three spinning classes a week apparently. Then there's Karen Doyle, our dead woman. According to the treadmill's data, she ran five miles without breaking a sweat. Both, of them, all of a sudden," I snapped my fingers, "dead."

The waitress appeared at my side. "Yes?"

"Oh, I'm sorry, I wasn't snapping at you." I blushed at my unintended rudeness.

"Yes?" she asked again, this time tapping her pen against her notepad, apparently nonplussed.

"Let's order," said Solomon, reeling off dishes as though Thai was his second tongue. Maybe it was. He had a lot of hidden talents and I made it my mission to try them all out. His food, too. "Lexi?"

"That one, that one, and that one," I said, pointing to the unknown dishes.

"Pleb," said Solomon.

"Show off," I retorted.

"Good choices," said the waitress as she collected our

menus. "All tasty."

"She was saying that to me," I told Solomon. "Yours? Not so much."

Solomon laughed; then his face grew serious. "Two dead bodies. Two potential heart attacks. One connecting factor... the gym."

"It's very suspicious."

Solomon smiled. "You have a suspicious mind." If I didn't know better, I would have thought that pleased him. Wait, I did know better. He was thrilled that I was suspicious. Intrigue made better date conversation than "How was your day, honey?"

"That's why you employ me," I said, reaching for his hand. It was warm, big, and very, very adept. I rested mine over it and tried not to think dirty thoughts while sitting precipitously on the tip of declaring the gym a double homicide crime scene.

"It's not why I date you."

I laughed and he turned his hand palm up, his long fingers wrapping around mine. "I think it could be a contributing factor."

"Maybe. Okay, let's say these two deaths aren't just really unlucky. Who'd want to kill them?"

I picked up my wine glass and took a long sip. "That, I don't know. But my gut tells me there's something iffy about these deaths; and I've learned recently when my gut tells me something, I should listen to it."

"All right then. Tell me more about what happened to the guy, the one in your spin class. Jim something," he said. I was sure he knew Jim's name and had already mentally filed every little detail I'd given him.

"There really isn't much to say. He was doing okay, although I think he was going a little slower than he was supposed to. It's a pretty tough class."

"How so?"

"Tough cardio for heart and lungs, and pretty hard on thighs too. Our instructor, Anton, pushes us hard and gets results."

Solomon nodded, but I suspected he'd never taken a spin class in his life. Not that his thighs suffered any for it; but I wasn't supposed to be thinking about that either. "Okay. Go on."

"So, Jim Schwarz was slowing down. He got off the bike, wobbled a little, then just collapsed onto the floor. Anton tried to help him, but there was nothing he could do."

"That's it?"

"Yeah. Oh, and his finger was bleeding."

"A lot?"

"No, like a bead, like he'd just pricked his finger."

Solomon mused over that. Finally, he said, "With the exception of the treadmill death, it still sounds like your first guy died of natural causes. Maybe he nicked his finger. It's probably not related."

"And the woman?"

"It's not absolutely unheard of for two people to die of natural causes at the same location in a narrow time frame. It's just really unfortunate."

We waited as the server arranged little plates onto the table, asked if we wanted our wine glasses refreshed, then gave us a little bow before disappearing.

"Unnatural enough for you to ask me if I wanted to find a new gym," I pointed out. The delicious aromas reaching my nose made me salivate. "But maybe I'll go to the doctors and get a health check."

"I have a stethoscope," said Solomon, looking up and smiling, with his eyes sparkling under his lashes.

"Really? Are you sure what you keep in your pants is called a stethoscope?"

The sultry smile remained on Solomon's lips. "Stay over tonight and find out."

"If you insist, but only because I need to stay healthy."

"I'll give you a full body check. Promise."

21

I shivered. I knew exactly what that meant: that I'd be very tired in the morning, albeit very satisfied. "Since you insist and while we're on the topic, I'll be doctor and you can be nurse."

"I'm a real man and I can be a hot nurse," said Solomon.

For no apparent reason, I wanted to eat our meal quickly, but Solomon's leisurely pace forced me to slow down. The dating thing was new, and great, and so far, only the two of us knew about it. Oh yeah, and Lily. And his sister, Anastasia. Okay, so that made four, but most importantly, our colleagues did not know, and the rest of Montgomery did not know, which meant my family couldn't bug me about it. It also spared me from having an awkward conversation with Maddox, who already knew that things had occurred between Solomon and me in the past, but not that they were now happening on a regular basis.

That said, I did have the occasional urge to shout from the rooftops that Solomon and I had been getting it on for the past two months, ever since he arrived at my house one night and asked to stay. Since then, we have enjoyed a series of movies, meals, and nights in at his place. He rarely slept over at mine when I had my apartment in West Montgomery, but I figured that was just because his home in Chilton was closer to our office. However, now that I'd moved, it would be nice to have him stay over in my home.

"You could stay at mine tonight," I suggested between mouthfuls of something savory. "You could still get to work easily tomorrow."

"At yours? The ranch?"

"It's a bungalow," I corrected for the millionth time. "And sure, why not? I've stayed at yours a bunch of times."

Solomon shrugged. "Okay."

"Oh, I didn't think you'd say yes."

"Disappointed? Worried what the neighbors will say when they see my car outside your house?"

"Not at all. Aidan will probably high five me."

"Aidan?"

"Neighbor. You've met him. Deaf. Got a crazy dog."

Solomon blinked. "Barney?" he asked.

"That's him. He really doesn't take any getting used to," I continued, "and I have breakfast."

"I'm already sold. No persuasion necessary. Why didn't you think I'd say yes?"

"I thought you might find a sleepover at a yellow bungalow emasculating."

"I already agreed to play the role of the nurse, how much worse can it get for me? Will there be any sex?"

"Absolutely."

"Then..." Solomon showed me his palms and stuck his head forward a little, eyes wide, as if to say "What's up?"

"Okay, you got me, what if one of the guys drives past my house and sees your car?" I asked, wondering why the hell this stuff came out of my mouth. I wanted him in my home. I just didn't think he wanted to be there, despite what he said.

"Why would anyone drive past your house in the middle of the night?"

"Why does anyone do anything? I don't know."

"Lucas doesn't like the outdoors. I know Delgado is staying with your sister tonight, and Fletcher and Flaherty went to a casino."

"I hope they're not robbing it."

Solomon laughed. "Me too. All the same, no one is around, so you're safe."

"So... you don't want to be seen at my house?" I frowned.

"I didn't say that. You invited me over, I said yes, then you... are we having an argument?"

"Not unless we can have angry, make-up sex."

"I thought you wanted to play doctors and nurses?"

"I want to be the patient now."

"And I want to give you a full physical and I don't care whose house it's in."

I looked over at the table next to us. The woman was staring at Solomon and rapidly fanning herself while her male companion droned on about his golf handicap. If I turned down a full physical by Solomon, I'd be letting the female species down. That would be wrong.

"You're on. Say no more. I'm glad you're sleeping over and really, *really* sorry you don't have any pajamas. You'll have to sleep naked. Yay!"

Our female neighbor gasped as she reached for a cracker.

"Glad you're happy. Are you eating that?" Solomon pointed his fork at my plate. "Can I?"

"Human garbage disposal."

"Thank you." And Solomon finished off my plate. I decided that was a good thing because he would probably need the energy. However, when we climbed into the car a little later, and Solomon did his cursory visual checks as always, I couldn't help wondering if he would have turned down my offer if any of the guys at work were likely to be in the neighborhood. The secret relationship thing was great in parts: no one to tease me, no one to imply I got my job through sleeping with the boss while I try to convince them that I wasn't when he offered me the job, and no one to get my mother's hopes up that she might have finally married me off — but it also had its downsides. We had yet to dine somewhere without worrying about running into other people we knew, not that I knew for sure if Solomon had any close friends, and we never made PDAs. Even hand-holding ran a risk of us being found out so we didn't.

A part of me kind of wanted to be exposed, perhaps so that Lily wouldn't be my only friend who knew, or so I could go public with the relationship and not worry about it affecting my work life. I just didn't know if Solomon felt the same. How I felt about that, I wasn't sure, but there was much less worry, dented pride, and even a tiny bit of relief at the lack of interference from everyone else.

CHAPTER THREE

When I awoke the next morning, sated and yawning, I could feel Solomon next to me, warmth radiating from his body. We slept in the guest bedroom downstairs while I finished painting my bedroom in the attic.. Although I missed my new, king-sized bed upstairs, at least the kitchen was downstairs and within staggering distance. The scent of coffee hung in the air so I figured he'd already gotten up, made a pot, and returned to bed, all without waking me. He was stealthy like that. Again, I was glad he was on my team and not out to rob me, because I really wouldn't have heard a thing.

I stretched until the tips of my toes touched the footboard and my fingertips the headboard, then rolled over and snuggled into him. His arms went around me and I smooshed my head against his muscular chest. My tongue stayed in my mouth by sheer force of will. I couldn't think of a better way to start the day. Or a much better way to end it either. After the past forty-eight hours, it was tempting not to get up at all.

"Can we stay here all day?" I asked, my voice

muffled against his skin.

"I heard 'mumph-mumph day'," said Solomon, tucking a piece of hair that had fallen across my face behind my ear.

I lifted my head, and looked sleepily up at him. Damn it, he'd already had a shower and brushed his teeth, while my hair was still stuck to one side of my face. Peeking under the quilt, I saw he was clad only in boxers. Tight ones. Hubba. I repeated the question, adding, "How long ago did you get up?"

"I wish, and around an hour. I had some phone calls to make. Speaking of calls, your phone keeps buzzing."

"Did you look?"

"No."

"What if it was another guy?"

Solomon raised his eyebrows skeptically. All the same, he said, "Your business."

"Might be a hot date," I teased, waiting for the reaction that never came. What was up with that? "You can look if you want. It's probably Lily. Or my mom."

"Has your mom taken up any new hobbies?" Solomon grinned. I remembered the one time I took him to a family dinner and my mother wanted him to enroll in a survival skills class. Like he needed it. He politely declined and I got lumped with both the class and the practical excursion. My mother's gift of a knife came in handy though, and I still had it, just in case I needed to cut anything or stab someone else.

I sighed. "I hope not."

"Have you taken up any hobbies?"

"Only you, and painting this house."

"I'm now a hobby?"

"One with infinite possibilities and many, many years of research."

"Years, huh?" Solomon wriggled away from me and slung his legs out of bed. "I looked through your kitchen cabinets. I'm making French toast with bacon." He waited.

I waited. He made a gesture with his hands, signaling he wanted a yes or no. "What?" I asked, "You think I'm going to say no to that?"

"It was fifty-fifty after your newfound commitment to the gym." Solomon leaned down, both hands on the mattress, and planted a kiss on my nose. "Get ready. Breakfast is in fifteen minutes."

"It's not newfound! I've had membership for years." I watched Solomon disappear around the corner, a pair of jeans in his hands. "It's waning though," I muttered to myself, trying not to think of Jim Schwarz or Karen Doyle.

While Solomon earned serious points in the kitchen, I headed upstairs to use the bathroom and gather my clothes. I got ready lightning fast, scrubbed my teeth, showered, and fastened my hair in a neat pony. A clean, white shirt, dark blue jeans and the cutest pink pumps in the world prepared me to face the day. My stomach started growling the moment the bacon aroma reached my nostrils.

As I descended the stairs, and passed through the small hallway to the guest bedroom, I grabbed my cell phone from the nightstand. Making my way into the sunlit kitchen, I had to rub my stomach in an effort not to scare Solomon with the internal baying for food.

Solomon had already laid the plates, filled the glasses with orange juice and poured coffee. He even found the maple syrup and added it to the table. "This looks amazing," I told him, joining him and sitting down. "And it smells delicious."

"Let's go three for three and hope it tastes good too," he said, moments before a heaped forkful landed in his mouth. I followed his lead. My shoulders dropped, my head dipped to one side. "Mmm," I murmured, the wonderful flavors swirling deliciously on my tongue. "Mmm-mmm-mmm."

My phone buzzed just as I dropped my fork onto the empty plate and reached for my coffee. I picked it up, reading the message from my new gym buddy, Lorena. It said *Call me ASAP. Need to talk. Lx.*

Scrolling through my phone, I saw it wasn't the first time she called. There were five text messages from Lorena, each with a variation of the same thing, starting from last night. There was one from Lily too, asking if I wanted to join her for a drink at her bar later; and one from my mother that I think she must have meant for my dad, because after reading it, my eyes flew open wide and I almost lost my breakfast.

"I need to make some calls," said Solomon, sliding his chair out and reaching for the plates.

"I'll clear," I told him, laying my hand over his for the briefest of moments, but long enough to give me that tingling feeling I always got whenever he was near. "Thank you. This was great."

"Anytime." He leaned over, kissed me again, this time on the cheek, then left the kitchen. He closed the door to the guest bedroom, and a moment later, I heard his muffled voice.

I cleared the plates, rinsing them in the sink, and leaving them stacked while I texted Lily a *yes*, my mother an *OMG!* and then Lorena, asking if she was okay. She called me right back.

"Hey, what's up?" I asked when I answered. "I got six messages from you. I was at dinner so I didn't check my phone."

"It's okay. I had some bad news and... I just need to talk to you," said Lorena, the urgency apparent in her voice. "Soon."

"Okay. Want to meet at the gym? Or did you want to take a run too?" I asked, hoping she would say yes. It would be nice to get my mind off Jim Schwarz and Karen Doyle. Lorena and I hadn't run together for a couple of weeks after she sustained a sprained ankle. I checked in on her every few days and she assured me she'd be better soon and was looking forward to taking a few light runs.

"Not today. I don't feel so great and I really need someone to talk to." Lorena sniffed and her voice wavered. Now that I thought about it, she really didn't sound so great, and though I hadn't known her for very long, she was usually a warm, bubbly woman. Something was definitely upsetting her.

"Has something happened? Is everything okay? Is it Marnie?" I asked, knowing she was previously concerned about her daughter away at college.

"No, Marnie's great. She got an A on her English paper. It's something else. Lexi, I can't talk on the phone, but I really need to see you. Can you come over now?"

"Where are you?"

"At home."

I estimated how long it would take me to kiss Solomon goodbye, throw a few things in my bag, and tidy the house before I left. "I can be there in under an hour."

"No, I need to speak to you sooner. It's really important, Lexi, or I wouldn't ask."

"Okay," I paused, noticing the tremor in Lorena's voice, the sniffle that could be almost a sob. Lorena lived in a small link house not far away from my old apartment. I could leave the washing for later and only needed to grab my wallet. "Twenty minutes. I'll leave right away. Do you need anything? Medicine or... tissues?"

"No, nothing. Just you. Please hurry, Lexi. I think... I think I'm in trouble."

"Don't worry. Try and relax. I'll be right over and we can work things out," I assured her. Truth be told, I was a little pleased that she called me to help her. Obviously, she thought a lot of our new friendship; and I decided I'd help her however I could.

"Okay," Lorena sniffed again. "Okay." She hung up without saying goodbye.

I stared at my phone, puzzled. Since meeting Lorena a couple of months ago at the gym, we'd gotten friendly. When she mentioned she was starting to train for a half marathon, something to motivate her towards eventually doing the Boston marathon, I told her I wasn't a particularly good runner, but wanted to be. We agreed to be running partners in order to motivate each other. Since then, we regularly ran twice a week, pounding the sidewalks of Montgomery before bonding over pots of coffee. She lived alone, her daughter Marnie only coming home for vacations, and was all kinds of interested in my job since finding out I was a PI. I didn't expect to be a person she called when she needed help though, so I wondered what was bothering her that she didn't turn to family or a closer friend. Still, I said I would be there so I ducked my head around the door to the bedroom and told Solomon I had to go.

He held one finger to his lips, said something into his cell phone, and hung up.

"Sorry, was I interrupting?"

"No. We finished. Did something come up at the agency?"

I shook my head. "A friend called. I think I mentioned her a couple of times. Lorena Vasquez. The one I've been running with? She's upset and wanted to talk. I said I'd go over."

"Are you coming into work?"

"I'll make the meeting."

"You sure?"

"Absolutely. I never miss one unless I'm undercover or on a job; but I filed my last report and I don't have any ongoing cases."

"Unless there's a shoe sale," said Solomon, ignoring that and focusing on a more valid reason why I might be late.

"How dare you!" I feigned mock anger. "I shop online. I'm still there *physically*."

Solomon just shook his head and reached for his sweater. "Let me grab my stuff. I can finish my calls at the office."

"I don't mind giving you a key."

"Nah. I'll leave with you."

I didn't get much of a lingering kiss, but on the porch, I received a fast and furious one and some stray hands, which nearly had us rolling through the front door and back into the house! That, however, would have made Solomon late for work, and me renege on my agreement to Lorena, so instead, we agreed to meet up for a lunchtime horizontal later in the day.

I called Lily as I drove to Lorena's place, cursing the slow traffic. "Tell me this," I said. "Are Solomon and I boyfriend-girlfriend or what?"

"Have either of you said you are?" she asked, her voice filling the car's speakers.

"Not exactly. I know we're dating but... I mean, who says 'are you my boyfriend?' It's so…"

"High school?"

"Yeah. So I kind of just call him my boyfriend in my head," I said, pausing at how lame that sounded. On the plus side, I could call all kinds of guys my boyfriend in my head and they could never complain. Win!

"So what's the situ? Did you have dinner last night?"

"Yeah, at some Thai place that no one we know goes to."

"Maybe he really likes the food."

"Maybe he doesn't want to be seen with me. He stayed over at my house."

"Oooh!"

"But I think it was because there was zero chance one of the guys at work would make an accidental driveby."

"Pfft," said Lily. "Do you care when you leave your car at Solomon's?"

32

"No. He made me French toast."

"He's your boyfriend."

"He kissed me on the nose this morning."

"Had you brushed your teeth?"

"No."

"He's still your boyfriend. And your problem is?"

"My phone kept going off and I said maybe it was a guy, and Solomon said 'your business' like he didn't care, and it didn't matter if I had another guy in the wings."

"What exactly were Solomon's words?"

"'Your business'."

"So he didn't say anything else?"

"No."

"Have you told him you love him yet? You know, since you two actually got together?"

"No! Okay, in my head. But he told me ages ago and he hasn't said it since."

"Maybe he's waiting for you this time. Be brave, Lexi. You don't need to wait for a guy. You are a modern woman. You can do whatever the hell you want, including making the first move."

"You speak sense."

"I know and I haven't even been drinking. When are you coming by the bar? We need to talk wedding dresses, bridesmaid dresses, and everything else wedding. Oh! The wedding reception!"

"At the bar? The reception is at the bar?" I turned onto Lorena's road and began the tedious search for her house. They all looked the same, which didn't help. "I thought it was at The Belmont."

"Talking about the reception at the bar," Lily clarified. "Where are you anyway? Are you going to work? Did you get a case? Is it juicy? Is it about the two people from our gym?"

"Schwarz and Doyle?"

"They sound like a coffee brand. Are you

investigating their deaths?"

"No, Maddox said Jim Schwarz's death was natural, and I don't think anyone even called the police for Karen Doyle, just an ambulance."

"Huh. Well, I guess, they're the experts. Wasn't Karen the same woman who sat next to Jim yesterday?"

That made me take notice. I did think she looked familiar. "Really?"

"I think so. Yeah, I'm sure she did. Oh, that's bad."

"I know. Really sad."

"No, I meant you'll never be able to find out where she got that cute top from now. Where did you say you're going again?"

"My friend, Lorena's house."

"Who?"

"My running partner. I told you. You met her last week. She called and said she needed to talk."

"What about?" Lily asked and I heard a smash in the background. Lily groaned.

"No idea, but I'm here now," I said, stopping at Lorena's house, right behind her Toyota. "See you at seven?"

"There will be a mojito with your name on it."

"I won't be late."

Lorena's house was the middle in a row of link houses all painted the same sandy beige with identical paths leading to the door and identical rectangular patches of grass. It was a new development, less than a decade old, and mostly populated by singles. I remembered Jord once looked at a house here and decided the area was too boring for a single guy. Lorena, as a mom, clearly had different priorities. I crossed the sidewalk, taking the pathway that led up to her steps and small porch.

My hand was already raised to knock when I noticed the door was ajar, not by much, maybe only an inch or so, but enough to make me frown. Lorena never left her door open, or unlocked, even when she was home since she'd had the uncomfortable feeling someone had been in her home a month ago... and she was expecting me. I pushed it open a little further and poked my head around. "Hello?" I waited a moment, then, "Hi, Lorena. It's me. Lexi."

Nothing.

I stepped inside. Lorena's purse was on the console by the door and her pumps underneath it. A radio played in the kitchen, pumping out a Bruno Mars track. Despite the upbeat music, a chill traveled through me. Something wasn't right. The house was too still.

"Lorena?" I called one more time, just in case she was in the bathroom. Still nothing. I remembered her telling me she just had a deck built out back and she liked to sit there some mornings.. I closed the door behind me, shrugged off my discomfort, and walked past the leather couches and the round, oak dining table. I veered off to the left into her kitchen. Stepping inside, I saw her; and a cold wave of fear gripped me, rooting me to the spot.

Lorena couldn't answer the door. She would never answer the door again.

She lay sprawled on the floor, facing the ceiling, eyes open and motionless. Judging by the stillness of her body, she clearly wasn't breathing. A knife handle protruded from her chest and her top was soaked red. The blood pooled beneath her, spreading into a vile puddle as I watched.

I gazed down at my dead friend, knowing there wasn't a damn thing I could do to bring her back.

It could have been seconds, or minutes, I didn't know, before I fumbled in my pocket for my phone and hit "speed dial." This time, I didn't call Maddox; I called Solomon. When his voicemail clicked on, I left him a calm message telling him my friend was dead and where to find me.

After hanging up, I slid my back down the wall until

I was huddled into a crouch, my arms around my knees. I was trying not to look, but unable to resist, being so close to Lorena and a whole world away. All I could do was sit on the cold tile and wait anxiously for Solomon to come.

CHAPTER FOUR

"One death is unlucky, two deaths a coincidence, and three is downright suspicious," said Solomon.

We were sitting in my living room, an hour after being finally allowed to leave the crime scene, but even my sunny, little house couldn't cheer me. Not after the brutal scene I stumbled upon.

Solomon came for me, as I knew he would. He entered the house, stealthy as always and found me staring at Lorena's body. After checking my vitals, he took charge, carrying me outside and settling me on the porch steps before calling the police.

Maddox arrived first, apparently back from the fraud squad to homicide, then my oldest brother Garrett, now a lieutenant. After them, came a stream of cops, the coroner, the morgue van — the guys driving it did a double take when they saw me, then waved cheerfully like we were old friends. Solomon insisted on taking me home before they removed Lorena's body. He hadn't left me alone for more than a minute or two since.

Now, there was just the two of us. Well, the two of

us, plus Delgado, Fletcher and Flaherty, the three other PIs at the agency. Lucas declined for reasons Solomon didn't share, and chose instead to text them several times to check on me.

With the exception of my colleagues camped in my living room, and the horrible scene every time I closed my eyes, all was normal in my world. I clung to it, seeking it out, taking comfort in all the things that hadn't changed. Next door, Aidan had some machinery running and Barney, his dog, was barking. Someone honked a horn. A cell phone rang. The aroma of coffee was fresh, the liquid hot on my tongue, but I could barely taste it.

I nodded at Solomon's declaration, noticing my three colleagues looked equally interested now that we had one murder and two suspicious deaths.

"How much do you know about Lorena?" Matt Flaherty asked. He was an ex-detective, no longer on the force after an unfortunate incident with a bullet rendered him an invalid, but he was still a great investigator. I wasn't sure how Solomon knew him, only that their friendship went back a long time.

"Not much," I told him. "We met at the gym and we'd been running together these past two months. She has an adult daughter at college. She's single. We didn't talk about her daughter's dad so I don't know what the deal is with him."

"You met at the gym," Delgado repeated, clearly pondering it. Settling himself in my oversized armchair, his massive body filled the whole thing. With a huge physique, he could look pretty scary if you didn't know him. Unlike my colleagues, I knew a softer side to him, which was recently revealed when he started dating my sister. My baby niece adored him and hers was an excellent seal of approval. "Did Lorena know the other two people that died?"

"I don't know." I tried to recall. Had I seen her

talking to anyone? Yes, yes, I had. "I think she knew the woman. Karen. The treadmill…" I used my fingers to mime two legs running, then flying off it. It wasn't much of a demonstration, but I never managed to find a temp job where I could have possibly perfected my skills at it. "I remember now. I saw them talking a couple of times so I guess they knew each other, but I don't know how well."

Delgado nodded. "It's a start. At least, it's a connection."

"And Lily said Karen was the woman who was sitting next to Jim Schwarz in our spin class when he died."

"That's damn suspicious," said Solomon amidst murmurs of agreement.

Opening my mouth to point out that's exactly what I'd been saying the last two days, my cell phone suddenly rang and I reached for it, recognizing the name that flashed across the screen. "It's Michael. He manages the gym," I said.

"Answer it," said Solomon and the room went quiet. Nosy bunch. All the same, I answered, "Hi, Michael."

"Lexi, is it true? Is Lorena dead?"

I took a deep breath. "Yes."

"I heard you found her."

"Also true."

"Oh, God. I just can't believe it. First Jim and Karen, now Lorena. Does it sound bad that I'm relieved she didn't die at the gym too? I'd be so much happier if she was alive, but… this is terrible. I'm really sorry you were the one who found her."

"Me too." We paused, and mine was silent and reflective. I couldn't blame him for anything he said. Of course, he didn't want another death occurring at the gym. Two was two too many already.

"Lexi, I heard you are a private investigator. Is that true, too?"

"Uh, yes."

"Then, I want to hire you," Michael said promptly.

"Say what?" I asked, as Solomon mouthed something incomprehensible.

"I want to hire you. The gym group has their own lawyers here in case we get sued by the families, but I want someone to find out what happened. I want someone I can trust to find out if there is anything up with these deaths. If it's... it's... I guess what I'm trying to see it's all too suspicious," he added, echoing the same words now coming from several others' lips.

"Hold on a second," I told Michael, before covering the phone with my hand. I locked eyes with Solomon. "He wants to hire me. He wants someone to investigate and find out what happened."

"Tell him to come by the office today."

I put the phone back to my cheek. "My boss says to come by the office today." I reeled off the address while he noted it down before he read it back to me to be sure he had it right.

"I'll be there. Thanks, Lexi. This whole business is giving me the creeps. Both Jim and Karen were fit, healthy people, and used to regular exercise. They couldn't have just dropped dead. And Lorena... I just don't know. Who would want to hurt her?"

"You're not the only one who's concerned," I assured him in the most inefficient way. After hanging up, I raised my eyebrows at Solomon, waiting for him to say something. When he didn't, I said, "Guess someone has to go back to the office."

He nodded. "You're coming too."

"I didn't say I wasn't."

"Just making sure. Don't want you going into shock all by yourself. Everyone, we'll meet you at the agency. We have a meeting to make and a potential new client to interview. Lexi, I want you to ride with me."

"My car is right outside," I said, pointing to my VW

in the driveway. Although I'd driven it home, with Solomon on my tail the whole way, I barely remembered the journey. Solomon gave me a look. "Fine, you can play chauffeur for the day," I conceded, secretly touched at his concern.

We waited as Delgado, Fletcher, and Flaherty exited my house, softly closing the door behind them before taking off in Delgado's car.

"How you doin'?" Solomon asked.

I grinned. "Better since your Joey impression."

"Who?"

"Joey, from only the biggest sitcom ever…" Solomon gave me a blank look. Right. He probably spent that decade killing people in the jungle or something. How could he have found the time to watch television? "Oh, never mind. I'm okay. I was just so shocked when I saw Lorena. It's so different finding someone you know murdered."

"You've found people you know dead," he pointed out, which, unfortunately, was true.

"This is different. I actually liked Lorena. She was nice and fast becoming a friend."

"I'm sorry you had to see her like that."

"She was the one who called this morning, you know, and last night. She kept leaving messages, saying she needed to talk, but when I called her after breakfast, she said she couldn't talk over the phone. She sounded worried about something. Maybe If I hadn't called Lily or there hadn't been so much traffic, I could have found out what was wrong and she might still be alive." It was the same argument that kept replaying through my brain. What, if anything, could I have done differently to change the outcome? The rational part of me said nothing. There was no other outcome.

"Or you could have walked in on her being attacked and be dead now too," said Solomon, his blunt tone sending a chill through my spine. "So don't question anything you did or didn't do. Lorena Vasquez is dead. You can't change that now."

"That's some straight talking, John." I rarely called him by his given name and when I did, he smiled, which is what he did now. Being rewarded with a smile like that, no wonder I saved his name only for special occasions.

"Yes it is, Lexi Graves."

"Okay." I nodded to show I understood, that I wouldn't continue to second-guess myself. "What next?"

"Now we go to the agency and see your potential client."

"Mine?"

"You're my best PI for the job. You know the people, you're familiar with the locale. You want point on this?"

I gave a decisive nod. "You bet."

By the time Solomon and I meandered over to the office, Michael had already arrived and was seated in the small boardroom we usually used for internal meetings or the occasional client. Mostly, we saw our clients in a suite of interview rooms a floor down from our offices, but they were currently closed for painting.

"When did he get here?" Solomon asked, pausing by Fletcher's desk. Delgado's was empty and a fresh take-out coffee sat on Flaherty's, so I guessed he was around somewhere. Lucas's monitors were blank, but his jacket hung over his desk chair. I looked up at the ceiling. Hmmm. Maybe he was up there, on the new, not very secret floor, but where very secret things happened. Secret things I made it one of my missions to find out about.

Fletcher jumped and looked up. I smirked to myself, glad I wasn't the only one Solomon could surprise. "Twenty minutes, boss. Said he'd wait, so I put him in there with a magazine."

"A nice one?" I asked.

"Your dirty ones are locked in your drawer," Fletcher quipped as I stuck my tongue out at him.

Solomon nudged my elbow. "Let's go talk to him."

I dropped my sandwich on my desk. I didn't have the appetite for it anyway. I could not get the image of Lorena lying dead on her kitchen floor out of my mind. I thought about the other two dead people I previously encountered, but they didn't hit me in the same way. I only knew them by face, not as friends. With Lorena, it was personal. Jim Schwarz and Karen Doyle's deaths were so much cleaner too. One minute they were there, the next... gone. I wondered if Michael was taking the ghastly trio of deaths personally. He was a friendly sort and I often saw him chatting warmly to members.

"Thanks for coming in," said Solomon, extending his hand to Michael's as we entered. Michael shook his first, then mine, and I saw the guys take a moment to size each other up while I introduced them. They were comparable in height, but Michael was broader and more muscular than Solomon. That was saying something as my boss was no weakling in any way, and definitely more handsome. All the same, the sight of Michael's bicep stretching his short-sleeved white t-shirt didn't bother me.

"I appreciate you taking the time to see me. Hey, Lexi. You okay?" he asked, his concerned eyes running over me.

"I've had better days," I said, taking the seat opposite him as Solomon moved to the head of the table.

"It's a damn shame. Lorena seemed like such a nice person."

"She was," I agreed.

"Tell us why you think we should investigate," said Solomon.

"Truthfully, I don't know," Michael said, giving us a shrug and a confused shake of his head. "I know it looks like Jim Schwarz and Karen Doyle died of natural causes, but two in two days? And now Lorena? It doesn't make any sense. I have a very bad feeling."

"Lorena's death was definitely not natural," Solomon pointed out.

"I know. I heard," Michael said, sounding somewhat distressed.

"How did you hear?" I asked. "You called me pretty quick."

"We have a few officers at the gym. They talk. I overhear."

"Can you think of any connection between the three deceased?" Solomon inquired.

Michael nodded. "Only the gym. That's the only connection. Here's my big worry: that someone at the gym targeted those folks and perhaps they're not done yet. I can't have a murderer killing off my clients. Maybe someone has it in for the gym."

"Most people would feel the same," agreed Solomon, "but there's nothing to suggest that Jim and Karen were murdered, or that your gym might be a target."

"Yet," said Michael.

"Yet," agreed Solomon.

"But don't you think it's suspicious too?" Michael waited, looking alternately at both of us.

There was a long pause in which Solomon leaned back in his chair, his hand under his chin as he assessed the situation. "I think it's something to look at more closely," he said and Michael gave a relieved sigh before slumping back in his chair.

"And you?" Michael asked, looking at me. I nodded too. "Then I want to hire you."

"It might not be what you think," Solomon warned, "it could be nothing. Or, it could be natural causes from underlying health conditions. It could be a problem at the gym, or with one of your employees, or even a member. We can't predict which one of those things it is. Are you sure you want to hire the agency, or would you rather wait for the police to finish their investigations?"

"I'm worried they might not investigate the deaths of Jim and Karen at all, to concentrate on Lorena since they know she was murdered for sure. Not that she doesn't deserve all their efforts. I hope they find the bastard that did that to her. I just don't want someone else dying in my gym while they're not looking, or if, when they finally look, there's no evidence. Or if every potential witness's brain goes funny and no one can remember what they saw or heard."

"You think like an investigator," said Solomon.

"I think like a man who wants to keep his job while making sure no one else dies," replied Michael.

"Can you afford us?" asked Solomon, predictably.

"Yes, I have access to discretionary funds. If something hinky is going on, the gym's owners will be glad I used the money to investigate. Whatever happens, you'll get paid. I promise you that."

"Okay, Lexi will run through the paperwork with you. You'll sign it, pay a retainer, and we'll get started. We can do all that at the end of the meeting. Right now, I need to know a few things. Are the areas where the two deaths occurred at the gym secure?"

"No one's been inside the spin studio ever since the police left. I had it locked up."

"Cleaners?"

"Not yet."

"No one touched anything?"

"Nope."

"And the treadmill?"

"Had it put in storage in the basement. Me and my assistant manager moved it, but we used gloves. The gym is still open."

"Good thinking. What about the possessions of the deceased?"

"The police weren't interested so we left their lockers be. Jim might have left something in the spin studio and, like I said, that's still locked up. There was a water bottle and towel on the treadmill Karen used, and they're both in my office."

"You called Lexi because you knew she was a private investigator. Is that common knowledge at the gym?" Solomon inquired, glancing at me quickly. I shook my head.

"I only knew because Lexi told me a while back," said Michael, looking toward me for confirmation.

I nodded. "Lorena knew too, and Lily. I don't think anyone else knows though. You've told me not to discuss it, which is why I don't. Lily and I have been going there for years so I'm a familiar face, um, occasionally."

"Did anyone know that you knew Lorena? Or the other deceased?"

I shook my head. "I only got to know Lorena recently and we met up outside the gym to run. We haven't though for the past couple of weeks because of her ankle injury. I didn't know the other two, but I did see them from time to time. Familiar faces, but not enough to talk to. No one would think I have any particular connection to any of them."

"Okay, so it's probably safe to keep Lexi at the gym so she can monitor the situation. She'll need to be the eyes and ears for anything suspicious that we should investigate." Solomon stood and took the few steps over to the door to beckon Flaherty in. The ex-detective appeared at the door. "Flaherty can liaise with the coroner and MPD here."

"Yes, boss," said Flaherty, giving a single nod before shutting the door behind him. A moment later, he was at his desk, on a phone and dialing.

"Lexi will fill you in," said Solomon. "Michael, what reason could Lexi have for explaining why she's at the gym so much?"

"I have a vacancy for a spin instructor now that

46

Anton's taking a few weeks off."

They both looked at me. "You have got to be kidding?" I spluttered. "Me? A spin instructor? All that cycling and going nowhere?"

"I know you spin," said Michael.

"Under sufferance!"

"Maybe you could just be an instructor," said Michael. "A trainee? Then it doesn't matter that you don't know much. You won't even have to teach any classes!"

I looked at Solomon and nodded; he shrugged, so I turned back to Michael. "I guess so long as I don't have to teach anything since I can't do that. Being on staff would be a good cover to talk to employees and clients."

Solomon placed his forearms on the table and nodded his approval. "That's settled then. Lexi, you start tomorrow. Michael, can you get everything arranged for Lexi to start so her cover is in place?"

"No problem."

"Again, I want to make clear we cannot control the outcome. We might find nothing or we might find out your most trusted employee is a maniacal psychopath."

"I kind of hope you do," said Michael, "find nothing, that is. That would be the perfect outcome for the gym if it were just sheer coincidence."

Despite his affirmation, as I looked at each of the men in the room, I knew that none of us thought this would be a clear-cut case, or that it was entirely a coincidence. Each of us smelled murder. The big question: was there a serial killer at my gym? And was another victim in the killer's sights?

~

"You? A gym instructor? Oh, please!" giggled Lily after I filled her in on my newest case. It was right after I told her about Lorena over my first drink. We were sitting at the end of the bar, away from the burgeoning after-work crowd and the mood was pretty heavy until now.

"You didn't laugh this much when I told you I was going to be a PI." I pouted as I reached for my melon mojito and took a sip. Lily's bar may have been the newest addition to Montgomery's social scene, but judging by the early evening buzz, it was already a success. That was due, in no small part, to having hired Ruby Kalouza, currently serving. Besides her many other surprising talents, she was also an amazing cocktail mixer. The mojito was delicious.

"That's because you are a natural PI. You are not a natural gym instructor."

"Michael said I could be a spin instructor."

"Oh stop!" screeched Lily. "You're making my sides hurt! I have to drag you into Anton's class."

"Anton's taking a few weeks off. Apparently, having someone die in his class really got to him."

"Can't say it did much for me either. I'm thinking of taking up road cycling."

"You don't even have a bike."

"True. Maybe I'll just get my cardio by treadmill..." She paused and we both thought of Karen Doyle. "Maybe not."

"We could do yoga," I suggested, "it's not at all dangerous."

"Or pilates," agree Lily. "Or aqua aerobics?"

"I don't want to get my hair wet."

"Good point. So when do you start?"

"Tomorrow. I don't even have to teach a class, just wear a tight t-shirt. Hey, did you tell anyone I'm a PI?"

"No. Why?"

"I'm going undercover. I need to question people to find out who might be a killer."

"If they make you wear one of those t-shirts that the female staff wear, no one will be able to think straight when they answer your subtle questions," said Lily, gesturing at my chest. The girls were currently ensconced in a very nice bra and not a distraction at all. I hadn't noticed my chest drawing anyone else's attention lately either, but I supposed that was just a matter of time. "Talk about weapons of mass distraction," she giggled.

I pulled a face. "Really? They're not that big and not everyone looks at them." I looked down. Yep, they were looking good. Props to me! "Maybe they're lonely. I wonder who I can ask to keep them company?"

"Heh!" Lily snorted. "Back up... Seriously? There's a serial killer in our gym?" Lily gaped at me. Her hand bobbed around on the bar, searching for her drink so I pushed the glass into her hand. She raised it to her mouth, taking a big gulp, never taking her eyes off me.

"That's what I have to find out."

"I might suspend my membership."

"I don't think anyone's going to kill you."

"Why not? Is the serial killer really picky? Doesn't he like blondes?" She tugged at a blonde curl, straightening it, and letting it go so it bounced back into a loose ringlet. I recalled the days when I was blonde, which were abruptly cut short when I had to dye my hair for a disguise. Since then, I let it grow out to my natural brunette.

"Okay, maybe they will kill you next," I decided in a rare moment of hair jealousy.

"Maybe I'll just cancel for now and rejoin when you catch him or her. Dammit, I have a pedicure booked at their spa on Friday. Do you think you could catch the killer before then?"

"Probably not, sorry."

"Can you at least try?" Lily pleaded.

"I will. I promise. Anyway, as Solomon and everyone else pointed out, it might still just be a really unlucky set of sad coincidences."

"Yeah, a knife in the heart sounds pretty unlucky to me too."

"Except Lorena," I conceded.

"Poor Lorena. I was going to invite her to the wedding." Lily looked down at her notepad where she listed the invitees to her forthcoming wedding. "Now who can I invite to fill her space?"

"I don't know. I'm sure you'll find someone. Ask Jord. You might have missed a relative."

"I'm not inviting *all* your relatives."

I looked at the list. "Are you sure? It looks like you are. Ohmygod, is that Grandma O'Shaughnessy? You can't invite her!"

"Why not?"

"She's scary."

"She's your grandmother!"

"That's not a get out of jail free card!"

"I can't *not* invite her."

"You could lose the invitation. Blame it on her. She's ancient and probably more than a little forgetful."

"Lexi, that's terrible. Anyway, do you want me to write John Solomon or plus one on your invitation?"

That had me stumped. Appearing with Solomon as my date to Lily and Jord's wedding would be about as official as it could get in Montgomery. Everyone would know, and those who didn't know would know by the next day. "I still don't know if we're dating-dating or just dating?"

"What's the difference?"

"Monogamous dating and calling each other boyfriend-girlfriend, or just casual dating."

"You still haven't asked him!"

"It never came up before! Then, Lorena died and I got hired to find a killer so I didn't have any time to mention it today."

"You need to ask him. Do not ruin my seating arrangements, Lexi. I mean it," she added, her eyes narrowing.

"Bridezilla."

"If you call me that again, I'll make sure you pay for all your future cocktails."

"I'll ask him soon," I promised as I finished my mojito and Lily ordered us fresh drinks. "If I drink too many of these, I'll ask him when I'm drunk; then I won't care if he just says it's casual. Tomorrow, I have another job anyway, and la-la-la, my life will be over." I lay my head on the cool bar and Lily stroked my hair.

"You really should never date the boss. Why couldn't you stick with sexual harassment?"

"Sexual harassment doesn't make French toast," I muttered. "Or look like sex on a stick. And I love him." I hiccupped. The alcohol that once seemed so warming, was now hitting me hard.

"I'm gonna leave your table placement until last," Lily decided. "Now as to the dresses... I was thinking pink as the final choice, but maybe we should get you black in case the serial killer gets to you first. Then it can double as your funeral gown. Black is very chic for weddings, so that's a good thing. I feel so frugal now I know you can wear it again."

"Screw my life," I said, lifting my head as the newest drinks appeared in front of us. I plucked a straw from the container, stuck it in the glass and took a healthy slurp.

"Just don't screw up my wedding. If you're a no-show and dead, that will totally steal my limelight. And don't be late for the fitting either! Promise me, Lexi, hand on heart: you will not let the killer get you."

I rose upright, straightened my back and placed my hand over my heart. "I promise to not let a serial killer get me or to ruin your wedding. Your wedding will be perfect." I didn't even think to cross my fingers.

CHAPTER FIVE

I had never been inside the gym after hours when it was closed. There was something eerie about the rows of silent machines, the neatly stacked weights and mats, the smell of cleaning solution still faint in the air. I couldn't quite equate it with the place where I sweated for years, with similar bodies heaving, sweating, and gasping for breath to a soundtrack of motivational tunes pumped through speakers.

Michael and I had arranged to meet an hour before the gym opened so I could investigate both the spin studio and the treadmill. I didn't really relish the idea of combing the areas for anything suspicious in the quiet, but it beat doing it when the gym was crowded with a dozen curious eyes watching me. "It's five a.m.," I said, glancing at my watch. "I should still be in bed."

"Sorry, it's the only time we have alone," Michael said, jingling a ring of keys from one hand. "I have to get the studio open. People are complaining it's shut and the gym is closed too much, even threatening to cancel their memberships. I think that's a good thing."

"It is. It means people want to stay."

Michael gave a half-hearted shrug. "What does that say about people's compassion though? Two of our members died here and they just want to get back in for their workouts."

"I couldn't say." To me, it said a lot about the gym members' dedication to good figures, and good health in the face of death, but not so much about being friendly neighbors. I patted Michael's arm as I hefted my camera bag strap onto my shoulder. "Let's check out the studio and get it over with."

"You sure you're up for this?" he asked, giving me a quizzical glance.

"I already wrote up my eyewitness statement for both events, and Detective Maddox took one when he was here too, so I'm good to go. This is not my first death scene," I told him, trying not to sigh. I didn't bother adding that it would be the first one I'd investigated alone. At least, Solomon was on the other end of the line in case I needed him. I bet he was snuggled up warm in bed, unlike me. He didn't stay over so I couldn't be sure.

"Okay," agreed Michael as he unlocked the doors, holding one open for me.

The spin studio had clearly been trampled and was left in a jumbled mess. Countless people must have been through here, none of them concerned that it might have been a crime scene. I mentally thanked Michael's thoughtfulness in sealing it off so that any residual evidence might not get completely obliterated. "I can't believe the police department doesn't want to investigate," he said. "Detective Maddox called and told me yesterday after our meeting."

"I'm sorry. They just don't consider it a possible murder scene."

"Like I said already, I really hope it isn't. I feel sorry for the poor guy, but I hope it was just a heart attack or an aneurysm. You know, something natural."

"Me too," I said, still skeptically fascinated at the probability of two natural deaths within two days, under the same roof.

Michael took one last look around and shook his head. "I'll wait outside. That okay with you?"

"No problem." Michael had no sooner opened the doors when I remembered something, "You said you picked up Karen Doyle's water bottle?"

"That's right."

I handed him a plastic bag from my kit. "Could you put it in here and be careful not to touch it, if you haven't already."

He took the bag and nodded. "Sure thing, Lexi."

I started with my camera, but first made sure I had a memory card inside. In lieu of something in particular to focus on, I snapped everything. Full scene shots and close-ups. Every item left behind in the rush to exit and every single bike. I snapped a shot of the doors, the closed windows, and the air vents.

That finished, I made a beeline for Jim Schwarz's bike, still lying on its side on the floor. I snapped a bunch of shots from different angles, not entirely certain what I was looking for. When I thought I was done, I lay my bag on the floor with the camera on top, just in case I needed it again.

I pulled on gloves and went in for a closer look at the bike. Nothing seemed out of the ordinary. On my notepad, I made a note of the gear position, adding a memo to see if Michael could get a digital readout of its last workout. Perhaps the heart rate monitor could provide something useful? Or maybe Jim was pushing the gears harder than Anton requested? Perhaps he simply overdid it and something inside his body just gave out. That would account for a natural death.

A towel still draped over the handlebars. No water bottle. I couldn't remember if I'd seen Jim holding one either. It would have been perilous to enter a class without one. Staying low to the floor, I looked around. There were a bunch of water bottles on the floor. Since any one of them could have been Jim's, I collected all seven and bagged them. I left the small stack of evidence next to the doors so as not to forget it upon my exit.

Returning to Jim's bike, I knelt down beside it. I started my examination with the stationary wheel and the mechanism. Nothing seemed out of the ordinary. Next the frame. Again, all seemed normal. The saddle was dry and I looked under it too. Nothing concealed. Finally I moved to the handlebars, which were set out in racing and normal riding formation. The towel was draped across the bars, concealing them, and since I'd already photographed it, I scooped it up and dropped it into another evidence bag. Turning back, I saw the strangest little thing. If I'd been standing over the bike, I would have missed it. But kneeling down, with the bike on its side, I had a clear view beneath the bars. I blinked and leaned forwards. Yes, on each bar were two thumbtacks, attached to the underside with the tiniest amount of tape, and almost impossible to see.

I reached for my camera and snapped a half dozen shots from the underside. Both bars together, then separately. Standing, I repeated the photo sequence from the top perspective.

When I was done, I set down the camera and stared at the bike. How would I get this piece of evidence back to the agency for analysis without destroying it? Knowing I was stuck, I reached for my cell phone and called Solomon.

"Sweetheart," he said, upon answering the phone, and I knew he was alone.

"Darling," I replied, smiling to myself, and restraining a giggle.

"What can I do for you?"

"Many, many things," I replied in a husky voice.

"Any of these pertaining to the job?" asked Solomon, a teasing lilt to his voice.

"The current request is…" Oh, how I wanted to play with him, but there was a job to be done. I had something unexplainable, which made me doubt the natural death theory even more. "I found something odd," I told him, quickly describing what it was.

"Any of the other bikes have something similar?"

"I haven't checked them yet, but I will. I'm guessing, no. I've never seen anything like it. The thumbtacks look like they're embedded into the handlebars; and if I pull the tape, I'm worried I could make a mess of the whole thing. Plus, I think I see a little smear of blood. And remember, Jim had a little cut on his thumb."

"Hmmm." Solomon paused and I waited for a genius idea. "Take off the handlebars," he said finally. "I'll get my forensics guy to go over it at his lab."

"What? All of it? How?"

"Yep. Unscrew the lot and bring it in. You're wearing gloves?"

"Yes."

"Good. Make sure you don't touch the bars themselves. I don't like the sound of this."

"Okay."

"Do you have a large evidence bag?"

"A couple are in my kit."

"Use them both and tape them shut. Catch you later."

My breath caught. "Does that involve you chasing me?" I whispered, though I don't know why because I was the only one in the studio.

"Is there a prize if I catch you?" Solomon asked, his voice smooth and inviting.

"Yes, but you'll have to catch me to find out what it is." Saying that, I hung up, leaving him to wonder what I might possibly do with him, which was just as well, since I hadn't worked it out yet either.

Retrieving a screwdriver from my kit, with a confident, happy smile on my face, I set about removing the handlebars. I found two large plastic bags to store them in and slipped one bag over each side before taping the middle closed. Just to make certain these were an anomaly, I checked the handlebars of every single other bike. Not one showed signs of a thumbtack or tape.

If Michael thought it was weird when he saw me taking the whole rack of handlebars, he didn't say. Instead, seeing my armful of evidence, he simply nodded as he added another bag on top. Inside was a blue water bottle with liquid that sloshed back and forth. A sticker on the outside read "Property of Karen Doyle."

"Is it okay if I get this studio cleaned up now?" he asked.

"Sure. There's no reason that you can't. There's nothing more for me to do and if MPD say it isn't a crime scene, then legally, it isn't. I did find something strange though." I showed Michael the handlebars, being careful not to let the thumbtacks stick me, and his forehead furrowed into deep frowns. "Do you know what these are?" I asked.

"No. Nothing like that should be on a spin bike. Ever! It's not safe."

"That's what I thought."

"You think this has something to do with Jim's death?"

"It seems rather odd," I said non-committally. "I'll take it to the agency and we'll send it to the lab for tests. These too." I held up the large, translucent bag holding the individual baggies of water bottles and Jim's towel. "It smells bad in there," I warned Michael.

"Of death?" He shuddered.

"I was referring more along the lines of pee."

"Great. Just great. Three dead clients and a pee odor. Sometimes I hate my job."

For once, I couldn't agree with him. I loved my job! Sure, it had its downsides, not the least of which were the endless hours of surveillance, random corpses, and bodily assaults I occasionally had to endure, but it had a whole bunch of positives too. I got to use my brain to solve baffling crimes, barely had to do any filing, and got to look forward to something different every day. As a double whammy bonus, my whole family was proud I'd finally found my calling, and it didn't fall too far from the family crime-solving tree.

Leaving Michael the unenviable job of setting the spin studio to rights, I took the stairs down to the first floor and exited the building. I carefully stowed my crime treasures in the trunk of my VW. Checking my watch, I saw there was still thirty minutes before my shift began, giving me just enough time to drop the evidence at the agency and return. I left the lot, looking back at the gym in my rear mirror. Did I made the right choice by taking an undercover assignment here? I didn't know the answer to that, but I did know there were three healthy people whose lives were cut short; and maybe, if there was such a thing as an afterlife, they needed me to find out what happened to them.

~

I arrived back at the gym with minutes to spare. The first cars of eager gym bunnies were already pulling into the lot as Michael guided me from the entrance to the office.

"Meet Fairmount Gym's newest fitness instructor," said Michael, flapping a pink t-shirt with the gym's name emblazoned across the front, at me. Unlike the men's version, it did indeed have a deep v-cut and I winced. Lily was right about how distracting my assets might become.

He spun me around to see my reflection in the full-length mirror in his office and wrapped the t-shirt across my front. It wasn't quite waist-length and I made a mental note to thank Lily profusely for all the times she motivated slash dragged me to the gym to firm up my abs. "It looks great!" he exclaimed. "You'll fit right in!"

Personally, I wouldn't consider it quite my shade, but who was I to argue? All I had to do was blend in and try to listen to all the members' conversations to learn anything that people weren't telling the cops. Someone here, I figured, had to know something about what happened, first to Jim Schwarz, and then Karen Doyle, not to mention Lorena's brutal murder in her own home. Someone must have seen something, however innocuous it might seem now, right before their deaths. My aim was to glean every last bit of information for Michael in order to prove that the gym was not negligent. Not only that but I desperately wanted to know who had killed my friend.

"You are aware that I know nothing about fitness, right?" I asked, taking the t-shirt and folding it over my arm.

"I know you come to the gym a lot with your cute friend," replied Michael. He moved around to his side of the desk and rifled through the mound of paperwork until he pulled out one sheet, which he passed to me. "This is your schedule. You don't have to stick to it exactly," he said, "you can come and go as you please. I'll find cover when you can't make it, so just let me know when you plan to be here. I need to square it with the permanent staff so they don't think you're getting preferential treatment. I'll tell them I have you for my personal assistant too. That means I can cover for you if you are somewhere they don't expect you to be. I can just say you're running an errand."

"And just to confirm, I don't have to take any classes?"

"That's right. I've told everyone you're a freelance fitness instructor, but you haven't taught in a while and you're just helping us out with some cover until Anton returns. If he returns," Michael muttered.

"You think he won't?" I asked, glancing up from the schedule. It didn't look too strenuous.

"I don't know. I've never seen a man appear so white."

"He's black."

"Exactly."

"I might need to interview him. He had a really good view of the room."

"Sure." Michael turned around and pulled open a filing cabinet. He plucked a slim file from it, opened it on his desk and grabbed the sticky notes by his desk phone. "Here's his address and phone number," he said, scrawling on the note before passing it to me. He hesitated. "What reason will you give for why you're asking? You've taken his class for a long time. He knows you're not a fitness instructor."

I tucked the address into my pocket. "It's unlikely I'll call but, if I do, I'll think of something."

"Great." Michael relaxed slightly in his chair. "You need to get changed. The gym is officially open for business. Are you ready for this?"

"Never more ready," I assured him. "How hard can it be?"

Michael grinned. "You've clearly never worked in a gym."

~

Never in all the time I have lived in Montgomery — which means my entire life barring a brief stint in Army boot camp, an ill-considered decision of badly dressed proportions — could I imagine just how many fitness fanatics this town contained. The gym was half full only minutes after the doors opened; the treadmills and cross trainers, rowers and steppers, all whirring to life while Lycra-clad people sweated and powered their way to the land of toned bodies. For the first couple of hours, I simply tucked myself away at the instructors' station on the gym floor. I waited for them to get on with their programs, and barely had to answer a single question. Even when I made the occasional rounds, tidying weights here and there, stacking mats next to people, and pausing to chat or eavesdrop, I didn't learn anything useful. By the time Lily came in, it was already noon. My shift was nearly over and my stomach was trying to eat itself.

"Cafe?" I asked Lily when she arrived at the station, clad in cute gray capris and a pristine white, form-fitted top. Headphones slung around her neck completed the look. She might not have worked out today, but her shapely arms and hourglass shape proved she'd been regularly paying her dues.

"Treadmill."

"Cafe," I said again, barely holding back a whimper. "If I don't eat soon, I'm going to bite the head off the next person who asks me to wipe 'em down with a towel."

Lily wrinkled her nose. "Yuck. Someone asked you to do that?"

"Three people. Why? For the love of anybody's deity, Lily, why would anyone ask me to do that?"

"Maybe they can't reach? Did you have to touch anything nasty?"

"No, but I accidentally whipped one guy across the butt with his towel, and he left me his phone number."

"Shame you're taken. Was he cute?"

"If you find age seventy cute. I have a newfound respect for fitness instructors. Plus, can you hear that?"

Lily cocked her head to one side. After a moment, she shook it. "No. What?"

"Huffing. Wheezing. Air con. More huffing. Oh God, the huffing never ends," I wailed.

"I think we better get you a protein shake." Lily grabbed me by the elbow and steered me towards the doors. "I'm worried you're starting to hallucinate."

I wasn't hallucinating but I probably was a little low on blood sugar. From the instructor-shirted side of the biz, I saw the gym in a whole new light. Far from a place to work out, hopping happily onto machines, then staggering off them, lifting a few dumbbells, and taking a few classes, all to keep looking good, now all I could see was sweat dripping onto the machines, a discarded water bottle rolling across the floor, and death at every turn. And someone even had the gall to put my neatly organized dumbbell stack into disarray.

"You do look pale," said Lily, pushing me into a chair at the small cafe before handing me a bottle of pale colored liquid. Next to us were two older ladies in pink sweats, who were deep in conversation. Otherwise, the cafe was empty. "Drink this."

"I thought I was getting a protein shake. What is it?"

"Vitamin water."

"Ugh... Oh! This actually tastes nice." I glugged some more of the vitamin water. "I guess I'm pale because I'm just waiting for someone else to die," I added. It could happen anywhere. Electrical outlet fault. Malfunctioning deathtrap machine. Air duct poisoning. Ugh, I hoped not to catch Legionnaire's disease.

"Awesome. Count me in."

"What?"

"I said 'count me in.' I only got to see two corpses. I want to find another!"

I leaned forwards, the cold bottle in my hand as I lowered my voice. "I'm supposed to be figuring out if there's a killer in here, not enabling another potential murder."

Lily leaned in too. She looked from left to right, before meeting my eyes. "I. Want. In."

"Ugh."

"You can't be everywhere," Lily continued. "Plus, I know, like, *millions* of people here and they all talk to me. I come here way more often than you do."

"Maybe you should ask Solomon for a job," I sniffed. She was right though. Not that there were millions of people, but she came religiously every day, paying homage to every machine and praising her body in the mirror, and it showed. Plus, she did know a lot of the members.

"I run a bar," Lily pointed out, missing my sarcasm. "I'm very busy."

"But with enough free time to go hunting for another body?"

"Do you want my help or not, hotshot?"

"I want your help," I said grudgingly, taking another sip. It tasted funny, but it was okay. It was... Just at that moment, a light bulb went off in my head. It didn't taste funny enough *not* to drink. Karen took a sip of her bottle right before she collapsed. "Poison," I said. "It's poison."

The women at the table next to us turned around. Their eyes fixed on my bottle. One of them got up and returned her unopened vitamin water to the counter. Her friend hurried over to the water fountain and emptied her vitamin water bottle.

"It's not poisoned," said Lily, smiling at them. It was a good move. Reassuring. How could anyone not trust a face like that? "Lexi is just thinking out loud. She got a new house. Rat problem."

"Big rats," I agreed, but my mind was whirring. Karen could easily have ingested something that harmed her. I trusted the labeling on the bottle even though it tasted a little odd. Karen could have done the same. Could she have ingested a fast acting poison? Then there was the tiny bead of blood on Jim's thumb, and the strange tacks taped to the underside of the bike. Was it conceivable that something entered his bloodstream too? Something powerful enough to kill him?

Could the two of them have been dosed with the same poison?

The problem with all my questions, was the biggest

question of all. The three lettered question. The one my nieces and nephews used to drive me nuts... Why? Why would anyone want to poison Jim Schwarz and Karen Doyle?

And if they were poisoned, why was Lorena stabbed?

Was this one big plot? Or three individual, unrelated cases? Did someone murder all three, or were we looking for a trio of murderers? Right now, I had more questions than answers.

"You've got that look on your face like you discovered something," said Lily, raising her voice a little louder for the benefit of our eavesdropping companions. "Like you discovered a really big rat."

"A really big one," I agreed. "Or three little, evil ones."

Lily frowned. "Nope, you lost me."

"I need to call..." I stopped and looked at the eavesdroppers. I couldn't say "my boss" given that I was wearing a staff t-shirt, or Solomon, because I shouldn't have mentioned him under any circumstances. After all, I was undercover. I had no connection to the agency. The eavesdroppers smiled encouragingly. One of them leaned over. "You need pest control, honey." She handed me a card, which she fished out from the oversized purse she held in her lap. "My son is the best rat-catcher in Montgomery."

"You must be so proud. Thank you," I said, taking the card and laying it on the table. The image of the dead rat printed on the card didn't do a lot for my appetite, but it didn't kill it either.

"He's single," the lady continued.

"A real catch," said her companion and they both giggled.

"Lexi already has a boyfriend," said Lily, "and she's very dedicated to her new job. She just started here. Relief cover for Anton."

"We love Anton," said Mother Rat-catcher. "He's the best."

"We heard what happened," her companion confided. "Such a tragedy. And that nice, young lady too. You know, I was in the gym that day. I actually saw her going into the gym. She looked so healthy with her towel and water bottle. To think she would be dead that same day. Tragedy."

"Tragedy," echoed her friend as they gathered their things. "Nice to meet you, dear. Good luck with the rat problem."

"Good luck! I'll tell my boy you'll call," added Mother Rat-catcher like I was making a date with him. I hoped he wouldn't sit by the phone because if so, it would be for a very long time.

We waited until they were gone, leaving the small cafe clear, before I called Solomon.

"How's your first day so far?" he asked.

"I don't think I want to work in a gym," I told him, honestly. "It's really not me."

"Okay. What have you discovered?" I started to tell him, but he interrupted me, "Not what you've discovered about why you don't want to work in a gym."

"Shame. That list is long. Anyway, it's not a discovery I'm calling about. More of a hunch."

"Go on."

"I told you the about the handlebars and the pinprick on Jim's finger, right? That there was something really strange about it. I think you should check for poison."

"Poison?"

"Yeah. Poison. Karen Doyle too. I don't know if she was poisoned, but I know she had a water bottle when she was on the treadmill and she drank from it. That would be an easy way for someone to get poisoned."

"Poison?" Solomon said again.

"Uh... yeah."

65

"Lexi, what did you think we were swabbing the handlebars for?" he asked, very slowly.

"Um..." I actually didn't think about it, and I began to color. "Poison?" I squeaked, pulling a face.

"You got it."

"Oh, right. Well, I think Karen Doyle's water bottle should be checked for poison too."

"It's pretty hard to poison someone with water."

"I don't know if she was drinking water. Maybe she had a protein shake or something. That would disguise the taste of anything weird. Her face went all puffy and her lips, too. Now that I think about it, it could have been an allergic reaction."

"Do you happen to have the bottle?"

"I gave the bottle to you with the other evidence I gathered."

"Okay. Flaherty caught a case so I'll make a call to the ME and suggest running a tox panel while they autopsy. I think she'll go for it since Karen Doyle was pretty young to die of natural causes. I'll suggest she looks at Jim more closely too based on the evidence you found."

"Great!"

"What about Lorena?" Solomon asked.

"Keep up, boss. Lorena was stabbed," I said before I hung up. I reached for the laminated menu that was sandwiched between the condiments. One side had smoothies, shakes, and blended fruit juices. The other side had healthy food. For a gym, it looked pretty good.

"What did he say?"

"My hunch was useless. He already planned on swabbing the evidence I collected from the spin bike for poison, but he is going to tell the ME to run a tox panel on Karen too. I think I embarrassed myself."

"Not the first time," said Lily. "Not the last either. I hope you brought nice clothes to change into. We have a fitting to make."

CHAPTER SIX

With Lily and Jord's wedding fast approaching in less than two weeks, we were at the final stages of dressing. I couldn't have been happier for my best friend and brother, finally finding true love with each other, although Lily discovered it at least ten years before. Jord eventually woke up and realized he could lose his perfect woman. Well, I was more than happy. I was thrilled, but distracted. The thrill was fine. The distraction would only dissipate after we cleared up the mess at the gym, but for now, as Lily tried on her wedding gown, that enigma was far from my thoughts.

"It's beautiful," I told her, for the umpteenth time. "Really beautiful."

"I know," agreed Lily, eyeing herself in the mirror. "So what if it's not the dress I really wanted? It's five thousand dollars less, and who can argue with that? I want to be independent, just like you. If you can do it, so can I."

"Exactly," I agreed, smiling at Lily's reflection, both of us avoiding the tiny trace of disappointment in her eyes. I had to applaud her attitude though, she could easily have gone to her distant parents and asked for more money, but she didn't, insisting that she didn't want them to just throw cash in her direction. I wondered if it had anything to do with Lily barely seeing her parents recently, as they rarely came home to Montgomery.

"But do I get the short veil or the long veil?" Lily asked.

"Try them all on again," I suggested, bouncing on the soft ottoman like a kid in a candy store.

"Or maybe a tiara."

"Both."

Lily glanced at me. "It isn't too much?"

"Pah! Who cares? Try them all. Excuse me! Miss! Can my friend try on your tiaras?" I asked, looking around for the assistant who had shown us in only fifteen minutes before.

A beige-suited woman appeared from behind one of the expansive swathes of curtains that draped the fitting studio. She was holding two flutes of champagne, which she set on a small table away from Lily's gown. Lily introduced us briefly. Her name was Sharon and I recalled she wasn't just a store assistant. She owned the Perfect Brides boutique. "Of course. Did you have something in mind?" she asked.

"Yes," said Lily, turning to her left and giving her skirts a swish. "All of them."

"An excellent choice," agreed Sharon, beaming as if she'd never seen an undecided bride before. "I'll gather some for you to try on. Short veil or long veil to accompany?"

"Yes," said Lily.

The woman smiled and nodded, resisting a laugh at Lily's infectious enthusiasm for all things bridal.

"Do you think Jord will like it?" Lily asked, smoothing a non-existent crease from the front of the skirt.

I stood next to her, a half-foot shorter thanks to the small podium, which added a good six inches to her height and we gazed at her dress in the reflection of the mirror. It was beautiful. A strapless, fitted, satin bodice, overlaid with creamy-white lace and a skirt that flared from her hips to the floor. Times had changed since the days when Lily wouldn't even look at the price tag. Her mother might have simply set up an account with the store and told her to buy whatever she wanted, but Lily steadfastly refused. I knew what Lily really wanted was some of her mother's time and that wasn't available.

"You're a knockout. He's going to love it," I assured her, knowing my brother would appreciate anything she wore.

"You're sure?"

"Knowing my brother, I am sure he loves you and he'll love anything you wear. Except a potato sack. We're from Irish stock and get a little sensitive about that."

Lily laughed and reached for my hand. I gave it a squeeze. "Who knew this would happen?" she said. "I marry Jord; we get to be sisters-in-law!"

"Don't forget I'm your bridesmaid too."

"Chief bridesmaid," Lily reminded me.

"The only bridesmaid!"

"Are you sure you don't want to wear white like Pippa Middleton?" Lily asked, pointing to the black bridesmaid dress with a white sash I selected from an array she deemed acceptable. It hung over the changing room rail, looking the right side of sexy for a wedding.

"No. If you were getting married in a cathedral to royalty, I would."

"Probably too late for that now," said Lily, after some thought.

"Next time," I grinned, dodging to the right before she could cuff me upside the head.

"Shame you're not exactly single," Lily mused.

"Why's that?" I asked, not thinking it was a shame at all. Since Solomon and I had finally gotten our acts together and decided to give "us" a shot, my romantic life was going great. Unfortunately, only Lily and Anastasia knew that. Anastasia had since left town for her job in the city, and Lily was sworn to secrecy. I had an inkling she told Jord, however, but he never said a thing. Come to think of it, Solomon and I still needed to have that chat...

"Have you seen Jord's groomsmen?" Lily asked, raising one perfectly arched brow.

"I have. I have also seen one naked, but I'm not saying which one."

"Tell. Me. Now." Lily fixed me with The Look, but I was saved from interrogation by Sharon returning with an armful of boxes, which she set on the ottoman I recently vacated. "Ooooh! Pretties," Lily exclaimed, and I knew I was safe for now. That meant the groomsman was also safe from my brother who probably wouldn't be thrilled hearing about that accidental night, which turned into an accidental weekend several years ago.

As I watched Lily rifle through the boxes, I mused on weddings, allowing myself to daydream a little. There's something amazing about weddings and how an event like that affects people. It makes people happy and hopeful and full of laughter and good memories. In Lily's case, it made her even more excited and enthusiastic about life than normal. Considering that she'd been through a really rough time recently, I couldn't have been happier. Plus, playing dress-up legitimately, and without anything that involved Spandex and embarrassing photos later, was pretty fun.

"This is the one," said Lily, pulling a tiara from the very last box. There were already two dozen spread around the fitting studio, at haphazard angles from where they'd been discarded in their boxes. Lily held it aloft. "This is the one for me." She placed it on her head, while the manager fiddled with the combs, tucking them into Lily's curls as she turned to the mirror. I couldn't argue. It looked perfectly elegant with the dress.

"Yes, it is," I agreed. "You don't even need a veil."

Lily looked wistfully at the heap of veils she'd tried on and discarded. "Shame," she said.

"Maybe next…"

"There will be no next time! One wedding and one wedding only!"

"Maybe I'll wear a veil," I said, picking one up and attaching it to the top of my ponytail, then fluffing it over my shoulders. "How's that?"

"Cute. Did Solomon propose?"

"Nope."

"Did you?"

"Nope. Remember, we're not telling anyone yet."

"I'm sure no one noticed at all that you and your boss are getting smoochy."

"No one noticed last time."

"You were pretending to be a married couple then. You were in your undercover role."

"And now, we're not. We're barely working this case together. I don't even know when we'll see each other next, thanks to the undercover aspect taking up all my time."

"But you are dating?"

"Yes. No. Maybe. Yes," I replied.

"And you actually go out on dates? When you're not going at it like rabbits?"

"Lily!" I pretended to be affronted, but it was so true. "Yes, we go out. To places no one can see us."

"I bet the whole of Montgomery has seen you."

"They're all being very quiet about it if they have, and this town is anything *but* quiet."

"Especially your family."

"You remember the last wedding?" I asked her. "My

cousin Sian?"

"She throws a good punch," said Lily and we both pulled faces. "Three hundred people and a six-tier cake. My wedding will not be like that."

"You wish."

"It won't. We're having a quiet, outdoor wedding in The Belmont's courtyard, then a civilized wedding breakfast, and after that, a big party with chocolate cake. The Belmont's security staff has been thoroughly briefed."

"Good to know."

"Try on your dress," suggested Lily, nudging me in the direction of my bridesmaid dress. "I don't want to hog the mirror," she added, admiring her reflection from every possible angle.

I checked my watch, noticing the time. The daily meeting would be over, but I still had to get to the agency's office to write my initial report; not to mention, start running background checks on the deceased. "I can't. I have to go."

"Where? Did you get a break in the case already?" Lily was off the podium and whirling around, trying to undo the dress before I could say no. "Really? Oh, that sucks. I don't want to be callous, but do you think it will be over before the wedding? I want you totally focused."

"I'll do my best, but I'm not sure the killer is working to accommodate your schedule."

"Stupid serial killers," said Lily, pouting.

"Tell me about it. Right now, we don't even know if the deaths are connected. I have to go to the office to run some background checks, and then, I need to go home and take a shower. Tomorrow, I have another shift at the gym. On the plus side, with all the extra exercise I'm getting, I will look a lot better in my bridesmaid dress!"

"Just so long as you don't get murdered. I don't have time to get a new chief bridesmaid. Can you help me out of this?"

I helped Lily unzip her dress, leaving her to shuffle into a large changing cubicle. While Lily dressed, I repackaged as many of the tiaras as I could. By the time she emerged, clad in blue jeans, t-shirt, and a smart blazer, the manager had reappeared.

"You didn't have to do that," Sharon said, noticing my neat pile of boxes, "but I really appreciate it; thanks. You have no idea how many times a day I have to re-package these things."

"You won't have to box this one again," said Lily, clutching her tiara to her chest. The wedding gown was draped over her shoulder and she was also trying to hold her purse and the straps of her heels. She might have had better success if she were an octopus. "Thanks," she said when I relieved her of her purse and heels. I pulled the dust bag from her purse and dropped her heels inside it as Lily handed her gown and tiara to the manager.

"Let me just check your final fitting…" said Sharon, taking the items and disappearing behind another curtain, only to reemerge empty-handed a moment later. "One week from today," she said, "I think it's perfect now, but we can do any last minute adjustments after you've selected your shoes. The full dress rehearsal. Are you excited?"

"Ridiculously so," said Lily. "Will the dress be secure here?"

Sharon stopped. Her face paled and her breathing seemed to hitch. "Yes," she stammered. "Yes, of course. No problem at all. We're very secure. Why do you ask?"

Lily shrugged and leaned over to pull on her boots. "No reason," she said and I frowned as Sharon gave a long, relieved exhale before recovering her composure.

"I'll show you out," said Sharon, guiding us from the changing rooms to the showroom. At the front door, she undid two bolts, then turned two locks. As she opened the door, I looked up, noticing the new security camera, safely hidden under the porch roof, aimed at the door. "Do call if you need anything before then. I'm afraid we're 'appointments only' now," Sharon added. We stepped onto the sidewalk and the door shut softly behind us. Even with the noise of the traffic, and the gaggle of teenage girls in prep uniforms walking past, I still heard the sound of the bolts sliding into the place, and the clicks of the locks turning.

"That was odd," I said.

"What?" Lily rummaged in her purse, before revealing her retrieved car keys.

"Do you think the manager was acting funny?"

Lily's forehead wrinkled. "Sharon? I didn't really notice."

"There's a lot of new security here. More than when we first came to see the dresses and when did they go to 'appointments only'?"

"I don't know. It's probably nothing. You're getting too used to crimes and weirdoes." That was probably true. All the same, I had a nagging feeling that all wasn't well with the wedding store as Lily leaned over and gave me a quick hug and air kiss. "Keep me informed of You Know What," she said, waggling her fingers as she turned to walk to her car, parked next to mine. "And ask Solomon outright what the hell is going on with you two!"

~

The array of databases I had access to, thanks to the Solomon Agency, was dazzling. Sometimes, they were really tempting, too. After all, I could look up the credit history of anyone I knew! But, despite being a career snoop, I knew Solomon frowned upon that sort of thing. So, as of now, I hadn't snooped on anyone that I wasn't supposed to. I figured my days were numbered. One could only be virtuous for so long. Since I probably should have started the background checks prior to beginning the undercover role, I figured the virtuous angle was already pushing it. However, time was of the essence and this was the first moment I found to delve into the potential victims' lives.

I had plenty to keep me occupied from thinking about Lily's burning question. Jim Schwarz, Karen Doyle, and Lorena Vasquez all needed to have their backgrounds crawled through if I were to get a well-rounded picture of who they were in life. Since they were dead, and I was trying to ascertain whether all three were killed, I figured they probably wouldn't mind, but I didn't expect them to say thank you.

Since I actually knew Lorena, I worried that digging through her virtual records might be more testing on my emotions than the other two potential victims, so I put her off until last. I chose to start with Jim Schwarz.

Jim was an unassuming man. He kept a steady job and was employed as a research assistant for a little over a year. Prior to that, he had a short gap in his resume after working nine years for the same firm of which he directed a lab. I wondered what might make him switch roles after nine years to take up a job so inferior to his qualifications. Was it a change of scenery or a change of pace? I doubted he received a better paycheck at his new job.

His Harbridge apartment was a two-bedroom that he'd been slowly renovating. That was something I picked up when combing through his phone records, noting several calls were placed to a kitchen and bathroom showroom. His driving license was clean and he paid monthly installments on a Toyota. An internet search revealed he was a keen cyclist and took part in charity races as well as long distance cycling vacations. He didn't subscribe to any kind of social media. His credit history was good. I couldn't see any evidence of a girlfriend or a boyfriend. Altogether, he seemed like a very average citizen. With the plain evidence of his life accumulated in the file on my desk, I failed to see any compelling reason for someone to murder him. Then again, as I'd learned over the past year, an awful lot of people conceal an awful lot of secrets.

I made my notes, added a few printouts and moved onto potential victim number two, Karen Doyle. She was thirty years old and engaged. That was easy to find out as she and her fiancé established an engagement website with details of their upcoming wedding. The photos were professional and she appeared both pretty and happy. The short biography told me she met her fiancé at work when she joined the company fourteen months ago and happened to take the desk opposite him. No one had updated the site yet, and the idea of someone having to do so made me incredibly sad.

Continuing to comb the website, I learned Karen had two sisters, both close to her own age, and that she and her fiancé loved hiking and camping, and had gotten engaged at Lake Pierce. Like Jim, her credit history was good. She had no outstanding debt except for two thousand dollars on her sole credit card. She had just moved into her fiancé's house, after leasing her smaller apartment to her younger sister. Her phone records revealed she sent a lot of texts. A few numbers appeared over and over and I made a note of them. She had a driving license, and the couple were registered for wedding gifts at two local stores. Perhaps saddest of all, she had just put a down payment on a dress at Georgina's Gowns.

I stared at the photo of Karen and her fiancé for a long time, thinking about how familiar she looked. I definitely remembered seeing her in the gym the day before she died, now that I thought about it. Like Lily, I was sure she was the same woman who sat on the bike next to Jim during our spin class. From my bike on the row behind, I only saw the back of her head; and apart from a brief moment when I admired her cute workout outfit, I hadn't really paid much attention to her. I confess being too focused on my own screaming thighs. She was definitely a similar height and build as the woman I saw Jim speak to. I added, then underlined two questions: *Where did she go when Jim died? Did Maddox catch up with her?*

I stared at the computer screen a long time before I typed Lorena's name, feeling a little guilty for snooping through her life when we'd only recently become friends. Lorena Vasquez was fifty-three and thanks to amazing genes, didn't look a day over forty. I knew a little about her already, which I noted in my file. Her father was Spanish, her mother American, and they met when her mother took her first trip to Europe. She returned with several tourist refrigerator magnets, a husband, and a pregnancy. Personally, I thought that was pretty terrific souvenir hunting.

Lorena had a younger brother, Marco, whom she'd been working with part-time for a year. She was divorced and had one daughter, Marnie, currently away at college. Lorena's house was paid off and she lived within her means. Judging by her credit history, she made just enough money to support herself and her daughter. I typed the daughter's name into a search engine and found her immediately in a puff piece for the *Montgomery Gazette*. She was a classic case of small town girl makes good, having won a partial scholarship. She majored in pre-law, and was currently in her sophomore year. Mother and daughter shared the same beautiful, wide, brown eyes and thick, glossy hair. I didn't find anything on the ex-husband so I added a question mark to the form I was filling out.

It took a few seconds of internet searching to find the phone number of Lorena's workplace. I dialed it and asked to speak to Marco, but the assistant told me he was out of town for a few days on bereavement and unreachable. I declined to leave a message.

Next, I called his cell phone, easily finding it on

Lorena's phone bill. I called but no one picked up. Hanging up, I redialed, and this time, it clicked through to his answering service so I left a message. I told him who I was, and asked him to call me back.

When I logged onto a photo-sharing site that Lorena had introduced me to only a week before, in order to print a recent photo of her, I saw it. Tucked away, a few dozen thumbnails down the page, was the photo that changed everything and made the big question mark hanging over the case even more intriguing.

Jim, Karen, and Lorena all knew each other.

Clicking on the thumbnail, it opened to full size. Filling the screen were the three recently deceased. Lorena stood in the middle, wearing a knee-length, floral shift and a boxy, white jacket. Jim and Karen both leaned in from each side, cheesy grins on their faces, glasses of wine in their hands. All three wore an employee identification badge, clipped to some part of their attire, with a photo and name. The caption read "Simonstech annual party," and was dated approximately two years ago.

I rummaged through my research notes, looking for information, and finding it, which really made my heart race. I leaned back in my chair, steepling my fingers under my chin as the pieces clicked together. Each one of the happy trio had taken new jobs within the last fourteen months. Two years ago, they looked carefree and friendly at Simonstech, their previous employer. Did something happen to make all three leave within months of each other? And did that mysterious something have anything to do with why they all died in the past week?

I grabbed the photo from the printer and knocked on Solomon's open door. He had his phone pressed to his ear as he waved me in, continuing to listen while I sat. After "yes," "no" and "keep me informed," he put the phone down, giving me his full attention.

"I've got something," I told him.

"Me too." He gave me a nod as he waved his forefinger. "You first."

"You look pleased with yourself."

"Tell you in a minute. What've you got?"

"Michael may have been onto something. Jim Schwarz, Karen Doyle, and Lorena Vasquez knew each other." I slid the print across the desk and Solomon picked it up, his eyes running over it. "They all worked at the same firm two years ago. Then, within the last fourteen months, they all took new jobs," I explained.

"This is good."

"I know!" I grinned. So shoot me. I was practically bursting from potentially breaking the case wide open. Not a murder, my ass! Take that, Detective Maddox!

Solomon lay the photo on his desk and folded his hands over the top. He leaned forward. "I just got off the phone with the ME. She ran a tox panel on Jim and it came back with elevated levels of something that gave her cause for concern."

"Such as?"

"She needs to run more tests to identity it. All she could say was it was a poison. When the results come back from the tests on the evidence you collected, I suspect we'll find trace evidence on the bike's handlebars as the entry point. Based on that result, the ME ran the same test on Karen Doyle."

"Same thing?" I asked, with a hopeful expression.

"Nope," he said and I deflated, my shoulders sagging at the news. "But, she was concerned enough to run a few more tests when I suggested it. Karen Doyle died of a severe allergic reaction to peanut oil. The ME was prepared to write that off as natural because Karen wore a medical bracelet, declaring her allergy. However, her water bottle tested positive for peanut oil too, which leads us to believe she didn't take it knowingly or intentionally. We're not looking at one murder, Lexi, we're looking at three, and you just found the connection that suggests one person might be responsible."

"That's…" I started to say, great, but as the gravity of the situation sunk in, I couldn't help gulping. Someone wanted those three people dead. "That's… bad," I finished.

"Very bad," agreed Solomon.

~

Before my shift started the following day, I had to tell Michael what happened in his gym was not at all his fault, as far as I could see; and actually, a helluva lot worse. It really wasn't a conversation that I looked forward to having, but he was paying the agency to get to the bottom of the deaths, and this major breakthrough was exactly the kind of news he needed to hear. Needed, but perhaps, not wanted.

I doubted he wanted to hear what I had to say at all.

"They've been murdered," Michael repeated, taking a deep breath and blinking. We were sealed up tightly in his office, far away from prying ears, but he still kept his voice low. Finally, he looked up and gave a shake of his head. "That's great!"

I squeezed my eyes shut and winced. "Not really."

"It's great that the gym isn't responsible."

"Even though they knew each other, it doesn't change the fact that all three victims were your clients and someone targeted them. No matter why, we can't escape *where*." I circled a finger in the air, indicating the whole gym.

Michael's shoulders slumped. "You're right. This sucks. Why would someone want to murder my clients?"

"Could be a crime of opportunity," I suggested. "We only know for sure that Jim Schwarz was targeted here. We don't know how or where Karen Doyle was poisoned, only that she probably was. It could be coincidental that she collapsed and died here."

"And Lorena?"

I shook my head. "I don't know. It doesn't fit that she wasn't poisoned, but it's early in the investigation yet."

"So what now?" Michael wanted to know.

I thought back to the conversation I had with Solomon before leaving the agency in search of a hot shower and a warm bed, when I asked the same question. I gave Michael the condensed version. "The ME will make the report to the homicide division and they'll open murder investigations into Jim and Karen. The inquiry into Lorena's death is already underway."

"And you? The agency?"

"If you want to end our investigation, we'll turn over our report to them, plus, any evidence we collected, and they can take it from there."

Michael ran a hand over his closely cropped hair and leaned back. He looked tired all of a sudden, like he hadn't been sleeping well. I concluded he probably hadn't. "What about the gym? The spin studio got cleaned already, and the treadmills get wiped down every night, along with all the other equipment."

"You've done nothing wrong," I assured him. "Detective Maddox was here right after Jim died, and he said it wasn't a murder and cleared the studio. Of course, you were going to clean it. What else could you do? Wait for him to change his mind? If it makes you feel any better, at least, you called the agency in to check things over. Plus, if it weren't for you, we wouldn't have started investigating, and Solomon wouldn't have called the ME and suggested running a tox panel. The homicide squad will probably thank you!"

Michael brightened. "You think they'll thank me?"

"Not likely, but there's always that small possibility." I held my thumb and forefinger an inch apart. On second thought, I moved them closer together, until there was barely a gap. I figured Maddox would probably be furious to learn he cleared a murder scene right after his boss finished chewing him out. "Listen, here's the thing, Michael. Montgomery PD is going to take over the investigation very soon. We can turn our evidence over and leave them to it. You pay the agency fees and we're done. Or…" I hesitated, letting him fill in the blanks.

Michael stayed quiet for several long minutes. Finally, he looked up and fixed his eyes on me, just when I stopped pacing his room and began to stroke one of his many trophies. "No," he said, "I want you to stay undercover. The police are only interested in catching the killer. As self-preserving and callous as it sounds, I'm interested in preserving the good name of the gym and I don't want a serial killer targeting my members. The minute that idea gets out, the members are gone and we're through. There're too many jobs at stake for that when you consider my employees too." I gave him a nod to show that I understood, and waited for him to continue, "Lexi, I want you to keep investigating and remain my liaison with the police. I'm grateful for everything you've discovered so far. Now you just need to find the killer."

I reluctantly left the trophy alone and took the chair opposite Michael. "What makes you so sure I'll find the killer here?" I asked, interested in any theory that supported the gym being a target, as much as the victims.

"Thanks to the poison on the spin bike, we know that at least Jim's death was set up to happen here. How did the killer get in, Lexi? When did he or she have an opportunity to plant it? We went to 'members only' two weeks ago so not just anyone could walk in. Only a client or a staff member could have had access to set up the trap for Jim. And," Michael continued, leaning forward excitedly, "someone also knew Jim's routine. I mean, which bike he used and when. I asked Anton. He said Jim always took that same bike and always on the same day."

Privately, I disagreed. There were probably a bunch of ways someone could sneak into the gym, and lucky me, I was probably going to have to discover them all. There was another thing that niggled at me though. Despite finding a connection between the three victims, it was only conjecture that they were all killed by the same person for the same reason. For that to be true, the Simonstech angle had to work out. Until we knew a motive, we just had a lot of questions.

"Okay," I agreed, "Solomon and I discussed this and we're happy to keep working the case. There's a few more things I'll need from you now that I have my bearings as an employee."

"Name it."

"A full client list, including anyone who left over the past year. Any records pertaining to the victims. They all filled out a member questionnaire, like I did, right? And I'll need copies of the security feeds from every camera you have for the twenty-four hours prior to the spin studio being used at the session when Jim died. Maybe we can catch someone on tape. Oh, and I need the security feeds from the day Karen Doyle was in the gym. Maybe we can see something there too."

"I'll have it all ready for you by the time you leave. What are you going to do now?"

"Find out if anyone saw the killer," I said, feeling glad he didn't ask me how. I hated to sound unsure, but I hadn't exactly worked out how I would do that yet.

CHAPTER SEVEN

So much for anyone seeing the killer. Despite all my subtle snooping while wearing the Fairmount Gym t-shirt, no one saw anything. Well, they saw a bunch of stuff, but nothing that pertained to my case. I did receive three complaints about gym equipment, the suggestion of Legionnaire's disease being transmitted through the air ducts, some gossip about two of the instructors secretly getting it on, plus, the offer of a luncheon date from a very bendy octogenarian. So, you know, excluding my secret relationship with my boss... I still had it!

Speaking of bosses, mine was strolling towards me at that very moment and it was all I could do not to sigh. There was something about him that made my stomach do the flippity-flip, while my fingers curled my hair and I giggled. Fortunately, I managed to muster some self-restraint as I was twenty years too old for that kind of stuff. I noticed a couple of women on the treadmills following Solomon over toward me and tried not to feel smug. I didn't try too hard because that defeated the object of having a hot guy.

"How's it going?" asked Solomon, his lips pursing ever so slightly as he blew a secret kiss only I could catch.

"Nothing yet," I told him, "though I now know a bunch of stuff I didn't need to know."

"Sometimes even the smallest, most inconsequential things can mean something later," he told me.

I waved to Mr. Ahearne as he ambled by the instructors' station, his knee-length shorts hitched up on one side to reveal surprisingly toned quads. He winked at me.

"He asked me out earlier," I told Solomon.

Solomon watched the older man shuffling out the door. "Want me to fight him for your honor?"

I laughed. "No, but thanks for offering. To what do I owe this unexpected pleasure?"

"Just came by to see how you were doing and if you needed any help?"

"Do you drop in on the guys and see if they need any help too?" I asked jokingly.

However, the jovial air disappeared as Solomon frowned and simply said, "No."

"Just me, huh?" I asked, wondering if Solomon knew my training wheels had come off a while back. Several corpses (not mine), bullets and stabbings (both mine), and a bunch of solved cases surely gave me some gravitas in the agency? Didn't it? Then again, I hadn't racked up as many cases as the other guys, who were all seasoned law enforcement professionals of some description or other. Except Lucas. He was a seasoned criminal-turned-good-guy that Solomon employed for his amazing computer skills.

In contrast, I fell into the job after literally falling over a former boss's body and getting sucked into his murder investigation. After the murderer was caught, Solomon offered me the best job I've ever had. "What if they notice the extra visits and conclude that we're having a relationship? I thought we were keeping this, us, secret until we were ready..." I trailed off, waiting for Solomon to get the hint and confirm our status as a couple. Somehow, asking outright seemed feeble, desperate even. I was neither. I could run in high heels, fight drug smugglers, and take on international fraudsters. That all took guts and perseverance.

"We *are* getting it on, and maybe I'm checking on my newest, least experienced recruit in a dangerous case. Or, maybe I just like seeing you a lot more than I like seeing them."

That really wasn't what I had in mind. "Bet you don't want to sleep with them either."

"Technically, I don't want to *sleep* with you."

I pretended to fan myself. "Whatever do you want with me, John?" Solomon smiled and my stomach did an Olympic-quality flip and dive, forgetting all about my relationship status woes. "Ohh! I get off shift in ten minutes."

"And straight onto your real job," Solomon reminded me in a low voice as he leaned in, causing his pecs to pop under his lightweight, cream sweater. It was an attraction I could have sold tickets for.

"Damn," I said, though I wasn't sure what I was damning: my lack of leisure time or his muscles.

"Want to grab dinner later?"

"If by 'grab' you mean, sit down at a nice restaurant and eat at a leisurely pace, then yes."

"What if I meant grab a hotdog while watching a suspect?"

I shrugged. "That works for me too."

"I'll pick you up at seven. Wear something pretty."

"Fancy hot dog stand, huh?" I quipped, suddenly remembering I had another date that day. "Can we make it eight? I have a dress fitting with Lily."

Solomon frowned. "I thought you already did that."

"We did, but Lily found her perfect shoes this morning and she wants to try them on with the dress to make sure they really are perfect, so I said I would go with her after she finished her shift at the bar."

"Are you ever going to show me your bridesmaid gown?"

"No. You'll have to wait for the wedding."

"Is it a meringue? Is it floral?" Solomon teased.

"No and no."

"Is there a headdress? Does it have sequins?"

"Yuck. I hope that stuff doesn't turn you on."

"Getting you out of it would."

"One track mind."

"Mmm. The right track." Solomon's eyes dipped down my body then back up again and I could pretty much figure out what he was thinking because Mr. Ahearne had the same look right before he asked me to his social club luncheon. Solomon checked his watch, probably noting the several hours between now and dinner. "Where are you headed next?"

"The office to take another look through Jim Schwarz's background, and Lucas said he left a bunch of reports for me. Then I'm going to do some checking up on Jim," I added, wondering if my colleagues spilled as much information on their planned whereabouts.

"I won't be there. File a report and don't do anything dangerous."

"Who? Me?" I feigned mock shock. "Never. A little light snooping, then trying on shoes and dresses, and after that, home to wait for you."

"I like that," said Solomon.

"What? Shoes and dresses?"

"Someone to come home to," he said, walking away, and leaving me wondering if I would like that too.

~

After my gym clothes were hung in the locker in the employee's room, I switched into cute, mint-hued pants, a black sweater, and the most gorgeous pair of pointy-toed black Louboutin pumps - a gift to myself for being fabulous. I hightailed it to the agency, but Solomon was nowhere to be seen. Only Fletcher was in the office with his head buried in a file. It was just as well Solomon was absent because I had a stack of paperwork on my desk to read through. I needed to concentrate, and not think about our romantic dinner - unless he really did want to grab a hotdog? - and whether he would stay the night. I mentally thanked the lingerie gods for having the fortitude to ensure I wore a matching set. Just in case.

Settling into my chair, I retrieved the victims' slim files from my locked drawer, and pulled the stack of papers Lucas left on my desk onto my lap. I set about adding the reports to the files of each victim. I returned Karen and Lorena's now thicker files to the drawer.

After a moment or two of paper shuffling, I turned to Lucas's almost empty desk and empty chair. Now that the upstairs section of the agency was up and running, he didn't spend much time down here anymore. I cast a casual glance at the ceiling and wondered exactly what they were doing up there. Wrinkling my nose and blowing out an exasperated lungful of air, I turned my eyes to the papers. Jim's credit report, his bank statement, his cell phone usage, a résumé; it was all there, and once again, I was amazed at the kind of information we could access on a person. Not all of it was strictly legally obtained, I suspected, given that we couldn't get the kinds of warrants the police could. But I wasn't looking for evidence admissible in court. No, I was just trying to connect the dots in a puzzle that currently was missing most of its pieces.

After perusing Jim's financial information - mortgage on a property, car payments, the usual grocery bills and a couple of restaurants featured on his bank statement over the past year, I concluded he didn't have any curious payments or deposits. He seemed sensible, a saver, probably a rainy day kind of man. That matched the sensible, straight-laced opinion I remembered having of him.

I tossed the stapled set of papers onto the desk and looked up again. Maybe... maybe if I just strolled on up the stairs, I could take a peek? Where was the harm in that?

With that idea in my head, nothing could stop me. Fletcher didn't look up from his reading as I left the office, and Flaherty said nothing on his way in with a paper bag and a takeout coffee in one hand. He held the door open, nodded and waited for me to pass.

"Thanks," I said and he grunted a response. Clearly, not a chatty day for him.

Out in the small lobby, I paused. A few months ago, there was a swipe card access point to ensure only agency employees got into the lobby, and from there, to our large, shared office. We also had access to a small suite of meeting rooms on the floor below where we met with clients away from our precious files, databases and whiteboards. Since Solomon had acquired the floor above, the lobby was opened up, revealing another set of stairs, presumably so employees could freely travel between this floor and the one above. So far, since I had no need to ascend, I ignored that particular staircase; but now I strolled casually towards it as if I were absolutely meant to be there, and tried not to race up. My heart sped slightly as I stepped from the stairwell into the next lobby. This lobby was plain and empty too, with a set of double doors across from me. I moved over, glanced through the windows, and saw a couple of workers, both men, judging by their thick necks and buzz cuts, with their backs to me. Several laptops lay unused on a few desks. One wall seemed to be covered with surveillance equipment, but I didn't have a good angle or superhuman vision, so I couldn't see what was on it. I reached for the handle and gave the door a tug, but it didn't budge. Locked, of course, I realized when I clocked the swipe card point next to the door. Just for kicks, I ran my pass through it and the light blinked red. Boo.

"Whatcha doing?" said a voice behind me and I spun around, my heart pounding.

"Nothing," I blurted out.

Lucas grinned. "How come you're plastered to the wall like that?"

"I thought I felt damp," I lied, spreading my fingers. "Nope, not on this floor though. All good! Hurrah! So... what are you doing?" I asked, figuring my best defense was to act suspicious of Lucas.

"Going in there." Lucas pointed to the double doors I just failed to access. "You?"

"Heading down. Uh... thanks for the reports on Jim Schwarz. Very... comprehensive."

"No problem. Later, Lexi." Lucas stepped around me, and leaned in to swipe his pass, disappearing through the door. He pulled it shut behind him before I could grab the handle and follow him inside. I heard the faint sound of locks clicking into place, and not just one. Solomon certainly had that floor securely protected.

"Damn," I sniffed, sulking all the way downstairs, my interest piqued and dashed, as I returned to my waiting files.

Jim Schwarz's reports didn't get any more interesting, so I placed them in a folder and typed up a brief report that I emailed to Solomon. With a little time to kill before the next dress fitting, and a lot of time to work up an appetite, I could have read all three files, which were now fuller, but what I really wanted to do was get out there. I needed to learn something about the victim that wasn't just paperwork. My first call would be Jim's house. Maybe there, I could "bump" into a neighbor or a relative who might shed some light on why this seemingly very average man would have been murdered in such a cold fashion?

My number one victim lived in a first floor apartment of a two-family home. It was neat and soulless, with a perfectly manicured lawn, and a small box hedge, approximately one foot tall all the way around. I looked at the neighbor's place to the left. They cut their taller hedge into something resembling castle ramparts, which was pretty hilarious because Montgomery never, ever had a castle and probably never would. I bet it looked brilliant on Halloween. I also bet it drove the fastidious Jim crazy. Even though I knew Jim was unmarried, and I got the impression he lived alone, I knocked on his door anyway. No one answered. I waited a few minutes, surveying the neighborhood. Harbridge was a nice area, very "up and coming" along with the prices, which had risen considerably in recent years. Jim's Toyota was missing so I guessed he'd driven it to the gym, which was too far to cycle or walk. I didn't see it at the gym so that meant it had either been towed or someone came to retrieve it. I crossed the Toyota off my mental list of things to check out, deciding it was a dead end.

The other cars in the area were all nice models, I noted as I looked around from my vantage point at his front door. Boxy, two-seater convertibles, small hatchbacks, and a couple of minivans showed a diverse cross-section of people who lived on this street. Turning back to the apartment, I peeked into the windows. A couple of squashy couches, a glass coffee table, a huge, flatscreen television, a couple of bookcases, heaving with books, and a large Yucca in a basket made up the single guy's living room. Everything was minimal, and neat, very much like Jim appeared in person. Returning to the door, I knocked again, just in case someone was there and didn't hear me. If I were lucky, the resident upstairs might appear.

"If you're looking for Jim, honey, you won't find him," said a voice behind me. I turned to see a short

African-American woman with cornrows smiling up at me. She wore a fashionable, pink scarf over a long navy dress and thick, gold, hooped earrings. "He's passed on, honey," she added. "Some kind of accident."

"Are you his neighbor?" I inquired.

"Sure am. I live right there," she said, pointing to the house on the right. It mirrored the size and shape of Jim's, but instead of plain grass, her garden had a glorious flowerbed, smack dab in the middle of the lawn. "I'm helping his family out, keeping an eye on the place until they decide what to do with it, especially with the upstairs apartment empty."

I stepped down from the porch and walked over to her so we didn't have to yell, as I pulled my license from my pocket. "Lexi Graves, Private Investigator," I told her. "I'm looking into Jim's death."

"I heard it might not have been an accident," she said, pursing her lips as she looked over toward the house and sighed. Then she stuck her hand out and pumped mine. "Jackie Bishop. Do you think Jim was murdered?"

"Maybe," I said, remaining purposefully vague to her very direct question.

"Good heavens. I wonder why anyone would want to hurt Jim." She leaned in, like he was waiting in the house and might hear us, and whispered, "He was a touch dull, you know. Nice, but dull all the same."

"What can you tell me about him? Did he have a lot of visitors? Did you ever hear him arguing with anyone? What was his attitude like?" I asked, sensing Jackie Bishop liked to talk.

"Well now, let me think. He seemed like a nice guy to me. Always polite. He often looked after my two cats when I'd go visit my son and his wife in Boston; and I take his mail and look after his houseplants whenever he goes away, not that he does, or did that often. He's kind of a homebody. Nobody had a bad word to say about him, though he and our other neighbor there—" Jackie pointed to the castle hedge " —don't exactly see eye to eye on that hedge; but we just had a barbecue two weeks ago, and they got on fine then. Jim makes a great potato salad."

"Did he seem out of sorts this week?" I asked, thinking about Lorena's call for help. I wondered if Jim might've made one of his own.

"Now you mention it, yes. He seemed a little preoccupied when I came by to give him some mail that got into my mailbox by mistake. I asked him what was wrong and he said it was nothing, but he looked down. The last time he looked that low, he'd lost his job. Oh, that was a bad time for him."

"How so?"

"Well, he lost his job," said Jackie, slowly, like I couldn't work out why that wouldn't put the downer on someone. Come to think of it, I'd lost countless jobs, so by the end of my temping years, I wasn't exactly overly concerned about losing another one. I would, however, be upset about losing a job I enjoyed… like this one.

"Of course," I agreed, nodding. "He got fired?" I said, lilting my voice so it became more a question than a statement. I didn't know the circumstances yet, but I intended to find out.

"Oh no. No no." Jackie gave a determined shake of her head, seemingly surprised by the idea. "He left of his own accord, he told me, but he was very unhappy about it. One night, when we had a few drinks, he said he'd done something bad, something he couldn't forgive himself for, though he would never say what. I asked him about it the next day, but he made some kind of excuse or other. Got depressed about whatever it was too." A male voice called Jackie's name and she half turned, shouting back. "That's my husband. We're going out. I have to go," she said, returning her attention to me. She hesitated, like she didn't want to stop talking, nor did I want her to. I wanted to know more about what was bugging Jim enough to make him leave his previous job. What could have upset him so badly that he preferred to leave, rather than stick it out?

I slid a business card from my wallet and passed it to Jackie. "Just in case you think of anything else," I told her. She took a look at it before tucking it into her jacket pocket.

"The only thing I can think to tell you right now is Jim Schwarz was a good neighbor and a good man. No trouble to anyone. If his passing was no accident, then he didn't deserve it. I hope you get to the bottom of this."

Me too, I thought, as Jackie strode away, her hem swishing around her ankles. Me too. I took another look at Jim's manicured lawn, a glance at my own unmanicured fingernails and climbed into my car, the wheels spinning in my mind. My next step for looking into Jim's death, I decided, was to inspect his car before delving any further into his past job. There had to be a clue waiting for me there. The connection was too intriguing to pass up. Jim, Karen, and Lorena had all worked together, and all quit at around the same time. Jim was deeply unhappy, after doing something he considered unforgivable. Could that be a coincidence? What could've happened to make them all leave? And did it have anything to do with why all three now lay in the morgue?

~

"Nice manicure," said Lily when she let me into the wedding store after I'd rung the doorbell several times. I was barely a few minutes late. "New?"

"Just had them done," I told her, holding up my perfect, hot pink nails to admire.

"So pretty," Lily cooed before her eyes widened and she gasped, "Don't touch anything! Do not get that gorgeous polish on any dresses. What shade is it? Where did you get it done?"

"That new place across the street. Nails by Monica. I was early so I thought I'd get a manicure. And a hand massage. It was divine. Smell my hands." Lily dutifully did, giving me an approving nod at the lingering rose scent. "That was an excellent use of your spare time," she told me, sounding distinctly like my mother. "You should have called me and I would have joined you."

"Except then you wouldn't have been able to try on your dress with the shoes without worrying about getting polish on... ooooh! Shoooooooes!" I cooed, forgetting about the potentially hazardous nail polish issue. I was pretty sure they were dry, but you never could tell until that gut-wrenching moment when it smeared. "They're so pretty. My shoes want to have their shoe babies."

Lily grinned and rubbed the snow-white satin pumps across her heart. She reached into her shopping bag and produced another bag. "I got you some too, but to match your dress."

"Thank you. I love you so much."

"You can thank my mom's credit card. She paid."

"Thank you, Lily's mom, wherever you are... Guatemala?" I guessed.

"Ecuador," said Lily, "as of this morning, apparently."

"That was nice of them to let you know."

Lily sniffed. "My father's secretary sent a text."

We both rolled our eyes at the sterile message and I unpackaged Lily's shoe gift. Not only did they match the dress, but they fit perfectly too. As an added bonus, they were black, stunning, and I knew I would wear them many times. Best of all, they were free! Lily slipped hers on and we paraded around the store. "Where's Sharon?" I asked. "Does she know we're here?"

"Yep, she let me in. She was acting all weird again, but she said she hadn't eaten yet, so I figured maybe she was low on sugar. She's in the back, getting our dresses." When Sharon did return, low on sugar wasn't what I would call her behavior. She was skittish and distracted, jumping when the phone rang, and again, when a dog barked outside the store. Leading us through to the changing area, she hung back, nervously checking the door every few minutes, and frequently disappearing from view, while letting us struggle with the serious business of lacing Lily into her dress for the final fitting now she had her shoes and tiara.

"You should get that polish again for the wedding," Lily told me as we both stood in front of the floor-to-ceiling mirrored panel. I wore my bridesmaid dress and I had to admit I looked pretty good. The whole outfit was much nicer than my previous incarnations as a bridesmaid, but admittedly, those occasions were during the decades style forgot. "It goes with your dress. Do you want your hair up or down? I have to let the hair stylist know."

"I don't mind," I said, just as Sharon walked through. The wall phone extension rang, the bell bursting the silence, and she jumped, dropping the boxes she was carrying. After a long moment during which all of us just stared at the spilled contents, Sharon burst into tears and sank onto one of the velvet pouffes, hiding her face in her hands.

Lily and I exchanged puzzled glances. "What's gotten into her?" Lily mouthed and I shrugged as the sobs got louder. Gathering up our skirts, we stepped off the podium and sank down next to her. I lamely patted the woman's shoulder while Lily produced a tissue from somewhere.

"I'm sorry," Sharon sniffed, taking the tissue before blowing her nose loudly. "I didn't mean to start crying."

"That's okay," Lily murmured, edging her dress away from any splashed tears. "I don't mean to pry, but is everything okay?" Lily glanced at me and I nodded, so she continued gently, "We noticed you seemed worried about something."

"Oh no, oh no, it's nothing, it's…" Sharon dropped her head onto her knees and cried even louder. I peeked through the drapes to the showroom, thankful that the doors were locked so Sharon wouldn't be embarrassed by any other customers discovering her in this moment of crisis. I looked at Sharon again and then back toward the door and the large array of locks and cameras. Hmmm. Edging in front of her, I knelt, putting myself in Sharon's view whenever she lifted her head. I placed a hand on her shoulder and told her, "I think you're very upset and I think it has something to do with all the new security here."

Sharon raised her head, looking up at me with red-rimmed eyes. Finally, she nodded. "Yes, it is."

"What's going on?"

"I'm just so worried," she wailed. "Four wedding stores in Montgomery were hit in the last month and I just know my place will be next."

"What do you mean 'hit'?" I asked, trading puzzled glances with Lily.

"Robbed. Someone is breaking in and stealing all the dresses. Do you know how many dresses I have here? Over a hundred. Not just store models either, but dresses women have saved for and paid deposits on. All those poor women who were customers at the other robbed stores don't have their beautiful dresses anymore. Some of my customers are those who've already lost their dresses. I've installed new locks, cameras, a security system, and switched to 'appointments only', but it's only a matter of time before this store gets hit!"

"Oh, gosh, I had no idea," gasped Lily. She smoothed her dress and grimaced.

"I haven't been sleeping," Sharon continued, the story spilling out along with more tears. "I've been staying at the store as late as I can, just so if anyone is looking, they can see someone is here; and I come in early, but I just can't do it anymore. I'm just so tired." Sharon shook her head, and sniffed again. At least, the tears were subsiding. "But I don't know what I'll do if my dresses are stolen. I'll probably have to close."

"Maybe we can help," said Lily.

"Uhh…" I said.

"I would really hate if any brides had their dresses stolen," said Lily slowly. Just to drive the point home, she pointed dramatically at her dress in big jabbing movements.

"And the bridesmaids dresses and all the shoes and the tiaras and the…" Sharon sniffed to a halt. "They take everything. Everything!"

Okay, I really got the point. The idea of Lily losing her dress mere days before her wedding was enough to want to get involved, not lessened by the idea of someone robbing the bridal stores in Montgomery, which really piqued my interest. What were they doing with the bridal gowns once they got them? Surely, someone noticed hundreds of dresses appearing where they weren't supposed to be? Or a crazed Bridezilla with rack upon rack of dresses?

"Okay," I said, glancing to Lily to see her reaction "if Lily helps, I'm in. You are not going to lose your business and you're going to get some sleep. We will find out what's going on…"

" — And we're going to find all the stolen dresses!" screeched Lily, excitement spreading across her face. I'd seen it often enough before. She loved the thrill of the chase. "We're going to take them down! And we won't find any dead dudes!"

"Dead… dudes?" whimpered Sharon.

"There will be no dead people," I assured her, glaring at Lily. She shrugged and pulled a face, reminding me I couldn't really guarantee that. I suppose she had a point. Three were plenty enough dead people for one week, not to mention my short career as a PI.

"Do you promise?" Sharon asked, looking from me to Lily, and back again. Talk about being put on the spot! I hated to make a promise I couldn't keep.

"Uh…" I started weakly.

Lily stepped in. "We'll find out what's going. Just let us get out of these dresses and you can tell us everything we need to get started. Piece of cake. Right, Lexi?"

"Yup," I agreed with a gulp.

"I can't pay you," said Sharon. "I've invested so much on security, I have no more cash."

"Let us worry about that," said Lily just as I began to wonder what we were letting ourselves in for.

~

By the time Solomon picked me up, my mind was still a-whirr with everything I'd done, seen, read… and agreed to. I could hardly believe Lily actually signed us up to a case, but even I had to admit it was for a good cause. We could save dozens, if not hundreds, of weddings. Maybe even save a few relationships. That was a hard opportunity to turn down.

"You look pretty," said Solomon, bending down to kiss me on the lips as he stepped inside my bungalow. He ran a hand down my back until it settled on my waist. He stepped back and added, "And preoccupied."

"Didn't realize those were your mind-reading lips," I quipped as I reached for my lip gloss and added a new sheen to my lips.

"Got your report today. It was…" Solomon paused, seemingly searching for a word, before settling on, "short."

"It wasn't that short."

"It read, and I quote, 'I got nothing'."

"Okay, it was short, but it was accurate. I did discover something new though. Jim Schwarz had some kind of problem at his previous job. He confided in his neighbor that he was unhappy and maybe did something unforgivable, but he didn't say what."

"That's disappointing. Is he the type of guy to sexually harass someone?"

"I don't get that impression, but who knows? You don't seem that kind of man and you sexually harass me all the time."

"Only because you like it." Solomon smiled as he checked his watch. "I made reservations. We have to go."

"It really is a fancy hotdog stand!"

Solomon's smile grew. "I only take you to the best places."

"I have something else to tell you," I told him as I locked up and we walked over to his Lexus. He parked it in the street, which was quiet this time of night. Lights dotted the windows of the houses around me and I raised my hand to wave to my neighbor, Aidan, out walking his dysfunctional dog, Barney. I say, walking, but Barney was currently in the process of doing some kind of belly flop and slide on the grass verge while wearing his hearing dog vest. Aidan gave me a half-hearted shrug and waited for Barney to get over whatever he was doing. As far as service dogs went, Barney was largely a failure; but he was sweet and loving and Aidan often admitted to being very attached to him.

"That dog still a nuisance?" asked Solomon as he opened the car door for me.

"Absolutely. He's less a hearing dog and more a noisy dog."

"Cute though. What's he doing?"

"Your guess is as good as mine. Anyway, you know I haven't taken on a pro bono case in a while? I accidentally took one today. Oops!" I reached for the door and shut it, leaving Solomon on the sidewalk. A small movement in his face was the only reaction I got. It could have been bemusement or pride or… it could have been anything really. I waited until he climbed in, switched on the engine, and pulled into the street.

"So?" he said finally, which was better than "no."

"Several wedding boutiques have been robbed."

Solomon glanced over. "Did Lily lose her dress?"

"No, but Sharon, the owner of Perfect Brides, is worried her store might be hit next. I'm going to look into it. Maybe I can even get the stolen dresses back to the brides affected."

"Okay."

"Okay?"

Solomon shrugged. "Okay," he repeated.

"Lily said she'll help. She's going to do most of the surveillance too and I'll help out when I can."

"Do I have to pay her?"

"No. She's doing it out of the goodness of her heart, and because her dress is in there."

"So long as it doesn't conflict with your job, I'm happy. Plus, it's good for business."

"How's that?"

"You get the dresses back, we give every bride a business card, and we wait for the cheating surveillance jobs to come in."

My mouth dropped open and I punched Solomon's upper arm. *Nice.* I kind of wanted to do it again, except gentler and with more stroking. "Solomon!"

"I'm joking!" he laughed, his face splitting into the most delicious smile. "Sweetheart, I'm joking!"

CHAPTER EIGHT

Beyond my initial research, I didn't know a whole lot about Karen Doyle. Now I knew she was allergic to peanut oil, and her death was premature after being poisoned by someone who also had knowledge of her allergy. I knew she didn't deserve to die on a treadmill. She was very fit and had a connection to my other two victims, but that wasn't nearly enough to form an hypothesis on why someone might want to kill her. Now that Jim Schwarz's neighbor had thrown in the idea that all wasn't right with his previous job, I had an inkling that I needed to look further into her recent history than just the past few months.

It was that inkling that ensured my butt was parked in my chair first thing in the morning, after arriving at the agency separately from Solomon, with her file open on the desk.

Karen Doyle was the same age as me when she died, something I found hard to comprehend. Right now, her smiling face was staring at me from her wedding website photo. I wondered how long the website would stay live, and just in case someone closed it, I printed every page. Her fiancé only appeared in her life fourteen months ago. That told me he may not know anything about what might have occurred with her previous employers, but it didn't tell me if they discussed other pertinent aspects of her life. However, I concluded, she might have confided in her sisters. She may even have known what was bothering Jim Schwarz. However, all that was simple conjecture until I delved deeper.

Although I didn't know where one sister lived, I did know that her younger sister was renting her apartment. It took me less than a couple of minutes to find the address. I logged my whereabouts onto the file, sent Solomon a text to that effect, and grabbed my jacket and purse, making my way down to the underground parking garage. Just as I entered the garage, I spotted Solomon talking to two people, a man and woman. The man looked like one of the thick-necked guys I'd seen previously. The woman held a folder that read Solomon Agency in solid white lettering across the middle.

"Boss," I said, nodding to Solomon. "Hi," I said to the other two who nodded in return.

The woman added, "Hi" and Solomon greeted me, but he made no moves to introduce anyone.

As I climbed into my car, I couldn't resist taking another look in my mirror. Since the agency was small and tightly knit, I knew everyone in it, from our four investigators to the doorman. These people, however, I didn't know, so I could safely assume they worked on the mystery floor. Now that I'd made contact and properly established my position by greeting another agency employee, perhaps I could corner one of them for some more information. I quickly glanced away when Solomon eyed me, firing up the engine. I adjusted the mirror and backed out, stuffing the in-agency intrigue into the back of my mind. That was one mystery I would have to solve on my own time. Or, at least, at a time when Solomon wasn't watching.

Karen's rented apartment was situated on the first block into Chilton. Even on the border, I could see it was pricey by the actual liveried doorman lurking inside the doors — since when did Montgomery get liveried doorman? — and the very stylish brick exterior. I had to park a block away and walk back, which gave me time to think about what my excuse would be for visiting. By the time I got there, I was all out of ideas, so I opted for the truth.

"I'm visiting Melanie Doyle," I told the doorman, who clocked me the moment I entered.

"Sign here," he said, pushing a pen and the guest book towards me. I signed and hesitated, waiting for him to ask me why I was there. When he didn't, I simply smiled and went over to the elevator. Melanie lived on the fourth floor, in one of four apartments. Hers was to the front of the building, I noticed. I looked out of the corridor window while waiting after I knocked, trying not to think about how rude it was for me to be barging in on a grieving young woman.

Melanie looked a lot like her sister. Same size, slightly bigger build, and very pink cheeks. She wore a dark floral dress and button-up cardigan, both suited to mourning, but just as likely, her everyday wear. "Hi, I'm Lexi Graves. I'm sorry to intrude, but I'm a private investigator and I wanted to ask you a few questions about your sister, Karen," I said, trying not to trip over my own tongue in my haste to assert myself.

Melanie blinked and frowned. "My sister died," she said simply and bluntly.

"I know, I'm really sorry."

"Why do you want to ask questions about her?"

"My client is concerned about her manner of death," I said. "I know this is hard but…"

"No, no, it's okay," Melanie said, surprising me by stepping back and opening the door wider. "I'm worried too. Please come in. Can I see a badge or something?"

I pulled my license from my pocket and she took it, perusing it closely before allowing me to step in. I wondered if she'd ever seen a PI license before, but she made a show of nodding that she understood it, like most people did.

The apartment was smaller than I thought it would be, given the location, and I wondered if that was how Karen could afford it. We passed through a small entryway painted in beige and white, thick, horizontal stripes, which, I had to admit, looked very cool. The door at the far end was closed, and we passed by a small kitchen before entering a cozy living room. Everything was scaled to fit the room. Small couch and a tub chair, a dining table and two chairs. The curtains were hung high and wide, giving the appearance of larger windows. Everything was stylish, and there was nice artwork on the walls; actual watercolors, rather than prints.

"Karen painted in her spare time," said Melanie, noticing me looking at a meadow scene stretched over a wide canvas. "She was really good."

"They're exquisite."

"I kept on telling her that, but she stopped painting over a year ago. Said she just didn't feel it anymore."

"Did she often stop painting?"

"No, never. It was weird actually. She adored painting, she used to go on these painting retreats and everyone always bought her oils or watercolors for birthdays and Christmas. Then, all of a sudden, she just wasn't interested anymore." Melanie shrugged, turning away. "Now she can't ever paint again."

"This must be a difficult time for you," I said, immediately wanting to narrow in on what could have stopped Karen from a much-loved hobby, but I stopped myself. It caught my attention that she stopped painting not long after changing jobs. That was exactly the sort of personality change that I'd learned to identify as a clue to a person's mental state, but it was too soon to get personal.

Melanie nodded and gave me a sad flex of her mouth. "So how can I help you?" she asked, indicating I should sit on the couch while she took the chair.

"I hoped you would be able to give me some background on Karen."

"Like what? She was a pretty private person."

"Can you think of any reason why someone would want to hurt her?"

"No. Honestly, I'm still in shock that someone would. She was, like, the sweetest person. She was just nice. She was nice to everyone. I really looked up to her."

"Were you close?"

"Very. You know, she let me rent this apartment when she moved in with Connor. She could have rented it and made a lot more money, but she only lets me," Melanie paused, her voice choking, "*let* me pay the minimum, just enough to cover the mortgage."

"That was nice of her. She was really excited about the wedding..." I trailed off, waiting for Melanie to fill in the blanks. Melanie nodded. "So, so happy," she enthused. "She was really depressed when she got that job and Connor made a huge effort to make her feel really welcome. She always said how she was so surprised there was anyone that kind in the world, like she wasn't, you know? She said, maybe it was meant to be. Maybe some good had to come out of..."

I waited, but Melanie didn't continue. Instead, she looked at her hands folded over her knees.

I decided to try a different line of questioning. "Do you know if Karen knew a Jim Schwarz or Lorena Vasquez?"

"Yes, they both worked at the same company as Karen. The company she left. I'm not sure if she kept in touch. How come?"

"Jim and Lorena also died recently."

"Oh, that's so sad. I don't think Karen knew them too well, but I think they hung out at work. She said Lorena was like a mom to everyone and I think she said Jim was really funny. Like I said, I don't know if she kept up with them. I think they all got new jobs around the same time."

"Yes, they did. Do you know why they all left Simonstech? Were they unhappy?"

"I don't know. Karen was unhappy about something. You know, I remember something odd. I came by one Saturday because we were going to brunch and Karen looked so white I thought she might be ill, or had too much to drink at the office party and was sick. But she kept crying and wouldn't say why. I knew something had really shaken her up. I asked her a few times after that… I guess I wanted to make sure someone hadn't hurt her and she didn't want to say, but she told me to forget all about it, that she just had a bad day or something, and then she got a new job and I guess I forgot. She was kind of anti-social after that party, so I remember being really pleased when she told me she had a new job. After that, she and Connor started dating."

"Is that when Karen stopped painting? After the party?"

"No, that was a little while after, but I know she threw away everything she painted around then. She said they were all awful." Melanie checked her watch and drew in a deep breath. "I have to go soon. I'm collecting my parents from the airport. They were on vacation in Bermuda and now we're planning Karen's funeral. That's not what you expect to do for your sister, is it? Last week, we were planning her wedding flowers. Now, we're using them for her funeral. Isn't that sad?"

I had to agree it was. "How were things between

Karen and her fiancé?" I asked getting up when Melanie rose.

"Great. He's the nicest guy and they were so happy. Karen said he was the best thing to ever happen to her and she's not usually the kind of person to make such statements. He's devastated. His parents flew in last night and we're all trying to support him too. I was at their house because we were scheduled to make the wedding favors together. The doctor had to sedate him after the police came."

"Did Karen have any problems with anyone? Anything she was worried about?"

"No, she seemed really happy. We were all relieved she got through her depression."

"Your other sister, too? I'd like to speak to her."

"Claire? Oh yes. She was really happy that Karen met Connor right before she went overseas. She works for a medical agency in Africa. She can't get a flight until the end of the week so talking to her won't be possible."

I figured I'd asked enough questions and I didn't want to make Melanie feel defensive by bombarding her with anymore just yet, so I thanked her and she showed me out.

"Who is your client?" Melanie asked at the door. "I didn't think to ask before. I'm kind of not thinking clearly right now. Who asked you to look into Karen's death?"

"Fairmount Gym," I told her," but I'd appreciate it if you kept that confidential."

"The place where she died?" Melanie frowned, then blinked. "Do they think we're going to sue?"

"That never came up," I said, not strictly honestly. Fact was, I didn't want to distress her just as much as I didn't want to plant that idea in her head. The Fairmount Gym was paying the agency fee to find as much evidence as possible to clear them of any wrongdoing, not paying me to get them sued.

"Can I ask you something?"

"Sure."

"Please don't question my parents if you don't need to. They're grieving. And Connor is really out of it. You can ask me anything else you need to know about Karen." Melanie took a card from the slim console table and pressed it into my palm. "If you find out anything, please call. We're still waiting on the coroner's report and the police can't tell us anything." She rummaged in her purse and came up with another card. "The detective we spoke to is called Adam Maddox, if that helps any?"

I assured her it did, and she added, "We just want to know what's going on so we can lay Karen to rest."

I nodded. "I'll be in touch," I said, which wasn't really a promise or a refusal, but Melanie smiled and seemed to think that was good enough. As I walked up the block to my car, again, the niggling feeling in the pit of my stomach told me Karen's upset had something to do with her previous job. The three of them were photographed at a party. What happened there? What could have been so bad that she couldn't confide in her sister? And was it enough to make someone kill for?

CHAPTER NINE

Thanks to Solomon giving me the okay to take a pro bono case, I met Lily at The Coffee Bean, a popular coffee shop and hang out location. We were ready to canvass our first store as planned. She had a huge, heavy looking purse with her, which she kept on her knees, her arms clasped around it. She was smiling when I entered, which worried me.

"What's in the bag?" I asked, bringing our coffees to the table.

Lily took a furtive glance to the left and then to the right. She narrowed her eyes at an older teen, tapping on his laptop's keyboard, and he averted his gaze.

"What's with you?" I asked.

Lily unzipped the bag and fixed me with a determined stare. "You never know who's listening. The walls have ears! The thieves could be here. Right! Now!"

I looked around. The Coffee Bean was close to empty except for the teen, now packing his laptop into his bag and clearing away his coffee cup and a crumpled muffin wrapper. There were also two elderly ladies, deep in conversation, and a young mother, with a sleeping baby on her lap. "I think we're good," I told Lily.

Lily inclined her head to the mother and baby. "She could be married to the thief." Next, she nodded to the elderly ladies. "They could be evil masterminds. Looks are deceiving you know. Just think about Lord Whatshisname and Ben Rafferty."

"I guess," I agreed halfheartedly, thinking about my last case, which didn't end exactly as planned. There were just too many con men involved and one of them was always one step ahead of me. I tried to let it go, but truthfully, it still annoyed me that Ben Rafferty escaped. "But," I continued, "I still think we're safe. What's in the bag?"

"Okay. So I have mace, a camera…" Lily started heaping things onto the table. "A notebook, wigs, three hats, sunglasses. I brought some for you too."

"Uh… thanks?"

"Let's see… what else? A dog bone. My wedding invitation sample. A recording device in case you don't have a spare wire. My phone. Spare charger. Oh, no weapon. Did you bring your gun?"

"No!"

Lily sighed. "Well, that's just plain bad planning."

"I don't normally bring my gun anywhere. It stays at home in a locked drawer where it belongs. I don't need to shoot people. I only shoot at the range."

"It's for protection. We might get shot at." Lily looked strangely hopeful with her wide eyes. "Should I get a bulletproof vest?"

"We're only going to look into the thefts," I told her, before taking a sip of the hot caramel latte. Delicious. "We're going to ask a few questions. Take a few notes. Observe a little. See if anyone saw anything. Out of the kindness of our hearts," I added, since we weren't getting paid.

"And so no one steals my dress," added Lily, less

altruistically.

"And we're definitely not getting shot at." I poked through the items she assembled on the table. The camera and the notepad were a good idea. The recording device and the cell phone charger, too. But... "A dog bone?" I held it up, glad it was encased in a plastic wrapper. "What's this for?"

"In case we break in somewhere with an attack dog that needs subduing." Lily paused, then added, "Duh!"

"O-kaaaay." I placed the bone back on the table and held up the wig and the invitation. "And these?"

"Disguises. We have wigs, hats, and sunglasses, in case we need to change our appearance. The invitation is in case one of us needs to pretend to be a bride and we can say, 'Yep, there totally is a wedding! Not faking!'. Genius, right?!"

"It has your name on it."

"Oh, crap. I didn't think of that."

"Besides, you *are* a bride so we don't need to pretend, and I don't think we need to dress up either. Why are there three hats?" I asked, poking them. "We only have two heads."

"In case one of us wants to change."

"Hmm." I held back a laugh and Lily pouted.

"This is going to be less fun than I thought it would be."

"Sorry, but you volunteered us," I pointed out.

"For a good cause. My dress! To think I was worried about a serial killer screwing my wedding. Having my dress stolen would totally blow it!" Lily scooped her items into her purse and zipped it shut. I hoped she didn't plan on lugging it around with her the whole afternoon because she would get a very sore shoulder, which would make her whine. The only whines I could tolerate needed de-corking. "Where are we heading first?" she asked. "What's the plan?"

I pulled my notepad from my purse and flipped it

open, checking the brief notes I'd made. "First stop is the bridal store down the street. Georgina's Gowns. They were raided first. My cousin, Sian, got her wedding dress there. I haven't been by since, but it's a good place to start. The second store is downtown, and the third one a block from there. The fourth store is in West Montgomery so we can go home after that." I stopped. I forgot that neither of us lived in West Montgomery anymore. I had my bungalow. Lily and Jord were still in her parents' house in Bedford Hills while their new house underwent renovations.

"We could go to my bar afterwards?" Lily suggested. "Jord gets off shift at six. He might join us."

"It's a date."

"Threesome!"

"Gross."

Lily giggled. We waited another ten minutes, talking strategy, until our coffees were nothing but frothy dregs. Fortunately, Lily decided to stow her bag in the trunk of her Mini before we made our way to Georgina's Gowns, just a few minutes' walk away. Having been recently burglarized, it was not apparent. The windows gleamed, the lettering was perfect, and the white awning overhead provided a light canopy over the window and door. I looked closely for a security camera and noted they had two, one fixed on the door and one that looked out onto the street.

"Good news, they have cameras," I said, nudging Lily as she added a hat to her outfit. "They might have caught something on tape."

"Hurrah. Easy case! Let's go crack this mutha open!"

I sighed, but followed her inside anyway, entering into a wooden-floored, roomy space with glass cabinets displaying shoes and jewelry across one wall, and racks of white dresses at the back. A couple of mannequins wore dreamy gowns and I had to stop myself from running an appreciative hand over them as we crossed to the cashier's desk where an assistant waited. Her nametag read "Cindy" and she was absolutely expressionless as I asked for the manager.

"Georgina isn't here," said Cindy. "Can I help?" She glanced over toward the shoppers, pulling out dress skirts and cooing, then back to us, her smile never leaving her face, but somehow, not exactly illuminating it either. I couldn't decide if she looked crazy or just super perky.

"It's about the robberies."

"Oh my! Oh yes!" Cindy exclaimed, putting a quieting finger to her lips. She lowered her voice and nodded to the other patrons. "We're keeping that very quiet. You must be from the insurance agency. I'll get you the forms you asked for."

"Okay," said Lily as she nodded. She beamed at me as Cindy crouched behind the desk. A moment later, she popped up with a slim folder and passed it to me.

"This is a list of all the items that were stolen, the deposits and balances paid. Some of the dresses were due to be picked up the next day, you know. We had to drive all over to get new, matching dresses, but we did it. We never," Cindy fixed Lily and I with a serious look, "never, ever, let a bride down." She straightened, smiling at us both. I couldn't help smiling back. Okay, maybe she was a little manic, but she was sweet, and helpful, and so what if her forehead didn't move? "Okay, if that's all you need...?"

"Your security tapes from the day of the robbery as well, please," I told her.

"Oh, I thought you knew." Cindy grimaced - somehow managing to still smile - and shrugged. "We only got the cameras installed after the—" here she dropped her voice again, "—you know what."

"Right, of course. Did anyone see anything suspicious? Maybe that day?" I persevered.

"No, I was here all day. It was a Friday and we had a

lot of new brides come in that afternoon, but nothing suspicious. I mean, no guys or anything. That's always weird when guys come in. I mean, we're a bridal shop! We sell bridal, bridesmaid, and mother-of-the-bride. No menswear here."

"Did you notice anyone outside the store?" asked Lily, leaning in. Despite leaving her bag behind, she somehow managed to extract a hat and was now wearing it.

"No, it's pretty busy here on Fridays. I didn't see anything unusual at all, but we were so busy, I didn't really look outside."

Lily's hat slipped over her eyes. She pointed one finger under the brim and pushed it back. I tried not to imagine her in a Western, but failed. "Any of the brides acting in a way you wouldn't expect?" she asked, oblivious.

"Not really. I mean, they're all so excited, right?"

"Right," we agreed.

"So... you'll be in touch? We'll get our insurance paid out?"

I waved the file as we turned to leave. "I'll make sure it gets to the right people," I told her, which meant precisely nothing, but she seemed to accept that.

Lily and I waited until we were in her car before we spoke again. "That was easy," she said, removing the hat and tossing it into the backseat. "We have a whole list of everything that was stolen. Shame about the security tapes."

"Yeah, that was a downer, but we can assume one thing," I decided.

"What's that?"

"Whoever cased that store was probably a woman."

"Riiight, because no guys go in there?"

"Nailed it," I said, and Lily high-fived me.

"So all we have to do is look for a woman, pretending to be a bride, who's hiding way more dresses than she needs. Hey, do you think maybe it's a really indecisive bride? Or maybe a kleptomaniac? Or maybe she couldn't afford her dream dress, so she didn't want anyone else to have theirs?" asked Lily.

"Good theories," I replied as I browsed the list of stolen items, "but I think we should stick with the theory that this is plain theft. The dresses from here alone come to a hundred and fifty thousand dollars!"

"Whoa. And with four stores hit? That's…"

"Maybe over half a million dollars."

"I should have opened a bridal store, not a bar," said Lily. "That's good money."

"Yeah, but people only get married once…"

"I hope!"

I continued, "but they carry on drinking."

"I'd toast that, but I'm driving."

"Safety first."

"Next bridal store?"

"You bet."

"Shuler and Graves on the case!" Lily yelled, gunning the engine.

~

We didn't have nearly as much success with the other robbed stores. The Bridal Emporium had a closed sign in the window, the lights were off, and both racks and display cases were empty. A "For Rent" placard sat on the window ledge inside the building. We went into the boutique next door and asked when the bridal store folded.

"They got robbed," said the sales assistant as she busied herself hanging clothes. I suspected she was having a slow day because she became very chatty. "The owner was thinking of retiring anyway so she took that bad luck as a sign and decided not to reopen. I hear she's gone on a cruise with her husband. Insurance money must have been good."

"Were a lot stolen?" asked Lily.

"All the dresses," said the assistant. "Fortunately, the brides managed to get dresses elsewhere, but imagine if that was your wedding day, huh? And how excited you would be about getting your dress? Awful."

"Really awful," I agreed. "Was it a weekend?"

"No, a Tuesday, I think, but I wasn't here. My little boy was sick and stayed home from school that week so I only heard from Jessica, our other assistant, the week after it happened."

"Did you notice anyone casing the joint?" asked Lily. She lost the hat, but had buttoned her mac all the way under her chin. And added sunglasses.

The assistant frowned, looking from Lily to me, then back again. "Who are you two? Cagney and Lacey?"

"Just curious," I asked. "My friend is getting married and she heard about this place."

"Oh. Okay. There's another store a few blocks away. I heard they got robbed too, but they're still open."

We thanked her and left.

"Cagney and Lacey?" said Lily. "Oh please!"

"Nothing wrong with Cagney and Lacey."

"Yeah, but we could be so much more modern."

"It could have been worse. She could have said Diagnosis Murder."

"Very true."

"Maybe we'll have better luck at Montgomery Bridal."

Montgomery Bridal was open just as we were told and this time, we found the owner right away. She wasn't quite as interested in helping us, or bored enough to, until she took a closer look at me and asked if I was Matilda Graves' daughter. When I confirmed I was, she was all smiles and introduced herself as Sally-Anne McLoughlin. "Your mother is such a nice lady. We take Tai Chi together on Sunday mornings. You should come along. It's not just for older folk, there're plenty of you young things too. Your mother told me you're a private investigator. That true?"

"Yes, I work for the Solomon Agency," I confirmed, glad that the lady decided to open up.

"How come you're interested in my store getting robbed?" Sally-Anne asked. "I told your mother and a few people. Did she ask you to look into it?"

"No, we heard that four wedding stores had been burglarized..."

"And you took it upon yourselves to look into it. You're kind-hearted girls, aren't you? Your mother is proud of you, Lexi. Bet your parents are awful pleased with you too, Lily."

Lily shrugged and looked away. "I guess."

"Are you a private investigator too?"

"No, I own a bar," Lily said, turning back, her composure recovered. "Lily's."

"My daughter goes there. Says you have the best cocktails in town."

Lily beamed. "Thank you. I test them all myself."

"So, you said four stores got robbed, including mine? I heard about the one near here. The Bridal Emporium. You know it? They didn't reopen."

"But you did..."

"Oh yes. I can't let all my girls down and their menfolk. We sell menswear here too, not just bridalwear."

"We're trying to find out who robbed these places," said Lily. "We don't think it's a coincidence four wedding stores were burglarized in such a short amount of time. Did you see anything suspicious on the day of the robbery, or maybe before?"

"Now, you mention it, there was one very peculiar woman. She wanted to know all about the dresses, if we had any stock kept in the back. She asked if she could make an evening appointment and I said we shut at six on the dot every night. Always have, always will. Except Thursdays, which is seven, and then we open late on

Friday, at ten a.m."

"Did she ask anything about prices?" I asked, sticking to my theory of it being high-end retail theft. "Or about the value of your stock?"

"No, but she seemed to recognize the designers right off. Very knowledgeable. Could tell the designer just by looking at the dress. Asked for the Monique Lhuilliers and Vera Wangs, then to see the Caroline Castigliano collection, as well as the new Melissa Sweet gowns. Later on, I thought, maybe she's opening a store here, and wanted to check out the competition. I didn't really think of her again until now."

"Do you remember when she came in?"

"Oh yes. It was about a week before the store was burglarized."

"When did that happen?" I asked, pulling out my notepad.

"Thursday night."

Lily and I glanced at each other. "I don't suppose you have cameras?"

"Yes, I do, but they aren't great. They record, but they're more for deterrent purposes."

I didn't like to point out they hadn't deterred anyone. "Can I see the footage from the night of the burglary? And if you have any from the day that woman came in?"

"Let me go check. Take a seat while you wait."

"This is interesting," said Lily. "I smell a breakthrough."

Sally-Anne got us the tapes, having amazingly saved both of them, and she gave the discs to me. In turn, I gave her my business card. "If you can find out anything, I'd be very grateful," said Sally-Anne. "My insurance hasn't come through yet, and I used my savings to restock. I'd hate to think this could happen again. I hear of it happening. Thieves watching you until you restock, then taking all that too. Honestly, girls, it would ruin me."

"That's why we're going to bust these creeps," said Lily, determination etched across her face. "Aren't we, Lexi?"

"I knew you could do it!" exclaimed Sally-Anne before I could give a less than optimistic answer, but who knew? The security footage might be everything we needed to present our case to MPD. "What wonderful young ladies you are! I can't wait to speak to your mother!"

"We are going to break this case," said Lily as we climbed into her car again, my heart sinking at the idea of Sally-Anne telling my mother about the investigation. Not that it was a secret, or that my mother's connection had gotten the lady talking, just the idea of disappointing one of her friend's was extra pressure I didn't need. "Look at all the breakthroughs we've had today. We've got a suspect *and* security tapes!"

"We have a friend of my mom, and tapes we haven't seen yet. We don't know where the stolen dresses are, or if this mystery woman is part of it."

"Blah blah details," said Lily. "Last store, then cocktails?"

The last store on our list was situated in West Montgomery, which meant crawling through rush hour traffic and arriving just as the store was closing. By the looks of it, for good. It was empty.

"Are you closing down?" Lily asked, looking forlorn as the middle-aged woman with a short brown bob turned the key in the door. A "Closed" sign bounced against the back of the glass. "I was looking for a dress."

"I'm afraid we are, so I can't help you. I can't keep the store open anymore," she told us, one hand pausing on the glass pane as if she were saying goodbye to the building.

"Because of the robbery?" I asked, getting right to the point.

"Well, yes, I guess you heard. It was horrible."

"You could restock," suggested Lily.

"It's not that. It's knowing that someone was in here at night, stealing from me and my brides. The police said someone probably watched the store for a while before robbing it. They probably knew my routine. It gives me the creeps being here all alone."

"I'm sorry," Lily and I both said.

"Well, one door closes…" the woman trailed off. "Anyway, I'm sorry I can't help you, but there're some other really nice stores in Montgomery so I'm sure you'll find a dress. Good luck." She left before I could ask her more questions. That was one thing that bugged me about my job: asking people questions when they simply didn't want to answer them. Sometimes, however, that was the only way to get the job done. It didn't mean I liked it and on this occasion I was happy to let it slide. We gleaned plenty of information from our other visits. Now, it was just a case of deciding what was relevant.

"Maybe they're all in on it," suggested Lily as we drove to her bar.

"Who? What?" I asked, looking up from my doodled notes.

"All the wedding store owners. Maybe they all got together and planned this."

"For what reason?"

"To get rid of their stock, claim the insurance money. Maybe they'll even restock the stores with the stolen dresses and double their money."

"That would be a good theory, if two of the stores hadn't closed shop."

"They could have fenced them? Cindy said they sourced all the same dresses. Maybe they got the other two to sell their stock?

"Maybe. Sharon seems too worried that she'll get robbed next for her to be in on any crime ring. She wouldn't have asked us to help if she were part of it."

"Maybe she's not part of it. It could just be the other four," Lily continued.

"Okay. I guess we can do some background checks on the owners just to make sure that there's nothing hinky in their past, like criminal records."

"Good call."

Two hours later, I called Solomon and asked him to collect me from Lily's bar. We sat in a booth in the back and watched him look around. He paused by the door, waiting several minutes before he clocked us. He stared, making no effort to approach us, and just stared some more. Lily and I giggled. After another couple of minutes, he walked over.

"What's with the wigs and hats?" he asked. "Why is there a dog bone on the table?"

This set us off into uncontrolled peals of giggles. "Don't ask," I hiccupped as the askew wig slid from my head and landed in an untidy red heap on the table.

"Sunglasses?" said Lily, holding out a pair. They had diamante pieces sprinkled around the frames. Solomon shook his head, very seriously. "Not my style," he said. Just then, Jord walked over, wearing a pair of pink sunglasses and a pink baseball cap. The lettering read, "Number 1 Mom."

"Hey," he said to Solomon, clapping him on the shoulder before sliding into the booth next to Lily. "How's it going?"

"I really have no idea," replied Solomon. If he were utterly perplexed, he didn't show it. Somehow, that made it even funnier as Lily and I leaned into each other, giggling. "What's with the "Mom" hat?"

"I'm a proud man in charge of my sexuality," Jord said, with a straight face. "I can wear a pink hat with 'Mom' on it if I want."

"Okay. I still want to know what's going on with the dog bone."

Jord shrugged. "They won't tell me. I figure it's some

kind of initiation thing."

I held up my hand to Solomon and he hoisted me up. "Please take me home?" I slurred. "I didn't bring my car. I'm also drunk."

"Didn't notice," said Solomon, hooking an arm around my waist. He picked up a pair of sunglasses and slid them over my eyes. "You might need these in the morning. 'Night guys. Never, ever tell me what the dog bone is for."

"One day you'll beg to know," Lily yelled after us as I stumbled, giggling, out into the open air alongside Solomon.

I didn't remember getting home that night, but I did remember Solomon tucking me in, kissing me on the nose and quietly letting himself out. I couldn't think about that though. It was all I could do to make the room stop spinning before I fell into a dreamless sleep.

CHAPTER TEN

I was glad for the light relief the night before because the absolute last thing I wanted to do was probe into Lorena's life more than I already had. To make it less sad, I reasoned that I was required to. She was my friend and someone hurt her. Someone ended her life and that wasn't okay. Even worse, the killer may well have killed her friends, Jim and Karen. At the back of my mind was another horrifying thought: what if there was another person out there who didn't know he or she was about to become a victim too? I had to find out what was going on and only wished I didn't have to do it with a thumping head and a queasy stomach. Just how much did I drink the night before?

I put it off as long as I could, starting on the background checks I agreed to make on the wedding store owners. Each report came back quickly, leaving me with nothing. Or more precisely, the whole load of nothing meant debunking the theory that the store owners were colluding in some sort of insurance fraud ring. None of the owners had criminal pasts to speak of, unless you counted one outstanding speeding ticket; and none of them came into a large amount of money recently. I emailed Lily, briefly summing up what I'd found, and asked her if she had a chance to look at Sally-Anne's surveillance footage yet?

Then I made a coffee, browsed the internet and finally, got myself into gear. I couldn't put it off any longer and I couldn't ask anyone else to do it for me. No, I had to swallow my discomfort and do my job like a pro. My preliminary search into Lorena turned up nothing of consequence, barring the photograph. I needed to see if there was more.

After I ran through Lorena's background paperwork again, sitting in the quiet, empty agency office, I still found nothing, but the obvious. Grocery bills. Two cell phones, which puzzled me until I worked out that one belonged to her daughter, now at college. One thing was clear, Lorena could afford day-to-day life on her part time job, but the college payments had to be stretching things financially. It seemed that attending the gym was her only recreational activity. I didn't see anything in her financials to suggest that she ever went out to restaurants or bars, or that she had any hobbies, and from what I remembered, she never said anything to that effect either. That didn't mean she didn't go out. She could have had a boyfriend who paid, but I didn't recall her mentioning one. All the same, Lorena was an attractive woman so I made a note to check into it. A lover could have killed her in a jealous rage, and she did say she wanted to talk to me about something important.

Before I hit the streets — or in this case, the gym — in search of answers, I had a call to make.

"How's my favorite detective?" I said when Maddox answered his desk phone.

"I don't know. Who is it this week?"

"Ha-ha. You, of course."

"Yeah, yeah," Maddox scoffed. I imagined him kicking back his chair and resting his feet on the decades-old desk he called home at the station. "What do you want to know?"

"Two things. First off, did you get to speak to Karen Doyle after Jim Schwarz's death?"

"Why?"

"I caught a case. Your case, my case. So..."

"I should have guessed. Let me check my notes." Maddox paused and I heard him open and shut a couple of drawers before the rustling of a few papers. "Found it. Hmm. Okay, I went looking for the woman who was sitting next to Jim, but couldn't find her. To be honest, Lexi, I didn't really try to find her. And yes, before you ask, I regret that now since she's dead and her case is on my desk. I need to call the ME later but she looks like an allergic reaction from the initial reports."

"Thank you," I replied, politely deciding not to rub it in that he missed an opportunity there. "Secondly, an update on Lorena Vasquez's case would be great, please."

"You know I'm not supposed to divulge this information," he said in a low voice.

"Oh, please. Why are you lowering your voice? I can hear no one is in the squad room. Where's everyone gone?"

"Lunch."

"Kind of early."

"They like to be first. It's burger day in the cafeteria."

"Why aren't you there?"

"I want to live."

"Good for you. Speaking of living…"

"I know, I know. Dead woman."

"The dead woman was my friend."

There was a long pause. "I'm sorry, I forgot. What do you want to know? I'm gonna assume you have plenty of background on her already so I'll share, then you share. Deal?"

"Deal," I agreed, wondering at his readiness to confer. Perhaps, he hadn't turned up any worthwhile leads yet. "Whatever you've got."

"Cause of death was the stab wound. The ME says it would have been very quick as it punctured her heart." I gasped at that and Maddox paused a moment before continuing. "She bled out within minutes and there was nothing, absolutely nothing, you could have done to save her, Lexi."

"Okay," I said, my voice small and weak. "She was dead when I got there."

"I know. Even if she weren't, there still would have been nothing you could have done. The knife went straight in and the killer pulled it up. The tearing of her aorta was extensive."

"Did you get a handle on the kind of knife used?" I groaned at my unintended pun. This was no joking matter and thankfully, Maddox let it slide.

"Medium blade with slightly serrated edge. Common with kitchen knives. When we processed the scene, a kitchen knife was missing, so that fits. The wound was angled downwards so the killer is taller than the vic."

"So, the killer didn't come armed?" I frowned at that. If the killer intended Lorena harm, why didn't he or she bring a weapon?

"Looks that way. Maybe the perp didn't intend her harm to start with. It could have been an argument gone wrong and he or she grabbed the knife. Either way, the knife is missing. I don't hold out any hopes of finding it, but I've had uniforms go through every trashcan in a five-block radius."

"What about anything linking Lorena to the killer?"

"Nothing. No hairs, no fibers. Apart from a small mark on her forehead, Lorena didn't have any defensive wounds and there was no skin under her nails, so we couldn't extract any DNA. You know what that means?"

I did and I sighed. "Lorena knew her killer and she wasn't afraid of him or her."

"Enough to trust that person to enter her home," Maddox agreed. "I found a single fingerprint on the doorframe but no hits when I ran it. This is my theory. Lorena knew her killer. He or she came to her house. Lorena let that person in, agreeing to talk. She had no reason at that stage to fear for her life. They go to the kitchen to get coffee or something and an argument gets heated. The suspect grabs the knife as the nearest weapon and stabs her, then flees."

"Maybe she opened the door, saw the killer and couldn't get the door shut. She could have run into the kitchen. There's another exit there," I suggested.

"Maybe. I thought of that, but a few things bother me about that scenario. First of all, her neighbors and friends say she's security conscious, and she's a woman alone in the house. She always keeps her doors locked. There's a peephole. She looks through the peephole and sees someone she doesn't trust, she doesn't open the door, right?"

"Right," I agreed. "She thought someone had been in her house recently so she was careful. Really careful."

"So, I check the front door frame and the lock, and there's no sign of it being forced. No scuffmarks on the door jamb to suggest someone prevented it closing, say with a foot. Lorena was confident and trusting enough to open the door, though maybe she was too confident. Plus, there's no sign of struggle, not on her person or in the house."

"Could it have been a service person? A delivery?"

"I checked into that too. There were no deliveries scheduled for her house that day and no services due. That doesn't mean there wasn't someone posing as a delivery person, or maybe she couldn't see the person clearly, so that's still a question mark. This leads me back to the most obvious scenario…"

"Lorena knew her killer and allowed him or her into her home." I paused, remembering something Maddox said. "What about the mark on her forehead?"

"You got it. Now I just have to work out who that person is. As for that mark, it's got me stumped. It's small and looks like two triangles. I have photos, but it's not clear. So far, that mark is my top lead, which gives me very little to work from. Your turn. Tell me what you know about Lorena."

"Not much more than I told you already. She was worried about something and wanted to talk to me and that's why I was at her house that morning."

"Were you close enough as friends for her to confide in you about personal things?"

"No," I decided. We never talked about anything in depth. We stuck to the usual mundane topics with an added dash of running, something Lorena was good at and I wanted to improve. "No. We were only just getting to know each other and really only talked about running and mundane conversations. 'How are you?', running, her daughter, that sort of thing."

"Do you think she approached you because of your professional capacity?"

"It looks that way. She knew I'm a PI and she approached me after Jim Schwarz and Karen Doyle died. She knew both of them."

"From the gym?"

"No, from before that. They all worked for the same firm, Simonstech, and they all left around the same time. I know Jim and Karen were both unhappy about something."

"Coincidence?" Maddox sounded surprised.

"Do you believe in them?" I asked.

"Not anymore, but occasionally, they happen. How come you brought up those two? Apart from their connection to Lorena."

"You haven't heard?" I asked, surprised that I was

ahead of Maddox on that one. Clearly he had only taken a cursory glance at Karen's file.

"Heard what?"

"The ME concluded both Jim Schwarz and Karen Doyle were deliberately poisoned. That they knew each and died within days concerns me. Maddox, this isn't just one murder case, it's three."

"Shit! No one made that connection here! Damn it, I cleared Jim Schwarz at the scene as a natural death. I informed the Doyle family of the death too and said we'd look into it. I thought I was looking at an allergy case, maybe a food contamination. My captain is going to chew me out on this!"

"Oopsie?" I held back telling him I had also processed the scene and a bunch of evidence. At some point I would turn over my whole file, but right now, I wanted to keep the conversation on track.

"Ah, hell. This is just what I need. What else can you tell me?"

"About Lorena?" I asked, waiting for Maddox to answer. When he did, I continued, "I don't see anything suspicious in Lorena's life. I don't think she had a boyfriend, but she was financially stretched trying to support her daughter."

"We contacted the daughter. Her uncle flew out to get her and they're flying in tomorrow. I'd hate to be her right now."

"Me too," I said, making a note not to leave anymore messages on Lorena's brother's phone.

A tapping noise on Maddox's end of the line had me thinking he was playing with a pen while he thought. "I'll make a few calls about their employer," he said, just as I was about to prompt him. "It's interesting that they all worked together and died days apart."

"That's what I've been saying!" I sighed but there was no point getting exasperated. "I'd say it's more than coincidence. I just don't know why."

"I don't suppose I can tell you to stay out of this? I know I'm not your boyfriend anymore, but I hope I'm your friend, and you'll listen to me and not just as a cop telling you not to. Three murders are a lot in one week, even with you involved."

"It's my job, Adam, and Lorena was my friend. There's no way I'm sitting this one out."

"Then make sure you don't take any risks. That time at the warehouse when you were kidnapped, I swear, my heart stopped. I don't want to find you in any worse situation," Maddox said softly.

"I don't see how it could get any worse."

"Dead is hard to come back from, Lexi. Remember that. Take Solomon with you, or one of the guys. Take Delgado. He'll have your back."

"They all have my back," I said, ninety percent certain that was true.

"I hope so. I do not want to be called upon to identify you in the morgue. Not that I would even get to the front of the queue. Keep me informed?"

We hung up, after I promised to be careful, and Maddox agreed to call me if there were any new developments while he tied the cases together at MPD. In some ways, even though he was my ex-boyfriend, it was easier to ask him to keep me in the loop, than any member of my family, of which many, many were serving on the police force. Maddox, at least, saw me as a grown-up, unlike my brothers who were programmed to only treat me like their little sister on a regular basis. Not that they ever thought I should sit a job out, but they often erred on the over-protective side.

I helped Maddox with a bunch of cases, and though he may not have always liked that, he respected how I got the job done and broke the cases wide open, leading to a number of convictions. Of course, since I helped catch several bad guys, my family grew more supportive of my career, and my colleagues were less snarky about my lack of experience. Finally, I found confidence after I proved myself and earned my place at the agency, but this case wasn't about that. This case was finding justice for three innocent people.

I scrawled a note for Lucas, asking him to investigate a couple of pieces of info on Lorena's bank records, and left it on his desk. Then I locked away my files, grabbed my purse and headed for the parking garage, ready for my gym-snooping shift. As I beeped open my VW, I thought about each victim's seeming innocence. Based on their reported worries, I was getting more than a little concerned about what I would find the further I dug into their backgrounds.

~

"Thank God you're here!" said the deputy manager when I entered the employees' locker room for my break. Though I'd often seen the tall, blonde woman around the gym during my member days, and knew her name was Kate, I had yet to speak to her in my new role. She was dressed in her uniform of black sports tights and pink t-shirt, under which her biceps bulged, but today, she didn't look her usual calm self. "I've been looking for you everywhere! We're an instructor down."

"O-kaay," I said, looking around for Michael, wondering what that had to do with me. Class instruction was not what I signed up for. It was effort enough to participate in a class, never mind stand in front of thirty hopeful people, anxiously awaiting to start their workouts. That, and I was absolutely not qualified to instruct. I only agreed to the undercover gig as the best way of unobtrusively snooping around the gym's members, and not to actually *do* anything. Unfortunately for me, Michael was nowhere to be seen. "I think I need to be on the gym floor. Um, watching people. So they don't break anything. Or themselves," I added, edging away from Kate and her clipboard.

"No, no, we've got that covered on minimal staff. We

need you to teach the aerobics class."

"I don't do aerobics," I admitted.

Kate looked at her clipboard, flipping a piece of paper over. "It says here on your form you do."

"Form?" I blinked, trying to remember filling one out. I had a horrible feeling Michael filled it out for me, remembering that he said he would square everything with the real employees.

"You know, the one every employee fills out," Kate said, without looking up as she ran a finger down the sheet. "Yours says you can cover spinning, aerobics, pump, combat, yoga. You're very accomplished. I guess Michael was thrilled to you could fill in for Anton."

My hopes of talking my way out of this plummeted. "I.. er.." I what? I couldn't do any of those things. Well, I could follow a class, and I was pretty awesome at riding a bike to nowhere while making my thighs scream, but teach? A class? No! What was Michael thinking when he ticked every box?

"Great! I knew you'd be dying for a challenge. These first few days in a new job can be pretty boring, even if you are just temp cover. This way. It's in Studio One!" Kate enthusiastically lunged for my hand, grasped it and dragged me after her.

"I... um..." I garbled, tongue-tied as to how to get out of this mess and following in her wake. I frantically searched for Michael as we headed towards the dreaded studio and a class full of people who all thought they were getting a qualified instructor. My protests either fell on deaf ears, or got more encouragement from Kate, and before I could think to hit the fire alarm button, we were through the studio doors and I saw thirty people turning to look at me. I fell silent under their gaze.

"Here she is!" yelled Kate, flapping a hand the full-length of my body. "And she's so excited. Aren't you excited, Lexi?"

"So much," I muttered, with a weak smile. Thirty

people stood between the doors and me. Terror filled my veins.

"Lexi has been an instructor for five years, and she 's new here! Aren't we lucky?" asked Kate, pumping my arm upwards, and squealing to a smattering of applause.

Wishing that telepathy existed, and for someone to get me out of this, I whimpered, "Save me!"

"I thought you worked out here with that blonde woman? The really happy one?" said a small, redheaded woman, turning to her friend who confirmed it with a nod.

"Yeah, I always see you two in spinning," said her friend, a super slim woman in her forties with amazingly toned calves. I envied her calves. Shame they wouldn't get a workout today. "I didn't know you were an instructor."

"Lexi has many hidden talents and she's filling in for Anton for a while," grinned Kate. "Have fun! Work up a sweat, ladies!" And with that, she banged out the door, leaving me quaking under the sea of eyes all trained on me.

"So…" I sucked in a deep breath and tried to calm my racing heart. "What are we doing today?"

"Advanced aerobics," said the redhead.

Just my luck. Why couldn't it have been beginners? Or even a nice easy activity like… I couldn't think of anything nice or easy. This was just as bad as doing sports at school. Even though I never got picked last, usually getting snapped up right after the popular, sporty girls were picked, it wasn't like I particularly enjoyed it. Physical exercise wasn't all about fitness for me; it was a means to an end: looking damn good in my jeans.

"And we're psyched!" Redhead, as I dubbed her, continued. With that, the class let out a collective "Whoop!" and spread into a formation of several lines.

I looked around for an excuse to cancel the class, anything to get me out of this nightmare. "I don't have any music!" I said, barely able to keep the squeal out of my voice as I spied the music system at the front of the studio.

"The music is all on the stereo," said Redhead. "It's preloaded."

Gah. I made my way over there, slipping just as I was steps away. I landed on the sprung slat in the wooden floor with a thump... and got an idea. "Oh no! I twisted my ankle!" I reached for it, allowing my lower lip to tremble in faux-pain.

"I'm a doctor," said Redhead, kneeling next to me and taking charge of my ankle. "No bruising or swelling. You're good to go. Hey, let me get that," she said as she hit the stereo button. Seconds later, thumping music pounded through the speakers and all my excuses were gone. I narrowed my eyes at the annoying redhead and she retreated into the crowd, taking a space at the front.

Okay then. If I couldn't get out of it, I would make them sweat, I decided, a bright idea hitting me. I thought about all the times I landed on my ass and got yelled at to get up again. I would take them through my Army boot camp training, one of the least fun bits of my disastrously short and ill-considered Army career.

"We're doing something different today," I yelled over the noise. Redhead stepped forward, grabbing something off the stereo and passing it to me. A headset and belt pack. Oh yippee. I hated Redhead and her determination to get the class started. "We're doing Boot Camp."

"What about aerobics?" asked someone at the back.

"You want to sweat?" I retorted. When all I got back were some mumbles, I yelled, "I said, do you want to sweat?" The class jumped as my mic-amplified voice echoed around the room. "Do you want to get fit? Do you want to burn that fat?" Finally, I got another

"Whoop!" and steeled myself for one of the top ten worst hours of my life. "Then let's do this! Star jumps, sets of ten, let's go! I said, let's gooooo!"

By the time I was done, fifty minutes into the hour, my class was a depleted array of sweaty, panting heaps. Pristine gym wear bore large sweat patches; there were droplets on the floor, the mirrors were steamed, and everyone's hair was plastered to their heads... I didn't look a whole lot better, but managed to bluster my way through. Between my shouting and running around, yelling enthusiastic idioms that sounded so much better when they were screamed, I made my class yell back as I took them through drills, and what I didn't remember, I made up.

"That. Was. Awesome," heaved the blonde woman as I instructed them to take mats and stretch. "I have to sign up for this class. Did you have fun, Amanda?"

The redhead, Amanda, looked up from her mat, and gasped something inaudible before flopping bodily back onto it. I wondered vaguely if I should take her pulse until she moved and groaned.

Surprisingly enough, some of the class thanked me as they limped out, utterly exhausted, and a couple asked when I would be teaching again. I told them to check with Michael.

By the time I mopped the floor of their sweat and went downstairs, my t-shirt was soaked to my back and Michael was waiting for me. "I'm really sorry," he said, " So, so sorry. I was in a meeting and didn't realize you got dragged into this until halfway through. I came to rescue you, but when I saw the class in progress, you were doing great."

"I think I'm going to die," I said, the wind temporarily knocked out of me. "I don't think my heart is supposed to beat this fast."

Michael peered at me. "Maybe you should take a lie-down in the locker room."

"Okay," I wheezed.

"And a shower. Then we can talk about you doing another class."

"Not on your life. This was a one off. Never! Again!" I squeaked, as I wobbled away on unsteady legs to lie down on a bench, in the quiet locker room, and try to live. By the time I got my breath back, my shift was almost over and I was shivering in my now cold, damp clothes. Grabbing a towel and flip-flops along with my wash bag from the locker, things I previously assumed would be little more than props, I made my way through the small, empty room to the showers. The heat of the water warmed me, and I scrubbed my hair and body, allowing the water to sluice the suds away before shutting it off, only moments before I heard footsteps entering the room. Just as I was about to call out, "Hello?" I heard one of the people say something that made me stop and listen.

"I shouldn't have taken the cash!" said a woman. "I needed it, but I shouldn't have taken it."

"Be careful what you say!" ordered a second voice. This one was female too.

"It's okay, it's empty."

"So how much did you get?"

"Five hundred dollars."

"Just for the key to the building?"

"Yeah. They said they'd give it right back and I figured if anything happened, I would just say I lost my set."

"Five hundred dollars is a lot of money. Why did they want the key?" asked the second voice, a vaguely Southern twang to her accent.

"I don't know. I thought it was to prank someone. I don't even know who it is!" There was some rustling, and I figured one or both of them were getting changed.

"I don't get it. How did they give you the cash?"

"I just got a note offering me the money. Here, read

it." There was a long pause before the woman spoke again. "See? It says all I had to do was leave the key in this place and the money would be waiting and I could pick up the key the next day. I figured no one would get hurt then…"

"What?"

"It was the day before that guy died in the gym."

"Yeah, but he had a heart attack or something."

"And the woman on the treadmill."

"So? It's not like anyone killed her, and even if they did, having a key means nothing. I'm sure it's nothing."

"Do you think? I really thought it was for a prank then that guy…"

"I'm positive. Listen, don't worry about it. You got the key back and no one knows." Locker doors started to shut and there was a rustling as bags were collected. "Just don't do it again. It's not worth losing your job over. My cousin works over in…" The main door opened and shut behind them, leaving me alone in the locker room.

I waited until they definitely weren't returning before toweling off, and walking cautiously into the locker room. There was no sign where they had been standing, or what lockers were opened, which was just as well as they definitely intended to have that discussion privately. If they had checked, I wasn't sure I could argue that I didn't hear a thing, what with the locker room being small and the acoustics ensuring even the smallest sound traveled. I was simply lucky they didn't remember to make sure the shower room was empty.

All the same, just in case they came back, I dressed quickly, blow-dried my hair until it was barely wet, and grabbed my bag, stuffing the wet things inside to take home and launder.

"See ya," I called to Michael as I passed the reception desk. He was hunched over one of the monitors and jabbing at the keyboard like it would bite him.

He looked up as I waved and held up some cards. "Got four comment cards saying your class was brilliant," he said. "If you don't do it again, I'm going to have to hire a boot camp instructor."

"Knock yourself out," I said. "It's not for me."

"Shame. You got some great reviews."

I thanked him, because you know, take credit where it's due. I hurried across the parking lot before I got stuck with anything else I wasn't qualified to do and threw my bag in the trunk. As I slid into the driver's seat, my phone rang.

"I got something interesting for you," said Lucas. "I ran the extra searches you asked for and I got something interesting on Lorena Vasquez."

"Like what?"

"One of the payments was for insurance. I looked into it and she took out a one million dollar life insurance policy."

"When did she get that?"

"Here's the fun part. Three weeks ago."

"Really. Who does it pay out to?"

"Her daughter." I heard another voice before Solomon came on the line.

"You got time to come into the agency?" he asked.

I checked my watch. I'd agreed to meet Lily later for a stakeout, but this was more pressing; plus, I had to think about what I'd just heard. Who wanted a key to the gym so badly they were prepared to pay five hundred bucks for it? And could that window of access have given the person enough time to set up both Jim Schwarz and Karen Doyle? "I just finished at the gym so I can come by now. I have some theories on what I want to look into next."

"Good. It's time we got a working theory on this. A life insurance policy like that tells me Lorena Vasquez expected to die."

Although I hated it, I had to agree with him.

CHAPTER ELEVEN

Solomon had already assembled the team in our small boardroom. I was last to arrive, but that sometimes happened when a team member was working a big case. I didn't have time for our daily meeting, which was pushed back into the late afternoon. Today, I counted my lucky blessings as my colleagues wrapped up thoughts on Fletcher's case — a seemingly simple surveillance job that ended up with him being shot at. Now that his shoulder was bandaged, thanks to a bullet just skimming the skin, and the shooter locked up in county jail, he was reliving the drama.

"Want to see the bullet wound, Graves?" he asked when I congratulated him.

"Does it involve you taking your shirt off?"

Fletcher's smile widened. He was handsome when he didn't look so stony. "Yep."

I pondered that. "Maybe later." From the corner of my eye, I checked Solomon's reaction. He was bent over a file, but I caught the merest hint of a smile.

"It's a date."

"Before you two get cozy, we need to get our heads together on Lexi's case," Solomon said, finally looking up. The room pulled to order quickly. Solomon simply had that presence. He didn't even need to raise his voice. I could hazard a bet that his voice had a very different effect on my male colleagues than it did on me. "You've all been briefed. Lexi, catch us up."

"Okay," I agreed, walking over to the whiteboard covering one wall. It was a recent addition and a useful one. Not quite as cool as a special ops-style electronic board but it was a lot more in agency budget. It felt like a real life murder board and as I wrote the three victims names across the top, I realized it was. "We have three victims," I told them, as I added more personal information, "initially it appeared all deaths were tragic, isolated incidents but I have a connection."

"And that is…?" asked Delgado, as he tapped his pen against the table.

"Close to two years ago they all worked for a company called Simonstech and they all left abruptly. Schwarz's neighbor says he was very regretful of something that happened prior to leaving his job. Doyle's sister had a similar story. She was depressed about something and it changed her behavior significantly."

"How?" asked Solomon.

"She stopped her favorite hobbies. Didn't want to see anyone. Stopped socializing."

Delgado gave a thoughtful nod. "Sounds like depression."

"I agree. What's pertinent is that the depression and behavior changes coincided with Doyle also leaving the firm. That brings us to Lorena Vasquez. I knew her, but not very well," I qualified, knowing that the personal aspect could be perceived as either extra insightful or judgment clouding. "She called me the morning she died, asking to talk. Our working theory is that she wanted to talk to me in my professional capacity." I waited for the derisive snort to emanate from one of my colleagues, but none was forthcoming. I resisted a smile and continued, "Lorena also left the firm at the same time, although we've yet to speak to anyone close to her."

"Any idea why they all left?" asked Fletcher.

I shook my head. "No, but I don't think it's a coincidence although I won't rule it out yet. That's where I am with the preliminary investigation. Our first theory was that it had something to do with our client, Fairmount Gym, since that's where Schwarz and Doyle died." I added these notes to the board. "Lorena, however, was murdered at home. We know now the first two deaths weren't by accident; both were poisoned, but Lorena was stabbed. The common employer connection gives this case a new focus."

"A change in MO is unusual," said Flaherty. As a veteran of the murder squad, his opinion was always useful to me. "Most murderers stick to what they're comfortable with."

"Lovely thought," I said, continuing, "the first two murders were public, in the gym during busy times. I don't know if that was by design or chance. What we do know is they were hands-off kills," I looked to Solomon, waiting to see if he knew anything to confirm or counteract my statement, but he waved me on. "Lorena's murder was in her home. We think she knew our killer."

"How was the poison administered?" asked Lucas. He was tapping away at his tablet and barely paused to look up.

Solomon took over and I waited, watching their reactions. "There was a cut on Schwarz's finger and he absorbed the poison through that. He got the cut from a thumbtack embedded on a spin bike's handle. When we tested the handle, it was dusted with the drug." A few eyebrows rose at hearing that. "Doyle ingested poison via her water bottle. Someone diluted a quantity of peanut oil into her bottle of water, to which she had a massive allergic reaction."

"So, we got two poisonings in which the murderer didn't need to get near his or her victims in order to accomplish. This guy, Schwarz, definitely the target?" asked Delgado.

I nodded. "Based on their connection to each other, I'd say yes. The murderer didn't need to get close, but he... or she, I guess... did know Schwarz's routine. I took the same spinning class, and as far as a I remember, Jim Schwarz always rode the same bike."

"So it's likely that the murderer is a member of your gym?"

"Um..." Thinking about it now, did I need that membership so much? On the positive side, maybe if I caught the killer, my membership might be free. For life. That was something I could mention to Michael.

"Lexi?" prompted Solomon.

"Oh, right... Where was I? Yes, the murderer knew Schwarz's routines and yes, that person got close enough to Doyle to spike her water bottle. It could be a member but I have another theory," I added, recalling the conversation I overheard.

"There's some creepy people around," said Lucas. "I'm glad I don't have a gym."

"How do you keep fit anyway?" I asked, because he was looking pretty buff lately. "What do you do?"

"Cardiosex," he said with a broad grin.

"Gross." I paused, fixing him with a stare. Even though I knew he was engaged, I asked, "With a blow-up doll or a human?"

"Guys, we're talking murder here, take it seriously," Solomon said, reminding us of the purpose for our meeting.

"Yes, boss," Lucas and I chorused.

"So the big question is what could be the motive to kill three people? And why? What spooked three professional people into quitting their jobs? Jim Schwarz and Lorena definitely took lower paying jobs."

There was a long pause. "That's easy," said Delgado. "Murder."

"Three murders to cover up a murder?" I asked, frowning. "Isn't that a little too much overkill?"

Delgado frowned this time, little wrinkles appearing around his eyes. "Is that a pun?"

"No! Okay, let's say they saw something… a murder months ago? Why now? Why get rid of three witnesses now, after all this time?" I asked.

"It's as solid as any other theory," said Solomon, nodding to Delgado.

"That's a long time to let three witnesses wander around without doing anything about them. Why get rid of them now?" I persisted, voicing my concerns as much to myself as to my colleagues while I erased the whiteboard, looking for something I might have missed.

"I think it's time we took a trip to their former employer," said Solomon, shutting his folder and leaning back in his chair.

"I'll get out there this afternoon," I told him.

"We'll get out there," Solomon corrected. "There's no way you're going out there on your own."

I shrugged. "It's just a few questions."

"And we don't know who we're going to freak out. Strength in numbers. No arguments. I'll make the call." He gave me a pointed look and after a moment, I nodded. This wasn't just about strength in numbers, I realized, it was more than that. The look he gave me seared my heart. This was about Solomon protecting me and I… I liked it. Then the look was gone and Solomon went from boyfriend to boss in one swift move. "Let's go scare up some answers, Graves."

~

145

Simonstech was an ambiguous-sounding name for an ambiguous-looking building on the outskirts of Montgomery. This was prime industry location, attracting employees from our town and further afield. Several years ago, I temped in a building I could just see in the distance, on the other side of the lake that spanned the building's rear. It was cheaper than the city to operate a business here, hence, the landscaped grounds around the four-story building. The wide-open location was probably the most attractive thing about the complex. The building was a flat gray, with an almost entire glass front, tinted, so we couldn't see anyone moving around inside. Attached to the top left corner was a white on blue Simonstech logo, with the outline of a butterfly perched on the "h".

Solomon and I sat in his Lexus in the parking lot, observing the few workers that strolled around the grounds. People went to and from the glass entryway situated in the middle of the symmetrical concrete and glass structure. A few employees were clearly leaving for home, but for the most part, the parking lot was packed.

"Pretty average-looking vehicles," he said, his eyes roaming over the cross section of hatchbacks, minivans, SUVs and a couple of cool-looking convertibles. I said nothing, because what do you answer that with? "I like the shiny one with the soft top the best!" Incidentally, I did.

"I'm going to bet even their Christmas party isn't exciting," I said. "The people look as concrete as the building. So much gray!"

"That one's a statue," said Solomon, pointing to the figure in front of the building. It rose from a plinth in the center of the small square. Around it was a wooden bench. A couple of women sat on it, their backs to us. I rolled my eyes and ignored him. He continued, "Something was exciting enough to scare the crap out of our victims."

"We still don't know for sure that it had nothing to do with the gym, which reminds me…" I then began to recount the conversation I overheard from the gym shower.

"You didn't think to bring that up earlier?"

"I forgot!"

"Lexi!"

"It happens!"

"What do you think it means?"

"Oh, damn, I wanted to ask that." I paused as Solomon took his turn to pin me with a look. Cautiously, I smiled, and when he did too, we both laughed. "Okay, fine, it tells me we shouldn't rule out something hinky at the gym until we've spoken to someone at Simonstech."

"Hinky? What is this? Scooby-Doo?"

"Seemed like a good word at the time, but I'll shelve it," I said, sticking my tongue out.

"Don't. It's cute. I like that necklace you're wearing."

"Gift from the man in my life," I said, picking up the pendant and playing with it.

"He must like you a whole lot."

"Yup," I agreed, as I leaned over and kissed him. It was brief, heart-pounding, and made me sigh.

"You taste like strawberries," said Solomon, licking his lips.

"It's my lip gloss. I also have apple, grape, and a lipstick that tastes like watermelon. Want to try them all?"

"So long as I don't end up looking like a transvestite, yes."

"Deal." I was about to root in my purse for the extra lip glosses when Solomon picked up his cell phone, tapping the screen. The smooch moment vanished, and I was barely able to restrain a disappointed pout. Damn work, getting in the way. Sure, I was dedicated to the job, but it wasn't like we had that much alone time and I didn't want to miss snatching any opportunity. Maybe if we weren't still pussyfooting around town, trying to keep our secret dating slash relationship under wraps, it would have been easier. That made me wonder: just why were we doing that? I'd come a long way in proving myself at my job and felt confident that my colleagues weren't all that interested in my sex life. After all, now I thought about it, they knew about Maddox, and that didn't bother them at all. Perhaps keeping our relationship to ourselves wasn't all that necessary.

Just as I was about to voice my revelation to Solomon, he said, "Dinner? Mine? Later?"

"I like a man of few words," I replied, nudging him with my elbow. "Very sexy."

"Sorry," he said, shaking his head, "My bad. Would you like to stay at my house after dinner and a movie tonight?"

"Yes, please. Sleepover? Shall I bring my jammies?"

"Yes, and no. In that order."

"Toothbrush?"

"You may as well leave one, one of these days."

"Whatever will I brush my teeth with when I'm at home?" I asked, purposefully giving him my most vacant expression. Solomon leaned over, ruffled my hair and kissed me on the lips. Then he drew back, his eyes heavily lidded, urging me to sigh, before going in for a longer, more delicious smooch that sent my heart a-flutter.

"Screw the case," he murmured. "Let's go home, right now."

"You're so unprofessional," I whispered against his lips. Before he could reply, and possibly have gotten me on the same wavelength, his cell beeped, and with a grunt, he pulled away from me and reached for it. Unfortunately, I didn't let go and had to disentangle myself from his arms before I ended up face first in his lap. Not that I thought Solomon would argue, but as far as public displays of affection, that would be off the chart.

"It's time for our meeting," he said, beaming as I blushed. "Come on before I change my mind and drag you home."

"You really wouldn't need to drag me," I told him as I slid out of the car and followed him to Simonstech. It was hard to resist reaching for his hand, but I did, as I figured Joseph O'Keefe, the vice president, and our scheduled appointment, probably wouldn't take two canoodling private investigators seriously. By the time we got to the entrance lobby and signed the guest book, the security guard said O'Keefe's secretary was on her way down. That gave us only a minute or two to scan the room.

While Solomon took discreet looks at the security, I found my attention drawn to a large glass display cabinet against one wall. Inside was a scale rendition of Simonstech, but the focus was on the land beyond and a small painted portion of lake, lapping at the shore. They even had clusters of purple flowers mixed in with the woodland. Above the model hung a landscape painting of the natural habitat sanctuary Simonstech had set aside for the local wildlife. There were some notes about how the land would never be touched, and thus, still available for employees and future generations to enjoy. I had just finished reading about it when the secretary joined us. She was mentioning the excellent PR aspects of the natural sanctuary as we followed her via a series of elevators and corridors to a large corner office on the top floor.

"Thank you for seeing us," said Solomon, shaking the VP's hand first. I got a swift handshake too before we were ushered to the visitors' chairs opposite O'Keefe's desk. He settled into his own leather, upholstered chair and leaned back, examining us as we surveyed him. He had graying temples on an otherwise full head of dark brown hair and the most delightful blue eyes. They matched the sky-blue tie peeking out from his gray suit. From his online biography, I had him pegged as sixty minimum, but he looked much younger.

"Not a problem. We don't often get a detective agency here, or ever, I'll admit, so I was intrigued and I had a little free time. You said it was something to do with one of our employees?" Before we could confirm, he continued. "We take the welfare of our staff very seriously here. How can I help?"

"It isn't a current employee," Solomon explained, "but some background on a previous one that we need in reference to a current case."

"What kind of case? You didn't say when you called."

"Homicide."

"Oh." The surprise showed in O'Keefe's eyes, but he concealed it quickly. "Recent?"

"Yes."

O'Keefe took that in, looking from Solomon to me. "Okay. Simonstech employs more than a thousand people at this site so I can't guarantee I know the names of everyone here now, never mind a past employee, but I'll do the best I can. What's the name?"

"Jim Schwarz."

"Why, you're in luck! I did know him. He was employed in the research division. A very pleasant man. Bright future. I was very sad to see him go. He's dead, you say?"

"He died a week ago," I said, taking point from Solomon, whom I saw watching the man carefully for any kind of reaction, or body language that shouted "I did it!" I didn't know what Solomon read from him, but I got nothing but surprise, and perhaps, a little shock. O'Keefe really didn't know his former employee was dead.

"I'm very sorry to hear that. Like I said, I hated to see

him go. Jim had a bright future here. He was one of the youngest heads of a laboratory in the history of the firm. What happened?"

"He was poisoned."

"What is this world coming to?" O'Keefe got up and paced to the window. He stuck his hands in his pants' pockets and stared out for a few moments, before looking at us over his shoulder. "Has the killer been apprehended?"

"Not yet," said Solomon, "but it's only a matter of time. We're mostly interested in the reason why Jim Schwarz left your employ."

"To be honest, I'd like to know that too. We'd just approved his promotion when he resigned. We figured he wanted more money, so I offered it to him personally. Quite a large pay raise, actually."

"Who's we?"

"The big boss, Carter Simons Senior, our HR director, Anne Mannering, and yours truly." O'Keefe shrugged, continuing, "But he said there was nothing that could convince him to stay. I wrote a reference for him myself and I told him if he ever changed his mind, there was always a place for him here. I remember he seemed quite touched when he shook my hand and told me it was a pleasure to know me. Things like that really stick in your head when you're the boss."

"Did he give any indication as to why he left?"

"Not to me. That's not to say he didn't say anything to his co-workers. We're a family firm, you know. Simons Senior is my brother-in-law and the founder. We're still privately held, and as such, Simonstech really values its employees. I advise all my managers to have good relationships with the staff. Leniency on letting them attend their kids' Christmas plays, birthdays, no hassle dental appointments, that sort of thing." Solomon nodded, while O'Keefe rested his back against the window. He, crossed his legs, seemingly relaxed as he chose his next words carefully. "I hate to say it, but I wonder if Jim got into it with his manager."

"Who would that be?"

"Carter Simons Junior, Carter's son and my nephew."

"Could we talk to him?" asked Solomon, rising. "I'd like to hear his take on Schwarz, then we'll be out of here. We really appreciate your time."

"Of course. I'll have my secretary take you there. I have to go to my next meeting and there's a car waiting for me downstairs." O'Keefe rounded the desk to shake our hands again before grabbing a leather portfolio case from the desk and tucking it under his arm. "I hope you catch the bastard that hurt Jim. Call my secretary if you need anything else," he said, waving in his secretary, who was now hovering by the open doors. "This is my junior secretary, Mark. Mark, can you take the investigators to Junior and tell him to help them however he can." Saying that, Joseph O'Keefe was gone, with a couple of assistants flanking him as he exited the office.

"Please follow me," said Mark, "We have to head over to the east wing; but it's only a few minutes' walk."

As we followed, Solomon asked Mark a few questions, but the secretary had only joined the firm within the past couple of months and didn't know the deceased. Solomon gave up, and together, we surveyed the building as we traversed it. There wasn't much we could see. Unlike modern, open plan offices, Simonstech was very much closed off, with office after office hidden away behind touch code doors. Within minutes, we passed through a glass-covered walkway, hovering in the air between a second building, unseen from the front parking lot. The outside scenery turned greener as we moved towards the back of the building, and I could just see the edges of the lake and a smattering of the purple flowers, just like in the model.

A tall, slim man was waiting for us, all smiles as we approached, shaking our hands firmly and inquiring after our health. If I didn't know he was Carter Simons Junior, I would have recognized him from the photo of his father, also posted on the company website. "Old Man O'Keefe says this has something to do with Jim Schwarz, huh? Nice guy. We were all sad to see him leave. What happened?"

"He was murdered," said Solomon, rather bluntly.

"Well, gosh, I never would have figured Jim for a murder victim. Honestly," Simons Junior said, leaning in as he pushed open the door to a small meeting room and gestured for us to come in, "he just wasn't that interesting."

Solomon ignored that, instead asking, "We're checking into his background and were curious about why he left Simonstech so suddenly."

"I never really asked, but it's always the same. More money, more vacation days," replied Junior, with a knowing nod. "We couldn't match his demands, so he left. His loss, I can tell you. Nice guy, but plenty of bright guys out there just waiting to catch a break for a smaller paycheck."

"Did he have any problems with any of the staff here?" Solomon asked.

"No, friendly enough. He never mentioned anything. I can check his employee file, if you like?"

"We'd appreciate a copy."

"If you leave your card, I'll have my secretary mail you a copy."

"Appreciated." Solomon produced a card and pushed it across the table. Junior studied it a moment, then pocketed it.

"What did Jim do to warrant the special treatment with PIs?" he wanted to know. "Aside from being murdered?"

"That's principally it," Solomon deadpanned. "Was

Schwarz... Jim... particularly friendly with any other employees here?"

"Not that I remember."

"How about Karen Doyle or Lorena Vasquez?"

The silence in the room was audible, and Junior hesitated for the briefest of moments before recovering, and shrugging like the question was nothing. "He knew them. We all did since they all worked for me. They left a couple of years ago."

"Were the three close?"

"I have no idea. I'm sure they wouldn't have killed him." Junior laughed. "Like I said, they're not here anymore, or you could ask them personally. I'm pretty sure no one bears a grudge nearly two years old."

"A grudge?" I asked.

Again, Junior hesitated before continuing, "Poor choice of words, I guess. I simply meant, that if they didn't get along, I'm sure none of them care about it now. Our Human Resources department might be able to put you in contact. However, we didn't stay in touch."

"That won't be possible," Solomon replied. "Karen Doyle and Lorena Vasquez are both dead."

"Damn shame," said Junior, not skipping a beat. He checked his watch, then glanced over his shoulder to the empty corridor. "Nice people. Listen, I have a meeting to attend. Anything else I can help you with?" He pushed back his chair, rising, and overtly signaling the meeting was over.

"We're trying to work out if there was any reason why three employees of the same division, in the same firm, would all leave at the same time, and then all end up dead," said Solomon, not rising from his chair. I stayed put in mine too.

Junior crossed to the door, opening it wide and holding it. He acted like he had all the time in the world, but when he looked from Solomon to me, his eyes were cold and angry. "I don't like what you're insinuating and neither would my uncle. I think you should leave now."

"Thanks for your time," said Solomon, surprising me by rising this time. That left me obligated to follow his lead.

"I'll take you to the elevators, then security will show you out," Junior told us. We followed him; Solomon quietly, and I... puzzled that Solomon wasn't more insistent in his questioning.

"One more thing," Solomon said, as the elevator doors opened in front of us. "Did Jim Schwarz, Karen Doyle, and Lorena Vasquez have any issues that involved Simonstech or any employee? Were they encouraged to leave in any way?"

Junior pointed to the elevator, the sleeves of his suit pulling back to reveal cufflinks with a raised butterfly, the same pattern as the company logo. "That's enough. I won't have you slandering the good name of my family's firm. I don't know how you wheedled an appointment from my uncle, but I can guarantee you won't get another. Out," he said, the color rising in his cheeks. "And don't come back."

Solomon inclined his head and we stepped inside, the doors closing on Junior's angry face. Sure enough, a thick set, uniformed, security guard waited for us on the first floor as the elevator opened into the lobby.

"This way," he said, without any of the pleasantries he exhibited toward us on the way in. "I've been instructed not to let you back into the building," he said, striding ahead of us. Halfway across the lobby, I nudged Solomon and nodded to my right where Joseph O'Keefe stood, along with an older man. He bore a strong resemblance to Junior, but with thinner hair. Still, he was an enigmatic, handsome man. "That's Carter Simons Senior," I whispered and Solomon nodded. In front of the pair were Maddox and his occasional partner,

Detective Rebecca Blake. They looked up and saw us. Maddox acknowledged us and Blake smiled with a nod at me. I didn't like her for a long time, but decided I didn't loathe her now. I tried not to grin at Maddox since we'd beaten him to the scene… again. I couldn't say it was a surprise to see them, but I was happy we got here first. Solomon Agency, one: MPD, zero. On the other hand, they had badges and warrants we could never get. A moment later, we were out on our asses.

"That was quick," I said, as Solomon and I strolled to his car.

"But informative. What was your take?"

"I love this bit. I deduce everything right and you realize I am your smartest employee ever."

Solomon laughed. "Prove it."

I thought about O'Keefe's demeanor and went with my gut reaction. "Joseph O'Keefe knew nothing about his former employees' deaths and was saddened to hear about Jim Schwarz. He appeared genuine."

"Agreed. And Carter Junior?"

"At first, I thought he didn't know a thing, but he stiffened when you mentioned Karen and Lorena. He knew about them, but didn't expect they would be brought up and it caught him by surprise." I waited, but Solomon waved me on, so I continued, "I bet he makes a terrible poker player. Plus, he lied about why Jim Schwarz left the company. Jim didn't want more money like Junior said. He'd already turned O'Keefe's pay raise down. One other thing, he confirmed all our victims worked in the same division."

"He lied about something else," said Solomon. "He didn't have a meeting. He wanted us out of the building the moment the women's names were brought up."

"How do you know that?"

"Because I just saw him watching us leave from a window. Don't look up," Solomon added as he beeped the Lexus open.

"Oops," I said because my head was already turned.

"He's gone. I'm going to have Lucas look into his background. Junior knows something about the victims, and whatever it is, he doesn't want us digging around."

CHAPTER TWELVE

"On a scale of one to ten, how embarrassed are you to be seen out in public with me?" I asked. I blurted out the burning question that had been bugging me on an epic scale. Lily would be so proud of my directness. Meanwhile, I would have liked for a gigantic hole to open up in the ground and swallow me up. How whiny did I sound? But since Solomon's idea of dinner and movie seemed to have morphed into takeout pizza and a DVD at his house, I had to wonder again, didn't he want to be seen in public with me?

Solomon looked around the small store front of Monty's Pizza, which currently was only occupied by the two of us, and frowned. We were waiting for a large, stuffed crust, barbecue pizza and my stomach kept emitting embarrassing little growls. That my question covered up the noises was pure coincidence.

"Zero," he said.

"Whoa, that's off the charts!"

"You asked. What's with the question anyway?"

I shrugged. "No reason."

Monty, the man himself, slid the box over the counter and took Solomon's money. We climbed into his car and headed for Chilton. I tried to not lick my way through the box to the delicious contents. Solomon placed a hand on top of it. "If you wait ten minutes," he said, "you can have a plate and a glass of wine."

"So formal? You spoil me."

"Don't forget, one comes with alcohol."

"Sold. Drive faster!" Faster, I decided, before I started pressing the question of our relationship too. Oh, what the hell, while I was embarrassing myself, I might as well continue. "So… are you my boyfriend or what?"

"What?"

"Really!" I half yelled.

"No!" Solomon glanced towards me, looking utterly confused, before returning his eyes to the road. "I meant what kind of question is that?"

"We've never really discussed it. I know we're dating, but… I don't know if you think this is casual sex, or a relationship or…"

"A regular booty call?" Solomon smiled. "With dinner on top?"

"Well, I guess you could put it that way," I replied sulkily, trying not to think about who or what went on top. Solomon had a great trick that involved a strawberry, which was enough to send me into a spin just thinking about it.

"I kind of assumed you were my girlfriend."

"Oh." We fell silent. After a moment, Solomon asked hesitantly. "You are my girlfriend, aren't you?"

"Yes," I said, mashing my lips together to compress the huge grin that tried to consume my face. "I think so. Yes. Fine, if you insist."

"So… this is settled?"

"Um…"

"What now?" Solomon sighed.

"Can I tell anyone?"

"Like whom?"

"Lily, for starters, and my family, and… What about at work?"

"Maybe we should just keep it between us. The last thing either of us needs are people sticking their big noses into our business. Okay with you?" I gurgled a very non-committal noise, and Solomon glanced my way again. "But you can tell Lily."

"Thanks," I said, even though she already knew everything and Solomon probably knew that.

"My sister knows. And my brother," added Solomon. "My whole family knows!"

"They are your whole family," I pointed out, remembering Solomon lost his parents some years earlier and pretty much raised his younger siblings.

"And Anastasia is thrilled. She thinks you're awesome." Solomon pulled onto his street, searching for a parking space. "Have you been worrying about this? About whether I was taking advantage of you?"

"No," I lied. "Never. Never even crossed my mind."

Solomon parked and switched off the engine. He unbuckled his seatbelt, leaned over and kissed me firmly on the lips. "You're a terrible liar sometimes."

With Solomon busy in the kitchen of his large, welcoming brownstone, nestled in Chilton and only a few blocks from Melanie Doyle's apartment, I browsed his small DVD collection in the living room. Surprisingly, there were no romances, or musicals, but he did have a couple of comedies and action flicks. There was one DVD that made my eyebrows rise so I put it to one side to confront him when he brought our pizza in. Really, I never took him for that kind of man.

When my cell phone vibrated in my pocket, I thought about ignoring it, but after seeing it was Lily, I answered.

"Want to go on a stakeout?" she asked.

"Not really. I'm at Solomon's, having pizza."

"Takeout?"

"Yep."

"Still doesn't want to be seen anywhere with you, huh?" said Lily, breezily.

"Lily! That hurts."

"What's for dessert?"

"Me."

"I don't wanna... no, I am not saying that. I know what you'll answer and that's just rude. Do you want to stakeout after? Or will your legs be too wobbly?"

"Wobbly, I hope. How is the Perfect Brides stakeout working out?"

"Like watching paint dry. Nothing is happening at all."

"I called you. Any luck with Sally-Anne's surveillance tapes?"

"Nope. I watched the in-store tape first, and yeah, there was a woman in there around the time Sally-Anne said, but she never turned her face towards the cameras. And on the night of the burglary, there was nothing but white noise."

"White noise?"

"Yep. I called Sally-Anne and told her and you'll never guess. Go on, guess!"

"No, I don't want to. Solomon will be back any minute so just tell me."

"Spoilsport. Sally-Anne checked and the wire was cut on the outside camera. I think the thieves did it."

I mused over that. It was disappointing that the tapes couldn't give us anything, but it was a good lead to start. "I agree. Anything suspicious reported at Perfect Brides?"

"Sharon says no. I've been sitting outside for an hour tonight and I've seen zip."

"Any reason why you're staking them out tonight? Did something happen?"

"Jord got me the crime reports from the burglaries

and I noticed all the stores were broken into during the evening hours. The ones with security recorded times that were all before midnight so I figured the store only needed watching for a few hours at night."

"I'm sorry I can't help out more, but good work!"

"Thank you. And there's more! Sharon said there was a woman acting funny in the store this afternoon. Ruby said she'd cover my shift at the bar and Jord is at work so I thought, why not? And here I am. I'm boooored."

"Tell me about it."

"Well, my butt's numb and I didn't bring any CDs, so I'm listening to the radio and... hey, Lexi, what do you do when you need to pee on a stakeout?"

"Scream usually."

"Good call. If you get bored of your hot boss, come find me."

"Not likely. We had the talk."

"The Talk. The baby one? Lexi!"

"No, the boyfriend-girlfriend one. We're so on!"

Lily squealed and I held the phone away from my ear. "Ohmigoooooosh," she finally squeezed out. "I knew it! I knew he wasn't embarrassed to be seen in public with you. After all, you're very stylish and popular."

"Aw, thanks."

"Oh! I see someone entering the store! Gotta go."

"Okay, and if you see anything suspicious, do nothing," I instructed Lily. "Do not confront them. Don't even let them know you're there. Just take a photo, make some notes, but do not approach!"

"No problem. I'm very inconspicuous," Lily said and hung up. Somehow, that didn't comfort me, now that I'd already seen her wigs and sunglasses.

When Solomon entered, bearing a large tray loaded with pizza, napkins, wine glasses, and a large bowl of popcorn, I scooped the DVD from the coffee table and held it up. "What's this?" I asked, raising my eyebrows in question. "Since when are you into this stuff?"

"I swear it's not mine," he said, setting down the tray on the coffee table.

"The entire series of *Glee*? C'mon on. Are you a closet Gleek? You can tell me. I promise I won't break up with you."

"It's my sister's, and no, I don't watch it." He grabbed the remote control and patted the couch cushion. "Come over here."

I didn't need asking twice. I dropped onto the couch and curled my feet under me as Solomon passed my plate. "So, eating take-out in. Yum!" I stuffed a slice into my mouth. Well, not the whole thing, but close to it, and my stomach gave a mewling grumble of delight.

"Did you want to go out?" Solomon asked, frowning, as he channel-surfed. "It's been a long day."

"No, like you said. Long day. Plus, Monty's is the best."

"I thought we could head over to Lake Pierce on the weekend. Get out of town. Make a day of it. Or we could rent a cabin for the night?" Solomon smiled, raised his eyebrows, and I thought how charming it would be to stroll around the pretty lakeside retreat... out of town... where no one could see us. "Okay, what gives, Lexi? Why the funny look?"

"What funny look?"

"That one. What's wrong? I know you're not happy about something. Is it us?"

"No, no. It's not us. Okay, it's a little bit us. I just wondered if we still needed to be careful about letting it get out that we're in a relationship. I was wondering if the guys would care all that much."

"I think Delgado knows," said Solomon.

"I think Lucas knows," I replied. We both chewed on the pizza. That was two, out of four colleagues, not counting the secret floor above.

"No one else knows though. Plus, I don't want anyone thinking I'm giving you preferential treatment. And, I thought we wanted to keep things between us. This is nice…" He waved his slice around the room. "Cozy. Relaxed. No one bugging us. I'll even let you pick what we watch if staying in is bugging you."

"No, you're right, this is fine," I said cozying up to him, "and I'd like to go to Lake Pierce. Maybe we can do a team outing there one day? Like… team bonding?" The thought gave me the shivers, but it could be fun, and I looked great in hiking gear. Actually, that was a stretch, but I gave my best effort. What I did have was some hot lingerie, just perfect for rolling around in front of a log fire. All I had to do was remember to turn frequently so I didn't burn on one side.

"We could, but I was planning on making love only to you in a remote cabin."

"Uh…" Really, the things that got into my boyfriend's head. "Maybe we could go with Serena, Delgado, and Victoria one day? After we've done the hot and heavy weekend?"

"Sweet. Heh, look, the food channel. Want to watch the stuff we're not eating?" Solomon suggested as the latest *Man Versus Food* challenge filled the screen.

"Awesome."

~

Solomon was gone by the time I got up, which would have been fine if I didn't remember my car was nowhere near his house. So, I did the only sensible thing I could think of after rejecting the notion of calling a cab. I called my best friend and made her come over and pick me up.

"How'd the stakeout go?" I asked, when I climbed in.

Lily yawned, covering her mouth only when it threatened to eat the rest of her head. "I fell asleep in the car, got a stiff neck, and drove home at one a.m. I drove by the store on the way here and it was open as normal, so I guess it didn't get robbed. My wedding dress is still safe."

"That's good news."

"It is, isn't it?" Lily beamed. "Speaking of good news, meaning my forthcoming wedding, you better not have forgotten the rehearsal dinner tonight. Is Solomon coming? I need to get the seating finalized with the wedding planner."

Oh... organic crapola! The rehearsal dinner. Not only did I forget about the dinner, I still hadn't asked Solomon if he would be my date.

"Lexi..."

"I'll be there," I said, "Didn't forget. Absolutely didn't."

"I can't believe you forgot!" Lily wailed. "I even added it to your phone calendar. Everyone is coming. You've known about this for weeks!"

"Uh... do I have to wear my bridesmaid dress?"

"No! Wear whatever you like. You do have something to wear, don't you?" Lily screwed her eyes up as we hit a red light and fixed me with a scrutinizing stare that made me want to shrink in my seat and apologize incessantly.

"Yes!" I replied indignantly as the light turned green and Lily pulled a left. I only just finished organizing my closet after the big move, and had a dress I was dying to wear. It even had the tags still on it, but I didn't remember buying it. I gave myself bonus points for shopping in my closet for free and snagging a find like that.

"That's a shame. I thought you might want to go shopping later," Lily replied as she pulled up outside the agency building. "Don't be late," she warned, and I hopped out. "And remember to think up an explanation for why you're wearing yesterday's clothes to work," she added as she pulled the door shut and maneuvered into traffic.

"Oh, sugarlumps!" I snapped as I realized she was

right. But then, a brainwave hit me. My car was in the parking lot, and in the trunk, was a magical receptacle called my gym bag, and inside that, was a spare t-shirt. With that lightbulb flashing, I hightailed it around the corner and down the ramp, jogging to my car. The t-shirt was there all right, and after a swift change in the backseat, I edged out, walking straight into Delgado.

"Are you sleeping in your car?" he asked.

"No. I'm just... oh, nothing." I tossed my bag in the trunk and slammed it shut. Sometimes the best defense was switching topics. "Are you going to Lily's rehearsal dinner tonight with Serena?" I asked.

He grinned, his mouth a shining beacon of white teeth. Did he get his teeth done? I wondered. Did my sister make him? Personally, I always thought he had nice teeth, but I wasn't the one doing the horizontal fandango with him. "Sure am," he confirmed. "We went shopping for Victoria's dress for the wedding. It's the cutest thing. Pink ruffles."

"You went to the baby store?"

"I went to seven. I didn't even get bored. Everything's so tiny." Delgado held his hands inches apart to demonstrate.

"Oh, sheesh. You're broody, aren't you?" I asked as he held the parking garage door open and I passed him, entering the stairwell.

"Don't you get broody around your niece?"

I had to admit I did. It was hard not to. She was a plump, scrumptious baby, but I wasn't at that stage yet. I was still at the "hold them and give them back" stage of life.

"You'll make a good daddy," I told him.

"Do you think I'll make a good brother-in-law too?"

"In all fairness, Delgado, there's not a lot to compare you to," I said, remembering my sister's now ex-husband, "but I think you'll do just fine."

"I appreciate that. And I just want you to know that I

166

really care about your sister. She's a very special woman."

"I'm glad to hear it. Please keep her as happy as she is now. The entire Graves family appreciates it." I wasn't even being sarcastic. Serena was a changed woman. Of course, it wasn't totally down to dating Delgado, but he was definitely a good thing in her life. I got extra points for sending him to her one day when she needed a security system installed at her home. Heck, I practically set them up. Good for me! Now I just had to concentrate on my own life.

"So... are you bringing a date tonight?" Delgado asked as we ascended the stairs.

"Maybe," I said, wondering just when I should spring the dinner on Solomon and what he would say. So much for keeping things just between us. Now, I was going to push him to reveal our relationship to everyone in my world.

"Just for the record," Delgado said as we reached the top. He placed a hand on the door, preventing me from exiting the stairwell. "I've known Solomon a long, long time, and he seems really happy. And on the record, item number two, you seem happy too. I hope it works out for you both." Then he pulled the door open and disappeared through, leaving me flapping my mouth at nothing. After a moment, I took a deep breath and followed him inside, wondering who else noticed the happy-meter rising around here.

~

Solomon assembled our small band of merry PIs in the boardroom. where yesterday's whiteboard beckoned me to use it again. After extracting my case files from my desk, they sat in a neat pile in the center of the table. "We need to get our heads together on this one," he said. "Lexi and I visited Simonstech yesterday and we were asked to leave. Working on a hunch, it's appears more and more likely that this has nothing to do with

Fairmount Gym, and very likely that something happened at Simonstech. Take a case file. I want you to go through the histories of each of our victims again and find out what happened right before they left Simonstech. Lucas, I want you to hack Simonstech and get me the employee files."

"There isn't a ton of information," I told them as each reached for a file. "Jim Schwarz didn't have any close relatives so I only spoke to his neighbor. Karen Doyle's family were out of town, except for her sister and her fiancé couldn't speak. Lorena Vasquez's brother didn't return my calls, nor has her daughter. Our victims don't have many people in their lives."

I looked at the files we currently had as they were opened. Delgado had Jim Schwarz. Fletcher got Karen Doyle. Flaherty had Lorena Vasquez. "Who've you got, boss?" I asked Solomon as he opened his file. "Carter Simons Junior," he said.

"Oh, boo. I wanted him."

"No you don't," said Solomon. "I want you to stay away from him for now."

"Why?"

"Because of yesterday."

"What happened yesterday?" asked Lucas, who had his laptop set up.

"We spooked him," I told him, realizing I didn't have a folder. I got Solomon's point. Yes, Junior did get angry, but I could hardly stay away from our current number one suspect. How could I do my job by ignoring a man that could be an important player in this murder game? "And he threw us out of the building. Where's my file?"

"I want you to get your Google-Fu on and start checking through the *Gazette's* records. Find any mention of Simonstech, especially in the months prior to each victim leaving the firm. It's a longshot, but you might find something suspicious. Something that can account for all of this." Solomon waved his hand over the table, and the murder files. "I think we can give the gym enough proof that what happened there was not because of them. I have a meeting with MPD later to discuss the case."

"What happens then?"

"Depends; as soon as we clear the gym, we'll turn our files over and let them take it from there."

"That's not fair. This is my case," I protested. "I've done a ton of legwork, including going undercover, which, by the way, is hard work at that gym, and I nearly got caught naked by two suspicious-sounding employees." I quickly realized what I just said as the room went quiet and four heads looked up.

"Naked?" repeated Fletcher, ducking his head when Solomon shot him a look, before turning to Delgado and Flaherty who also swiftly looked down, although smirking.

"I'd just finished taking a shower when I overheard the employees talking," I mumbled. "Solomon, I told you about it."

"Were you alone?" asked Fletcher. "Any other chicks?"

I threw a pencil at him. "Shut up, Fletch."

"Just askin'. Setting the scene..." He looked up and caught Solomon's stony gaze. "Okay, I'll shut up."

"Our directive was to clear the gym of any foul play, not solve the murders," said Solomon, indicating we should get our heads down and do just that.

Before Fletcher got into it, he leaned over and said in a low voice, just the right volume for everyone to hear, "No offense intended, Lexi."

"None taken from your pervy mind," I whispered back with a roll of my eyes. Delgado laughed, and the atmosphere went back to normal, even though Solomon took another glance around, but his eyes were dark and unreadable.

I set up my laptop on the table, and for a while,

enjoyed the benefits of having the agency put their heads together to help solve the case. I still didn't agree with Solomon that we shouldn't go that extra mile to catch the killer too. To me, that was the ultimate way to put the gym completely in the clear. Probable doubt simply wasn't enough. All the same, we took turns taking coffee runs and raising pointers in our victims' lives for debate, occasionally adding something to the whiteboard. I'd eaten three donuts by the time I looked up from my screen.

"Guys, I think I've got something."

"Shoot," said Solomon, pausing. I noticed no one else did. He was the only one not reading, instead adding a series of photos to the whiteboard. I tried not to look when he pinned a photo of the mark found on Lorena's head but I couldn't help myself. It looked familiar, like I had seen it somewhere before.

"Avril Sosa, twenty-seven, a lab assistant at Simonstech was reported missing fifteen months ago. She attended an office party, but never made it home. There's a small report here about it. I think I saw her name somewhere else—" I tapped her name into my search engine and a few more local newspaper reports popped up. "Yeah, I did, but those reports didn't mention Simonstech. That's why I nearly missed it."

"A missing lab tech," mused Solomon. "Jim Schwarz was head of a lab."

"She went missing right before all three of our victims left," I said, scraping my chair back so I could move over to the whiteboard and point to the office party photo. "This could be from the same event. What if they all knew something about her disappearance?"

"Find out what else you can about the missing woman and her disappearance," Solomon instructed me, "and put in a call to your contacts at MPD. See if they've got anything. Maybe she's been found. Guys, look out for the name Avril Sosa while you're doing background checks."

"I got through Simonstech firewalls," announced Lucas. "Want me to grab her file too?"

Solomon nodded. "If you can do it without setting off any alarms, yes."

I printed the few short reports I found in the *Gazette* before returning to the browser's search page. Nothing else came up for an Avril Sosa so I excused myself, and left the room to place a call.

"Hi, Garrett," I said when my oldest brother picked up his desk phone.

"What's up?" he asked. "What do you need for me to do, and more importantly what are you prepared to pay for it?"

"Er…" I burbled, stumped, having only mused through the questions I wanted to ask. "What's with the cold questions?"

"It'd be nice if you just called to say 'hi,' you know," said Garrett with a sigh.

"Hi!" I said. "That's twice now. What makes you think I want something?"

"Past experience."

"Oh, fine, well… you're not wrong," I said, deciding to go with the truth. "I wanted to know if you had any background on a missing person."

"What's her name?"

"Avril Sosa."

"Give me a minute while I try not to think about what rules I'm breaking." Garrett paused and I listened to the tap of his keyboard along with the calls flying across the squad room. "Okay, it's still an open case, but it's gone stale. What's your interest in her?"

"She came up in connection with a case I'm working. What can you tell me about her?"

"Not a lot. The detectives looking into the case drew blanks at every turn. Seems this woman just disappeared without a trace."

"How could that happen?"

"It can't. It just looks that way. Things like this happen all the time, unfortunately." Garrett spoke with the jaded tone that reflected too many years of missing people, and victims, and cases that went didn't turn up any viable leads.

"Avril Sosa was a twenty-seven-year-old lab tech, not a teen runaway."

"All the same, no one saw anything. Says here they interviewed a bunch of people the night she apparently disappeared, and no one saw anything. Her car was found dumped and burned out off the interstate thirty miles away, which indicated foul play. Says here her boss saw her leave in her car around midnight, but no one else remembers seeing her after eleven-thirty."

"Anything else?"

"Not much. The detectives assigned to her case followed up a bunch of the leads, but everything resulted in a dead end. Her bank account was never touched. She didn't show up at any hospitals. They even checked the homeless and women's shelters. They had nowhere left to turn and the case got iced."

"What about her family?"

"They're adamant something happened to her, but they couldn't tell us much. I'm just looking through the interview notes and it says she was quiet, shy, and didn't have a boyfriend since splitting up with her college boyfriend after she graduated. She'd just gotten her first apartment and didn't have many friends. She spent a lot of time at work, apparently on some secret project, but when they asked, no one at Simonstech knew anything about that."

"So she was hiding something," I concluded.

"Could be."

"Who was the lead detective on the case?"

"Ah, well, you're not going to like this."

"Who was it, Gar?" I asked, hoping he wasn't about

to say Maddox.

"Couple of old timers called Martin and O'Hare. Martin died of a heart attack a year ago and O'Hare retired to Florida."

"Great." My heart sunk. That was no help.

"Speaking of detectives, I hear you're working an angle on the Vasquez murder.""

"Yeah? Who said that?"

"Maddox."

"Oh, great. Since when did you two get friendly?"

"Always liked the guy, except for the brief moment that I didn't," Garrett explained. "Plus, the Schwarz and Doyle murders passed my desk. Just for kicks, I gave them to Maddox too."

"I think they're connected."

"He briefed me. I'm a step ahead of you here, sis."

"Pfft," I replied rudely. "I don't see you catching the murderer."

"Twenty bucks says we get there first. Want me to get your ex to call you?"

"No. I'll call him."

"I don't mind."

"It's fine, really. We're friends," I told him. "We chat."

"So long as he respects that you're just friends."

"He does. Anyway, it's not your business. It's mine. Thanks for your help. I'll take it from here and that twenty is mine!"

"Before you go, the price is…"

"I know, I know! When do you want me to babysit? You can't say tonight because it's Lily and Jord's rehearsal dinner."

"I was going to say you have to come to the range with me. I've got time tomorrow."

"Oh." I was taken aback. I didn't mind babysitting at all — I loved hanging with Garrett's kids — but that was usually Garrett's price for feeding me information.

Shooting was a new thing and I liked it. I could already shoot, but Garrett made sure I got my license and a gun when I first got involved in police business. It had been several weeks since I went to the range, however, and I appreciated him looking out for me. "Okay," I agreed.

"When was the last time you fired a gun?" he persisted, not just taking my ready agreement at face value.

"Er..."

"Deliberately."

"Well..." I had to really wrack my brains. Unfortunately, I came up with nothing.

"Just like I thought. I'll pick you up and we'll go shooting and make sure your skills are honed. Then we could go to lunch. Traci wants to hang out too."

"Cool. I'd like that. Thanks, Garrett."

"No problem, sis. Got to make sure you can look after yourself without resorting to creative measures."

"I don't know what you mean. Anyway, I do learn from my mistakes."

"Just so long as you do."

"Pfft," I said again, but this time, with affection. I knew Garrett just wanted to keep me safe. Funny, there was a lot of that going around right now. "See you later."

Returning to the boardroom, I shut the door behind me. "The case is still open into Avril Sosa's disappearance," I told the guys, quickly filling them in on the details Garrett supplied as I added the new name to the whiteboard. "And she's the only major event occurring right before our victims resigned. If we can connect her to them, we'll crack the case. She's the key," I told them. "I just know it."

CHAPTER THIRTEEN

Intruding upon a grieving family and interrupting their private moments gave me a horribly uncomfortable feeling in the pit of my stomach, but with a lead as hot as this, I just had to shove my personal feelings aside. During the whole drive over to the Sosa's house, I worried about what to say, without bringing them any false hope. As I parked in front of their spacious, freestanding home, I decided I just had to suck it up and get on with it. They might even appreciate that someone was looking into their daughter's disappearance, I told myself, just to appease my fizzling nerves, but somehow, I doubted it.

The Sosa's Harbridge home was in a very nice part of the town, an area that had experienced a rapid rise in housing prices in recent years. It looked like the kind of classic, all-American home that kids draw in school. Two windows flanked the front door on either side and there were a total of four windows spanning the second floor. The brick was neat and tidy and the windows featured elegant, white-painted shutters. There were no signs of children anywhere. other than an old basketball hoop. nailed above the garage doors that were recessed at the rear of the property. Twin Hondas were parked on the driveway and there was still space for a third car.

It was the same address given on the missing persons report so I guessed Avril must have grown up here. I wondered if they still waited for her to come home. I also wondered if parents ever gave up hope on a lost child, even if she were an adult.

Before I got too miserable, I grabbed my purse and made my way to the front door, giving the knocker a sharp rap. I didn't have to wait long before a woman with graying, shoulder-length hair answered the door. She wore a half-apron over her jeans, her shirt was rolled to the elbows, and there was a light dusting of flour on her wrist. She had been baking and the smell of something sweet followed her.

"Yes?" she said, smiling at me before looking at my hands.

I held them palms up, so she could see I had nothing to sell or try and sign her up for. What I did have was my PI license. "I'm Lexi Graves from the Solomon Agency. Your daughter's name came up in connection with a case we're investigating and I wondered if I could talk to you for a moment."

"My daughter's missing," Mrs. Sosa said abruptly, her breath sharp. I knew I surprised her and it showed as she struggled to keep her composure. "She's been gone nearly two years."

"I know and I'd like to talk to you about that."

"Do you know something? Do you know what happened to Avril?" She looked over my shoulder, like her daughter might appear behind me.

"No, but I'm investigating it."

Mrs. Sosa gave me a disappointed smile. "I'm glad someone is. The police did nothing."

"I'm aware they didn't find any viable leads."

"Viable leads," sniffed Mrs. Sosa, with a sad shake of her head. "I can give you ten minutes, but my husband is due home soon and I don't think he'll be very happy to find you here. He's not a fan of you people," she told me as she invited me in. "What do you want to know about my daughter?" she asked, indicating for me to take one of the upright chairs bordering a slim console table. She was polite but not exactly welcoming but it was enough that she would talk to me.

"I want to find out what project she was working on at Simonstech and what her working life was like there," I told her, cutting straight to the point. I sensed Mrs. Sosa liked plain talk and that she was pleased, in a small way, to know someone had taken an interest in her daughter's unsolved disappearance.

"The police asked the same thing when she went missing. All she told us was she was working on a secret project and had to work late some nights. There were occasional overnight trips too, but Avril said it was for her career and she was always very focused." Mrs. Sosa pointed to a photo above the console of a serious-looking, young woman holding a scroll and wearing a gown. "I said at the time we were really pleased she seemed so happy there. She always concentrated so much on school that she never had many friends. We were really glad when she finally got a social life. Balance, you know?"

I nodded, showing that I did. "Did she ever mention the names of her friends at Simonstech?"

"No, not that I remember."

"What about Jim, Karen, or Lorena?"

"Maybe, but I don't remember."

"How about a Carter?"

"I know Carter Simons was her boss. He sent a nice card when she went missing, saying they'd hold the job open for her. We really appreciated that. Like I said, she never really talked about her friends much. She was just a lot happier. She was going out to dinner a lot and she started making more of an effort on her appearance. I guess the girls at work were a good influence on her."

"When did she start changing her appearance and going out more?" I asked, curious about the gradual change in Avril. Had she really seen the benefits in a friendship group after so many years as a lonely bookworm?

"Oh, maybe six months before she… before she disappeared. You know, the more I think about it, the more I think maybe there was a boy she liked, in that crowd. I did think all the late nights working was too much and that maybe she was dating, but didn't want us to know about it. Her father was a little over protective in her teens. I didn't want to ask until she was ready, but I was hoping she'd bring him home soon." Mrs. Sosa glanced at the portrait and sighed. "I suppose I'll never know now. That's one of the worst things about when someone you love goes missing. All the questions. The never knowing. We just want to know where Avril is, if she's okay, if she's happy, or if…" Mrs. Sosa trailed off and we both knew what she would say next, but neither of us needed to voice it. We both realized there was little chance Avril was alive after all this time.

"I'm so sorry," I said. "I know this is very hard."

"No, it's okay. Really. What else do you want to know?"

"I wanted to know if Avril was unhappy about anything at Simonstech? If she mentioned any problems with the other employees?"

Mrs. Sosa shook her head quickly. "No, never. Like I said, she seemed really happy there." Mrs. Sosa paused. "There was one girl she talked about. She had an Irish last name. O'Donagh? No. O'Doyle! Karen O'Doyle, that's it. They were friends, I think. Didn't you mention a Karen? Maybe she could tell you something."

"Thanks," I said, my heart sinking. It was a lead, but it led to a dead body. Mrs. Sosa didn't need to know that.

A noise at the door had us both turning our heads, and a moment later, a man stepped through. He looked from Mrs. Sosa to me, and smiled, though it didn't quite reach his dark eyes. Mrs. Sosa scrambled to her feet and walked over to him, kissing him on the cheek. "This is Lexi Graves, a private investigator. She came to ask about Avril."

His manner changed instantly, his face going from welcoming to angry. "Unless you've got news about our daughter, we have nothing to say to you."

"I was just asking a few…"

"Questions. Always questions. We had so many questions, but could the police find anything out? And we called and called and they just ignored us. Avril's dead. We know it, they know it, but not one of you can find her!"

"We don't know that," said Mrs. Sosa, reaching for him, her voice soothing and sad still.

"There's only one reason Avril wouldn't come home to us and that's because she can't," he snapped. "Get out. Get out of my house and don't come back until you know where her body is."

"I'm sorry to intrude, I'll leave my…" I fumbled for my card, dropping it on the console.

"Just go!" Mr. Sosa said, his voice breaking as he turned away to lean one hand on the wall, his shoulders shaking.

"Try Avril's friend," Mrs. Sosa urged as I crossed the threshold. "I'm sorry, I… we…"

"I understand," I told her, and gave her hand a quick squeeze before I stepped onto the porch, the door banging shut behind me.

I called Solomon from my car, wishing I could sound more enthusiastic, but after seeing a man so broken, and a mother so lost, it was all I could do not to cry for them. "Bingo!" I said, by way of greeting. "Avril did know Karen at least and there's more news. Oh no!" I gasped, catching sight of the dashboard clock as I fired up the VW's engine.

"What? What happened?"

"I just saw the time. I have to get to Lily and Jord's rehearsal dinner, and I'm going to be late. I have to get home and put on my dress."

"Where are you?"

"Harbridge so I'm close and I forgot to ask you to be my date to the dinner!"

"I can't come. I'm in the lobby at MPD. I have a meeting with Lieutenant Graves and Detective Maddox in two minutes. Why didn't you ask me earlier?"

"I forgot!" I tried not to think about my boyfriend, my brother, and my ex sharing a meeting together. Mostly, I was grateful I wasn't there. The small talk would be excruciating.

"Lexi!" Solomon sighed, exasperated. "What was your other news?"

"Huh?"

"Avril," Solomon reminded me.

"Avril might have had a secret boyfriend. Her mother was suspicious about all the late nights and overnight trips and she thought maybe it was a guy. Her mom thought Karen might know, but I didn't have the heart to tell her Karen was dead."

"Better they don't know. It might still come to nothing."

"Her dad said they knew she was dead."

"Unfortunately, I'm leaning towards that conclusion too."

This was depressing, but then, lots of elements of my job were, and I couldn't disagree. Everything we'd learned so far about Avril pointed towards foul play. Now, I suspected our first three victims might also have known something pertinent about her disappearance, something worth killing them to keep quiet.

On the plus side, at least, I wasn't working at MPD, picking up cases like this every day, which would absolutely ruin my general good humor and social life. Speaking of which, "Will you be my date to the wedding?"

"I gotta go," said Solomon at the same time I asked. "Your brother is here. We'll talk about this later. Call me after the dinner." He hung up before I could agree, so all I had left to do was try not to break the speed limit all the way home, then have a breakneck-fast shower and change into my dress, before tearing over to the dinner.

~

"You're late," hissed my mom, as I slid into the shadows around the room, searching for my seat. Lily had commandeered the restaurant next to her bar and the small tables were arranged to form several long tables. The lighting was low, the bar was well stocked and the scent of food gave me a tummy rumble that was, thankfully, barely audible over the chatter.

"Barely," I replied, sliding into my chair just as a bow-tied waiter deposited my entree in front of me. My mouth immediately watered at the scent and it was all I could do not to dive in with my fingers. But, like a well brought up lady, whose mother wasn't opposed to rapping the knuckles of her adult children, I held back. Just. My two youngest nephews weren't so polite. No sooner did their plates hit the table, than Ben had his fingers on the baby meatballs. Sam went one further, sticking his face in the plate. A moment later, his mother's hand gripped his collar and straightened him up, all without breaking conversation. I sighed. It was just like another family dinner, except we were in a far nicer restaurant and no one got lumped with the washing up. "How did you get here before me?" I asked Garrett. "You had a meeting."

"We spoke really fast, there was some glaring, a little file sharing, and then we were done," he replied, stabbing his fork through a shrimp with uncharacteristic violence.

I grimaced and turned away. "What did I miss?" I asked my second oldest brother.

"Just a speech by Dad on how great it is to get married just once," said Daniel, rolling his eyes. He'd been married briefly once before Alice, and didn't like to be reminded of it. Much like I didn't like to recall my broken engagement. Everyone knew that incident sparked my sensible decision to run away and join the Army. That chapter in my life ended with me dumping the Army and taking up temping. My decision-making skills had improved a lot since then.

"I'm going to get married a whole bunch of times," said my little niece, Chloe. "And I'm going to wear a different dress every time!"

"We're only paying for the first one," said Garrett, "Though if he's a dunce, you might luck out on a second wedding."

Chloe patted my arm. "Yes, sweetie?" I asked, looking down at Garrett's youngest child.

"Are you going to get married like…" Chloe started, then looked around. "Like everyone!" she finished loudly.

All eyes went to the empty seat next to me. "Mmm, great food," I said, ignoring them. "Yummy."

"It's okay to be married more than once," said my dad, raising his voice so that Daniel, several seats away, could hear him. "Daniel, it's okay that you've been married twice. We thank God everyday for Alice." We raised our glasses in salute to Alice and she smiled and tried not to look completely uncomfortable. I tried not to be pathetically grateful that everyone's attention had turned from me to Daniel, though come to think of it, he did manage to marry twice, while I still scored a fat zero on that count. And that was totally fine by me. Marriage wasn't the ultimate goal in every woman's life now, though I liked to think I could have the option one day.

"Don't remind me," groaned Daniel, reaching for Alice's hand. The whole table grimaced at the reminder of Daniel's first wife, then crossed themselves. Delgado, seated next to Serena, didn't cross. Instead, he gave me a quizzical look, but when he caught Serena's glare, he did.

"What's with the crossing? No one here is Catholic," I said, adding after a moment, "no one is overly religious either."

"I'm Catholic," said Delgado.

"You didn't cross!"

"He would if he knew," said Dad. "We all turned religious when Daniel got divorced. We all thanked God regularly that the harpy was gone."

"What's a harpy?" asked Chloe, choosing that moment to pay attention.

"A mythical thingy that flies and sings," said Alice.

"I want to be one." Chloe nodded sagely. "Or a kindergarten teacher."

"Mommy, are you a harpy too?" Rachel asked Alice. Ben, her brother, and a couple years older, sniggered.

Alice's eyes flashed. "No, darling."

"Is Daddy's other wife my mommy too?" Rachel persisted.

Alice gave a strangled noise. "No," she croaked.

"You only have one mommy and one daddy," Daniel explained, lifting Rachel into his lap.

"Boring," yawned Ben. "Jake, in my class, has two moms, and Louisa, in Rachel's class, has two moms *and* two dads." He dropped his mouth open as he looked around the table. His expression matched that of my parents.

"Lots of families are different," said Alice, attempting to diffuse the situation. Meanwhile, the rest of us waited for the finale of this line of conversation with bated breath and hopeful expressions.

"Don't die, Mommy. Joey's mommy died. She died and went to heaven," said Rachel.

"No, she didn't," said Alice, frowning.

"Did too."

"No, I saw Joey's mommy just yesterday. She went to the spa and said she died and went to heaven."

"But..." started Rachel.

"It's not the same thing!" Alice yelled, her voice rising above all others in the room.

"Oh." Rachel stuck her thumb in her mouth, and for a moment, the table was quiet while we contemplated all the different families in the world, and, most of all, our food, which we finished pronto.

The peace was short lived. "So, if Uncle Daniel got two wives—" Sam started.

"At different times!" yelled Daniel.

Sam ignored him, continuing, " — And Mom and Dad have been married forever... foreverer... foreverest..." He paused, trying to decide on the best way to describe a time frame he couldn't even comprehend.

"Since the dinosaurs," said Chloe, looking interested again as she wiggled in her chair and smiled. "I like dinosaurs."

"Yeah, since the dinosaurs," agreed Sam, "and Aunt Serena is working on husband number two..."

"Sam!" exclaimed Serena, looking appalled, probably because he got it right. Delgado just grinned.

"That's what Dad said! And Uncle Jord finally got a woman — Dad said that too! — how come Aunt Lexi can't get a date?"

"I didn't say that!" said Garrett, patting a napkin to his mouth before reaching for his wine glass. "Or any of the other stuff," he mumbled, quietly adding, "exactly."

"Is it because you shoot men?" Sam asked me, just when the table got quiet again.

Everyone looked at me. "Urgh!" I choked.

"I definitely do not give him those ideas," said Garrett. "Anyway, you haven't shot that many!"

"Knew it," whispered Sam to Ben. "Many means 'some'." They gave me approving nods.

"Me either," said Traci. "Wild imaginations, these boys. Pass the wine, honey." Garrett passed her the wine bottle and she filled her glass to the brim.

"But Mooooom!" wailed Sam.

"Let's have a kid's table," suggested Mom. "All in favor?" All hands were raised. There was only so much we could take of the innocence of youth and we had only eaten the entrees. The wine had barely been opened. I passed my glass to Garrett as, across the room, Lily caught my eye. "Help me," I whispered just as my mother leaned over.

"I'm taking a journalism class. We're on the blogging segment. You could write a blog about your dating life. Maybe you would get a book deal? Oh!" Mom's eyes widened and she extracted a notepad from her bag, writing notes furiously. "I had a better idea," she said, pausing to look up at me. "I'll write a blog about your dating life and maybe we can get you some nice dates! I think I'll let the *Montgomery Gazette* know. Maybe I could write an article for them. It'd be like *The Bachelorette,* but on paper."

"What happened to Tai Chi?" I wailed. "Why can't you have a nice hobby?"

"I love Tai Chi, but I'll love getting you married off more. Next year, this wedding could be yours!"

"Can I be bridesmaid?" asked my nieces simultaneously.

I looked at the empty chair next to me. "Urggghhh," I squeaked and took a big swallow of my wine before setting it down. This was going to be a long, long night and I had to drive home, so I couldn't even get through it by pickling myself with alcohol.

CHAPTER FOURTEEN

After the dinner, Jord took off for a shift, explaining he was saving all his vacation leave for the honeymoon. My sister and other brothers took their kids home. Since I was dateless, and Lily too inebriated to drive, I volunteered to be Lily's ride and somehow, somewhere along the way, coincidentally right around the time I filled her in on the break in the case, we decided to stake out Carter Simons Junior's house.

I tried not to question the wisdom of stalking our top suspect as we watched his large, double-fronted house on the outskirts of Montgomery, from quite a way down the street. There were a bunch of cars on the driveway and parked on both sides of the street, and judging by the raised level of noise, as well as people entering and exiting, there seemed to be a party going on.

"This is great," said Lily, staring at the entrance through her binoculars, a recent addition to her kit. Admittedly, they made more sense than the dog bone. "We can sneak in, mingle, and take a real good look around."

"No, we can't. I met this guy, remember?" I reminded her as she passed the binoculars to me. I watched a couple walk up the path and turn towards the door. The man was Joseph O'Keefe and the woman had a gorgeous wave of dark blonde hair that fell around her shoulders. They were holding hands so I figured she must've been his wife. They disappeared through the open front door and away from view.

"He might not remember you."

"We pissed him off," I reminded her, mentally picturing Junior's angry countenance as he insisted we never return. "He'll remember me."

Lily looked over her shoulder at her bag. "Disguise?"

"Hell to the no."

"You are such a spoilsport. I remember when you were all for breaking and entering."

"I know, but this one is different."

"Yeah?" asked Lily, pulling a face. "How?"

"Well…" I paused, feeling stumped. I could have said "this guy is alive" unlike the first house I'd ever broken into. There, the missing corpse of my dead boss had unexpectedly turned up after his killers left it there, far from the murder scene. My most recent snooping adventure was prowling the rear yard of my neighbor, Aidan, whom we suspected might be a serial killer. As it turned out, he just had a weird dog that liked watching horror movies, and a career in furniture-making that required all manner of scary-looking tools. I'd barely gotten away without being seen, and still wasn't sure if he knew the extent of my snooping. He made me a bench as a housewarming gift though, and we went to dinner twice, so I figured he liked me regardless.

"See? I knew you couldn't think of a thing. Let's go crash this dude's party and find out what he did to this Avril chick."

"We don't know if he did anything. We didn't even ask him about Avril because we didn't know about her then. Maybe he's just super defensive and private about his family's company and didn't want us snooping around."

"Yeah, right. He's guilty."

"Who made you judge and jury?" I continued scanning the area. The sidewalk was empty, the front door was still open and every so often, someone passed by, just brief blurs of shapes.

"Me, and I do it well. What's with the lack of confidence?"

"I've got it wrong before, you know."

"The Lord dude?"

I set the binoculars in my lap. "No, I got that right. He was a fraudster."

"Oh, then the other guy? The cute one."

Ben Rafferty, or whatever his real name was, had certainly thrown me. I wavered back and forth on his guilt, eventually accusing him, only to find evidence pointing to another guy, and nearly destroying the case. As it turned out, they were both guilty; but for a while, my confidence was rocked. I should have trusted my gut in the first place. Today, it told me that Carter Simons Junior wasn't a man to be messed with. He became angry too quickly and I didn't want to do something stupid, that in turn, made him do something even more stupid. Like calling the cops on me.

"I don't want to talk about Ben Rafferty," I sulked. "He sucks."

"He's still on the run."

"Yeah, but the FBI are running after him now. Anyway, I solved the case and Solomon and the client were happy with the outcome."

"You don't have to justify it to me. Now are we gonna keep discussing this? Or can we sneak in and go through Junior's drawers?"

"We are not going though his drawers. Or his wardrobe or anything else," I added after catching Lily's

188

eager expression. "We're not going in... period."

"Maybe a little snoop around the outside?" Lily suggested. "We came all this way and it's dark, so the chances of us getting caught are zero. We could take a walk around the perimeter. Maybe we could overhear something?"

"Fine," I conceded. "Just a little exterior snoop. We're not going to get close... hey, wait for me!" I yelled as Lily scrambled out of my car. I hightailed it after her as she power-walked to the Simons' house in four-inch heels.

"Isn't this great? No electric gates. We can just walk right in!"

"No! We just can't anything. We talked about this, Lily. We're just going to take a walk around the block and... Lily?" I stopped, suddenly alone on the sidewalk. I turned around, just in time to catch a flash of Lily's dress as it disappeared past the fence. I jogged in my heels back to her. "Damn it!" I said as I watched her walk right into the Simons' house. "Heel issues," I said to the couple giving me a sly look a moment later as they stepped around me, following Lily inside. I waited until they were gone before I backed away, cursing. Lily was inside and she wasn't coming out.

Since I couldn't risk following her, and would have looked odd to anyone who saw me by just standing there on the sidewalk, I needed to make a plan fast. I couldn't wait and I didn't want to walk back to the car without Lily. I reached for my cell phone as it began to ring in my little purse, hoping I wasn't about to get chewed out by Solomon. How he would know Lily had just gate-crashed our chief suspect's house, I didn't know, but he always seemed to know all kinds of stuff.

As it happened, it was Lily. "You gotta come in here, the house is sooo nice," she cooed. "I'm taking photos."

"Oh my God! Has anyone seen you?"

"Oh, sure, like all the guests. It's a birthday party for

189

Julia. The cake is gorgeous. I think it's from the same bakery that's doing my wedding cake. I'm sending you a photo. They have the cutest butterfly spray on top."

"Who's Julia? Where are you right now? Can anyone hear you?"

"Duh!" sniffed Lily. "I'm in the powder room. I think I'm going to ask for the interior designer. I'd love to have them do my house."

"No! No, you cannot do that!" Someone passed by the front door and I sidled backwards behind a large bush, holding a palm to my head. The last thing I needed was Lily mingling, though I had to concede the photos could be a good idea. It was also, I believed, very unlikely, Lily could be murdered inside with so many witnesses.

"Why not?"

"Because you're not supposed to be there. Come out and don't get caught."

"Pfft! I am not going to get caught. I'm just going to have a little look around, eat some cake, make some small talk, then leave. Or you could come in?"

I gave a strangled noise as Lily hung up. I took three whole seconds to consider joining her before deciding she was on her own this time. That left only one other option. I turned away from the house and started walking, sticking to the task I suggested. The house occupied a corner plot, so all I had to do was walk the length of the front yard, round the corner, and follow the noise coming from the garden. It was pretty sedate really. No loud, thumping, music, just some popular tunes at a moderate decibel level through speakers, and no yelling. Just conversation and people in good spirits. I walked the entire garden, concealed by the tall fence, looking for some place to peep through and found a knot in the wood that created a little hole just at my eye level as I doubled back. Pressing myself to the fence, I peeped into their garden, feeling like a total creep.

Most of the guests were gathered on the patio, the other side of the small kidney-shaped pool, from my vantage point. I could see a couple of waiters circulating with wine glasses, as well as people who were crossing in and out of the house via the French doors. I couldn't see Lily yet, so I just hoped she wasn't doing something stupid, like getting caught.

While much of my side of the garden remained shrouded in dusk, the house lights spilled plenty of illumination onto the patio and there were a dozen candle-lit lamps dotting the environs as well as fancy patio heaters. I could see O'Keefe and his wife chatting to another couple, but I couldn't identify any of the guests or recognize anyone from Simonstech. That didn't mean there weren't any there. Solomon and I didn't see too many people when we visited. I figured if it was Mrs. Simons' birthday, maybe the guests leaned more towards her friends and family than her husband's. Just as I thought that, Simons Senior stepped through the French doors, a striking woman on his arm. She was the Simons matriarch, and apparently quite a well-known local philanthropist. A younger woman in pearls and a fitted, sheath dress followed them outside to the chorus of "Happy Birthday!" and a burst of applause. She held her hands to her chest and swished her hair around, beaming under the spotlights, both visibly flattered and delighted. Could this be Julia, the guest of honor this night? Behind her, more waiters stepped through, bearing trays with little plates, which they began to circulate. As I watched them, I saw Junior approach and whisper something in her ear. She nodded, and followed him inside.

The only problem was, while I could guess plenty, I couldn't hear a thing, much less   question anyone. Pulling away from my little peephole, I leaned against the fence and texted Lily, *Where are you?*

Seconds later, my screen flashed. *Coming out*, it read.

Meet you out front.

I took one last peep, assuring myself there was nothing more to see, and speed walked around to the front to meet Lily. I didn't have to wait long before she joined me on the sidewalk. "I had to come get you," she said, grabbing my arm. "I found that Carter guy and his wife, Mrs. Carter... "Ohmygosh! Mrs. Carter! He's married to Beyoncé?" Lily squealed. "Oh, the look on your face, Lexi! I'm joking. I know she's not Beyoncé. Their house would be way bigger if she was."

"I'm not surprised you found them. It's their house. I just saw them on the patio."

"Yeah, but they came inside when I was looking at one of their paintings and I think they're having an argument."

"What about?"

"I don't know. He had her arm and they went into the study." Lily stared at the house thoughtfully. "I think this way," she said, grabbing my hand and tugging me around the other side of the house. This side bordered with a neighbor's and there was a narrow, paved, service path leading to the garden gates. "The study is on this side of the house and they shut the door, but I went in there earlier when I was looking for the powder room and there's a window. We should go listen."

I brightened. Maybe this wasn't a wasted trip after all. "Okay," I agreed, following Lily as we hurried along the service path, my heart beating faster when a light came on in the neighboring house. We paused, and froze mid-step. After a moment, a shadow of a figure passed by a window, then the light went off.

"There's the window," whispered Lily, pointing to a rectangular opening just above our heads, a few paces away. Then she pointed down at the pebble bed, spread a foot from the house. I nodded, showing I understood her warning not to step on it.

"Let's go." We snuck in closer, then pressed our upper bodies against the wall, careful to keep our feet on the path, all the while listening intently. With the party concentrated in the backyard, and rear of the house, this side of the house was much quieter and the two voices were easily overheard.

"Honey, I told you. It's nothing for you to worry about."

"But Carter, I still don't understand. I got the ring made just like the picture you gave me. They looked exactly alike. I didn't know there was an engraving inside."

"It's a simple mistake. Let's just enjoy the party."

"Kelly doesn't think it's a simple mistake."

"Just stay out of it."

"What if she finds out you asked me to make a new one?"

"I think she already figured out it's a new one," Simons replied, obviously agitated the more his wife persisted. "Let's go back to the party."

"What if Kelly brings it up?" Mrs. Simons persisted.

"Who's Kelly?" whispered Lily.

"Carter Simons' wife."

"I thought that was Julia?"

"No, the other Simons. Senior."

"Oh, right." Lily nodded, turning away again. We froze as Lily's foot crunched on the pebble bed between the path and the house, the bed we were so carefully avoiding standing on until now.

"Shhh," Junior hissed and we all quieted, including his wife.

"What is it?" Mrs. Simons asked after a moment or two. I could imagine them both standing very still inside, as Junior listened.

"I thought I heard something," he said and Lily winced.

"It's probably the party," Mrs. Simons said. "I don't

hear anything."

"Wait here." There were footsteps, then a door opened, and I heard Mrs. Simons say, "Huh?"

"We need to go," I mouthed to Lily. She nodded quickly, as she extracted her foot and let the pebbles slip back into place before edging past me, eager to get away. We hurried in tandem along the service path and ran straight into Junior. His surprised expression turned into extreme annoyance in a matter of seconds.

"What the hell are you doing here?" he asked, his voice rising as he struggled not to shout.

"Who are you?" said Lily, all innocence. "Is this Tony's house?"

"I should be asking you that!" he snapped.

"Why? Are you looking for Tony's house too?" she asked.

"Don't play dumb with me." Junior took a step towards her, and to Lily's credit, she didn't move one bit even though he towered over her by several inches. "I know who you are. You're both from the Solomon Agency and you're snooping."

"I am not from the Solomon Agency," said Lily. "I have a proper job. I inebriate people!"

"I should call the cops on you two. What were you doing back there?" He looked past us, and while I was sure he knew the study was located there, I could only hope he hadn't realized yet that the window was open and we were listening to his private conversation. "What did you think you would find?"

"Tony's house," Lily quipped, persisting in her lie. I just hoped it was enough to get us out of this before Junior drew unwanted attention.

"Cut the bullshit. I want you two out of here now." He pointed off the property, taking me right back to the moment he threw Solomon and me out of Simonstech. He was clearly big on the pointy gestures. I suspected he must've taken a management seminar on them. "Get out of here!"

"What's going on?" asked a female voice. When Junior whirled around, I caught sight of the woman I guessed earlier was his wife. She was much prettier up close. "Carter? Who are these people?"

"No one," he said. "They were looking for another house. I was just giving them directions." He turned again and speared both of us with a very threatening look. "They were just leaving."

"Why are you on our service path?" Mrs. Simons wanted to know, just as Joseph O'Keefe stepped around the corner, a small medicine bottle in his hand.

"Forgot my Warfarin medication, Julia, thanks for reminding me. Got to keep this old heart in good working…" he started to say, before seeing Lily and me. "What…?"

"It's nothing, Joe, these women took a wrong turn," said Junior, staring at us. "Julia, go inside."

"Wrong turn," I agreed, finding my voice as we edged past them both.

"Who were they, Carter?" Mrs. Simons asked as we walked away. "Don't give me the directions thing. Was that her? Carter? Answer me? Was that her? Why was she at…" The rest of her questions were lost to us as we were beyond earshot of their voices, leaving the Simons to their argument and a confused-looking Joseph O'Keefe behind us.

Our heels weren't made for jogging, but we beat a fast pace to my car and climbed in. I hit the lock button and exhaled my relief. Even when I pulled my seatbelt around me, my heart was pounding.

"Here," said Lily, passing me a small, tissue-wrapped parcel.

"What's this?"

"Birthday cake."

"You stole cake from the Simons? Lily!"

"Not just any cake. Birthday cake. Mmm, delicious!"

she exclaimed between bites. "Plus, I really thought it through. I'm sure there are absolutely no laws on stealing birthday cake. None whatsoever."

"Oh, screw my life!" I wailed, leaning my head against the steering wheel. As Lily made appreciative noises over the cake, I thought about what we'd overheard. It could have been nothing, but Junior tried his best to brush off his wife's concerns about a ring. Then she seemed to think one of us might have been "her". But who was that? Did Junior have a mistress? Junior was a good looking man, had a lovely wife and a great life. Would he risk it all to have an affair? Did our victims know about it?

"Hey." Lily patted my back. With her other hand, she pulled back the tissue to reveal the triple layer slice. I hated to admit, but it smelled divine as I took it from her, peeling back the last layer of tissue and noticing the iced butterfly pattern. The tissue paper had butterflies on it too, I realized as I looked closely. The Simons seemed to have a thing about the pretty winged creatures and it seemed to nudge something in my memory. Something I had seen on the whiteboard at the agency. The strange mark on Lorena's forehead... its pair of triangles could be a tiny butterfly, the same size as the one I'd seen on Junior's cufflinks. "That worked out a lot better than my wedding store stakeout. At least, we got *something* out of this!"

"A lot more than just a slice of cake," I agreed.

CHAPTER FIFTEEN

I arrived on my doorstep, dejected, an hour later. After dropping Lily at her temporary residence, I drove home to my bungalow and pulled onto the dark driveway. Sure, I had good memories in abundance of the dinner, but the crumb-filled tissue crumpled on the passenger seat was a reminder that anytime now, Carter Simons Junior could be informing someone of Lily's and my excursion, uninvited, onto his property. I did not look forward to having to explain it to Solomon when he called me out on it, especially when we didn't even discover anything really useful. Lily's photos were blurry, except for a couple of cake shots, and one of the powder room wallpaper, and the conversation we overheard was more perplexing than pertinent. And the mark... it could have been anything, I reasoned. Maybe I just wanted it to be a butterfly.

Grabbing the napkin, I threw it in the trash on my way to my front door. The path was dark and I pulled a face at the lamp, which failed to turn on, then nearly tripped over something large and heavy in my way. I squealed when something thumped my foot.

"Barney! What the hell?" I said loudly, looking down at my neighbor's assistance dog, currently sprawled on my doorstep. His tail thumped my foot again.

"Ruff," said Barney, scrambling to his feet and thrusting his nose first into my palm, then into my jacket pockets. When he didn't find anything, a little stream of drool fell from his mouth.

"No food for you," I told him, grabbing his collar. "You're going home and you're going to be quiet all night so I can sleep in peace. No horror movies, no howling, no nothing." I continued telling him exactly what he couldn't do all the way to his own door. I pushed the doorbell, and it rang loudly and flashed too, just in case Aidan wasn't wearing his hearing aids. I waited while Aidan appeared.

"Hey," he said opening the door a crack, then wider when he saw whom it was. He had a TV remote in one hand and a tub of popcorn in the other. I pointed down. "How did he get out? And where did you find him?" he asked, tossing a piece of popcorn into his mouth.

"On my doorstep."

"Aww. He went to visit you. Sweet."

"Delightful," I said, sounding anything but. "We've had a talk and he's going to behave all night."

Aidan made a rude noise, which summed up the probability of that as Barney strolled past him and flopped across his hall carpet. "I came by earlier to see if you wanted dinner, but I guess you went out. You look pretty." He ran his eyes over me in appreciation. I knew he'd inquired after my relationship status once, but I never viewed him that way. It was hard to when my mind was full of Solomon, and nowhere near my mind when I had a handful of... well, never mind. He was nice though, had a charming face, and was extra helpful about the house. I would have been happy to introduce him to my single friends; unfortunately I was short on the single friend front.

"Thanks. My brother and best friend are getting married and I was at their rehearsal dinner."

"Got a date?"

I pulled a face, heaved a breath, and rolled my eyes.

"That's girl-speak for 'no,' isn't it? I'll be your standby," he offered. "I look great in a tux. Want to watch the rest of *Predator* with me?"

"Thanks and no thanks. 'Night, Aidan. Goodnight, Barney," I said, waving at the dog. He raised his head, gave me a doggy grin and laid it on his paws again.

"Later, Lexi. Hey, I noticed your porch light is out. I'll come by tomorrow and fix it."

I gave him the thumbs up as I left, glad of the offer even if it was just so I didn't get surprised by Barney again, and the door banged shut behind me.

Back home, I locked my front door and flipped on the lights, going through the motions of closing the drapes and making myself a hot chocolate. I was wondering if I should get a pet to keep me company on lonely nights. As I passed by the fridge, I gave the magazine cutout I held up with a magnet there a stroke. It was a fluffy white cat that looked ridiculously high maintenance. Stroking the picture was the closest I got toward looking after an animal. That, and talking to Barney whenever he visited. Once, barely a week after I moved in, I arrived home to find him asleep on my couch! I still don't know how he got in.

I went around checking all the window catches before I retired to my guest bedroom, and changed into my pajamas. I read a book for a while, and made a few case notes. I thought about Solomon not making it to the dinner, even though the meeting had clearly been cut short. I wondered if he would be my date for the wedding, or if I should accept Aidan's back-up offer. I worried if I should have been clearer in what I wanted from Solomon, and not expected him to just know. I window-shopped on my cell phone's browser before the calendar reminded me of my appointment with Garrett to go to the shooting range. Hopping out of bed, I retrieved my gun from its safety box and checked it over, just to make sure it was in good working order. I noticed I'd forgotten to unload it. I set the safety, and placed it on my nightstand so I wouldn't forget it the next day before switching off the lamp.

Amidst the stillness, and gentle creaks of the house going to sleep, I heard a single bark from Barney before I fell fast asleep.

~

I don't know what woke me, but all of a sudden my mind was on. My body, however, lagged a few steps behind. Looking through my lashes, I could see shadows cast around the room, and the dark chink between the curtains told me it was still the dead of night. The world that was Bonneville Avenue in the early hours of the morning was still. No vehicles moved. No dogs barked. The kids a few doors away were quiet. But in my bedroom, a floorboard creaked and I knew I wasn't alone.

It may have been something in my subconscious, sounds that I'd heard in my sleep and not yet processed, or maybe even my sixth sense, but I felt a presence that wasn't welcome, and knew it wasn't Barney paying a visit. My first instinct was to throw back the covers and scream. My next instinct, and the one I followed, was to stay very motionless and pretend I was still asleep until I knew what was going on, or what I faced. It would be just my luck to assault Solomon on a surprise visit, not that he was in a habit of doing that, and certainly never while I was asleep in bed. So, I took a few seconds to allow my body to wake up while I inspected what I could see of the room from behind my eyelashes. My dresser, the cute velvet tub chair I found on sale, my day clothes folded over the arm, the open door... the pair of legs.

The legs stepped closer and from behind them came a gloved hand, and a glint of steel.

My heart thumped wildly.

Another step closer.

The body leaned in.

I sat up, and screamed as loud as my lungs would let me before belting the intruder with a pillow that I grabbed with my left hand. I watched in terrified satisfaction as my assailant stumbled backwards, probably bewildered. But a pillow certainly wasn't enough. As I threw back the bedding and scrambled to my feet, he lunged towards me, and this time, his ski-masked face came close to mine, the head-butt glancing off my cheekbone and sending me crashing against the wall. My knees threatened to give way and my body pounded as I cried out, wincing with the pain that shot through my shoulder where I jarred it.

I kicked out as he approached, planting my foot squarely on his chest with a resounding slap, and knocking him backwards. He stumbled, grunting, and came at me again, slashing the knife. I barely heard the whisper it made as it cut through the air, but I screamed again and again. Blocking his hand with my left, I punched with my right, the blow glancing off his forehead. I dropped to my knees, however, when he landed a punch with his closed fist.

As I fell, I spied the gun. Grabbing it, my thumb scrambled at the safety, missing it once, twice... got it! I fired.

"Oh, fuck!" screamed the man, staggering backwards, his attention now on his side, which clasped. He looked up and I saw his eyes, just the whites of them against the dark. "You bitch! You fucking bitch!"

I raised the gun, and steadied it, as I got shakily to my feet. I looked down on him, both of us frozen. "Next time it's between the eyes," I warned him, my voice steadier than I felt. Whether I was bluffing or not, I couldn't be sure. Crucially, neither was he. "I won't miss," I cautioned him, hoping my legs would support me for a few minutes more.

He gave a grunt, walked unsteadily backwards, and started to leave the room. A moment later, he returned, except this time, he was... retreating? Despite still having the gun pointed at him, he didn't turn around.

From my vantage point on the bed, my back pressed against the wall, I couldn't see why he didn't turn around to face the danger that was before him — me. Then he stepped to one side and I saw a figure in a hockey mask holding a chainsaw. He ripped the cord and the damn thing powered up, the sound vibrating through the room.

"What kind of freakshow is this?" yelled the knife-wielding assailant at the hockey-masked chainsaw guy. "Are you frickin' nuts?"

Assailant number two stepped inside the room and waved the chainsaw at the knifeman who lunged this side and that, stepping backwards. With one last look at me, the knifeman turned and leaped through my window. One curtain ripped from the pole, and glass splintered in all directions as he escaped. He didn't look back, but took off at a run.

That left me with a chainsaw-wielding intruder. I raised my gun again. "I shot him!" I yelled. "I'll shoot you too!" Barney padded in and sat down. The hockey mask dipped as the figure looked down at him. "If you hurt the dog, I'll definitely shoot you!" I screamed.

The chainsaw stopped and the man carefully set it down on my bedroom floor. He stayed low, rubbing Barney on the head as he reached for his mask. When he stood up, I could have screamed in relief if I hadn't been all screamed out. "Aidan!" I wailed, lowering my gun.

"Barney woke me. He knew you was in trouble, I

think," he said. "He brought me a copy of my *Jason* DVD and wouldn't stop jumping on me until I followed him. I saw someone moving in your house so I grabbed my chainsaw and came right over. I followed Barney and your kitchen door was open."

"Oh, thank you, thank you. Barney, you brilliant dog." I scrambled from the bed, lurching towards them.

Aidan stepped back and pointed at the gun. "I promise not to shoot," I told him. "I'm all done shooting tonight," I added as the police siren cut through the still night air.

"I called the police," Aidan said and Barney's tail gave a thump.

"I hear them."

"C'mere." Aidan held his arms out and I stepped into them, allowing him to fold me into his warmth for a couple of minutes, right up until half of MPD burst through the doors. They threw Aidan to the floor, diving on him. After the last man landed, Barney climbed on top and rested his head on a police officer's back.

Daniel was the next man through the door. He looked at the tangle of bodies, then at me, then down again. I followed his eyes, feeling like I was having an out of body experience. "Sis, you're bleeding," he said. I responded by blinking before I went dizzy, and Daniel caught me just before I hit the floor.

~

"I didn't faint," I said, ten minutes later, as we sat at my small kitchen table. Daniel looked up from the bandage he was taping to my forearm and raised his eyebrows. "I didn't lose unconsciousness," I continued to protest. "I just wanted a ride to the kitchen. All that breaking, entering, and fighting was hard work."

"You're lucky this was just a surface wound. Glad you see the funny side," said Daniel.

He didn't get to finish because a voice behind him said, "I sure as hell don't."

I looked up and gave my next visitor a weak smile. "Hey, Maddox."

"Hey, yourself," said Maddox, squeezing through the officers, now crowding my kitchen. They'd given us a little room so Daniel could clean my small knife wound, and someone had smartly cordoned off my bedroom after ten officers, one sore Aidan, and Barney trooped out. Aidan had the third chair and Barney was safely under the table where no one would trip over him. The gun was between us. I didn't know where the chainsaw was. Maddox rounded the table, and after checking Daniel's handiwork, pulled me into a fierce hug. "You have no idea how scary it was hearing your address being announced over the radio."

"I bet it wasn't as scary as a man with a knife in my bedroom at three a.m."

"What the hell happened?"

"I don't know. It's all a big blur, and it happened so fast. I heard something, or maybe it was my sixth sense. I don't know."

"Oh sweetheart, that's not sixth sense, that's common sense. If someone is in your bedroom uninvited, he's not there to turn down the covers and kiss you goodnight."

"Yeah, okay, well, something woke me up and there he was. How did he get in?"

Maddox looked over his shoulder. " Anyone? How did this creep get into Lexi's house?"

"I found tool marks on the front door lock," said a uniform somewhere in my hallway, past the small crowd that had gathered. "Is cousin Lexi okay?"

"Siobhan, is that you?" I called back.

"Yeah, it's me. Oh, Jord is here. Hey, Jord!"

"Hey, Jord," the crowd chorused as my brother made his way past them.

"The kitchen door was open," said Aidan, who was following the conversation keenly. "That's how I got in."

"Guess he tried the front, couldn't get it open, then

went in the back," said Daniel, abandoning my arm to check the door behind me. He pulled on a fresh pair of gloves, opened it and examined the damage. "Looks like your lock is busted. We'll get them both dusted for prints," he added, retrieving an icepack from the fridge for my cheek on his way back.

When Jord finally made it to the kitchen, he was in uniform, although his days wearing it were numbered since passing his exams with flying colors. All he needed now was a spot to open up and he'd be joining our other brothers in suits. "What the hell?" he said, looking at me, then at Maddox. "There's an ambulance out front. I thought you were dead."

"Surface wound," I told him, holding up my arm. I got some "ohs" and some "aws" from my audience, which abruptly silenced after a scowl from Maddox. It was nice that they all cared enough to stick around, although I had to admit, this was prime gossip material for the station too.

"She was lucky," said Daniel, again. "She fought off her attacker."

"I shot him," I said, bluntly.

"Did you hit him?" asked Jord.

"You bet. I kicked him too."

"I meant with a bullet."

I nodded. "Yep." There was a small round of applause as I confirmed my shot.

"Who processed the bedroom?" asked Maddox. There were some mumbles and a few looks around, but no one came forward. "Out!" he yelled, backing them up as he pressed forwards. "This is now a crime scene. Out. Every single one of you is corrupting the evidence here. Get out!"

"You heard him," said another familiar voice. This time, Garrett appeared in the doorway. "This is like a Graves family convention. Hey, Uncle Dermot! Siobhan, good to see you. One shooting and they all come running," he said, upon entering the kitchen. "I've seen three of our uncles and four cousins."

My cousin, Siobhan, edged through the doorway, looking serious. "I've got uniforms perusing the perimeter looking for evidence," she told us. "Uncle Dermot is going to stand guard on the kitchen door and Uncle Luke is posted at your bedroom window. I'm taking the front."

"Who died and put you in charge?" asked Garrett, reminding me of their familiar childhood bickering.

"I put me in charge since you're all hanging out, doing nothing," replied Siobhan.

"Can I make you a coffee?" I asked and she nodded.

"Can I get a coffee too?" asked Garrett.

"Are you doing anything?" I asked, pausing on my way to fill the pot. "Don't give me that mean look. Siobhan is organizing everything here. She gets coffee."

"Dammit. I was across town, Lexi. In bed. I got here as soon as I could. You're taking this real well, I might add. And just so you don't think I'm mad at Siobhan, I recommended to her superior that it was about time she took her exams. She'll make a great detective."

"That's nice of you, she'll appreciate that." I added a filter and ground beans and made sure there was enough water. "I don't know how else to take all this. I've never dealt with something like it before. I don't know what else to do." I turned the coffee maker on and resumed my position at the table.

"Maddox, we'll split the duties on this one, okay? Since I'm guessing you're not planning on leaving," said Garrett. Both men looked toward me, waiting for me to say something.

"I'm happy for Maddox to stay. The more the merrier." I looked around my full kitchen to the dark presence of my Uncle Dermot at the kitchen door. As if realizing he was being observed, he turned and waved. I waved back. Truth be told, I wanted everyone here. I

206

wanted the house full of people. People who would never raise a hand to me, let alone a knife. I put my hands in my lap to stop them shaking as I realized the longer people were here, the longer I could delay the time when I would have to stop and think about what I'd been through. I hated the idea of being alone tonight. I hated the idea someone got into my home and the possibility that the outcome could have been so much worse.

"Maddox, you take Lexi's statement and see if anyone else heard anything. Lexi, Daniel and I are going to go through your room and the house, looking for evidence until the forensic team gets here."

"You might find blood splatter in my bedroom," I said, pretending not to notice as my brothers and Maddox tried not to wince when I added, "Mine and his."

"I'll take Aidan's statement," volunteered Jord, and Aidan nodded his agreement. Now I thought about it, I felt the two of them would get on pretty well. Who knew that all it took to get a pair of bros together was an attempted murder and a chainsaw-wielding rescuer?

"We can go to my place. Barney has to go to bed or he'll sleep all day," he explained. "If you need anything, just scream your head off, okay, neighbor?" he said, nudging me with a reassuring smile. I stood and hugged him, looking up at him so he could read my lips as I said, "Thank you for coming to my rescue."

"Anytime." Aidan gave me one last squeeze, then Barney sniffed my knees and licked my palm and they were gone too, along with Jord. With the rest of the force outside, Garrett and Daniel processing my room, and the kitchen empty, Maddox sat in the chair adjacent to me. Lifting my hand, he took a deep breath.

"Did anything happen that you didn't want to tell your family about?" he asked, his voice low and serious.

"Like what?"

Maddox flapped a hand and sucked in a breath. "Did he assault you in any way? Did he…"

"Sexually? No. No, he didn't."

"Okay. I had to ask. Okay, then." Maddox exhaled, seeming relieved. "I need to take your statement. We've done this before. Try not to think about it too much. Just start from the moment you woke. Ready?"

"Is anyone ever?" I asked.

"Not always, but they usually brave it out anyway."

I nodded, starting, "I woke up and I sensed someone in the room…" I was just finishing explaining to Maddox what happened, pausing several times to answer his questions — Did the guy call me by name? Did he issue any threats? Did he say anything? — when I looked up, and found Solomon staring down at me. Normally, he had a poker face, utterly unreadable, and though tonight was much the same, I saw the veins on his neck standing out, and his chin appeared stiff, while his mouth was set in a thin line. I had never seen Solomon looking so alarmed before, and we had endured some pretty dire situations. Maddox glanced over, following my gaze, and nodded a greeting. He turned back to the statement he'd written, studying it.

"Are you okay?" Solomon asked, slowly and seemingly unsure.

"Ninety-nine percent fine. Just a small cut to my forearm and a bruise on my cheek," I told him, knowing he would want those details before anything else.

"I got here as fast as I could." He looked over his shoulder. When he turned back to us, there was a small smile on his face. "Along with the rest of Montgomery. Bonneville Avenue is gridlocked."

"First time for everything."

"I met your cousin, Siobhan. I met some other cousins, but there's too many of them to remember names. I need one of those family tree things to carry around with me," he said, his gaze landing on me. He stepped forward and I saw the worry in his eyes. Not to mention the fear.

Solomon seemed very afraid for me.

"My uncles are here too, and I think some aunts, and my brothers."

"Your sister wanted to come with Delgado when I called him, but I told them to stay at home and we'd let them know anything. Fletcher and Flaherty are here too. They're parked out front. Lucas is at the agency, crawling over every piece of traffic camera footage in the area."

"Thanks, I appreciate everything you're doing. I don't want the baby to see all this, and it's nice the guys came. What about my mom and dad?" I asked, realizing out of everyone, they were the only ones not here, but then again, they were probably asleep. Everyone else must have caught the night shift. I also realized something else: these guys really did have my back.

"I already called them and left a message," said Garrett, ducking his head around the door. "I figured they probably already have plenty of calls to wake up to. They just texted me that they made up your old room if you want to stay over. We're done in your bedroom. I tried not to mess anything up but... it's a mess. Your window is broken."

"We're done here too," said Maddox. "You did good, Lexi. He might not have called you by name or threatened you, but he did attack you. I need to get a list of everyone you interviewed recently just to see if this has something to do with your case; but there's still a lot to work with right here. DNA, maybe fingerprints."

"Really? I didn't think I gave you much, other than it was a white man and I only know that because I saw some skin. I didn't recognize his voice. He was taller than me, I think, but I was on my bed, so I couldn't give his height exactly. I think that narrows it down to how many tens of thousands?" I asked, not meaning to sound sarcastic. I was just exasperated that I couldn't see more and it was hard not to berate myself for it. Most of my job rested on my ability to notice things.

Maddox began to answer, but Solomon simply said, "Can you all give us a minute?"

I nodded to everyone that it was okay, promised to email Maddox a list of my interviewees, starting with anyone angry with me, and they retreated. Garrett shut the door behind them and I heard him say something to Maddox before their footsteps faded away.

For what felt like forever, Solomon and I stared at each other. Then, when I felt like my knees might wobble, he was across the room in a flash, sweeping me into his arms and hugging me so tightly, my ribs felt like they might pop. Settling me on the floor, I realized he'd literally just swept me off my feet, as he leaned in to kiss me.

The kitchen door banged open and I jumped.

"Whoops!" said Lily. "I see you're okay so I'll be right back." She stepped out again and pulled the door shut. "She's okay," she yelled to whomever else was out there. "Absolutely, totally doing fine."

I couldn't help laughing as I leaned my head against Solomon's chest. The laugh gave way to a few tears and I wiped them away with my hands. "Tonight was scary," I mumbled, my voice sounding muffled against Solomon's sweater. My cheek throbbed, as did my arm and my back and... everything ached. I knew I would feel like I'd been in a fight the next day, one I barely managed to win.

"You did good," Solomon told me, his large hands brushing my hair and resting on my back as he held me. "You didn't panic. You defended yourself."

"He could have killed me."

"No 'could haves' about it. This *was* the outcome, so it's the only outcome. Don't think about anything else."

"When did you become so philosophical?"

"When someone tried to kill my girlfriend in her own home."

I gulped. "Yeah, it's a so different from when people tried to kill me elsewhere."

"I should have been here."

"It's okay. I had my gun." I rested the side of my head that didn't hurt over his heart and listened to it beat as Solomon wrapped his arms more tightly around me.

"Lexi, I'm lost for words," he whispered, his words muffled against my hair.

The door creaked open and Lily stuck her head around. "It's okay, you can come in," I told her as Solomon and I stepped apart, like we automatically did when we weren't alone. She entered and I noticed she wore her coat over her pajamas, and her feet were stuffed into a pair of boots.

"I broke every single driving rule getting over here," she told me. "I'd have to attend traffic school for weeks if I were caught."

"Thank you." I reached for her hand and squeezed it.

"On the plus side, your Uncle Luke got me a great discount on my wedding flowers. Did you know his wife's sister's niece is a florist?" she asked.

"Probably, but I forgot."

"It's just plain lucky I ran into him here. Do you want to come home with me?" Lily asked. Behind her, Jord nodded. "You can stay in one of the guest rooms."

"I was going to take you to Mom and Dad's," said Garrett, joining them.

"You can take my spare room," said Maddox, stepping next to the trio. "It's no trouble."

"You can pretty much have any room you want in Montgomery tonight," added Daniel with a grin. "Or my couch. Your choice."

Problem was, I didn't want to be in any of those places, although I appreciated the options. I wanted to be home. I didn't want to leave my house in case I was too scared to ever return to it, or the trauma of the memory ruined it for me. Part of me wanted to run, of course it did. A big part of me wanted to take sanctuary with my family and friends, but I valued my independence too. It was a major part of me and I wanted to be brave, even when I didn't need to be. I couldn't let an unknown assailant ruin everything I had worked for, and I wouldn't.

I didn't dare look up at Solomon, the only person in the room who hadn't spoken. So I could barely do anything, but nod inanely when he said, "Or we can stay here. In your spare room, and I'll stay with you as long as you need." His hand crept into mine, his fingers folding over my own, and I looked up, my heart pounding as the sound of my other would-be-rescuers finally edged away, leaving no one, but Solomon and me.

CHAPTER SIXTEEN

I woke to find Solomon, Delgado, Fletcher, and Flaherty standing at the foot of my bed in the unfinished upstairs bedroom, all in short sleeves and flexing their muscles. If I were into that sort of thing, it would have been the best wake up... EVER. Since I wasn't, my first instinct was to see if my pajamas were on. The second, to ask "What the hell?" and the third, to shoot them.

"Garrett took your gun," said Solomon, as my hand patted down the nightstand. "Just in case."

While I pondered my brother's foresight, Lucas walked in, a smart tablet in his hand. He grinned. "Nice jammies. Ponies?"

I looked down and sighed before pulling the covers over my head. Of all the pajamas for my colleagues to catch me in! Even worse, as my fog of memory swirled into reality... Did most of MPD see me in my check shorts and singlet jammies last night too? They had been bagged as evidence leaving me with the pony option.

"Oh God," I murmured. "I'll never survive this."

A weight landed on my bed and the covers were

tugged down a little. I pulled a face at Solomon's smiling one. "What?" I mumbled sullenly.

"No one is going to remember your pajamas," he told me. "Get up. Breakfast is made. We have work to do."

"Okay, but..." I looked past him to my colleagues poking around my room. "What about...?"

"They can go downstairs while you shower and get dressed."

"Guess the cat is out of the bag?"

"Guess so," said Solomon, smiling. He didn't seem at all upset about that.

I nodded and took a deep breath, strangely unconcerned that my private life was now out in the open and subject to criticism from the people I strived daily to impress since taking the job. Of present concern, my heart started to pound the moment I thought I'd be truly alone. Sure, we decided to sleep upstairs in my unfinished bedroom, rather than amongst the broken glass and blood spatters in the guest bedroom, but it was still the same house. My home, my space, had actually been violated and that thought unnerved me more than I could say. "Can you..." I started, trailing off, not sure what I wanted to ask him, and trying to avoid appearing weak. Hadn't I been through much worse already?

"Stay?" murmured Solomon. "Yes," he said, and nodded. "You're not alone."

After my colleagues trooped out, I headed into the bathroom. True to his word, Solomon stayed with me, leaning against the windowsill while I showered. He disappeared only briefly before returning with my clothing and my small medical kit. After I dried, he examined my wound, and applied a fresh dressing to my arm before pressing my cell phone into my hand, and telling me it had beeped several messages. I checked them. There was one from Lily, reminding me of my promise to help Sharon. Another one pointing out there were a lot of wedding dresses to save. The third message from her was a photo message of the two of us in our gowns, just to drive the point home that Lily didn't want to lose her dress either. Maddox also sent a message reminding me to send him my interview list. There were a bunch of messages from my parents, sister, and one from my oldest nephew, Patrick, asking if I'd really lost my arm in a knife fight.

"What is everyone doing here?" I asked while I dressed in the jeans and light blue shirt Solomon picked out for me.

"Fitting a security system for you," Solomon explained. "No one will be able to catch you unawares again. You'll be totally safe."

"Thank you," I answered, surprised. "I'll..."

"Don't even suggest paying for it. This is on me. I got you into this, and I'll protect you."

"You didn't get me into anything."

"I gave you this job. I've put you in harm's way. If you'd stayed a temp..." Solomon turned away, his hand covering his eyes as if he couldn't face looking at me.

"Whoa! Hold it right there. I took the job because I wanted it. I'm good at it. I... Dammit, Solomon, I'm good at this and I'm not going to give up my job because some asshole broke into my house and tried to kill me!" My voice continued to rise as I reached out, turning him towards me. Couldn't he see I was fine? "He is not going to ruin my life, and everything I've worked for." My heart continued to pound as I stopped, my breathing heavy. When I looked up, Solomon was nodding, his fingers tracing the rough coloring of my cheek where it bruised.

"You got it," he said, determination etched on his face. Although what he intended to do, I wasn't sure, suffice to say, I would hate to be my assailant if Solomon got hold of him first. "Breakfast," he said, softly, "then back to work."

"Okay."

"Okay. Maybe you could do some surveillance with Lily? She must want company and you did take the wedding case." He gave my arm one last check. "Garrett is in the kitchen."

"Oh, shoot! Uh, no pun intended, but I agreed to go to the range with him today."

"That's off. Your gun was used in a shooting last night, remember? I turned it over to Garrett and he logged it in at MPD."

"Oh."

"I made bacon and eggs."

I brightened. "And the world is okay again."

Garrett was sitting at the kitchen table, a full plate in front of him. He also had the local newspaper, and a coffee in one of my mugs. He looked up when we entered and gave me a glance over. "You look okay," he said.

"Better than the other guy," I quipped. "Have you found him yet? And did you tell Patrick I lost my arm?"

"No, and what the hell? No, I don't know how Patrick got that idea." Garrett sliced his bacon and chewed it, then took a sip of coffee, licking his lips sumptuously. "All hospitals in the county are on alert for anyone with a gunshot wound and all the local doctors too. If he turns up, and he will, we'll get him."

"Solomon told me he turned over my gun," I said, taking the chair opposite.

"You'll get it back. I thought we'd skip the range since you already got your shooting practice in." Garrett balanced a forkful of scrambled eggs into his mouth. "These are good," he added, returning to the bacon.

"Don't look so forlorn, Lexi, your breakfast is coming up," said Solomon, moving over to my stove.

"Did you make this?" I asked him, trying to see what was on my plate.

"Fletcher," replied Solomon, spooning food from the pans onto a plate and setting it in front of me. "But I sent

Flaherty out to the store to fill your fridge."

"Aww." Another pressing question entered my mind, one I should probably have asked before. "Am I going to get arrested for this?"

"For shooting the man who attacked you in your own home?" asked Garrett. "No. Not in a million years. Here. I've been answering your calls." He pushed a notepad towards me. "You've got a bunch. Uncle Dermot is sending his boys by to fix your lock and the bedroom window. Dermot says he'll get them to paint your porch too. Siobhan and her husband are doing your yard work."

"So I see," I said, running my finger down the list. "Why is Aunt Mary offering to paint my fence?"

"Everyone wants to help out," said Garrett with a shrug. "Mom and Dad will come by later and paint your living room. It needs freshening up. Traci and I already cleaned up your room and we took the sheets to wash since they got... Well, anyway, Daniel and Alice left some medical supplies for your arm, but you were sleeping and..."

"This is too much," I told him, looking up from the list. It continued almost to the end of the page. "No one needs to do all this stuff for me."

Garrett shrugged. "Everyone wants to."

"But..." I started to protest.

"Let them," said Garrett. He gathered his knife and fork and took them with his plate and coffee cup to the sink. "It makes everyone feel better to help. Well, I gotta go too." He leaned over and planted a kiss on my cheek. "Oh, what are you doing after lunch?"

"Nothing. I have a short shift at the gym... that's my undercover thing," I added when Garrett looked confused, "then I guess I'll be at the agency." I looked to Solomon for confirmation, but he appeared very focused on the bacon sandwich he was fixing. Too focused actually. I smelled a rat.

"So you're free? Great! I volunteered you to talk to Chloe's class later today. They're all amped up to meet a real life lady detective."

How sweet... "Wait... what?"

"All the details are on the notepad. Don't be late!"

"Why can't you meet them? You're an actual detective."

"I'm investigating an actual crime!"

I gaped at my brother. "What do you think I do? And before you answer that, calling me a lady detective is sexist. Why cares what doodahs I have so long as I get the job done? Two, I'm not a detective. I'm a private investigator."

"Whatever," said Garrett. "Be there at two. I squared it with your boss. You need a day off and something to distract you temporarily."

I turned my narrowed eyes on Solomon, who took that moment to join me at the table, coffee mug in hand. "I can't take a day off. Michael is waiting for me at the gym. I need to talk to him about the conversation I overheard."

Solomon simply shrugged. "I thought you'd like spending some time with your niece. Take it easy for a few days," he said. After a long stare from moi, he added, "Some light relief?"

"You call a class full of kids light relief?" I wailed, turning back to Garrett. "I'm going to kill you."

"Can't. I have your gun. Good luck! Don't let all those kids down!" He edged out the door, laughing. I suppose this was his way of getting me back for some sibling infringement. Well, two could play at that game. This was something I would not forget.

"Argh!" I wailed, but it was half-hearted as my eyes moved to the notepad and the long list of things both my near and distant relatives had offered to do for me around my home. I felt a little overwhelmed as Solomon picked up the list and perused it. "You guys filled my fridge, made me breakfast, and are installing a security system?" I said in a low voice as tears prickled at my eyes. "And everyone in my family is pitching in to fix my house up."

Solomon laid his hand over mine. "You're very much loved," he said simply.

I had to agree. I really, really was.

~

My colleagues were still installing the security system by the time I had to leave for the gym and my scheduled shift. Fortunately, my shift was a short one, which was lucky because 1) I got very little sleep and the idea of being in an energetic atmosphere was doing the exact opposite of making me feel perky; and 2) it was a lot duller being a gym employee than I thought it would be. The clients moaned about everything; no one tidied after themselves' and the talc on the changing rooms floor... I couldn't fathom why, beyond a vague idea, the members were striving so hard to preserve themselves in some way. 3) Most importantly, since the lead on the missing Simonstech employee, I thought we were barking up the wrong treadmill with the gym. And that was exactly what I planned to tell Solomon when I caught up with him later. Right after I mentioned annoying Carter Simons Junior, the man currently at the top of my list of potential attackers. Was his fury at my snooping after our interview enough to attack me? Given that I'd asked Maddox to take a closer look at the suspected butterfly mark Lorena's killer had left, a mark that I attributed to Junior's cufflinks, I had to concede it probably was.

Taking charge of the gym floor was not only a pretty safe place for me to be right now, but it gave me plenty of opportunity to think about the things I'd seen and heard here. The one thing I kept coming back to were the voices I overheard in the employees' changing rooms. I needed to know exactly who the two women were so I could interrogate them further. Someone definitely paid one of them for the key, and if that person also committed the crimes, the mystery women might be able to tell me something that would lead to the killer. Of course, it didn't escape my notice that if said person was the killer, after offing three people, perhaps four if I counted Avril, the murderer wouldn't hesitate to get rid of anyone who might identify them. I had to get there first.

Another thing crossed my mind. Michael would be very pleased to have the gym cleared of any wrongdoing, but I didn't think he'd be thrilled at the idea of an employee being involved, even if it were in only a minor way. All the same, I was sure he'd be glad to see me close the case; and I'd be pleased to return to my normal routine of not being attacked by madmen, wielding knives, and wearing nicer gym wear than my current cut-off polo shirt and leggings combination.

"Hey, can you man the floor for a minute?" I asked, the moment I spotted another employee. When I got a nod in the affirmative, I edged away. "Five minutes, okay? Maybe ten. Thank you!" I whipped through the doors and power-walked to the reception desk. The receptionist was talking on the phone so I took up position behind a monitor and logged in, using Michael's special all access log-in. It was less exciting than it sounded, but it did give me a chance to look at the employee work rota. I called up the file and browsed through it, until I found what I was looking for. Fifteen employees were on staff the day I overheard the conversation. I knew the voices were both women, so I immediately discounted the men. That left nine. Three signed on a couple of hours after I'd taken my shower, so logic dictated it was unlikely to be them. Seven. Two were lifeguarding at the pool and could be discounted. Five.

I had five potential suspects.

Unfortunately, there was no way of narrowing it down to which two had the conversation. I noted the names on a piece of notepaper and closed the program, logging off the system. Checking my watch, I saw I only had a couple of minutes left before good will ran out, so with a sigh, I made for the gym.

"Lexi, do you have a minute?" Michael called as I stepped into his doorway and prepared to knock.

"Yes, lots," I confirmed, lowering my hand. He beckoned me in and indicated for me to shut the door.

"Where are we?" he asked.

I looked up curiously. "Your office?"

"No, I mean, where are we on—" he stopped, and looked around. I looked around too. I had no idea what he was looking for. When I looked at him again, he mouthed, "the case."

"I'm following up a lead, but I'm a little stumped." I took the chair and sat down, uninvited. "I overheard a conversation that might be pertinent to the case, but I don't know who was talking." I pushed the notepaper with the names across the desk and Michael picked it up. "I checked the employee roster for the time I heard it, and deduced it has to be two of these people." I explained how I knew they were women, and what I heard, and Michael's face went from incredulous to furious in one quick step.

"Okay. How do you find out whom?"

"I don't know. I don't know any of them well enough to recognize them from voices alone."

"Did you hear any accents?"

That was a good question. I thought back. Did I? Not really. No, that wasn't true. One of the voices was vaguely Southern. "One of them was Southern, I think, but not a very strong accent," I told him.

"That's AnnaBeth. She's on your list. She's the only one from the South. The other four grew up in Montgomery."

"Is she close to anyone? It's the other woman I'm interested in mostly."

"She's tight with Kate, our deputy manager. She's on your list too. What was their conversation about? Could either of them have something to do with the murders?"

"No. At least, not directly." I thought back to the few times I'd heard Kate speak. It could be her. Now I thought about it, I was sure it was. "Let's assume it was Kate. I overheard her tell AnnaBeth that she took money to leave the key in a safe place. She told AnnaBeth she needed the money and left the key as instructed, and it was returned to her a day later. She didn't know what the person wanted it for so assumed it was for a prank."

"Shit! You don't give a key to someone you don't know, for cash, and expect nothing bad to happen!" Michael ran a hand over his eyes and tipped his head back. He pinched the bridge of his nose and closed his eyes. "That means someone has a key to this place," he added.

"It looks that way. My guess is they got it copied and returned it before anyone could know it was missing. There might still be a copy out there."

"They could have taken anything. Changing all the locks won't be cheap. I know, I know. Bigger picture. My deputy manager hands out a key, and within days, two of my members get killed on the premises."

"Kate said close to the same thing."

"What do I do now? Kate isn't due in until later when her shift starts."

"I'd like to let Solomon know their names, then inform the murder squad working the case at MPD," I told him, realizing how bad things could get for Kate and AnnaBeth. My sympathy was very faint. Kate did the deed, and now she had to deal with the consequences, harsh as they may be.

"What are you going to advise them?"

"To pick Kate and AnnaBeth up. Kate might have

some other information that she didn't tell her friend. AnnaBeth might know more than what I heard. There's a possibility Kate could be in danger, especially if she knows anything that could identify the killer. Can I use your phone?"

Michael waved a hand at it. I called Solomon first and told him what I planned to do and he agreed it was a smart move. Next, I called Maddox; and after assuring him I was still alive and fine, I told him my assumptions, and he reminded me again to send him my interviewee list.

"It's as easy as that, huh?" asked Michael.

"Yes."

"What now?"

"Now I finish my shift. I could be wrong," I told him, erring on the side of caution.

"Are you wrong?"

"I don't think so."

"I guess I'm looking for a new deputy manager. Let me know what happens with Kate, will you? And AnnaBeth too? I want to believe Kate wouldn't do something too dumb, but then I'd like to believe two people weren't murdered in my gym, and I know that happened. Why didn't Kate come to me if she needed money? Why didn't AnnaBeth tell me what Kate did?"

"I wish I could answer those questions, Michael, but I can't. All I can say is, don't do anything just yet. I could still be wrong and I don't want Kate or AnnaBeth alerted."

Michael sighed. "No, you're not." He was quiet for a few long minutes and just when I got up to leave, he asked, "Are you coming back?"

"To work here? No, I don't think so. I have other leads so I think the gym is a dead end, excuse the phrase, as far as this case goes. In the several shifts I've taken, I haven't learned anything useful except this. I'd appreciate it if you kept my spot open, just in case, but I don't think I'll get the answers I need here."

"Damn shame." Michael opened his desk drawer and pulled out a couple of discs. "Here's the surveillance footage I promised you. I haven't watched it so I don't know if it's of any use."

"Thanks."

"If you ever think about leaving the PI biz and want to get into the fitness industry, give me a call. I could do with someone I trust. Someone who can shake things up for the members." Michael stood and walked around the desk, offering his hand. I shook it. Even if I wouldn't take up his offer, it was nice to be appreciated. "I could do with someone just like you."

Michael's words were still ringing in my ears as I threw my gym bag in the trunk close to an hour later. I called Solomon, gave him the names, then cleaned out my employee locker, changed into black pants and a nice blouse, and was just leaning in to retrieve the surveillance discs to slot them into my purse for viewing later, when an SUV drew up alongside me and stopped. Since several cars had entered and exited the lot in the minutes since I arrived, I ignored it in favor of searching for my phone, which I'd dropped in the trunk. It was only when I found it, and noticed a pair of legs a step back from mine, that I jumped, hitting my hid on the lid.

"Shit, sorry," said Maddox.

"Owie," I whimpered, reaching a hand to my hair. No wet spots meant no blood, which was good news since I'd seen enough of mine to last me several decades. I took in Maddox's sharp suit and striped blue tie as I reeled back and asked, "Since when do you sneak up on a woman who just shot an intruder? My nerves are shot!"

"My bad. I'm really, really sorry. How's your head?"

"I'll live. What brings you here? I'm incognito, you know."

"I came to check up on you."

"You did that already. What's the real story?"

"Maybe I'm just being extra nice?"

"In that case, I'd appreciate flowers." We both looked down at his empty hands.

"Okay, I was checking to make sure you were okay and I came to give you the good news and the bad news. We picked up Kate Holm and AnnaBeth Chabot at their homes fifteen minutes ago. You came up good. Kate confessed the moment the cuffs were slapped on."

"To the murders?" I asked hopefully, wondering who "we" was. Maddox was never dressed this smartly for work; plus, he'd gotten here way too quick after making an arrest.

"No," said Maddox, ignorant of my silent questions. "She had an alibi for that. She told us she supplied a key and she still had the money and the note arranging the deal. We're checking it for prints. It'll take a while."

"And AnnaBeth?"

"She took a little longer, but when we gave her the cliff notes of the conversation you overheard, she opened up. She's got an alibi too. Looks like she was just a confidante. Neither of them are the killer."

"Ugh. That's disappointing, but not exactly unexpected." I felt my head again. No lump. What a relief. It was hard enough covering up the bruise on my cheek.

"It's one step closer than we were."

"So that's the good and the bad news covered."

"Actually, that was the good news. The bad news is Carter Simons Junior filed a complaint against you. Apparently, you were caught trespassing on his home property, harassing him."

"I was not!" I exclaimed.

Maddox raised his eyebrows. "Kind of funny, a guy from Simonstech files a complaint when you were just at that place." He waited. I waited. Someone had to break the silence, but it wouldn't be me. It was a technique I perfected during my many years of temping. Eventually, my opponent just told me whatever it was he or she wanted, or gave up. Maddox, however, was a tougher nut to crack. "Fine," he said, after several long minutes and a no blinking competition that I wasn't sure who triumphed over. "What were you doing on his property?"

"Taking a wrong turn."

"Pure coincidence, huh?"

"Absolutely."

"Didn't think so. Whatever you're not telling me... this guy is on my radar now. Would I be a genius if I guessed he was on your interviewee list?"

"No, you're not a genius; but yes, Solomon and I interviewed him."

"Assumed as much."

"For what it's worth, Junior is at the top of my list of potential attackers. Did you match the mark on Junior's cufflinks to Lorena's head?" I asked.

"No, because I don't have enough evidence to get a warrant." Maddox sighed as my face fell. "I will ask him where he was last night," he assured me.

"Great. And about the..."

"Listen, don't worry about the complaint. Nothing will happen. Just do me a favor... don't go back to Simons' house and do not approach him."

"Thanks, I appreciate it. At least, I would if I'd done anything, which I haven't! So... where are you going?" I asked, turning around to shut the trunk, and avoid Maddox's devilishly handsome grin. He seemed pretty pleased with himself in semi-catching me in trouble while conducting an investigation. It was annoying that Junior filed a complaint, but I should have expected it. It was only a matter of time before Solomon found out. With a sinking feeling, I realized I had to tell him first.

"I have a date."

I gulped, and blinked. What? Maddox had a date?

And he thought I wanted to know about it? "Oh, I..." I stuttered, turning to face him.

"No, I shouldn't have... I don't have a date, okay?" Maddox flushed.

"It wouldn't matter to me if you have a date."

"Of course not. You have a boyfriend."

"I have a boyfriend." I paused, adding, "Solomon." I don't know why I felt the need to confirm it there and then, but I did and now it was out there. Talk about awkward moments as we stood there, facing one another. Maddox did a little toe kick to the dirt and I checked around us, for anything that would give me something else to talk about.

"I figured," said Maddox, eventually, and very, very casually. Another long pause, then, "I have a job interview. The gym was on the way and I saw your car so I thought I'd drop by, just to check in on you." Maddox looked at his watch. "I can't be late. I thought you'd want to know your lead came up good."

"I appreciate it."

"Thank you." We stood, still awkwardly, looking at each other, our conversation having grown stilted until Maddox gave a little nod and stepped backwards. He walked around to the driver's side and opened the door, pausing as he rested his arms on the roof. "I'm happy for you," he said. "Still wish I hadn't screwed us up, but I'm happy for you. Solomon's an interesting guy."

"He's one of the good guys."

"Let's hope so," said Maddox as he got into his car. When he drove away, I wondered what the hell that meant and what kind of job Maddox was interviewing for. Maybe he was due a promotion, I decided. He'd been having a good run with his own cases lately. I didn't have to think about it too long because my cell phone rang, causing me to jump again. I answered it as I got into the driver's seat. "Hello?"

"Lexi Graves?" asked a woman. "My name is Marnie

Vasquez."

"Lorena's daughter? I've been trying to call you."

"I know. I got your message. I'm in Montgomery and was hoping we could meet. I'd like to talk to you."

"Yes. Yes, definitely. Where would you like to meet?"

"My mother's house. If that's okay with you?"

"Well… yes, okay. Are you sure you want to meet there?" I asked, hesitantly.

"I have to go there sometime. I really need to talk to you about what happened. To my mother," she added, as if I could ever erase the awful scene I discovered there. I hadn't been back and didn't plan to, but I couldn't turn her down. I needed to talk to Marnie. "We don't have to go inside if you don't want to," she added, surprisingly tactfully.

"Whatever you're comfortable with," I replied, because no matter what I'd seen, I couldn't imagine anything worse than losing your mother so horrifically.

"Honestly, I'm not that comfortable there either, but I have to go there sometime," she said again. "I'd like to get it over with. It was my home. It still is, I guess. I'm not staying there. I'm staying with a friend and her family down the street, but I'd like to talk to you privately so I guess the house will do. I'm sorry, I'm rambling. I'm a little…"

"It's fine. I have an appointment I can't get out of now, but I'm free after four," I decided, after factoring in time to talk to the class, then grab some food. I might not get a chance later on. "Is that okay?"

Marnie agreed it was fine and hung up, leaving me with a heavy feeling that our conversation would be very hard.

I made it to the school a few minutes before — not exactly thanking Garrett all the way — I was due to arrive and introduced myself to Chloe's teacher. She already had the kids assembled on the floor carpet, in a horseshoe shape, and I gathered they'd just finished a story or their discussion time. I wasn't sure. The kid thing baffled me and awed me. How could one person manage so many of them? I wondered. Wasn't it similar to herding cats?

The teacher didn't appear too frazzled as she ushered me to a lumpy armchair at the front. I settled in it and smiled at the hopeful little faces in front of me. I waggled my fingers at my niece and she waved back.

"We're really, really excited to have Detective Graves here today," said Mrs. Nguyen. "Isn't that right, class?" She led a little round of applause and I started to enjoy myself. The kids were all so eager to learn and wait... what? Detective?

"I'm not a detective," I said.

"Sure you are," said Mrs. Nguyen.

"No, I'm a private investigator. It's like a detective, but I don't have a badge."

"Do you have a gun?" asked one little boy. "Can I see it?"

"Yes, I do, and no, you can't. It's... at the police station." I didn't dare explain why.

"So you *are* a detective," said the little boy's friend. They nodded to each other.

"No. I'm really not."

"Can I see your badge?"

"I only have my investigator's license, but you can see it." I fished it from my purse and held it out.

"Boooooring," said the little boy.

"That's enough, Peter. Okay, settle down everyone. Private Investigator Graves is going to tell us a little bit about her job and how she solves mysteries." She waved at me to continue as another adult appeared in the open doorway who beckoned her. She mouthed, "five minutes" to me as she edged away, exiting the room before I could protest. I wanted to whimper, "don't leave me" but hey, how bad could it be? They were only kids and this was supposed to be relaxing. Maybe it would even be fun, I decided, smiling at their eager faces.

"Are you Nancy Drew?" asked the girl who sat next to my niece. She had the cutest bunches on either side of her head and her sleeves were spattered with red... oh, it was paint. Phew!

"No."

"Is your name Nancy Drew?"

"No," I sighed, holding up my license. "See here, on my license it says Alexandra Graves, but everyone calls me Lexi."

"Is too Nancy Drew. You solve mysteries and so does Nancy."

"Well, yes, I do solve mysteries."

"Knew it!"

"But I'm not Nancy..."

"Are too."

"Like I said, I'm..."

"Do you have a TV show?" piped another kid before I could win that argument.

"No, sorry."

"Nancy Drew has a TV show," said the little girl.

"See, I'm not..."

"Dog, the Bounty Hunter, has a TV show!" yelled Peter.

"Ahh, well, I'm definitely not a bounty hunter."

"You suck," said the shortest kid in the front row, who had a surprisingly loud voice.

"I thought your aunt was Nancy Drew," sighed the little girl next to Chloe, a fat tear sliding down her cheek. She sniffed and a tear slipped from her other eye. Chloe looked up at me, absolutely appalled. I knew how she felt.

"I thought you were cool," she whispered.

"Oh, my life!" I sighed as the barrage of disappointment hit me to the tune of a dozen little kids singing Dog's theme song.

CHAPTER SEVENTEEN

"How did it go at Chloe's school?" Lily asked when I joined her. She was parked down the street from Perfect Brides and listening to a local radio station while looking utterly bored. I had to move three candy wrappers, a pair of binoculars, and a water bottle before I could sit on the passenger seat. "Feeling all maternal?"

"No," I wailed, searching for more candy. I knew Lily had to have more somewhere. She reached over, opened the glove box, and handed me a Twix. "They hated me. They were expecting Nancy Drew and I totally disappointed them. You should have seen their faces. It was like I told them Christmas was canceled."

"Big whoop. I'm Jewish."

"Hanukkah, too. And you celebrate Christmas. I've seen you."

"I celebrate anything with gifts."

"I need sympathy."

"Ahh..." Lily paused.

"Oh, come on!" I waved the half-eaten candy bar at her.

231

"To be honest, I'd be disappointed too if I was expecting Nancy Drew and got you instead. You probably ruined Chloe's life. Have you apologized?"

"No! She's only little! She knows what I do for a job." I rested my head in my hands, still chewing. "What do I do?"

"Easy. Get your own TV show!"

"You know I was nearly killed last night. I could have talked about that and terrified them." I waved my injured arm at Lily. I was lucky. After swallowing two painkillers, it barely hurt, and I could take some satisfaction that the other guy came off a lot worse than I. I would be really satisfied when he was caught.

"They would definitely remember you. I noticed last night you had a really nice manicure. It lasted really well. Not even a chip!"

"That's what you noticed last night?"

"That, and I remembered I was still pissed you didn't ask me to come with you to the manicure bar. Oh, and I also noticed that your house is a really good party house. The amount of people in there, the flow... have you feng shui'd it yet?"

"No. I IKEA'd it instead."

"I thought you got a new plant. So when are we getting manicures?"

"You're really not going to ask how I am?"

"Nope. You shot the dude and you're barely hurt. You totally won."

"You don't seem very concerned about me nearly succumbing to a mad man." Just what did one have to do for sympathy around here, I wondered. Or was my life now so crazy that even my best friend didn't blink an eyelid after hearing a psycho came after me in my own home?

"You've succumbed to loads of mad men and you're still here. Anyway, I doubt this one was mad. Besides, I came over wearing a onesie! In public! How much more concerned can you get?"

"Well... I guess... wait! No! Be more concerned! I'm your best friend."

"I was concerned!" Lily exclaimed, turning to watch two women as they entered the wedding store. "Right until I got there!"

"So what changed?"

"Apart from you actually being alive? Lexi, you were wearing those PJs. Anyone who's watched a huge amount of crime TV knows that the killer only goes after the hot girls who wear nothing but matching bras and panties along with full makeup." She waved a hand at my figure. "You were in no danger. Your hair wasn't even done."

"Are you saying my jammies saved my life?"

"That, and we should go shopping. Stat!"

"Until then," I said, thinking about how far my paycheck would stretch, "are we any further on the wedding dress thefts?"

"Nope. I've been watching the place every evening, and so far, nothing. I've also been checking in on Sharon, who hasn't noticed anything either, besides that one woman. She's still antsy so I said I'd watch over the store this afternoon too. Hey, since I'm stuck here, can you get me a drink and a snack from across the street? I'm hungry and you ate my chocolate."

"Sure. And I'll take the next shift," I told her, feeling simultaneously magnanimous and guilty that I hadn't helped Lily more. "Solomon said I should take it easy for a day or two."

"Cool. Maybe Jord and I will go out for dinner, Hey, what about the gym?"

"Dead end," I confirmed. "Well, sort of. There was a little break in the case. I'll tell you later." I waved away her money and crossed the street to get Lily her snacks, feeling rather pleased that I volunteered to take over her shift. Truth be told, it wasn't easy watching the wedding store when I had another case that was growing more confounding by the moment, but maybe a change of scenery could reboot my brain. That Lily managed to put in the surveillance hours already, around her wedding arrangements and running her bar, was commendable. She deserved a night off to hang out with Jord.

I pulled two drinks from the tall refrigerator and grabbed a couple of candy bars, and some chips, moving to the front of the small store. As I reached the stand, the front page of the *Montgomery Gazette* caught my eye. "Oh no," I groaned, reaching for it. "Damn, damn, damn."

"You read it, you bought it," said the little woman behind the counter, fixing me with angry eyes as I scanned the front page.

I pushed over a few bills and hightailed it back to the car. "We've been watching the wrong store," I told Lily as I slid inside. "Another bridal store just got hit in Chester."

"No! You're kidding!" Lily wailed, taking the paper from me and skimming it. "That's thirty miles away. Look at all the designer dresses they stole!"

"Maybe this is the last one," I suggested, "Maybe the thieves have enough dresses now."

"What do you need with that many dresses anyway? Do you think it's one of those illegal bridal rings?"

Sometimes Lily had great ideas, sometimes they made me say, "Huh?" This was definitely a "Huh?" moment. "Huh?" I said.

"Maybe they need the dresses for fake brides to have sham weddings to get visas?"

"I don't think they'd go so far as to let the sham brides choose their sham dresses."

"I totally would," decided Lily. "I'd keep it and sell it afterwards. I'd insist on a honeymoon, too, just so it looked really real. We could go together!"

"You've been thinking about this sham wedding a lot."

"Not much else to do when you're sitting in a car for hours. I passed a lot of Candy Crush levels, too, but now I'm out of lives."

"Wait... what did you say about selling the dress? After?"

"I'd sell it. There's good money to be made from a high-end wedding dress. Between the auction websites and the seconds websites, you can almost make your money back."

My original suspicion was that the dresses were stolen and the re-sale value confirmed that, but the volume of thefts puzzled me. "But I don't think you could sell that many dresses without arousing suspicion. We're talking three to four hundred dresses missing, and they have to take up a lot of space."

"Where else could they go?"

That had me stumped. I couldn't see the thieves setting up a store, and it would be no easy feat to fence that many dresses from a trunk. For a start, barely ten dresses can fit in the average trunk, and that's providing they weren't puffy meringues. "I don't know. I'll think about it. I have to run. Lorena Vasquez's daughter wants to meet me at her house and I don't want to be late. Call me if there's any news?"

"Don't hold your breath. Hey, give me the newspaper. Maybe I'll call the store that just got burglarized and see if I can get any clues," said Lily, thrusting her shoulders back with newfound conviction that she could save the day. She gave her hair a sexy swish as she grabbed her cell phone and spread the paper over the steering wheel. "I bet I can sweet talk some information out of them! Just because Perfect Brides hasn't been burglarized, doesn't mean it won't. We are still on this case!"

I hugged Lily, told her that was a great idea, bid her

CAMILLA CHAFER

goodbye and hotfooted it to my VW, pointing toward the direction of Lorena's house. I wasn't looking forward to the meeting. For one, I hadn't been back to the house since finding Lorena, and the idea of being there made me extremely uncomfortable. It wasn't because someone died there; that kind of thing didn't creep me out. It was because Lorena died there, violently, and I liked her. I knew that whatever I felt, her daughter had to feel a hundred times worse, and she deserved to know what was going on, even that her mother's death might be part of a larger crime. I tried to imagine going to my family home, knowing my mother was no longer there, and my throat caught. By the time I pulled up outside the house, my sniveling subsided and I got myself under control.

Lorena's daughter needed the truth, and yes, my sympathy, but she didn't need me making things any worse for her. I gave myself a little shakedown, checked to see my mascara didn't run, and climbed out, turning to face Lorena's home, a home that was now someone else's.

The door opened just as I raised my hand to knock. The woman framed in the doorway was the image of Lorena's younger self. She had the same big eyes and glossy hair, and I had no problem immediately identifying her as Marnie. She had clearly been waiting for me, but somehow I doubted it was eagerly. All the same, I admired her courage as she shook my hand and introduced herself, before inviting me in. I took a forced breath and stepped over the threshold.

"Can I get you a drink?" the young woman asked, politely and pleasantly, almost like I just stopped by for a social visit. "There's a shelf full of coconut water in the fridge that my mother kept stocked for after her daily runs, and I think there's coffee too."

After declining Marnie's offer of a drink, I couldn't conceive going into the kitchen, and was grateful when

236

she suggested we sit on the couches for our talk.

"I was with my father when he had his heart attack and died. I'm sorry you had to find my mother like that," said Marnie, indicating I should sit opposite her. The door to the kitchen was closed, I noticed, and nothing was moved in the living room, barring the plastic bottle of coconut water on the coffee table, which Marnie reached for, drinking straight from the neck. Except for a wilting plant on the bookcase, it was like time stopped still.

"I just wish I could have gotten there... here... earlier. I'm so sorry for your loss. I liked Lorena a lot," I said, hoping she sensed the sincerity in my voice. Marnie nodded and gave me a weak smile, making me wish there was something I could do for her, something more practical. I hoped her uncle and friends were taking care of her and that she wasn't alone.

"She mentioned you a few times. We talked every other day on the phone, you know. She liked you too. My mom was really impressed to have a friend who was a private investigator. She said she wished she had the guts to take a job like yours."

"It takes more patience than guts."

"I imagine it does." Marnie clasped her hands together and fell silent.

"I don't know how I can help you, Marnie, or what I can tell you, but I'll try," I told her. "You can ask me anything you want. If it's okay, I'd like to ask you a few questions too."

"I only really want to know what happened. The police came to my apartment when they informed me of her... her..." Marnie took a deep breath, but couldn't finish. "When I got here, I went to the police station with my uncle to find Detective Maddox and he told me what happened to my mother and said that you found her. He called you a friend of his and my uncle said you left a couple of messages. I guess I just wanted to hear it from you."

"In my own words?" I asked. Marnie nodded. "Okay. I'll tell you and you can stop me any time and ask any questions you like. Okay?"

"Okay."

So, I told her everything that happened from the phone call that morning to the very end, when I called 911. Marnie asked me to repeat some parts, and had a few questions, but mostly, she stayed quiet while I talked. It wasn't easy reliving the experience, especially now that I could totally relate to a home intrusion. I tried to speak carefully and clearly without getting emotional. When I finished, Marnie was frowning, and she stared past me, although I didn't think she was looking at anything. She appeared deep in thought.

"What was it my mother wanted to talk to you about?" she asked, finally looking at me again, the confusion still etched all over her face. Whatever Lorena wanted to talk about, even her daughter had no clue.

"I don't know. She wouldn't say over the phone, but she said it was urgent."

"Do you think it had to do with you being a PI?"

"Maybe. Do you think so?" I asked, hoping she might have some insight. Perhaps her mother mentioned something, however incongruous, that she could relate to me now.

Marnie shrugged and reached for the plastic bottle on the coffee table between us. She unscrewed the cap, took a long draw, and screwed it back on again, making sure to place the bottle on a coaster. I wondered if it was a habit Lorena instilled in her daughter, and if Marnie was struggling to make sense of things by sticking to habits and rituals if only to keep some sense of order in her shattered world. "I'm not sure. I think so. Something was bothering her for a while. Whenever I asked her what was wrong, she just shut me down. She wouldn't talk about it. Told me to concentrate on college and that she would look after herself. Maybe she wanted your opinion."

I nodded in agreement. That was plausible; even more so, given what I knew about Jim Schwarz and Karen Doyle. They had troubles too. There was only one way to find out. "Do you recall your mom ever mentioning a Jim Schwarz or Karen Doyle?"

"Oh, sure. From her old job at Simonstech. I think she still saw them from time to time. Karen was the one who recommended Fairmount Gym to my mom. Why?"

"They both died recently."

Marnie's hand flew to her mouth and she gasped. "Oh my gosh. Really?"

"You didn't hear?"

"No," she replied, sounding flustered, "but I only just got home and all I could think about is my mother. I'm sure my mother would have mentioned something like that... Wait, they both passed recently?"

"Yes," I said simply, not wanting to tell her just how recently.

"Oh, that's awful. I don't know why you brought them up though. Does their passing have something to do with my mom?"

"I don't know yet. I'm interested to see if there's a connection with each other. Are you okay?" I asked, noticing Marnie leaning against the couch cushions, one hand rising to her heart. She coughed and blinked, then nodded. "Yes, I'm fine. Just a little under the weather, I guess. What were you saying?"

"Just that I was interested in Jim and Karen's connection to your mom."

"All I can tell you is, they all got on well as far as I knew, but after Mom left Simonstech, they didn't see each other so much. It was right around the time that other lady disappeared. April? No, Avril. My mom was really upset about that."

"Avril Sosa?"

"Yes, I think that was her name. I remember it was in the paper and I asked Mom about it, but she told me never to mention Avril's name again, and to forget I saw the article. Don't you think that was odd?"

I agreed it was and asked if Lorena said anything about Avril recently, but Marnie answered no. She was about to say something else when she leaned forwards and grabbed the bottle, her hands shaking as she all but wrenched the cap off. She glugged a few mouthfuls, her hand still trembling when she returned it to the coffee table, almost missing it altogether. She blinked rapidly and coughed again. Her skin suddenly took on the oddest pallor.

"Are you okay?" I reached forward and touched her hand when she didn't respond. "Marnie?"

"I… I…" she choked. "Lexi, I…"

"Maybe this has been too much," I suggested. "We can talk again another time. I didn't mean to upset you."

"No, it's… I… oh, God, I think I'm gonna…" Marnie pushed against the sofa with her hands and wobbled to her feet, stumbling forwards. I leapt up and caught her as she stumbled again, her knees banging into the corner as she tried to avoid the table.

"You really don't look well," I said, but I don't think she heard me. Her eyes were glassy and she'd paled considerably.

"Help… me…" Marnie whimpered. Her eyes rolled into the back of her head, her knees collapsed, and she sank to the floor, taking me with her as I held onto her arms. I called her name a few times, but she didn't respond, so I wriggled out from where she'd fallen on me, and put her on her side, trying to remember my first aid training. Her airways were clear, and there was nothing to hurt herself on, so I stroked her hair and talked to her for a few moments, but she didn't come around.

The longer the seconds ticked by, the more concerned

I became that Marnie hadn't simply fainted. When I saw the trickle of blood sliding over her lip, I was sure all was not well.

I dialed 911 and called an ambulance, telling them I had a suspected poisoning, and waited in terror for the EMTs to come.

~

"How is she?" I asked when the doctor, a short, black woman bearing a badge that read, Dr. Marcus, approached. Marnie Vasquez was treated quickly and efficiently in the ER before being transferred to the third floor to be observed on a twenty-four watch. Her stomach was pumped and I nearly threw up when I saw them inserting the tube. I figured Marnie was very sore, but oh so very lucky to be alive. It was a thought Solomon shared the moment he joined me, arriving just as the ER doctors finished working on her. We'd been waiting an hour to speak to someone, and my heart was beating a fast rhythm.

"She's going to recover," Dr. Marcus told me. "Your friend is very fortunate."

"What happened? One minute, she seemed fine. The next, she collapsed."

"We've taken blood for tests, but my theory is that she was poisoned."

A cold wave ricocheted through me. I didn't want my assumption to be true, but there it was in plain language, from a medical professional. That worried me.

The doctor nodded, a simple confirmation of my fear. "From the way the poison acted, I think she probably ingested it. Was she upset about anything? Could she have taken something deliberately?"

"No. Absolutely not." I shook my head, and then again, when Solomon gave me a pointed look. "She was upset that her mother died recently, but she showed no intention of taking her own life. She wouldn't have invited me over if she planned on doing that."

"If it was accidental, your being there probably saved her. If you didn't get her to the hospital when you did, the outcome wouldn't have been positive. Do you know what she ingested? Could she have mixed products up accidentally?" Dr. Marcus continued, scrutinizing me as she did so.

"I don't think so," I said decisively. I might not have known Marnie long, but she didn't give me any indication that she might hurt herself. She wanted answers. "She's a smart girl. She wouldn't have pulled the bleach out from under the sink and drunk it, thinking it was juice, if that's what you're suggesting."

Solomon took my hand and I gently squeezed his fingers. I suspected he was telling me to cool it, so I did, though my breaths came in short, sharp rasps. I was angry, not at the doctor, but at whoever would have tried to hurt Marnie. I was also grateful for the sheer luck that I was there and managed to prevent her possible demise.

"No, of course not," the doctor conceded. "Plus, whatever it was, it wasn't bleach."

"We'd like you to send a blood sample to MPD," Solomon said, taking over. "And you should call Detective Maddox. He should be informed of this."

"I already logged a call with the police and took a sample," Dr. Marcus told us, which surprised me. It shouldn't have, and when I thought about it, I was glad that the doctor had the foresight to take a blood sample.

I tried to recall earlier that evening. Marnie offered me a drink, but I declined. There was a half full bottle of coconut water on the coffee table, which she kept sipping from throughout our meeting. "She was drinking coconut water right before it happened," I told them. "She said her mother drank them after running, and there was a shelf full of them in the refrigerator."

"I doubt a health drink would have caused this," said the doctor. "If you find anything, let me know. We've called her uncle and he'll be in to sit with her soon. There's nothing more you can do now."

"Poisoned," I said to Solomon as we watched the doctor walk away. "Why would anyone want to poison Marnie Vasquez? If the Simonstech connection is the common factor with our victims, Marnie doesn't fit."

"Maybe it was an accident." Solomon took my elbow and guided me over to the windows, away from listening ears. Not that I could actually see any, but he was taller than I, and could easily see over partitions. Besides, he hadn't just saved someone's life, so he wasn't feeling antsy, and I figured it was better if we erred on the side of caution. We leaned there with our backs to the outside world and our butts perched on the sill. From here, I could see through the observation window. Marnie was lying in her hospital bed, the covers pulled up to her waist. She looked pale and sickly in her hospital issue gown. An IV tube led from her wrist to a bag on a pole next to her, and she seemed to be sleeping. "We know that Schwarz's killer knew his routine. The killer could have known Lorena's too, and exactly what she would consume every day like the coconut water after her run. Maybe the poison was intended for Lorena, and when she didn't die fast enough, the killer changed his plan," Solomon said.

I looked at Marnie as I answered him with a weak, "Really?"

"I think we need to take a closer look at that coconut water."

"Shouldn't we stay? What if Marnie is still in danger?"

"I think she's collateral damage, but if it makes you feel better, we can wait until the uncle gets here." Solomon nudged me and inclined his head towards the dark-haired man approaching us. "Coincidentally, I think that might be him. Let's go."

We took a few minutes to talk to Marnie's uncle,

Marco, before we left. The doctor had already filled him in on his niece's condition, but again, I gave my account. I assured him that I was positive Marnie didn't do this deliberately, and at the end, he hugged me and thanked me for saving his niece. He also expressed his concern for my own health, after being the one who discovered his sister, which I thought was extremely kind of him, considering his own loss. When I asked him who he thought could harm his sister, he shook his head sadly. I tried asking him about Simonstech too, but all he could tell me was that his sister told him she was scared of something. He was pleased, he said, to have her work with him and she seemed much happier.

"Can you find out who tried to hurt my niece?" he wanted to know, after telling me that his sister had mentioned my name a couple of times. He reached into his back pocket, coming up with a leather wallet. "I can pay."

"We're already on the case," said Solomon, waving away the bills the man extracted. "No charge, but it would be helpful if we got your permission to look around your sister's house."

"Do whatever you need to do," Marco readily consented, producing a key from his jacket pocket and pressing it into Solomon's palm. "I heard my sister called you the day she was killed. Do you know what was worrying her?"

"I wish I knew," I said. "I'm still trying to find out."

"Now I think about it, I'll bet everything I own that it has something to do with that creep at Simonstech," he said, shaking our hands. "You should try asking them why he scared the shit out of my sister so badly, she had to leave her job." He pushed through the door and was gone. Picking up his niece's hand, he mashed his lips together, looking like he was about to cry. I turned away, loath to observe his grief.

Solomon and I looked at each other. "All the roads

keep leading back to Simonstech," I said.

"Too bad Carter Simons Junior has alibis for the murders."

"How do you know that?"

"It came up at my meeting with your brother and your ex."

"You could just call them Lieutenant Graves and your former colleague, Maddox."

"Works either way." Solomon was silent as we walked out to his car and didn't speak again until we were on the road. "I want you to stay away from that Simons guy," he said. "His name keeps coming up and I don't like it. I have a bad feeling."

"Is this a bad time to confess Lily and I went by his house?"

Solomon slammed on the brakes and we lurched to a stop. "You. Did. What?" he asked, very slowly.

"It was just a short visit, and I didn't even go inside!"

"Lexi!" Solomon slammed his hands on the steering wheel and looked dead ahead. Someone behind us honked and Solomon seemed ready to explode. After what felt like forever, and three more impatient honks, he shifted into drive and we took off. "What happened?"

"Nothing much. We overheard a conversation."

"About?"

"Junior and his wife were talking about a ring. A new one she had made, but it wasn't right or something."

"Were you seen?"

I gulped.

"Lexi?"

"Yes."

"When was this?"

"Right before someone broke into my house," I said softly, trying not to cringe at how bad that sounded. I darted a glance at Solomon. Yup, he looked thrilled. Really delighted. Perhaps I wouldn't mention the complaint. It would only make things worse.

"Lexi!"

"There's nothing that ties Junior directly to any of the murders, and you already said he had an alibi... What exactly were his alibis?"

"At Lorena Vasquez's murder, he was having brunch with his father across town. Simons Senior confirmed it. He has alibis for Jim Schwarz and Karen Doyle too. Both times, he was in meetings with ten other people to vouch for him."

"Damn." I let that sink in before I said, "So far, we only know Junior knew the victims when they were alive, but there's been nothing to suggest he's seen them since. I mean, yeah, he knew all three of our victims, and he knew Avril Sosa, but there's no evidence to link him to any of them. Maybe our hunch that he is hiding something was wrong," I concluded, trailing off. It was a major disappointment. More so, that I suddenly seemed to be defending my number one suspect.

"Evidence can be wrong."

"Don't let the writers from *CSI* hear you say that!"

"Okay." Solomon smiled. "Let me rephrase it. Sometimes, when we don't have all the evidence, the evidence we do have tells us a different story from the real one."

"So we need to find more?"

"You got it."

"Let's go."

"Not you, Lexi."

"But..."

"No arguments. You can help at the Vasquez house, but I want you to stay the hell away from the Simons and anywhere they might be or go. I do not want you pissing them off, and I don't want you getting hurt. Besides, I told you to take a few days off. Work your pro-bono case. You cannot get into any danger with that."

I tried to argue, but Solomon refused to debate my

insistence that I had to see this through. The more annoyed I got, the less coherent I became, so eventually, I gave up, deciding to work on him again when he calmed down. I hoped some new evidence would be exactly the sort of thing he needed to make him realize that taking me off the case was a bad idea.

More evidence is exactly what we found at the Vasquez house. I pointed to the coffee table where Marnie dropped her bottle. Solomon pulled on gloves before picking it up, while I took a deep breath and went into the kitchen. I tried not to look at the faint stain on the kitchen floor, and had to pinch my nose from the lingering scent of bleach. Instead, I went directly to the refrigerator. "There're seventeen unopened bottles of coconut water here," I called out to the living room. "A half full carton of orange juice. The fridge looks like it was cleaned out."

"Check the trash," called Solomon.

I did. It was empty except for one bottle, identical to the one Marnie was drinking. "I see one bottle."

"Don't touch," said Solomon.

"I wasn't planning on touching it," I said, still annoyed, and now sniffy at his assumption I would make a rookie move like that. As he walked through, his hands gloved, he set the bottle he was examining on the countertop and reached inside the trashcan. He extracted the empty bottle, turning it this way and that until he nodded and beckoned me closer.

"See this?" he said, pointing to the neck.

I peered at it. "Nope."

"Closer."

"Okay, but still no. I see nothing. What am I supposed to see?"

"There's a tiny pinprick hole just here, in the neck of the bottle. It's barely visible, thanks to the short, fat neck. I think poison was injected into this bottle, just under the cap rim, and the same as that one. Someone planned to make Lorena Vasquez very, very sick. I wouldn't be surprised if there was enough poison to kill her slowly over time."

"That's treacherous!" I bent at the waist, my hands on my knees as I stared at the first bottle. Sure enough, there was an identical pinprick in the neck, again, barely visible. "But Lorena wasn't drinking the water. She sprained her ankle and hadn't been running, and I know she only drank this stuff immediately after exercise; otherwise, she said it was too calorific."

"So she didn't die as expected," surmised Solomon. "This stuff just sat there."

Thinking of how calculated her death was made me sick. Not to mention, imagining how someone planned to kill Lorena slowly. "The killer couldn't wait. That bastard! She was healthy and wanted to talk to me and he came here to speed up her death. We need to get all the bottles to the lab and have them analyzed. Maybe the killer left a fingerprint."

"Call one of your contacts at MPD and get him to pick everything up. They'll need it for building the case. Before we discovered this, the killer could argue manslaughter of Lorena, a heat of the moment kind of killing, but this changes things. This is murder one."

I made the call to Garrett and told him what we discovered. He agreed to send someone from the forensics lab over right away. Thirty minutes later, we had the unopened bottles packed up in a crate, two tampered bottles bagged and tagged, and one grateful detective in the guise of Maddox himself. I let Solomon deal with him. It was bad enough I had one guy mad at me, never mind two.

"What now?" I asked Solomon when we locked up and returned to his car. Solomon stuck the key in his pocket, resorting to silence once more. "Where do we go from here?"

"Since Maddox just told me about Junior's complaint

against you, you are going to take a few days off and keep a low profile. Give some attention to that pro bono case you accepted and dumped Lily with. How many nights of surveillance has she undertaken?" Solomon asked, his voice belaying annoyance. "Your life isn't in jeopardy on that case."

I swallowed with a gulp. Was there any point in arguing right now? The easiest thing to do would be to absolutely ignore his advice, but the safest thing to do was follow it. That left me with an impossible decision, one that was probably going to blow up in my face no matter which path I took. "Actually, I meant literally. Where are we going?" I asked, as we passed the exit to my house.

"My place," he said.

"What about my place?"

Solomon glanced at me. "Let's assume someone thinks you're getting too close to the truth and knows where you live."

I gulped. "They could break into your house too."

Solomon huffed. "Not a chance. You'll be safe at my house while I get to the bottom of this mess."

CHAPTER EIGHTEEN

Although Solomon called staying at his house "relaxing," it felt more like I was under house arrest. While I poked around his kitchen and rifled through his bookcase in search of some easy reading, he took the opportunity to return to the agency and solve my case. On the plus side, he arranged for my car to be brought over from the Vasquez house. Now it was parked outside his house, so at least, I wasn't completely housebound.

"Solomon's solving my case," I told Lily. "He said, and I quote, 'Lexi Graves you are off active duty'."

"The bastard!" Lily screeched.

"I know, right?"

"Like, how dare he? I am incensed, Lexi! I am outraged!"

"Calm down."

"I can't! I'm burning with fury. Why did he take you off the case anyway? Is it the psycho? Would Solomon lock himself up if someone broke into his house?" Lily asked, without absolute conviction that no, Solomon would not.

"His house is more secure than Fort Knox. If someone broke into his house, he'd probably offer the guy a job. And no, it wasn't the psycho. Someone poisoned Marnie Vasquez. I had to call 911."

"Is she okay?"

"She's in the hospital, still recovering."

"That's not your fault! Are your really letting Solomon take over your case and solve it without you?"

"Hell no. He might be digging for dirt, but there's still plenty of work for me to do," I said, remembering the discs safely ensconced in my bag. "I have surveillance footage to watch."

"That's the spirit," agreed Lily. "That may be as dull as sitting on your ass and watching a bridal store for four hours straight, but you might see the killer!"

"And you might catch a thief!"

"We rock," said Lily. "We rock hard. Call me if you see anything."

I agreed I would and hung up. I had just loaded the surveillance disc into Solomon's DVD player and set it to "play" when Lexi called back. "I need a break. Want some company?"

"I thought you were going to spend the evening with Jord?"

"Me too, but he said he can't make it as he caught an extra shift. He's looking at the burglary division. He said if he puts in some hours covering a shift there now, they might request him when one of the detectives retires next month."

"Good for Jord. Come over."

"I'll be there really fast, just as soon as I get some feeling back into my legs."

I watched the tapes in "fast forward," which was okay since very little happened. I had a few notes of what to look for. One of them was Kate Holm. Maddox hadn't told me where she left the key or retrieved the cash, but I figured it had to be somewhere close to the gym. If I could see where she left it, I might be able to see who picked it up. If I spotted Carter Simons Junior on the tapes, and could prove that he had access to the scenes of the poisoning, I would be ecstatic. Now, that would be the sweetest piece of evidence to take to the team. It would exonerate the gym. As much as I watched though, I saw nothing on the camera feed covering the gym's front entry. Sure, there were plenty of other people, entering and leaving, but no Junior.

I did see Jim, but failed to recognize him at first since it was the back of his head. When he turned to look back, I grabbed the remote and hit first "rewind," then "play," slowing the tape down so I could watch him in some of his final movements. Jim exited the building, wearing jeans and a jacket with the hood pushed down. Over his shoulder was his gym bag and something small dangled in his hand — his car keys, I realized when he stopped at a blue Toyota. He looked over his shoulder, and paused, like someone might've called him, then raised a hand. A moment later, a woman came into view... and Solomon's doorbell rang. I paused the disc and let Lily in.

"I'm at a crucial moment," I told her. "I just found Jim on the gym's video footage the day before his death."

"Is anyone killing him?" Lily asked.

"No, that was the next..."

"Then I gotta pee," she interrupted, dashing past me to the half bath. "Let me know what happens."

I resumed "play" and watched. Jim and the woman were having a conversation. She had dark hair in a ponytail with her back to the camera, and they both seemed a little tense. Finally, the pair of them hugged briefly and Jim got into his car. The woman turned around and my breath hitched.

"Is that Lorena?" asked Lily.

"Yeah. I just watched her and Jim have a conversation. I wish I could read lips." Had I seen Lorena and Jim talking before, ever? I didn't think so, but I didn't spend a lot of time at the gym, so that meant nothing. Marnie said they were in touch and the tape confirmed recently.

"That would be so awesome."

It would be beyond awesome and it disappointed me that I lacked the skills to lip read. I wasn't sure anyone else could do the job either. The camera wasn't that clear, the clarity far from high definition. However, what I could see told me the pair of them were engaged in a tense conversation, but parted affectionately enough. It also told me the two of them were still in contact, despite both having left Simonstech. Had something bound them together still? Seeing them talk definitely added to my theory that the two of them knew something about what happened to Avril Sosa. Perhaps they were discussing what to do next? Another thought occurred to me... Had they previously approached whomever was behind Sosa's disappearance?

Lily and I watched as Jim drove away and Lorena walked off camera. Thirty seconds later, her car passed by the camera, heading towards the exit. I made a note of the time on the tape, and hit "fast forward," my eyes glued to the screen. Nothing else happened, and eventually, the disc popped out. I exchanged the disc for another that came from the camera covering the rear of the building and the employee parking lot.

"You know, if the cop TV shows showed how long you guys have to spend sitting around doing nothing, but staring at screens, no one would ever watch them," said Lily. She found popcorn in the kitchen somewhere, microwaved it, and the two of us shared the bowl between us. We watched as we munched. "Also, next time we hang out, I'll pick the movie."

I hit "pause," then "rewind." "Got something."

"Yay. About time!"

"Only because I started the video just before Kate Holm's shift ended." It was risky to skip so much of the footage, but I figured I could watch the rest later. Now I had one piece of evidence, I was keen to find another, anything that would get me back on the case.

"Good call. You're a good investigator no matter what your boyfriend says."

I blinked. "Did he say I wasn't?"

"Noooo!"

"You'd tell me, wouldn't you?"

"You're my best friend, I tell you everything, even the crappy stuff."

"Thanks."

"Now let's find out what that moron, Kate, did." We watched Kate walk across the parking lot, past the car I knew to be hers and pause before the dumpsters. She pulled something from her pocket, then a small strip of what looked like tape before reaching around the back of the first dumpster, and seeming to pat it on the back. Her hand came back with an envelope and she opened it. "She's going to get fired," said Lily.

"I think so," I agreed. "That looks like she left the key and collected the cash."

"Mmm-hmm." Lily stuffed another piece of popcorn into her mouth. In her pocket, her cell phone beeped a tune and she reached for it, wiping her butter-glazed fingers on the tissue I passed her. "It's Sharon," she said while I continued to watch the tape. As Lily spoke, I watched Kate stuff the envelope into her pocket, get into her car, and drive away. I made another note of the time and hit "fast forward," and the scene quickly moved from daylight to dusk, shrouding the parking lot in darkness.

"That was Sharon," said Lily. "She said a van has passed by the store six times in the last hour and she's just about ready to leave."

"Why is she there so late?"

"She felt bad that I sat there all afternoon for nothing."

"That's nice." I contemplated the strange van. "Maybe it's a delivery driver looking for someone."

"She thought that until the fifth trip when she closed the store. She tried not to make it obvious she was watching, but she said she felt like they were casing her store."

"What made her think that? Did they slow down?"

"No, just a feeling she got."

"Hmm. Hold that thought." I almost missed it, but when I rewound the tape, there he was, a dark-clad figure, moving in the shadows of the building, and almost completely hidden from view. I had to concentrate to follow him, but again, there he was, passing under a sliver of moonlight, to approach the dumpster. He wore his jacket collar turned up and a beanie pulled down low over his ears, his face never turning towards the camera. It was like he knew it was there. He reached around the back of the dumpster, retracting his hand a moment later. Keeping his head down as he turned, he jogged back towards the building, disappearing under the camera. "That's our guy and he just went inside."

"Is it Carter Simons?"

"I can't tell." A few minutes later, the feed cut out, the tape dissolving into white noise. "I have to get this stuff to the agency. Maybe they can clean it up."

"On the way back, maybe we could watch the wedding store for a little while?" Lily checked her watch. "It'll be like old times!"

"I guess." I looked around Solomon's warm and inviting living room. What else was I supposed to do? Wait at home for my boyfriend to return and ask him how the case was going without me? No, I couldn't do that. Plus, didn't he suggest that I spend some time on my pro bono case? I'd already left Lily doing enough monotonous surveillance so I owed her the company. I ejected the discs and slipped them into their plastic wallets. "Sure, let's do that. Let's go."

At the agency, I parked outside before Lily and I went to the reception desk, rather than heading upstairs. The last thing I wanted to do was risk running into Solomon if he were in the building. Instead, I left the discs with the doorman, along with the note about the times to check, and called Lucas, asking him to come down and get them.

"Where are you going?" he wanted to know. "Solomon said you're not working the case anymore."

"I am, just not actively. And I'm hanging out with Lily tonight," I told him without divulging where or why. "Do you think you can do anything with the footage?"

"I won't know until I see it, but there's an AV specialist upstairs in the new suite. She might be able to work her magic on it."

"Why do we need an AV specialist?" I asked, thinking about the woman I'd seen with Solomon in the underground garage just a few days ago. Was that her? "And why is she upstairs?"

"To do extra cool stuff with audio and visuals. There's more space up there. You should see the gadgets! And the computers!" Lucas reeled off a list of things to do with terrabytes and processing speeds and other things I never heard or conceived of. I wondered again at the new division. Why did our investigations agency need so much high tech stuff? What was Solomon expanding into? More importantly, given how badly I'd annoyed Solomon, would there be a place for me in the agency after the expansion?

"Sounds great. Is Solomon up there?"

"No, he's in the boardroom with Delgado. They're going over your case, trying to find hard evidence to link this Simons guy to your victims and the other Sosa chick. Want me to tell them you called? Any message?"

"Just show them the discs and no message," I said, hanging up, hoping I didn't sound as peeved as I felt. "Let's go," I told Lily and she simply nodded and followed me out.

There was no sign of the mystery van when we reached Perfect Brides and we got there just as Sharon was locking up. With the businesses closing, there were plenty of parking spaces, but little cover, so I parked a few stores away rather than sitting on the store, which would immediately give us away. A few minutes later Sharon's car pulled around the corner and she waved as she passed.

"I pick up my dress next week," said Lily. "I said to Sharon, maybe I should pick it up today, but she was finishing a few alterations on another dress, and said she couldn't do the last bits on mine until tomorrow."

"Don't panic. Your dress will not get stolen. You're going to look gorgeous on your wedding day."

"I know."

"So we'll watch the store tonight. Everything will be okay," I decided," and tomorrow, you can get your dress."

"And yours," Lily added.

"And mine," I agreed. "And then all we have to do is wait for the wedding."

"And my bachelorette party!"

"That too. See? It's all going to be fine." I settled into my seat, pleased at just how positive I sounded. Not only that, but Lily would be able to relax for a few days before her bachelorette party. Then, providing she didn't lose her eyebrows or get taped to a street lamp, she would make it to the wedding, looking perfect. Not that I wanted to take any credit for ensuring her dress's safety, but I gave myself a virtual pat on the back anyway.

We had been sitting there for an hour, chatting occasionally, talking about the cases, and fantasy weddings, when Lily grabbed my arm, quieting me. "There's the van," she said, as a mid-sized, white van slid past. "Exactly as Sharon described it."

"Yeah, but it's not stopping. It just took a left."

"I kind of expected the store to get ram-raided tonight," said Lily. "Is it bad to admit I was almost hoping it would? Then all those nights I sat here, watching the store, wouldn't be for nothing."

"A ram-raid would be exciting."

"Yeah. Guess those concrete posts in front of the store are there for that reason."

I nodded, looking at the defensive pillars. As I turned my head, noticing how all the businesses, barring a couple of restaurants further down the street, had closed for the night, it occurred to me that every single store front had its own set of thick, cement guard posts, installed to prevent vehicles from mounting the curb and crashing over the sidewalks into their stores.

"All the stores got ram-raided, right?" I asked. "That's how the thieves got in?"

"Yep. Smashed and grabbed."

"But this one can't. Look! You said it yourself, no one can enter from the front."

"Does that mean we can go home?" Lily asked, looking hopeful.

I put my palm to my forehead and groaned. "No, it means we've been watching the wrong side of the store."

"There's a back entrance," Lily said slowly, pulling a face to match my own. "Sharon told me she parks her car in the back."

"Let's go." We buckled our seatbelts, I gunned the engine, and we drove around back. I pulled onto the side street when Lily pointed out the entrance to the rear parking lot that spanned the length of several stores. "I don't see the van. We need to get closer."

"What if we drove in?"

"If they're in there, stealing stuff, they might crash into my car, trying to get out. Or worse." I shuddered to think about that. I really didn't want to get hurt again in the line of duty by solving a mystery. My arm was already healing nicely and didn't look like it would scar. No reason to tempt fate.

We jogged over to the wall that blocked our view, and, with our hands in pockets, strolled past the gates, like we were walking home after being out for an early evening dinner. As we passed through the gates, both of us took a not-so-casual glance inside. "There's the van," squeaked Lily, grabbing my injured arm. I winced, but she didn't notice. "That's it. That's definitely the one! This is so exciting!"

"Keep walking," I told her, urging her on, looking for somewhere we could hide and watch, unobserved. "The alley will do." We passed the gates, allowing another wall to conceal us before we ducked into it. It smelled rotten, predominantly because of wet leaves, and I didn't want to think about what I could be stepping in if I were really unlucky. We had to walk fifty feet or so before we could peek over the wall, and through the chain link fence that rose above it. The van was parked next to an open door, but I couldn't quite make out which store it was.

"Maybe they're making deliveries," I suggested.

"Uh-uh." Lily shook her head vehemently. "Just wait."

We waited. After a few minutes, nothing happened and I had to lean down to rub the backs of my calves, which were now aching a little after standing on my tiptoes. "Here they are," whispered Lily furiously, her fingers gripping the top of the wall. "They have the dresses and they're loading them."

I sprang up, reaching again to see. Lily was right.

Two men had several garment bags in their arms, and all of them were white except for a pink bag. Lily gasped and grabbed my arm. "That's my dress!" she hissed. "They got my dress! It was stored in a pink bag!" As we watched them tossing the dresses through the doors, one of them stuck his head inside the building and I caught the sound of his voice, but lost what he said at being such a distance away. After a moment, a woman exited, pushing the door to the bridal store closed with a slam of her shoulder. The two men shut and locked the van doors and all three of them climbed into the cab.

At the same moment, my phone quietly buzzed in my pocket. I kept one eye on the van as I extracted it, glancing down. Solomon. Whatever it was, it could wait. I hung up.

"They're getting away," said Lily. I grabbed her before she could run after them. "We have to stop them!"

"We could get run over. Let them go."

"Nooo! My dress is in there!"

"We'll follow them." My phone vibrated again, and once more, I hung up, returning the phone to my pocket. The van passed us before we jogged to the end of the alleyway, leaving us free to sprint across the road. I beeped my car open and we clambered in.

"Follow that car!" yelled Lily, her voice rising somewhere north of hysterical. "Follow! That! Car!"

"I am! And it's a van."

"I know it's a van!" she screeched, grappling with her seatbelt. It clicked into place and she flopped back in the seat, her breathing heavy. "But haven't you always wanted to say that?"

I admitted that I did, but the next best thing was being the awesome driver who caught them! With that thought in mind, we shot off after the van, turning left around the block and catching sight of them fleeing toward the end of the street. With no traffic between us,

I cooled it on the gas and followed slowly.

"They took a right," said Lily, as the van turned right.

"I see it." I gripped the steering wheel, my knuckles turning white. Should I speed up and risk being seen? Or slow down and risk losing them? Those questions crossed my mind more than once as we followed the van through several turns until it hit the highway heading out of town. Amongst traffic, I felt calmer. There was less risk of them spotting us, with my car being just one of many. I had to hope they were confident enough in their heist that they weren't worried about being followed. All the same, I matched my driving to theirs: calm, maintaining my speed just under the limit, carefully obeying every sign and signal. We followed them for several miles, past residential areas that gave way to industrial units and further still.

"Where are they going?" asked Lily, searching the signs as they appeared.

"Beats me. There isn't much out here," I recalled, this route being so far off my usual stomping ground. "We're heading the wrong way for the city and we missed the turn for the freeway."

"Maybe they're meeting someone else to transfer their bounty."

"They're not pirates," I said as the sign for the docks flashed past and the van, several cars ahead, indicated it was taking the turn. "Actually, maybe they are."

"Huh?"

"We're going to the docks."

"I don't think fisherman are wearing white this season," Lily quipped and I had to laugh.

"Or tiaras. Anyway, this is where the tankers come into port. There're lots of storage containers there. Maybe they're planning on storing the dresses in one. They're big enough. Who would ever search for them there?"

"Not I," Lily replied. "But then, I'm not a gangster. Also, how lucky is it that you turn up for surveillance and Perfect Brides gets hit?"

"You wanted it to happen!"

"I changed my mind!"

The van's headlights disappeared as it turned after heading through the docks. Now that there were only the two of us entering the shipping yard, I held back, advancing slowly. We passed through the gates and braked, searching for the van. The yard was vast. Row after row of containers, some packed three and four deep, the alleys between them, dark recesses.

"There," said Lily, pointing and I caught a flash of headlight.

"We can't keep driving," I told her, "It's too suspicious. We'll follow on foot. We won't be seen that way."

I turned the car in a half circle, and parked it between two other vehicles, in the semi-full lot, figuring it was less conspicuous there. One of the cars had a flat tire so I assumed it must've been there a while, and the other probably belonged to a dockworker. Even better, we were pointed toward the exit in case we had to make a fast getaway. As I climbed out, glad I'd switched my heels for sneakers, Lily reached into her purse, extracting two flashlights and handing one to me.

"No dog bone?"

"I gave it to Barney. He was such a good boy, rescuing you."

"Aww."

"And you didn't think that bone would come in useful! Now, let's rescue my dress."

It took us twenty minutes of searching before we found the van. By the time we got there, it was empty. After a few minutes, spent observing it from the darkness of an alleyway, we came to the conclusion that no one was returning. "Watch my back," I told Lily.

"Why?"

"I'm going to see if the dresses are still in the van."

"And if they are?" she pressed.

"I'm going to call the cops."

"I was hoping you would get my dress first, then we could call the cops."

"Just make a diversion if you hear anyone coming."

"Okay."

Before Lily asked me how, I jogged across to the van and peeked into the passenger window. Nothing was in the cab. No people and nothing to suggest who they were. Keeping my shoulder to the van, I jogged around the side to the back and tested the handle. It opened easily, the door swinging backwards. I took one look, eased the door closed, and paused when I heard a voice. Someone was approaching. I waited tortuous seconds before I heard a footfall on the far side of the van. Quick as a flash, I moved around to the other side of the van, and crouching low, ran back to Lily, sliding back into the shadows as Lily's flashlight flickered off. Two men stepped out from the other side of the van. One lit a cigarette and said something in another language and the other laughed.

I took Lily's hand and drew her away.

"What did you see?" she whispered as we stopped at the other end of the container.

"Nothing. It was empty!"

"Where's my dress?"

I waved my hand in a large arc. "My guess? In one of these containers."

"How do we know which one? There're hundreds."

"Maybe thousands," I agreed, realizing my estimate wasn't helping matters albeit too late. "It can't be far. They wouldn't have parked too far away. If we circle around, we'll find it, I'm sure." I looked up at the container. It was a dark, rusted red, the same as the one opposite. Above us, I thought the container was dark blue, but it could have been because of the dim lighting. It hardly mattered, since the containers were unidentifiable. "We need to find a number or something," I told Lily, "otherwise I can't tell the cops where to look."

"The doors have numbers painted on them. I noticed when we were looking for the van."

"That's great, Lily!"

Lily beamed. "Not just a pretty face, but an amazing body, and an exceptional mind!"

"Funny, I was going to say the same about me, but I was waiting for the right moment."

We probably walked back on ourselves a couple of times before we caught the sound of voices and cautiously moved towards them, ending up in the alleyway, opposite an open container. We hung back, and the position of the moon enabled us to see them, but they couldn't see us. I didn't want to test that theory so I insisted we only peek around the back of a container. There were five of them: one woman and four men. I recognized one of the men as the man I heard talking by the van, and the woman from outside Perfect Brides, but I still couldn't make out their accents, not to mention identify their language. Occasionally, one of them said an English word, but mostly, their conversation was lost on me. Beyond them, in the container, were dozens of boxes and garment bags, the long line of them receding into the dark. Several more garment bags were tossed on the floor outside, not yet loaded. Another container lay open, but it was cast in shadows and I couldn't see inside.

"Let's go," said one of them clearly after some kind of discussion in which they nodded and gesticulated while pointing at the container. "Ten minutes, okay?" he added, resuming his own language again. Whatever it was, they all followed him, leaving the container wide open.

"Where did they go?"

"I don't know."

"My dress has to be one of those!" Lily said, pointing to the heap on the floor. "Let's get it. Come on. We'll be gone before they even know."

"We can't. It's too risky."

"I know, but we need the container number," Lily pointed out, "and we can't see it with the doors open."

"Okay," I conceded, my heart thumping. "Okay, I'll get the container number. You grab your dress and then we run faster than we've ever run before straight back to my car. Deal?"

"Deal."

We sprinted to the container. I rounded the door, searching for the number. It wasn't there! I lurched around, racing to the side, and around the door. There it was. Letter J, number 341. I repeated the code as I stepped out. Lily had a garment bag in her hand, but as she turned to me, her face fell. "I could only find your bridesmaid dress," she said, looking past me. "Mine is still in there."

"We should go. They said ten minutes."

"We have seven more minutes," Lily said, "it has to be just inside. There it is! Lexi, there it is! I see it. It's the only pink bag. Here, put this on!" She thrust the bag into my arms as she raced past, reaching for the pink garment bag.

"What?"

"Put it on," she insisted, wrenching open the bag and pulling out her dress. "I am not losing these again!" She stepped inside her dress and pulled it on over her jeans and sweater. "Put it on, Lex. You won't drop it if you're wearing it and it keeps your hands free."

That seemed like a good idea to me, but later I would claim not to know what was going through my mind at that moment. I pulled on the dress, getting it up to my hips when I heard feet on the tarmac, and footfalls that were heading towards us. Then one loud voice, followed by another. Across the small clearing, came another set of footsteps, but their echoing made it impossible to hear from which route they came. If we crossed the clearing now, we risked being seen by whoever was behind us, or running into whomever was ahead of us. There was only one thing to do. I grabbed Lily's hand and pulled her into the container, pushing her into a crouch behind a bulging rack of garment bags. I put my fingers to my lips, trying not to jump as a faux fur stole landed on my lap. I was tempted to wrap it around my neck for warmth, but instead, I flicked it onto the floor.

"Maybe we should have called the police after all," said Lily.

"That's what I'm doing," I hissed back, my hand shaking as I set up a text message. *J341 docks*, I typed, then *911*. I typed Maddox's name and hit "send," just as the garment rail was yanked forcibly over, and all the dresses landed in a fluffy mess in front of us. Right then, a beam of light flashed into my eyes.

CHAPTER NINETEEN

I've been through a lot more scary things than looking down the barrel of a gun. I probably would have been more afraid if I had actually seen the barrel of the gun; but it was a small model, and not quite as terrifying as being threatened by a sawn-off shotgun. I fully intended to rethink my fear response later, assuming I lived through this.

"Get out. Very slowly," said the man in an unidentifiable, but heavy accent. He held a flashlight in one hand, the gun in his other and used the flashlight to motion us forwards. His face was hard and angular, his chin covered in several days' stubble. A knit cap was pulled over his hair, covering it completely and he had a black windbreaker zipped right up to his chin. "Get out of container and put your hands up."

I darted a glance at Lily to see how she was taking it as we rose, shuffling past the stolen dresses in our own finery. Instead of appearing frightened, she looked furious. Her chest was rising and falling quickly and her cheeks were pink. Her hands were perched defiantly on her hips and her lips pursed. "If you —" she began, addressing the gang spread before us. Of the four men and one woman, each had a gun trained on one or the other of us, and their faces were inscrutable, which didn't bode well. Lily continued, " — If any of you even think about shooting this dress, I will kill you. If even a drop of blood gets on it, I will not only kill you, and very slowly, but I will haunt you. Forever. I will move the furniture in your homes, I will pinch you, I will throw crockery at your heads, and you will never ever get away from me if you hurt my dress!" she screamed.

"She'll do that if you hurt me too!" I yelled after her because righteous indignation seemed perfectly timed for this moment, and what else was I supposed to do? "And I'll help her haunt you! We will scare the living shit out of you forever because that's what besties do!"

The gunman looked over his shoulders at his gang and made a slow, circular movement around his ear. How rude!

"Don't make me come over there and smack you!" yelled Lily, "I am not crazy. I'm getting married and bloodstains just don't cut it when you're walking down the aisle. You stole my dress and I'm stealing it back. I knew I should have insisted on taking it home," she said as an aside to me. "Next time, make sure I take it home."

"There won't be a next time," I assured her, turning to the gang. "I'm her bridesmaid. Bullet holes are not good accessories on bridesmaids!"

"You two are nuts," said the gunman. "Shut up or I'll shoot you. Her first, then you because she is crazy one! Though maybe you crazy too!"

"I am not!"

"You're really trying my patience," yelled Lily. "I might just go Bridezilla on you!"

"Enough!" yelled the gunman, seemingly at a loss as to whether to shoot us or keep yelling.

"Shoot them and throw them in the bay," ordered the woman. Her voice was heavily accented also, but her

English was pretty good. I suspected there would be a few bridal store owners who could recognize her in a lineup. "We don't have the time to waste for this."

"I'm not shooting them," said the man. "I steal stuff. I don't kill people. Plus… you heard her." He waved his gun at Lily, but she didn't flinch.

The woman sighed. "The crazy girl cannot haunt you. She will feed the fishes."

"Actually I'm going to get married. And we don't have time for this either. Lexi, let's go." We started to walk away. I don't know what made Lily think that would work, or why I should follow, but the important thing was: we tried. For a moment, the gang members were too stunned to do anything, then a bullet exploded against a nearby shipping container and the shouting resumed. "Stay where you are!" yelled the man.

"Take off your dresses!" yelled another male voice.

"Shoot them!" screamed the woman.

"Make up your minds!" yelled Lily.

"Maybe we should take off the dresses," I suggested softly. We were frozen to the spot. Too scared to move, too incensed to want to stand still. Plus, one of the gang really wanted to shoot us, and I suspected the others weren't too far behind. "It's hard to run and hide while we're wearing these."

Lily looked appalled at hearing that. "No way! I paid for this dress. It comes with me."

"We need to go," said another man, his gun pointed at my chest while he spoke to the woman, who was clearly the leader. She replied in their language and he shrugged. "Let's forget the dresses. We have enough and the ship is departing soon. If we don't get the container loaded, they'll leave without us."

Again, the woman spoke rapidly. Again, he simply shrugged, turning to the others who also gave disinterested shrugs. I had the awful feeling something was decided and it wasn't to release us.

"You," said the woman, advancing closer. "Get in a container."

"Are you kidding me?" said Lily. "We just got out of one."

"You're not coming with us," the woman explained. "You get in empty container. I can't sell dresses that smell of American corpses." She fired a shot into the ground a few inches from Lily's feet and Lily shuffled backwards.

"I'm a little bit Irish," I said, holding my thumb and forefinger up. The woman turned the gun on me and I edged backwards too. It was bad enough that we were backed into a corner, but as I glanced over my shoulder, and saw the dark depths of the empty container, my stomach flipped. So what if the container wasn't scheduled for loading on this particular ship? It was going somewhere eventually. Or nowhere. I didn't fancy the chances of anyone looking for us. All Maddox had was the number of the container holding the dresses. A quick glance at this container showed me the numbers weren't sequential. We'd be dead before they found us.

"We have to run," I murmured to Lily. "We cannot get into that container. If we do, we're toast."

Lily hitched up her skirts and nodded. "What's the plan?"

"You go left, I'll go right."

She straightened up and fixed me with an incredulous look. "That's it? You couldn't come up with something better?" The woman yelled at us, interrupting our quiet, but tense conversation, and we edged back a little more, stalling for more time while we still could.

"Um... then run. Run really, really fast." When unarmed, outnumbered, or utterly unable to fight back, and/or wearing a really fabulous dress, sometimes running is simply the best policy.

"Can't you ninja-kick them? Then we could tie them up."

"Are you kidding me? All of them? Despite there being five of them and me, with only two legs, I am not a ninja!"

"Fine," agreed Lily, reluctantly, "We'll run."

"On three. One, t... Lily!" I yelled just as Lily ran left and a bullet exploded, hitting the container behind the gang. Someone yelled, "Police! You're surrounded!"

Raising his weapon, our captor returned fire. There was nothing else to do, but run for it, so I grabbed my skirts and ran to the right. Behind us, the shouting started, then the bullets, flying to my left and right until I was around the corner. The shooting continued, but as I pressed against the sides of the container, I realized they were no longer being fired at us. I edged quickly away as a stream of SWAT moved past me, their weapons raised. One waved at me. I waved back, simply because it was polite and I didn't want to be rude, even under pressure. Plus, from what I could see of his jaw, I was pretty sure we dated briefly. Terrific kisser. The things he could do with a... where was I? Oh yeah. Time to run!

"Police! Put your weapons down!"

I plastered my hands to my sides. The SWAT team rushed forwards, and suddenly, I was alone again in the dark and cold. I knew I should have grabbed the faux fur stole when I had the chance. As the last man passed, I paused briefly to think about my options. There was no way on this earth that I would go backwards, amidst the gunfire that seemed to be subsiding against shouts of "Get down!" and "Throw down your weapons!" No, I did not want to attend that show. I didn't even care that much anymore who came to save us. All I wanted to do was find Lily, get in my car, and go home. I longed to make a hot chocolate and hide under my covers, pretending none of this ever happened.

My plan set, I edged along the container, letting my fingers trail across the corrugated surface. "Lily?" I whispered. "Lily?" I continued my progress, weaving around the container and onto the next, then the next, and the next. There was no sign of Lily. With my heart falling, and the moonlight slipping behind the clouds, I had to concede defeat. I could search all night and not find her in this maze. If I were really lucky, I might even manage not to fall into the docks.

Another thought occurred to me. What if I couldn't find Lily because she was hurt? What if she were bleeding somewhere in her beautiful white gown? What if she thought I abandoned her?

"Liiiiily!" I wailed as I turned around and edged my way backwards. "Lily? Lily? Can you hear me? Lily?" I crashed into something hard. I tried to skirt around it, but the something hard placed two massive hands around my waist. I screamed and one of the hands landed on my mouth.

"Lexi?" said the oversized object. "Lexi! Stop screaming!"

"Umfugalumph!"

"What?"

"Umfugal..." The hand dropped from my mouth. I squinted upwards, but couldn't make out much more than a mouth and the whites of eyes. Not that I needed any visual. I knew that voice. "Maddox? What are you doing here?"

"Came to save you, of course."

"How dare you! I don't need saving!"

"Um..." Maddox paused, at a loss. "You seemed lost."

"Did not!"

"Where are you?"

"In a shipping yard."

"Can you narrow it down?"

"To?"

"To exactly where you are?" Maddox asked, a hint of amusement rising in his voice.

272

There was a long pause during which, I'm sure, we both wondered how I was going to regain my wounded pride. Eventually, I said, "Maddox, are you lost?"

Maddox tutted before grabbing me by the hand. "This way."

"If you insist."

"I know you're lost…"

"Let's not dwell on it. What are you doing here? How did you find me?"

"Funny story," said Maddox. A beam flashed onto the floor and whirled a couple of times. Our footsteps followed in its wake as Maddox guided me forwards. "The burglary squad was looking into a series of thefts from bridal stores and have been watching other local stores in hope of catching the thieves. They got really interested after they noticed a car consistently outside another bridal store. So they started watching it. Can you guess who that car belongs to?"

I had an uncomfortable feeling that I could, but I hated to ruin Maddox's fun story. "Go on," I whispered into the dark as we turned a corner.

"It was a turquoise blue Mini owned by none other than Lily Shuler!" Maddox announced like I just won a prize on a game show. "Anyway, some of my colleagues noticed the driver in a VW, the same night that store got hit. The VW, with two female occupants, took off after the van and ended up here."

"They followed us?"

"Lucky, huh?"

"They shot at us!"

"There was only the two of them. They waited for backup!"

"Were you guys on a donut break or something? They wanted to throw our bodies in the docks."

"The SWAT team would never have let that happen. They had money on you getting out of it before they got here anyway."

"Really? Awww." Warmth hit me, dead center, in the chest. It was nice someone believed in us. "How come you're here?" I asked. For him to have arrived so quickly, he had to have been here before I even sent that text.

"I tagged along for funsies the moment I knew you were involved after your plate was called in. When I got your text, I figured you'd be pleased to see me."

I punched him lightly in the chest. Yes, I was pleased to see him. We were quiet for a few moments, simply following the flashlight's beam, while I thought back to all the things that Maddox called fun. To be honest, tagging along after Lily and me, in the hope of a shootout, wasn't too far off base. It was exactly the sort of thing Maddox liked to do.

"Did you find Lily?"

"Yeah, she's fine. She said you were responsible for the two of you getting out of there."

I smiled. "Kind of."

"You were." Maddox gave my hand a squeeze and I squeezed it back. His palm was warm, dry, and very comforting in the dark.

"You know we had nothing to do with the robbery, right? I took Perfect Brides on as a case and Lily was doing our surveillance," I added, just in case the burglary team wanted to look at Lily and me a little more closely. Come to think of it, now that Jord was interested in a job on their squad, maybe we could put in a good word? Or maybe it was better if we didn't interfere at all.

"Figured that out already."

"Oh."

"Lily wearing a wedding dress wasn't much of a clue," Maddox continued. "It was actually a little incriminating, but she won't take it off. It's pretty. Good job Jord isn't here. Bad luck, you know."

"You call him seeing her in the dress bad luck after

everything we've been through tonight?"

"Yep." The flashlight's beam scanned over me. "Are you wearing a wedding dress too?"

"No!" I exclaimed, following with a mumbled, "it's my bridesmaid dress."

"I can't really see, but it looks cute."

"I was hoping for sexy."

"That too."

"Thank you for coming to find me."

Maddox squeezed my hand again. "Anytime," he said. "So... holding hands in the dark, huh? Lots different from the last time."

Last time we held hands in the dark, it was on a date and I remembered what a beautiful evening it was. I wondered if he wanted me to remember that, how happy we were while dating, or if he was just trying to distract me. "I wish things were different," he said with a sigh.

I didn't reply to that, because what could I say? If I agreed and wished things were different, I wouldn't have Solomon. If I wished things had remained exactly as they were, did that mean I never cared for Maddox enough? I was left with the revelation that "what ifs" didn't exist. My time with Maddox was ruined and that was that. So, when Maddox stopped and turned towards me, letting his hand alight on my cheek while his thumb stroked its way across my jaw, I knew the right thing to do.

"You are absolutely in my heart, Adam, you have to know that, but I'm not going to act on anything. I saw a future with you once, and now... now, I don't. I hate saying it, but it's true." I choked the words out before I lost my nerve, even though I knew I was hurting him, which was the last thing I wanted to do. "But I don't mind one bit saying I see a future with Solomon," I finished.

"You know, that's okay." Maddox's thumb brushed

CamillaChafer

my cheekbone. "We're still friends, Lexi. Always. In some ways, what you just said makes everything easier."

I stepped away, breaking the closeness between us. "How'd that interview go? The one you were all dressed up for?" I asked, just to be conversational as we stepped around a container and into the light.

"Tell you later," Maddox answered as we looked around the same clearing I escaped from only minutes before. The thieves were all on their knees, their hands behind their backs and judging by their stiff shoulders, all were handcuffed. SWAT surrounded them, but that didn't stop Lily from getting in the middle of them, walking in short strides in front of their faces. As I got closer, I could hear her lecturing them on how mean they were to steal wedding dresses and destroy people's dreams. One of the gang was weeping silently, but the others looked bored.

Maddox dropped my hand. I turned to ask Maddox what he wanted to tell me, but he was already walking away. When I called his name, he turned, smiled, waved, and continued walking. A little part of me knew whatever was between Adam Maddox and me was irretrievably lost. That was something for me to think about later. I couldn't dwell on it, or my sudden melancholy again, when I had to make absolutely sure Lily was okay.

"Lily?" I called as I moved towards my best friend.

She wheeled around and threw out her arms. "Lexi, I was so worried about you! I couldn't find you. Then Bryce said he saw you—" She waved at a SWAT guy - how she could tell them apart, I had no clue — and he waved back "—and then Maddox got here and then... You're okay!" She stepped closer and reached out to me. I held my arms up to hug her, but instead of hugging me, she dived at my dress, smoothing out the pleats. "Oh, thank God! It would have been hell to camouflage

276

bullet holes in this sheer material. See what you could have done?" she yelled, turning on one heel to face the burglars again. She pointed to my dress. "Bad people! Bad! Selfish!" She turned back to me. "Let's get it dry cleaned anyway."

"What's going on here?" I asked, turning in half circles to look at all the people gathered nearby us. There were local police and SWAT surrounding the gang, who remained on their knees, the focus of it all.

"It's utterly amazeballs! We cracked an international crime syndicate!" Lily pointed at the open shipping container. "There are hundreds of dresses in that one alone. They think there're lots more containers with dresses from all over the state. The dresses were being shipped somewhere in Europe, then sold on the black market. They would have made a fortune and we stopped them! Cool, huh?"

"Very. You know what's an even cooler idea?"

"Taking on another case? Opening our own agency? Happy hour at my bar?"

"Going home."

Lily nodded as if I just said something incredibly wise. She gathered her skirt in her hands and I hooked my arm through hers. "Let's vamoose."

We didn't go home right away. Instead, I called Sharon and asked to meet her at the wedding boutique. As it turned out, she was already there, talking to a police officer who was taking her statement. By the time we arrived, he was gone and Sharon was sitting on her cashier's chair in the middle of the debris.

"I don't have the heart to clear it," she said, when we entered. It probably didn't help matters that we gingerly came through the open front door and crunched over the broken glass left behind from a shattered display case. She didn't even ask why we still wore our dresses over our clothes.

"We have something to tell you that will make you

feel better," said Lily.

"There's nothing that could make me feel better right now," replied Sharon. "I've lost everything. The insurance money will never come through in time to get my brides their... what are you wearing?" Sharon peered more closely at us. She got up and stepped nearer, her mouth dropping open. "Is that your wedding dress?"

"Yep," said Lily, breaking into a smile.

"But... how?"

"When you asked us to investigate, you were right. The same gang of thieves were targeting the other local wedding stores. Tonight, they did this," Lily waved her hand around, and grinned "and we were here at the right time, ready to follow them."

"You got my dresses back?" Sharon looked from Lily to me for confirmation and we both nodded proudly.

"Yes, we got all of them," I told her. "The police caught them before they could transfer all your dresses. There're a few missing, but almost everything they stole from here will be easy to identify. I can make some calls and try and speed up the process."

"I don't know what to say. How can I ever thank you?"

"Don't thank me, thank Lily," I told her. "She did all the work. I just caught the grand finale."

"I thought everything was gone, everything except..." Sharon stopped and gasped, her hand flying to her mouth as she looked at Lily. "I know exactly how to say thank you. Come with me." She barely seemed to care as we crunched over the glass, tracking some of it into the fitting room. We followed her through the curtains, into the storage area beyond, and then to a door. She unlocked it, ushering us into a small room. We stepped inside and Sharon flicked on the lights, illuminating a stunning dress on the dressmaker's model. I recognized it immediately as the dress Lily had turned away because it was too expensive. Sneaking a look at Lily, I knew she recognized it too.

"I saw a little tear in the lace so I brought it back here to repair earlier today. That's why I couldn't do the last alterations on yours until tomorrow." Sharon pointed to an area on the lace, and I saw nothing but perfection. "I remembered you liked this one more than the dress you chose. Please, take it. I'll refund you for the dress you already bought."

"I couldn't," Lily breathed. "It's too much. It's…"

"Yours," said Sharon. "Free. Take it as my thank you."

"No, no, I really can't," Lily insisted. "Thank you, but I can't. Lexi investigated really and I just…"

"I barely did anything. It was Lily," I told Sharon. Sure, I asked a few questions and undertook some surveillance, but Lily bore the brunt of the workload. It would be unfair of me to take any credit. "I just got shot at a couple of times after pissing people off."

"That's true," agreed Lily.

"Please take the dress. I want you to have it," Sharon insisted. "You've earned it."

Lily nearly bowled Sharon over when she threw her arms around her. "Thank you, thank you," she whispered over and again. "I love it."

My cell phone rang as Lily shimmied out of the dress she liberated from the thieves so I excused myself. I walked from the little dressmaking room where dreams came true into the fitting room. The number was unregistered, but that wasn't new for me. My number got around in my daily business. Speaking of which, I had two messages from Solomon still to listen to and a lot of explaining to do.

"Hello?"

"Lexi? It's Marnie. Marnie Vasquez."

"Marnie! Hi! How are you feeling?" I asked, pleased that she sounded so strong.

"A lot better. The doctor says I was really lucky. I was poisoned, you know."

"I know. We think it was in the coconut water you drank."

"Yeah, I guessed as much. It was the only thing I drank at my mom's house and it got me thinking. There's not a lot you can do in the hospital, you know."

"Tell me about it." I didn't mean that literally, but Marnie continued. "I'm sorry to call so late. I was thinking a lot about my mom and I remembered she gave me something when she visited me last month. She said I should hold onto it, just in case something ever happened to her. I asked her what she meant at the time, but she didn't want to talk about it; and then we got busy doing other things, and I didn't really think about it again. Recently, I remembered it and now I believe this must have been what she meant. In case anyone hurt her."

"What did she give you?"

"A DVD."

"Have you watched it?"

"No, but I have it here with me at the hospital. My uncle brought my bag and some clean clothes and it's in there. I have my laptop here too, but I wanted to tell you first. I thought if I watched it, and didn't like it, maybe I wouldn't want to tell anyone about it, and Mom always brought me up to be honest."

"You did the right thing. Does anyone else know about it? Your uncle?"

"No. No one."

"Okay," I said, the wheels in my mind spinning. Whatever was on that DVD was important enough for Lorena to hide it. Perhaps she meant to use it as insurance since we already agreed she knew her life was in danger. It could be the key to everything. If the killer even suspected Marnie had it, however, her life could be in danger again. It was imperative that I immediately went to her to discover together what the DVD revealed. "Don't say a word to anyone. I'm on my way."

CHAPTER TWENTY

I asked Solomon to meet me at the hospital, promising to explain everything when I got there. If he were pissed that I'd gotten into danger – again – and ignored his calls, it didn't show once we were finished watching the DVD.

The quiet in the small hospital room was significant as we each digested what we saw and heard. I sat on the edge of Marnie's bed, who was tucked under the covers, one arm resting on top and the IV bag off to her side. Solomon leaned against the wall, his arms crossed, his face thoughtful.

Marnie broke the silence. "My mother should have taken this to the police months ago. She might still be alive."

"She was scared." I took her hand and held it as we all retreated into our own thoughts again.

I couldn't imagine how Lorena Vasquez got through the past couple of years. Her story was long and detailed, but it gave us everything we needed to go to the police. She told us about the night she and two friends, Jim Schwarz and Karen Doyle, witnessed a murder during a Simonstech party that was in full swing. There was nothing they could do to prevent it. They were in a third floor corridor, looking down and talking about how nice the grounds were, and how lucky they were to work for such a great company that really looked after its employees. It was then they noticed their colleague Avril Sosa running across the garden, a man behind her. As they watched, he grabbed her, his hands going around her neck.

Lorena told us that the killer looked up when his victim stopped fighting, and stopped clawing at him, and his hands loosened from around her neck, when he saw them in the window, looking down on him like judges. But she wasn't sure until later that the three of them were actually seen. She described how they watched the killer take Avril Sosa's body away. As she spoke, she wiped away tears and struggled to continue. "He ran away and then he came back," said Lorena, " and he just carried her away. We told each other Avril was drunk, that she just passed out. We were drinking too. Karen videoed it all on her cell phone."

As the three friends were discussing what they saw, frightened and panicking, they decided they couldn't be sure what it was, or if it had somehow gotten embellished. They finally agreed perhaps they hadn't witnessed a murder at all. Maybe Avril just collapsed. Maybe she was drunk. After all, everyone had more than a few drinks that night and Avril was upset earlier. Karen recalled finding her crying in the restroom after Simons Senior's speech. It could have been lots of things, they decided. They weren't even sure whom they saw with Avril. But later, after they sobered up and were heading home, they saw Carter Simons Junior driving away in Avril's car. Alone.

When Avril didn't come to work the next day, or the next, or any days after that, they knew. They were all sure they witnessed her murder and failed to report it.

Carter Simons Junior approached each of them individually over the next couple of days. His threats were subtle. They saw nothing, or were mistaken, he said, or it would come back on them. They were accessories, now, and he would make sure they went down with him for it. They would never see their families again. He would make sure their names were permanently tainted. They would be unemployable. They would lose everything and everyone dear to them.

None of it could bring Avril Sosa back.

Lorena, Jim, and Karen could not live with their guilt and they gradually lost their affection for the company where they previously loved working. Jim took a lesser-paying job, Karen switched careers, and Lorena initially went on unemployment rather than continue working there. They kept in touch though, despite Junior's warnings. It was there, months later, that they started to discuss whether they should do something about Avril's murder. They knew Avril was still considered a missing person. They wanted to give her family some peace by telling them where her body was, if nothing more. They figured she had to be buried on Simonstech land. Jim argued the evidence might tell the police who the killer was, but Karen thought it was too long ago, and any DNA would be compromised. Maybe they wouldn't be prosecuted like Junior had threatened.

Lorena didn't know what to do, so she made the video, just in case, insisting Karen gave her a copy of the cell phone video to include. They all agreed they should give Carter Simons Junior the opportunity to turn himself in. Perhaps, they thought, with the three of them as witnesses, he would do the right thing by Avril's family. Perhaps he was wrong that they would all be charged as accessories. Eventually, the truth had to emerge.

Lorena looked forlornly at the camera as it cut out,

making way for the cell phone footage which we watched silently.

And now that we had the truth, we had to make the decision of what to do next. There were two choices: turn the evidence over or bury it, like Avril got buried for the past two years. I knew what my conscience wanted and what the right choice was.

"We need to turn this in," I said, looking at Marnie, but the statement was really more for Solomon.

"What if my mother gets implicated?" she asked.

"She's already dead," I said as softly as I could. "Nothing can hurt her now. You asked us here so you wouldn't have to make the choice."

"Plus, the circumstances of her death along with this DVD are enough to clear her of any wrongdoing," Solomon added. He reached over and popped the DVD out of the laptop, tucking it into its plastic sleeve, and then inside his jacket. He turned to look at Marnie. "Do not tell anyone you saw this. Do not contact anyone mentioned on this video. Are we clear?"

Marnie nodded. "Clear. He killed my mom, didn't he?" Marnie said, looking at me. "And he killed Avril too."

"I'm sorry, I think so."

Marnie closed her eyes and rested her head on the pillow. I wondered how great a toll this would be on her.

"I'll speak to the uniforms on your door and make sure no one comes in except your uncle. You're not to discuss this with any of them either," Solomon continued.

She opened her eyes. "Just... catch that guy, okay? I hope he rots in hell for this."

"What do you think?" I asked Solomon as we exited the hospital.

"I think multiple counts of murder one look pretty good."

"And Lorena? Do you really believe her name will be cleared?"

"I think the so-called evidence hanging over her head, as well as Jim's and Karen's, was shaky. Fear was the main motivator for them not to say anything. They couldn't know if what Simons said wasn't true. They would never have been charged as accomplices or accessories."

"So they could have just come clean when Avril was killed?" That was depressing. They spent their last two years living in fear. Avril's family never found closure. Ultimately, Jim, Karen and Lorena paid for their silence with their lives.

"Yes."

"Don't you ever want to go into a happier business?" I asked a few minutes later as we hit the road, heading towards the Montgomery police station. I felt tired suddenly, like I could sleep for weeks and never get enough rest.

"Like what?"

"Floristry? Balloon animals? Cake pops?"

Solomon smiled and shook his head. "Cake pops don't give closure to families that need it."

"Taste good though."

"You want to go into cake pops, whatever the hell they are? Investigating isn't for everyone."

"I didn't say that. Are you suggesting that?" I asked, studying him. "You pulled me off a case."

"And if you would check your messages, you would hear me saying that the surveillance footage you pulled from the gym was good. We cleaned up the images and we have one that bears enough likeness to Simons Junior to convince a jury to believe it is he who gained access to poison Jim. Maybe Karen too."

I brightened. "So I'm back on the case?"

"I don't think you were ever off it, no matter what I said. What I will ask is are you at some kind of crossroads here? This isn't a job where you see people happy and at their finest. We deal with people who are sad, miserable, at the end of their ropes as to what they can do for themselves. It can be depressing, but also great. Can you continue to do this day in, day out?"

I didn't need to think about it. "Yes!"

"Then let's try and give some families a sense of closure. Let's help them lay their loved ones to rest. And after…"

"After?"

"After this is all over, we'll go to dinner and I'll make sure there's cake. Deal?"

"I can go one better," I told him. "I know a place where the food will be great and the dessert is wedding cake. Will you be my date to Lily and Jord's wedding?"

"Thought you'd never ask."

~

For the second time that night, I watched Lorena Vasquez's confession. This time, I had the murder squad for company, along with Maddox, who returned to the station some time before, and my brother, Garrett. The moment it ended, the room exploded into activity. Lorena's claims were checked and corroborated, but it was nothing new to Solomon and me. With Junior's now shaky alibis covering the other deaths, the only thing left to do was find Avril Sosa's body.

"I don't hold out much hope," said Maddox as a team was dispatched to Simonstech the moment the warrant came through. Meanwhile, we were in the squad room, a map between us where we pinpointed the body's location per Lorena's description. It was the early hours of the morning and it showed on each of our faces. "Lorena saw this two years ago. She could have mis-remembered details, or maybe the body was moved after that. Even the local landscaping could have changed."

"No," I said, jabbing my finger at a map of the

building. "This is where they saw Avril's murder. The only parking lot is out front, and carrying a body there is too risky, especially with people all over the place, thanks to the party. But here, this area is earmarked as a wildlife reserve. It's unlit at night and there're plenty of trees for cover. With the party being held on the other side of the building, this would be where I would hide a body. Plus, it was supposed to remain untouched while the landscapers replanted the rest of the gardens."

"How do you know that?"

"There was a display in the main lobby. I saw it before we interviewed Joseph O'Keefe." Another thought occurred to me. "The night Lily and I went to Simons' house, O'Keefe had to be reminded to take his medicine. Want to bet he's taking Warfarin and that's what they used as poison?"

"I'm a step ahead of you there," said Maddox. "Jim Schwarz's tox panel came back with aconite. It's a fast acting poison. Death can be instantaneous once it hits the bloodstream."

"That explains the thumb tacks on the spin bike's handlebars." They had puzzled me and I was glad to have an answer. "Wait, I've seen aconite before."

"Where?" pressed Solomon.

"At Simonstech. That model in the lobby of the wildlife reserve. They grow aconite on the land, something to do with lab testing. They even had little painted flowers representing it. No one would go on an area overrun with aconite if it's that deadly. I'll bet that's where Avril Sosa is buried."

"That's another tie to Junior." Maddox took a deep breath. "We still have to sit tight until the body is found."

"Shouldn't we just go and arrest Junior? Right now? If he gets wind of this, he might run."

"We have eyes on his house. He's not going anywhere."

So, we sat tight. We waited and drank coffee and tapped our fingers impatiently, and when I thought I couldn't take the waiting any longer, and my eyelids were starting to droop, the call came in.

We met the morgue van as it arrived and I had to look away when the body was unloaded. "You can't see anything," said Maddox. "She's bagged. They found her near aconite. Good call, Lexi."

"All the same," I said, facing the wall because I didn't want to see it by accident. I don't know why. It wasn't like I hadn't seen a dead body before. Maybe I just didn't want to see another one. Maybe I didn't want to see what happened to a body after a person spent two years beneath dirt and grass. Maybe it's because Avril would almost have been the same age as me now, if she had lived.

"Come on. We'll wait outside," said Solomon. He gave me a push in the small of my back and we were gone, beyond the claustrophobic walls of the morgue.

"Several possessions came in with her," said Maddox, joining us a few minutes later. He had them on a metal tray and poked at them with a pencil. "Cell phone, some jewelry. I checked her missing person's report and the same jewelry is mentioned, but due to the advanced state of decomposition, we'll need dental records to confirm it's her. She had this in her hand." He poked his pencil into a small object and held it up.

"Is that a ring?" I asked.

"Yeah."

"It's too big for a woman's hand," I said, taking the pencil. "Avril was a small woman." I knocked a little dirt off it with the back of my hand and it swung on the pencil for a moment. Something was scratched on the inside and I squinted at it. Writing. Writing that made my eyebrows rise as my mouth dropped open.

Maddox had his cell phone in his hand and was dialing. "We're ready to make the arrest," he told the person on the other end of the phone. "What do you mean, he left already? Follow Carter Simons Junior, and do NOT, I repeat, do NOT lose him." He looked up at me as I waved my hand to get his attention. "What is it?" he asked, frowning.

"A curve ball," I said, holding the ring to Maddox so he could read it. When his eyes met mine, I knew he was just as surprised as I was.

CHAPTER TWENTY-ONE

Carter Simons Junior was yelling at a bunch of uniformed officers in the parking lot by the time we arrived at Simonstech at seven a.m. Unfortunately for him, he also managed to attract a mob of bystanders, employees all arriving to start the day. They stood around looking helplessly bewildered while he went red in the face, pointing, and yelling. That there was a Bobcat digger parked in his reserved parking space probably didn't help matters a whole lot, but that was the least of his troubles.

"Sir?" said Maddox, approaching him. "Sir, if you could calm down please."

"Calm down?" yelled Junior, redirecting his anger at Maddox. "Are you kidding? I got here and there's a friggin' digger in my space and the gardens are all torn up, with holes and tracks everywhere and crime scene tape. What the hell is going on?"

"I think you know the answer to that, sir," said Maddox, his voice smooth and strong enough to be heard over the bystander noise.

"Come on inside, son, and let these people deal with it," said Simons Senior. "They'll inform us soon enough."

"They can't do this. Where's your warrant?"

"It was served on your night security several hours ago. I assure you, sir, the search and excavation were done legally," Maddox replied as the night watchman walked over, holding a piece of paper in his hand. Junior snatched it away from him, reading it.

"Excavation?" asked Junior, looking around as if he truly had no idea. "What the hell for?"

"The warrant authorizes them to search for a body buried on the land," said Simons Senior. "It's a damn shame. Poor person. It's an outrage someone would do this!" There was a ripple of shock and disbelief through the bystanders as the information was hastily retold. "Carter, son, let these people do their job." To Maddox, he said, "Anything you need, officer, you just let us know. I'll be with my staff in the boardroom. Son, we have to help these fine officers do their jobs."

Junior seemed to admit defeat with a fall of his chest and an angry shake of his head. "Fine," he said. "Fine."

"Actually, sir, we can't let you go inside," said Maddox, stepping forwards as the two Simons turned to leave.

"What? Don't you even think about telling me there're bodies in the building too! Isn't it bad enough that you've torn up the land and turned my family's company into a circus spectacle?" Junior pointed to the one lone reporter on the sidelines, making frantic notes.

"No, we don't believe that there are any more bodies here," said Maddox. His shoulders squaring off as though preparing for battle, which, seeing the fuming Junior, might well have happened. "Carter Simons Junior, I have to inform you of your rights. You are under arrest for the murders of Jim Schwarz, Karen Doyle, and Lorena Vasquez, and the attempted murder of Marnie Vasquez."

"You've got this all wrong!"

"Not even slightly," said Maddox, standing his ground. "Your plan was complex, but it wasn't good enough to remain unsolved. You poisoned Jim Schwarz." Maddox looked over at Joseph O'Keefe, who had just pushed his way through the crowd to stand behind the Simons.

"What's going on?" he asked, looking from the two men to Maddox. O'Keefe looked so utterly perplexed, I wondered if his nephew was successful at hiding everything from him. Could he really not know what was going on right under his nose?

"Your nephew used powdered aconite from the land, and his research knowledge, to poison your former employee," Maddox said, taking in O'Keefe's shocked looks as the crowd resumed their incredulous whispering. He returned his steely gaze to Junior. "You knew Karen Doyle was fatally allergic to peanuts, and all you needed was peanut oil, something you could buy at any supermarket, and access to something she would ingest. So you bribed a member of her gym for access. All you had to do was pick the lock to her locker and lace her water bottle. You also tried poisoning Lorena Vasquez, but unfortunately for you, she sprained her ankle and stopped running, and wasn't drinking the coconut water you laced with Warfarin. Unfortunately her daughter drank some. It's the same Warfarin your uncle takes for his heart medication. Isn't that right, Mr. O'Keefe?"

"Well, yes, I do take Warfarin but my nephew would never... he would never..."

Maddox cut him off with a wave of his hand, returning his attention to Junior. "You knew it was only a matter of time before she contacted the police after hearing of her friends' murders, so you opted to stab her instead. The officers searching your house found blood on your sneakers and I've no doubt that it will be an identical match to Lorena's. We have other evidence linking you to her murder."

Two uniforms stepped forwards, catching Junior by the arms. He struggled, lashing out and yelling for his lawyer, but he was no match for the cops. They had him in handcuffs and tightly gripped his upper arms as he wailed and shouted.

"One more thing," said Maddox. "Lift your shirt."

"You have got to be kidding me!" Junior screamed. "You make up this bull and now you want the shirt off my back?"

"I want to see the gunshot wound you sustained when you attacked Lexi Graves in her home," said Maddox and my heart stopped. "We will match the blood at the scene to you."

"Go to hell!"

"My lawyer will have my son out before you can pick up your unemployment check," growled the senior Carter. Behind him stood Joseph O'Keefe, still utterly bewildered.

"Your lawyer will be the only one picking up checks for now," said Maddox, turning to the older man. "Carter Simons Senior, you're under arrest for the murder of Avril Sosa."

"You can't be serious!" Simons Senior yelled as all eyes turned on him, and more than a few mouths dropped open. O'Keefe seemed totally lost for words.

"Deadly serious," hissed Maddox. "We have witnesses. We have evidence."

"There's no evidence. There's no damn DNA on the body you dug up to tie Avril Sosa to me!"

"Funny you should mention DNA, since no one said whose body we dug up," I said, and the two Simons looked just about ready to pop at hearing that.

Maddox grinned, knowing his case was solid the moment we read the inscription on the ring Avril had taken with her to the grave. "That's where you're wrong. You buried Avril with your wedding ring. Lovely inscription from your wife. Her parents thought she'd met a nice man, but in reality she met you. At first I thought maybe she was having an affair with your son but once I put the evidence together... Avril crying in the bathroom after your speech at the office party in which you expressed your love for your wife... then there's the video of her murder. It was you Jim, Karen, and Lorena saw. Not your son. Take him away." Maddox nodded to the uniforms, who marched father and son toward separate squad cars. We watched them being loaded into the back seats.

Solomon nudged me. "Case closed. Do you want to explain all this to Michael?"

I nodded eagerly at the thought of how relieved Fairmount Gym's manager would be now that the gym was in the clear. "You bet!"

"Maddox is waiting for you and I want to talk to the VP. We'll head to the gym after. Good work, Lexi." Solomon moved over to O'Keefe, to talk to him. I held up five fingers as I turned to follow Maddox back to his car, away from the dispersing crowd. Five minutes, that was all I needed to process this.

"Good work, Lexi," he said as we paused by his old sedan. "That was a good catch."

"Do you really think it was Junior who attacked me?"

"Without a doubt. His car got a ticket not five minutes from your house right before you were attacked. He took his car to the garage later that day, where we think he'll try to pretend it was. We'll play with him a bit, work him up a little, then we'll run the traffic cam footage of him driving it."

"Wow."

"Don't thank me. Thank Lucas. He found the camera evidence. I don't know how he hacked in, but since I just signed the agency on as consultants to this case, I can get around that. I only found the ticket."

"I think I'm still in shock. It's not just the attack, I thought Junior killed Avril Sosa until I saw that ring. How could Lorena have gotten it so wrong? She identified the son, not the father."

"They never really saw who killed Avril Sosa," Maddox reminded me. "They assumed it was Junior when they saw him driving away in the woman's car. Senior himself just admitted he knew it was Sosa buried back there. When we analyze the video recording Lorena made on her cell phone that night, we'll know more. I suspect when the video is cleaned up, we'll see Carter Simons Senior, because they were the ones having an affair. He's so old!"

"You bluffed!"

Maddox grinned. "It happens."

"Some women like older men, you know. So, she snatched his inscribed wedding ring during the fight and he didn't realize it was gone until later, when she was buried, and by then, it was too late," I added, my theory for the ring found on Avril Sosa's body. "I overheard Junior and his wife talking about getting a new ring made, and that she didn't realize there was an inscription until her mother-in-law saw the new ring. Senior must have asked his son to commission it. Neither of them could risk disturbing the body to look for the ring."

"He must have known the body would be found eventually."

"Not while he was in charge at Simonstech. Her gravesite would always remain a wildlife have and with the aconite planted around, no employee would go near it. He'd see to that. Plus, Junior got rid of the only witnesses that could tie his father to Avril Sosa's murder."

"Why would Junior help his father? He murdered a woman. The right thing to do was turn him in. The things that motivate people never cease to amaze me."

"Why do people do anything?" I asked, glad Maddox didn't lose his sense of injustice. "Familial love? Greed? Maybe his father promised him the company one day? Maybe he didn't want Simonstech stock to nosedive, thereby leaving him with nothing."

"Maybe we'll never know. This will go to court and trial could be a long time away. Three murders committed just to hide one comes down to collateral damage. I expect Junior, when and if he confesses, will say he couldn't let them go to the cops. I expect he saw them together one day, or maybe they contacted him, and he freaked out. MPD will keep digging. His alibis aren't as rock solid as they first appeared. With Lorena, we only have both men's words on where they were, so that's BS and Junior didn't have to be present to kill his other victims. We know he had access to the crime scene. Both the Simons are going away for a long time."

That made me glad. I hoped it would help the victims' families, and I wondered what it would do to the Simons' families too. "Let me know? Especially if it was him in my house."

Maddox dug one toe into the curb and kicked it lightly a couple of times. "I might not be around," he said. "I'll make sure someone contacts you, but I'm positive Junior attacked you. You must have really scared him when you showed up at his house."

"Good. So... vacation?" I quipped. "Long one?"

"More like a job offer."

"You got promoted?" I grinned. "Maddox, that's great!"

"Not exactly. I was offered a job with the FBI. You remember my contact, Special Agent Matthew Miller from way back?"

"Our very first case," I said, with a nod. "How could I forget?"

"He called me about a month back, said something

came up and was I interested…"

"And you were," I finished. I took a deep breath, thinking of the right thing to say. I would miss him. I would miss working with him, but maybe this would give him a fresh start. A fresh start we both needed, actually. "Congratulations," I said, hugging him. "I'm really, really happy for you. You'll make a great agent."

"We'll always be friends; remember that," said Maddox, pulling his door open. "And I'll still be around. You won't have time to miss me."

"Promise?"

"Promise."

CHAPTER TWENTY-TWO

"Alexandra Graves, release that newspaper and walk down the aisle!" said my mother, yanking the *Montgomery Gazette* from my hands and replacing it with a bouquet of white roses.

"Hey! I was reading that!" The front page story on the Simonstech murder had the whole town talking. It was the stuff that sold newspapers: an illicit affair between a young woman and a much older company president, that ended with her brutal murder. His son had aided in a cover-up, and the only witnesses were terrified into silence and murdered to prevent them coming forward. The undeniable evidence tied the perpetrators to the murders once the police knew exactly where to look. I heard the story was syndicated nationwide. My cell phone was ringing off the hook with reporters wanting to know how a small town PI managed to crack the case, thanks to Maddox giving me credit as a police consultant. Even though it had a nice ring to it, I declined to speak to any reporters. It wasn't that I didn't want to blow my own trumpet, I did, but the important people already knew. Besides that, I knew how difficult my job could become if my face were plastered all over the newspapers and television stations. I guess I'd have to kiss my TV show goodbye. Anyway, ultimately, it was a team effort.

Most of all, like Solomon said, we brought some peace to the victims' families.

Junior confessed the moment he was faced with damning evidence. His fingerprints were found on the envelope with the cash for Kate, he had access to the Warfarin and aconite, and he knew about Karen Doyle's peanut allergy. The bloodstained items found in his home just sealed the case in the eyes of the law. Garrett told me later that Junior helped bury Avril Sosa's body when his father came to him for help, knowing he'd been seen. Junior bullied the victims into silence, believing they would stay mum, until he saw them all together about a month ago. When they contacted him, telling him they would grant him the opportunity to turn himself, he panicked. He didn't want to lose everything because his father had an affair and killed the young woman when she broke it off. His father once told him that he never had any intention of leaving his mother. After expressing his love and gratitude for his wife in his speech at the party, it was enough for Avril to tell him it was over.

Carter Simons Senior would go to prison for murder, along with multiple counts of perjury, and other felonious crimes. His son would serve time for three murders, attempted murder, and as an accessory to a crime.

Just as Maddox suspected, Junior was my attacker. The gunshot wound ensured he couldn't argue that fact away and the blood evidence simply confirmed it. Despite everything else he was charged with, he was damn lucky he escaped the station alive after his panicked attempt at shutting me up. There were a lot of angry Graves that claimed his head after my attack. Me? I was just relieved to have him off the streets.

The respective Carter Simons households were reportedly horrified and refused to give any statements to the press. I understood. It was horrible to be a victim, and downright awful to be related or married to murderers. The Carter Simons probably wanted to fade into obscurity, eventually distancing themselves from the tainted corruption of their menfolk.

It was uncertain what would happen to Simonstech. The employees were all being counseled for grief as the enormity of the situation engulfed them. Four of their colleagues were murdered, and it was only by luck they hadn't seen anything that could have made them victims too. I wondered how heavily their guilt sat with them. I couldn't imagine many being happy while working every day, with an unmarked grave close by, especially after numerous reporters swooped on them for stories of the unimaginable evil that once existed there. I heard through the grapevine (okay, my mother) that Joseph O'Keefe was appointed president and I wondered how long he would last.

Needless to say, Michael and the Fairmount Gym were relieved that they hadn't been at fault, even if both Kate and AnnaBeth lost their jobs. Anton returned but I had yet to take another spinning class. Rumor had it, a new boot camp class was hugely popular with the members.

Somehow though, despite all of that intrigue, a blurry photo of Lily and me in our rescued dresses managed to make page seven of the newspaper a week earlier with the title "Crime-solving Brides." No one else picked up the story and that was all the fame I needed.

The "Meringue Gang," as the burglars were dubbed by the press, were tried and later incarcerated for their part in a string of robberies that spanned three states. Most of the dresses eventually were repatriated to their owners, but many of them, those which the insurance had already paid out and/or the bridal stores had closed, were donated to a community program for low-cost resale. The brides who eventually received the dresses couldn't have been more delighted. It was the best outcome from a crime that struck directly at the hearts of so many couples.

"You don't need to read that," snipped Mom. "This is a much more flattering photo of you than the time you were dressed as a pony," she added. She took a closer look at the newspaper before filing it in the trashcan, and gave me a tacit warning to get on with the wedding program. "You solved the case. Those awful Simons men are going to prison forever, and the weddings of Montgomery are safe from the Meringue Gang! Meanwhile, we have less than an hour for the service. Talk about rent-a-room."

"Okay, okay. I'm going!" I took one last look at myself in the mirror, smiling at my reflection. The gown was lovely, the shoes perfect, but a few yards behind me, I caught Lily's reflection and she made my heart melt. Her new gown was the most gorgeous dress I'd ever seen and she looked stunning with her hair teased into loose waves, topped by a sparkling tiara. "I still can't believe you're marrying my brother," I told her, giving her hand a last squeeze while my mother fussed around us.

"I promise to never consummate the wedding," said Lily, the corners of her mouth barely holding back the laugh she stifled. "I want to put your mind at rest about that."

"I can see in the mirror that your fingers are crossed."

"That would be because I'm lying."

"I'm not listening," sang my mother, her face a lighter shade of purple than her modest, two-piece suit. Lily plucked a rose from her bouquet and pinned it to my mother's lapel as my mother stuck her fist in her mouth and tried to hold back a sob.

"Oh please, Mom. You know what goes on. You've had five kids!"

"I still don't know how," said my mother. "That's my story and I'm sticking to it. And don't ask your father for advice. He's blissfully unaware too."

I doubted that, but I did remember a very awkward "birds and bees" discussion when I was twenty-five, when I had to abashedly inform him how many years too late he was. All the same, he pointed at the service revolver on his hip, told me he had some excellent tips from Montgomery's lowest on how to hide bodies, and could I remind any boyfriends of that if they got too frisky?

In the courtyard, the music started. On the other side of the doors stood Jord, waiting for his bride. Between him and us were dozens of Graves and friends of Lily's and Jord's. Somewhere in there was Solomon, and the idea of me as the bride in a white dress walking toward him gave me heart palpitations. I couldn't tell if they were the good kind or bad, so I felt glad my dress was black.

"Your turn next," said Mom. "Maybe you should do the modern thing and ask your nice man."

"Mom!"

"It's not like you aren't old enough, honey. And how old is Solomon? You've been dating a while now and if you leave it too long, you might not have enough time to have babies. Your ovaries will wither away. How many do you want anyway?"

"Moooom!"

"Garrett has three children, Daniel has two, Serena has one," Mom said, counting them on her fingers. "Five kids and only six grandchildren."

"I'm definitely having babies," said Lily. "Maybe a honeymoon one conceived in Hawaii. That would be awesome. We could call it Waikiki and it would be a really cool story."

"Waikiki Graves?" I mouthed at Lily as she stuck her tongue out.

"You should definitely have two," said Mom, very seriously. "Five is a handful. I've gotten through more crockery than two dozen Greek weddings thanks to all those boys. Thank God we're Irish."

I had no idea why being of Irish extraction had anything to do with crockery, other than my mother hoped not to buy anymore. "No more baby talk, Mom. Solomon and I haven't dated that long."

"You're right. Plus, there's always that lovely Adam Maddox as your back-up choice. He looks very fertile. That said, Serena will probably get married again before you go down the aisle. Isn't Antonio nice?" my mom said, turning to Lily for support. "Hispanic-Irish babies are quite the fashion now."

"Wonderful," said Lily, giving me a "WTF?" face that mirrored my thoughts.

"And so good with the baby. Do you think they'll have babies? Lexi, Solomon will make beautiful..."

I pulled the door open and walked down the aisle before my mother could pester me anymore or the idea of Solomon's babies got stuck in my mind. I was right though, I decided, as I proceeded down the aisle. It was too soon. We were only just getting used to dating each other. Even if our colleagues did now know, I certainly wasn't going to ask him to marry me.

As for the motherhood thing, there were way too many gorgeous shoes in the world for me to contemplate walking in them with swollen ankles. Instead, I decided I would count my blessings. I had a warm, loving family, the home of my dreams, and after my family finished helping me fix it up, it would be perfect. I had a cool job and a great boyfriend. I had a best friend who was always there for me through anything and would now be my sister-in-law. I had another friend I would truly miss, but who would always be in my heart.

I scanned the courtyard as I got closer to Jord, and sure enough, there was Solomon in the second row, seated beside my sister and Delgado. Victoria was crawling into Solomon's lap and she cuddled up to him, the flouncy ruffles of her dress pouring over his legs. He looked down at her chubby face briefly, then up at me, and smiled.

I revised all my plans immediately.

Turning away, I scanned the rest of the courtyard. There was my mother, scooting down the outside of the chairs and taking her place next to my father in the front row. My brothers took up the third and fourth rows with their families, and there were a few members of Lily's family on the bride's side. I didn't see her parents, but then I was almost at the altar and all eyes were turning away to look for Lily.

My heart jolted when I saw Maddox sitting a few rows back with a couple of Jord's friends. He looked gorgeous in his suit, the hue of his tie matching the eyes that once turned me into a babbling wreck. His hair had grown a little and stood in tufts as he ran a hand through it, smiling when his eyes connected with mine. I smiled back. I was going to miss him more than I realized, and my heart gave another little pang at the thought as I turned away, continuing my slow progression to the altar. Stopping opposite Jord and his groomsmen, I wiped away the tear before I turned around.

I didn't remember much of the service later, just how pretty Lily looked when I turned to watch her walk down the aisle, how thrilled my brother was, how the guests cheered when they kissed, how Solomon took my hand and smiled brilliantly at me when we followed the procession outside, and I really couldn't remember a more wonderful day.

Later on, just as the day was giving way to dusk and the sky was a cool, inky blue, punctuated with bright stars, I found myself on the terrace of the Belmont, sipping a flute of champagne and gazing upwards. My tummy was full of food, my veins pumping equal parts of alcohol and blood, and I was feeling merry. In the room beyond, the party was in full flow and the band played loud covers of all Lily and Jord's favorite songs. A brief blast of music had me turning around before it was dampened again by the closing of the terrace doors.

"Didn't think I'd find you out here," said Garrett. He pulled a packet of cigarettes from his jacket pocket and tapped out a stick of death, holding, but not lighting it. "Enjoying the party?"

"It's great. This wedding has been a blast from start to finish."

"With you there," Garrett agreed.

"Hey, do you know where Lily's parents are? I didn't see them at the ceremony or at dinner. Their places at the table were filled, but it wasn't them."

"She didn't tell you?"

"Tell me what?"

"They didn't come. They sent her flowers this morning and a note saying they had some last minute trip with an ambassador of somewhere or other and told her to have a great day."

My mouth dropped open. "No!"

"Yep."

I turned away from the party, annoyance seething through my good mood, sobering me right away. "This is high school graduation all over again."

"Except way worse. How can you miss your only daughter's wedding?" said Garrett. "Horrible people. At least, she's got us, huh?"

"Always," I agreed. "But then she always has."

We stood silently for a while, while Garrett stuck the unlit cigarette in his mouth and didn't smoke it. "I'm quitting," he said, moving it from his lips. "Absolutely, this time. Otherwise, I might not see my kids get married."

That was a depressing thought. "I'll remind you of that anytime I catch you smoking," I told him.

"Please do." Garrett took the cigarette from his mouth and tucked it into the packet, which he returned to his jacket. "Cake?"

"You bet."

"Throwing of the bouquet?"

"One thing at a time!"

Garrett grinned. "Your turn will come. We have a sweepstake on you."

"You've got to be kidding me!"

"Not even a little. You don't want to know the odds on who you're going to marry."

"There're options?"

"Oh, yes." Garrett laughed.

"Who's in?" Garrett pretending to count on his fingers, then pretended to lose count and start again. "Okay, I get the picture. Don't tell me."

"Didn't expect to see Maddox here," he said, changing the subject. Or staying on the same one. It was hard to know which.

"Lily invited him a while ago."

"He left twenty minutes ago."

"Oh?" I said, sensing Garrett wanted to say something else.

"He watched you and Solomon a while. Don't think he's over you. Not by a long shot."

I nodded, because I didn't want to say anything. I didn't know if Garrett was telling me something, warning me, or just noting what he saw.

"He's leaving," I said, after another few quiet minutes. "He got another job."

Garrett reached for my hand, squeezed it. "I know."

~

Solomon, as it turned out, really knew how to dance. I had to thwack the hands of several of my female relatives when they got a little bit too close as we spun past, but it was all in the name of saving him from them, so I figured he would be grateful. The longer we danced, the closer we got until the music came to the closing bars. As I looked up at him and we drifted to a stop, the lights seemed to dim, the room appeared to empty, and there was just the two of us, holding each other close.

"Have I told you how beautiful you look tonight?" Solomon whispered.

"Three times, but I love it, so keep going."

"You. Are. Beautiful. And I love you."

"I love you too," I murmured a millisecond before his lips landed on mine. His kiss burned my lips, sending my pulse racing. I wrapped my arms around his neck and he pulled me closer. When we pried apart from each other, there was a loud "Whoop!" and applause. We look around and Solomon gave a sheepish smile. "Guess we're out," he said.

"I think pretty much everyone already knew," I told him.

"If my team didn't realize it the night I stayed at your house, I'd have to fire them for being so unobservant." Solomon grabbed my hand and tugged me after him as we exited the dance floor to another round of applause that sent the color rushing to my cheeks.

"You want to file a sexual harassment suit against this guy?" asked Delgado as we passed. "You didn't look like you were enjoying that. The first time, the second, or the third!"

"Trust me, she loved every minute," said Solomon and we laughed. We circled some more, we spoke, we laughed, we drank, we snuck away to quiet corners and kissed, and after a while, Serena came to find me, insisting that I follow her.

"Don't tell me anything I really don't want to know

about Delgado," I warned her as she looped her arm through mine. "I have to work with the guy."

"Fine, but he's an excellent lover and I've never been more fulfilled in my life." Serena beamed.

I cringed and I hoped it showed. "Jeez."

"Bouquet," she said, pointing ahead as she yanked me forcibly into a group of women. I looked up to see the bouquet flying through the air as well as the wave of female hands reaching for it. It was coming right at me, probably through my mother's sheer force of will. As it careened towards my face, I stuck one hand up and batted it at Serena who caught it, her mouth dropping open in surprise.

"Guess it's your turn again," I said, swiftly slipping away as she held it aloft.

Solomon was just where I left him, talking to a man in my absence. I vaguely recognized him as a distant cousin, someone on my father's side.

"You didn't catch it," he remarked.

"Butterfingers," I said, with a shrug. We turned to watch Serena approaching Delgado, the prize bouquet in hand. She held it out to him sheepishly. Delgado plucked a rose from it and slipped it behind her ear. "He took that well," I remarked as the music started up again.

"Some men are born romantics."

"Speaking of which, what's going on upstairs?" Just so he didn't think I was inquiring about nocturnal activities, I added, "I mean the new secret division of the Solomon Agency?"

"Thought you'd never ask." Solomon grinned as he led me onto the dance floor. "I assumed you'd keep poking around until you found out. It took you forever to ask me." Just when I was about to give up hope of him ever explaining, he said, "Risk management and intelligence gathering."

"What does that mean?"

Solomon dipped me, holding me securely, not that I could ever imagine him dropping me. He was a skilled and graceful dancer. Who knew? "Interested in finding out?"

Duh. Was I ever? "Maybe," I said, playing it cool.

"Then I've got a case for you."

"Do tell."

"First things first. Are you in?"

"Always," I said, immediately wondering what I was agreeing to. Still, not knowing had never stopped me before. It was part of the job, part of the excitement.

"It could be dangerous," he warned.

"You don't like putting me in danger. You keep checking up on me."

"Did it occur to you that maybe I just like coming to see you and a case is a good excuse to do that? Besides, you've shown me over and over that you can handle yourself. This is higher risk. Can you cope with it? Can you deal with danger when it's headed directly your way?"

"Count me out."

Solomon whipped me up, spun me out and reeled me in until we were cheek to cheek. "Really?" he said, sounding surprised. I pulled my head back a little, his hand firmly on the small of my back, holding me close to him. His eyes met mine, and after a moment, he smiled.

I winked and settled next to him once more, feeling his body pressed against me, as well as the surge of excitement of the unknown, the anticipation. "Nah. Totally, absolutely, one hundred percent in!"

LEXI GRAVES RETURNS IN

LAUGH OR DEATH

COMING SOON!

ABOUT THE AUTHOR

Author and journalist Camilla Chafer writes for newspapers, magazines and websites throughout the world. Along with the Lexi Graves Mysteries, she is the author of the Stella Mayweather urban fantasy series as well as author/ editor of several non-fiction books. She lives in London, UK.

Visit Camilla online at www.camillachafer.com to sign up to her newsletter, find out more about her, plus news on upcoming books and fun stuff including an exclusive short story, deleted scenes and giveaways.

You can also find Camilla on
Twitter @camillawrites
and join her on Facebook at
http://www.facebook.com/CamillaChafer.

35656226R00195